# THE BEAST OF THE NORTH

THIEF OF MIDGARD – BOOK 1
ALARIC LONGWARD

**Hardhill Adventures**

THE BEAST OF THE NORTH

**The text and the story copyright © 2015 Alaric Longward**

(www.alariclongward.com)

**All Rights Reserved**

**Cover art by Eve Ventrue**

(http://www.eve-ventrue.com/#/)

**Design by The Cover Collection**

(http://www.thecovercollection.com)

**ISBN: 978-952-7101-16-2 (mobi)**

**ISBN: 9781517768706 (paperback)**

This book is a work of fiction. Names, characters, places, and incidents are the product of the author's imagination or are used fictitiously. Any resemblance to actual events, locales, or persons, living or dead, is purely coincidental.

All rights reserved. No part of this book may be reproduced or transmitted in any form or by any means, electronic or mechanical, including photocopying, recording, or by any information storage and retrieval system, without the author's permission.

*Dedicated to Odin for the gift of learning.*

*To Lumia, my beautiful, super talented daughter.*

*And to my wife, a true Aesir goddess, the goddess of patience.*

# A WORD FROM THE AUTHOR

Greetings, and thank you for getting this book. I hope you enjoy it. The second book for this series will be **The Queen of the Draugr**, and should arrive early 2016.

Please note, that **The Dark Levy** and upcoming (fall 2015) **Eye of Hel,** books one and two of **Ten Tears Chronicles** are related to **the Beast of the North**.

I humbly ask you **rate and review** the story in Amazon.com and/or on Goodreads. This will be incredibly valuable for me going forward and I want you to know I greatly appreciate your opinion and time.

Please visit

www.alariclongward.com

and **sign up for my mailing list** for a monthly dose of information on the upcoming stories and info on our competitions and winners.

## OTHER BOOKS BY THE AUTHOR:

**THE HRABAN CHRONICLES – NOVELS OF ROME AND GERMANIA**

THE OATH BREAKER – BOOK 1
RAVEN'S WYRD – BOOK 2
THE WINTER SWORD – BOOK 3
BANE OF GODS – BOOK 4 (COMING 2016)

**GOTH CHRONICLES - NOVELS OF THE NORTH**

MAROBOODUS - BOOK 1 (COMING WINTER 2015)

**THE CANTINIÉRE TALES – STORIES OF FRENCH REVOLUTION AND NAPOLEONIC WARS**

JEANETTE'S SWORD – BOOK 1
JEANETTE'S LOVE – BOOK 2
JEANETTE'S CHOICE – BOOK 3 (COMING LATE 2015)

**TEN TEARS CHRONICLES – STORIES OF THE NINE WORLDS**

THE DARK LEVY – BOOK 1
EYE OF HEL – BOOK 2

**THIEF OF MIDGARD – STORIES OF THE NINE WORLDS**

THE BEAST OF THE NORTH – BOOK 1
QUEEN OF THE DRAUGR – BOOK 2 (COMING EARLY 2016)

## TABLE OF CONTENTS

| | |
|---|---:|
| **THE BEAST OF THE NORTH** | 1 |
| *A WORD FROM THE AUTHOR* | 5 |
| *OTHER BOOKS BY THE AUTHOR:* | 6 |
| *TABLE OF CONTENTS* | 7 |
| *MAP OF NORTHERN MIDGARD* | 9 |
| *NAMES AND PLACES* | 10 |
| *PROLOGUE* | 12 |
| **BOOK 1: THE GRIM JESTERS** | 13 |
| *CHAPTER 1* | 15 |
| *CHAPTER 2* | 23 |
| *CHAPTER 3* | 31 |
| *CHAPTER 4* | 38 |
| **BOOK 2: MORAG'S FOES** | 48 |
| *CHAPTER 5* | 50 |
| *CHAPTER 6* | 65 |
| *CHAPTER 7* | 79 |
| *CHAPTER 8* | 97 |
| **BOOK 3: THE BLACKTOWERS** | 105 |
| *CHAPTER 9* | 107 |
| *CHAPTER 10* | 122 |
| *CHAPTER 11* | 126 |
| *CHAPTER 12* | 138 |
| **BOOK 4: QUEEN'S BANE** | 151 |
| *CHAPTER 13* | 153 |
| *CHAPTER 14* | 163 |
| *CHAPTER 15* | 169 |

| | |
|---|---|
| CHAPTER 16 | 189 |
| **BOOK 5: THE TIDE** | **192** |
| CHAPTER 17 | 194 |
| CHAPTER 18 | 200 |
| CHAPTER 19 | 211 |
| CHAPTER 20 | 227 |
| **BOOK 6: HEL'S HORDE** | **234** |
| CHAPTER 21 | 236 |
| CHAPTER 22 | 248 |
| CHAPTER 23 | 252 |
| CHAPTER 24 | 257 |
| EPILOGUE | 259 |
| AFTERWORD | 261 |

## MAP OF NORTHERN MIDGARD

**Northern Midgard**
2505 AFTER SUNDERING

Falgrin
Ygrin
Red Midgard
Dagnar
Bay of Whales
Callidorean Ocean
Aten
Malingborg
The Verdant Lands

## NAMES AND PLACES

**Ann** – Sand's unhappy sister.
**Arrow Straits** – the body of water between Callidorean Ocean and the Bay of Whales.
**Aten** – grand harbor of the Verdant Lands.
**Baduhanna** – Aesir, a demi goddess, general of the humans.
**Balan Blacktower** – head of the Tenth House, a historian, and father of Shaduril and Lith. A conspirator and Maskan's host.
**Balic Barm Bellic** – the High King, lord of the Verdant Lands.
**Beast of the North** – the title of the ruler of the Red Midgard.
**Brinna** – a knight of the Danegell's.
**Callidorean Ocean** – the grand sea of the west.
**Crec Helstrom** – Lord Commander of Red Midgard and Dagnar, head of the Second House.
**Dagger Hill** – the ancient name of Dagnar's prominent hill.
**Dagnar** – the capital of Red Midgard.
**Dark Grip** – ancient giant artifact.
**Dverger** – dwarves
**Draugr** – wily, intelligent undead, masters of disguise.
**Falg Hardhand** – servant to the queen, slave from the south.
**Falgrin** – allies of Red Midgard, one of the Fringe Kingdoms of the north.
**Gal Talien** – Lord of the Harbor, Lord of Trade, head of the Seventh House.
**Gray** – butler of the Blacktower's.
**Hawk's Talon** – one of the four brigades of Red Midgard.
**Hel** – goddess of the dead, mistress of rot, and the one whose war sundered the Nine Worlds from each other. She is forever seeking her eye.
**High Hold** – land of the Blacktowers.
**Jotun** – giants of Jotunheim, populating many worlds, including Muspelheim, Nifleheim, and Jotunheim. Often foes to the gods, to the Aesir and the Vanir, but sometimes not.
**Kallir** – Bear's henchman.
**Larkgrin** – Morag Danegell's stolen staff.
**Lithiana "Lith" Blacktower** – daughter of Balan Blacktower, a conspirator and Maskan's temptress.
**Hammer Legion** – High King's experienced, brutal armies.
**Maskan** – a thief and a ruffian with a surprising past and even more surprising future.
**Magor Danegell** – King of Red Midgard.
**Malingborg** – capital of the Verdant Lands, home of the High King.
**Mellina Danegell** – Queen of Red Midgard.
**Mir** – Maskan's mother and more.
**Molun** – Bear's henchman.
**Rose Throne** – throne of the Danegells.
**Sand** – son or the Bear, Maskan's partner in crime.
**Shaduril Blacktower** – daughter of Balan Blacktower, a conspirator and Maskan's love.

**Shakes** – master of the "Lamb," a tavern of Bad Man's Haunt.
**Sorrowspinner** – a magical artifact, a ring of dark metal and a blue stone.
**Taram Blacktower** – arms master of the Blacktowers. For to Maskan.
**The Bear** – also called the "Uncouth Lord." A highwayman and Sand's father.
**The Crimson Apex** – home of the Blacktowers.
**The Harlot** – executioner of Dagnar.
**The One Man Cult** – a cult of the High King, denying the existence of the gods.
**Thrun** – a dverg lord.
**Tower of the Temple** – Danegell's mighty fort on top of Dagnar.
**Valkai the Heavy** – brute leader of the Grim Jesters criminal outfit.
**Verdant Lands** – the holdings of the High King, rich and powerful lands.
**Ygrin** – allies of Red Midgard, one of the Fringe Kingdoms of the north.
**Ymritoe** – nation of the giants.

# PROLOGUE

A war was waged in the elven world of Aldheim.

A slip of a girl, Shannon, fought a magical duel in the midst of a terrible battle. She released a complicated, dark spell of a forlorn, mad goddess, Hel. It was a perilous spell of unknown results, but it was the girl's only hope, and so she cast the spell and the worlds suffered.

And goddess Hel smiled on her bed of rot.

The spell changed the ancient world of Aldheim profoundly, but it was a spell that would alter the fate of all of the Nine Worlds. In one of these worlds, in Midgard, the home of humans, that day had been unusually bright and warm across the realms. The gods had been gone for thousands of years, men ruled, and there was war, and there was peace in Midgard. Death and birth marked that day and night as any other day.

The night the spell struck this land, a thick, ominous darkness shot across the sky from the west. Night guards of the Midgard's many realms screamed warnings; bells tolled as a peculiar, strange storm front seemed to materialize from the thick, dark air. People were used to seeing all kinds of weather, but the dark storm rushing from the grand Callidorean Ocean was vast and terrifying, driving waves and winds before it. Ships sunk with all hands, towns were swallowed by waves, walls crumbled, and fires broke out as people fled to the higher grounds. Hel's spell danced across Midgard. Stone cracked. Flesh burned. Thousands died. Whole kingdoms were gone, and others changed forever.

Then, the storm abated. The strange darkness vanished as if it had never been, and it was called the Cataclysm ever after.

Something had changed, in Aldheim, in all the Nine Worlds and even in Midgard. Twenty years later, some of it would be clear.

Listen.

# BOOK 1: THE GRIM JESTERS

*'There are no noble houses here in the shadows. But that does not mean there are no lords in the dark.'*
**Shaduril to Valkai**

# CHAPTER 1

Alrik, the rogue, was choking to death.

His back was arched in hopeless panic and excruciating pain, and his face was a reddish mask of horror. His tongue flapped on his chin as he wheezed for breath. Then he wet himself. That indignity was not lost to most of the crowd as his legs began kicking around in the air, seeking something tangible to save his life. There was nothing. He was being executed. He was dying very slowly and with no mercy.

'Bastard,' Sand breathed. 'She's a rotten piece of gristle, isn't she?' He nodded at the woman in charge of the hanging.

I nodded in full agreement. The fat executioner was called the Harlot, and she was a brutal, fat woman who got rich off her former husband's profession; one she had perfected. Now she was squinting up at the victim, as if she was sorely disappointed by the gruesome death and the ineptitude of the principal actor hanging from the thick rope.

'She should pull on his legs,' I said softly and supported my rough-faced friend, Sand, who was being shoved around in the thick crowd. It was an apt name for the wide boy of seventeen. *He was much like the hung man was*, I thought, *blond, rough, and tough.* Many young men in the north looked like Sand, for the north bred men of dour, harsh disposition, and perhaps it was the long winter that made it so. I gazed around at the crowd. The large group of rogues and the poor, stinking and starving people were the usual specimens of northern dregs. *Family. They were that. Of sorts,* I thought. Most were thieves, swindlers, smugglers, and just petty criminals. All were sullenly watching the execution. The Butcher, Lord Captain Crec Helstrom commanded many such executions and the Lord of the Harbor, a thin official looking man oversaw them, and he was there, sitting on his horse. What part the king had in the process, was uncertain. The rumors said few lowborn even met an Elder Judge and was that not something the king should look after, if not Lord Helstrom? Alrik was dying too slowly. And he had not seen a judge either. That's what everyone said.

Finally, the suffering of the man, the terrible indignity of the piss-sodden, choking death made some people mutter out loud. One such person was louder than the rest. 'Odin curses the filthy fat bitch!' a woman yelled from the back of the crowd. At that the Lord of the Harbor grunted at the Brother Knights. Two huge, armored men obeyed and turned their heads towards the sound, and so did their gigantic dark horses. They guided their beasts forward and hefted their weapons. That nearly silenced the crowd. They were Brothers, of King Morag Danegell's house, and his bodyguards. There were perhaps ten of them altogether though only the two attended the execution. All were darkly armored in magnificent, rare plate and chain, and even their horses wore chain mail to match their master's somber, deadly looks. All were individually crafted helmets, and none had names. These two were White and Black Brothers, and horsehair of appropriate color was hanging from their helmets. Both were deadly bastards with wide shields hanging on the flanks of their horses. Lord of the Harbor guided his horse away from them while glowering at the crowd under his open-faced helmet, pulling at dark hair that wind blew over his mouth.

'Who called for a god?' the White Brother yelled, his voice muffled by the dark steel helmet, white horsehair twirling aggressively as he turned his head from side to side. In his hand coiled a whip studded with sharpened bits of steel.

'There are no gods, you curs,' the Black Brother echoed his comrade surprisingly gently. Despite the calm, cold voice, there was clear danger lurking behind the menacing mask. His spear was tall and wide bladed with a glittering tip, and that weapon drew looks. 'There are only kings, as has been decreed by the High King of the southern land and his subject, our King Morag Danegell as well,' he added. That prompted a small ripple of complaints from the crowd.

*Gods and kings,* I thought. *All trouble.*

Sand agreed. He leaned on me. 'We are not supposed to talk about gods, and we should all press our foreheads to the mud for kings, but they can't explain the temples, eh?'

'No,' I agreed. There were temples, gates if you like, dormant now, scattered across the lands. We had myths, legends, of war between goddess Hel and Odin, our supposed creator. The elders whispered of the battles that shattered us from the other eight worlds well over two thousand years past, but the king Danegell had lately passed laws to ban worship of the gods as requested by the High King. 'They cannot force the starving and the wretched to forget the gods, Sand. No.'

Sand spat into the dust, braving the attentions of the hulking Brothers. 'Everyone says the gods gave the kings their crowns and let them govern for them. And that temple by the Tower,' Sand nodded up the tall hill of Five Rings, the Dagger Hill, 'is a gate to another world. It is. The High King Balic of Malignborg and our fawning bastard Danegell and the One Eyed priests of the High King can hump themselves.'

'The High King,' I agreed, trying to calm my friend down as the knights were apparently looking for troublemakers, 'of course, wants to set himself on top of the gods. Who wouldn't? Who is there to punish him? Ours just does the same.' What was certain is that our king was attempting to force the religion of the High King to us all. That's why I wanted to leave the land. That and the fact my father had once been a nobleman and mother said the King had murdered him when she was pregnant. We were fugitives, had been all my life. I didn't even know my last name. I was born into Bad Man's and never been high. Father's skull adorned the Sun Court, where it was hung from an ancient tree with hundreds of others, and was painted red.

Sand shook his head as the hanging man twitched like a bass on a hook. ''Ann said it was not always so. Twenty years? That's how long this mad cult of One Man has spread around from the south. 'Ann was Sand's sister. She was beautiful girl I was afraid of. Sand wanted us to fall in love, but for some reason I had no such feelings for her. There was something wrong with me. But Ann would know such details, as she was clearly the smartest of all of us. It was evident as a knob on a forehead.

Around us, many people were cursing the Brother Knights for their words and the king for his cruelty. The king might not be there, only the Lord of the Harbor, but the king was to blame.

I sighed. While the kings were trying to oust the memories of the gods, I had a hunch our king was in a very disadvantaged situation. 'We have the Fringe Kingdoms here in the North, Sand,' I said. 'Fringe. That says it all. Poor if severe. I think our king bows to the High King and embraces his laws, but he does it to survive. So do the many other smaller lands all across the continents. I'm sure it is lip service to his madness, and King Magor Danegell won't let the High King hump our ass. Our king is not looking for trouble with the High King, so he makes concessions, but we can still believe. Silently.' *I was defending the killer of my father,* I thought. *I was sick, indeed.*

'Don't they say King Danegell is going to war with our allies Falgrin and Ygrin?' a strange man noted over my shoulder.

'They do say that,' Sand agreed with the man. 'Mad kings all around.'

I pushed the stranger away and leaned on Sand. 'Who knows what is true. But the fact remains that the north will remain free.' Sand did not look convinced and chortled a bit.

'Fine speech. You should be a general,' he said with a mocking bow. I pushed him, but he mimicked me with a sonorous voice. 'The city of Dagnar and Red Midgard will go on, and we will stand fast.' I was about to push him over when everyone went quiet. The hanged man had apparently died, for the Harlot was reaching for a body that was no longer moving, but then, to our growing anger, he began wheezing pitifully once more.

'Odin!' we heard him gasp.

'Silence the blaspheming bastard!' Black yelled, and the Harlot took a stick and slapped it across the hung man's face, drawing blood and ripping the skin. She did it efficiently, with little emotion, but the crowd was fuming now.

It was too much.

An old, terribly wrinkled and ugly man was shuffling at the back of the crowd, his blond and gray beard foamed with ale. He yelled out. 'Oi! Isn't the old Magor Danegell a heretic then? His shield bears the words! Kill Alrik! Or let him go!' Men and women yelled encouragements to the man from the crowd, and Black turned to look for the old man, who disappeared into the thick of the pressing flesh. The king did have the words "Sword of the Goddess," in his shield, indeed. They were there on the shields of the Brothers as well, ancient words of the old house, and everyone in the crowd saw them. 'Hypocrites!' the old man yelled from out of sight.

'Silence! Or join Alrik!' the Black Brother yelled back, his surprisingly gentle voice carrying easily through the murmurings and shouts.

They were not silent. It seemed everyone had forgotten the hanging man.

The White Brother scowled and pointed a finger at the Harlot, apparently telling her to hurry it up. She did not, but turned her back rebelliously and scowled at her victim.

There was a movement of the crowd, a subtle, very tiny movement, almost unthreatening, and yet, somewhat so as the people took a step closer to the Brothers and the rank of troops behind them. The White Brother whistled, the soldiers snapped to attention at a barked order of the Black, their round shields rattled, a hundred tall, tapering spear points rested on top of the shields, aimed at the crowd. A skull and sword symbol was painted on their pauldrons and shields. The red-caped, conical helmeted men looked nervous but steady. The White Brother let go with his whip. It went up and slapped down, and blood flew. A man shrieked and held his bleeding chest in agony. He stumbled away through the crowds.

Silence reigned.

The two dangerous Brothers glowered at the barely cowed crowd. The hanging man kept dying, very slowly, and I decided his plight was more important than the gods and the kings, and unconfirmed rumors.

The crowd was silent, but still fuming. It might turn ugly in a moment.

*Damn Alrik*, I thought. The bastard had been seen sneaking out of a high noble house in the Third Ring. He should hang. And people were now in danger for him.

'Alrik didn't pay her or the bastard on a horse anything before the show, so she's making a point,' Sand told me morosely. 'Many unfortunates from this crowd are likely to be up there one day, and she makes some of her upkeep from the poor souls hoping for a quick end. He should have paid her. Anything but that.'

I nodded, swiping at a bothersome fly. 'He likely had nothing. And nobody brought him coin before this atrocious show. That much loyalty his gang has for him.'

'Probably has enemies in his guild,' Sand grumbled.

I took a deep breath. I waited until the two tall knights turned away to look at Alrik and to whisper to the Lord of the Harbor, who dismissed their soft pleas to end it quickly.

Then I made up my mind, and flipped a silver coin towards the Harlot.

It flew in the air, twinkling in the oppressive heat of the morning and landed at her feet. She eyed it in surprise, and then looked around. Her eyes met mine. Uncannily she had guessed I had thrown the coin, but she was the Harlot, and they said she could smell money. She saw a man with a dark beard, deep brown eyes, and short hair. She grinned at me, but I made no movement, nor did I acknowledge her quizzical look. She nodded gratefully anyway and turned away to pick up the coin. The Master of Trade had turned for the crowd to try to catch the man who wanted to hasten the fun or perhaps to demand more coin, but I did not look at him or the knights, who seemed happy to have the torture cut as short as possible. I sensed the Lord of the Harbor was now staring enviously at the silver in the Harlot's hand.

Then he looked back to the crowds and spotted me. My skin crawled.

'What in Hel's name did you do?' Sand asked me in morbid stupefaction as he stared at the woman ambling away. 'That was silver. It was. Wasn't it? The piece we earned last week? Good, well deserved silver, gone. Eh? Alrik never knew us. You will never get out of here if you waste your fortune. And neither will I, as I cannot leave you alone to starve.'

'Yeah, I know,' I said. 'It was your coin, anyway.'

He grunted as a wounded animal would, his hands tapping his pouch. He found it open and looted, and I whistled softly as he balled his fists. 'Look—'

I grinned at him disarmingly. 'Relax, just wanted to test my fingers a bit. You'll get mine,' I told him. We had robbed a box of misplaced wine from the harbor, our favorite haunt for trouble. We sold it at some profit to a drunkard butler of some noble house at the gates, where such transactions often took place. The man had been out to find something to cover his thievery from his master. He paid a lot though not as much as the load was worth. We were good thieves but bad businessmen.

'Don't want yours. Want mine. Yours is yours. Mine is—'

'Shh,' I told him. 'Look.'

The Harlot bowed to the sullen crowd, the tall, chain-mailed men of the Mad Watch stepped away from her, their spears rattling. She ambled for the piss sodden legs dancing in front of her.

She grabbed them with no further ceremony. Then she jumped on him, pulling him down so hard, we all heard the nasty cracking sound as his neck broke.

He died. The Harlot struggled to her feet and bowed my way.

A meek servant adjusted the red tabard of the Lord of the Harbor and then the man moved forward to stare at the crowd, covered by a cordon of burly house guards and the two Brothers whose horses stepped in front of the Mad Watch. *Seventh House?* I thought. I could not remember where the Lord of the Harbor was from, and it bothered me. The man took off his helmet. 'Ann thinks he looks like a thin version of you,' Sand snickered, and I pushed him so hard, he nearly fell. We had seen him often enough at these events.

The man was a sleek noble with dark curly hair, thin face, and a cruel, grating voice as he stood up in his stirrups and addressed us over the shoulders of the two knights. 'Let it be known, scum, that King Magor Danegell, the Beast of the North, will hang any thief and their family should the raids in the Silk Streets and Blue Doors Districts continue. Rob the poor and eat each other, vermin, but leave the better folk alone. You have no business beyond the Fourth Ring.'

'What happened to Alrik's family?' someone yelled at him mockingly from the crowd.

'He didn't have any,' the king's man stated impatiently. 'The records—'

There was a slow murmur of laughter rippling through the crowd. 'We are all orphans, my lord! None of us are married nor carry children. Barren and forgotten we are, as a gravestone! We are but turds!' another voice yelled, a blonde, teary woman I knew was the dead man's wife. People cheered her bravery as she wiped away tears. The Black Brother was pointing at her, speaking to the White, who shook his head tiredly. *She would live,* I decided. No need to inflame the situation more.

'Silence!' a gorgeously armored Captain of the Watch yelled; his men were rattling their spears and pulling at glittering swords as the crowd cheered the woman. They had scarlet cloaks and black bronze shields but were citizen soldiers in truth. Their aggressive display didn't help the situation, and none went quiet as ordered. Not even White's whip would help the situation now. The vocal threats rose in volume, and even the Brothers decided not to challenge the crowd and the soldiers began to withdraw from the scaffolds, slowly and with dignity, guards forming steel fisted ranks around the official and the Harlot. They would be back. The knights led them up the hill towards the gates for the Fourth Ring and beyond all the way to the top, to the Tower of the Temple, the Sun Court and the barracks of the First Ring.

'Shit snuffling, wart-ass toy soldiers. Damned robber-nobles!' Sand yelled with barely controlled rage. He had a dangerous, violent streak in him, like his father did, who was a highwayman called the Bear. They often reacted violently to setbacks, except when Ann talked sense to them. The Bear was also my mother's boyfriend. Boyfriend, for mother was forty-five, and he was ten years younger than she was. It was strange, sometimes, but that strangeness had brought Sand and me together. We were like brothers.

I saw the Lord of the Harbor turn on his horse at Sand's voice. He leaned down on three of his men and pointed a finger at Sand and then at me. He wanted something with the man who paid fat silver for a rogue and with the boy who defied them so loudly. It would not be pleasant. I had made myself a target. So had Sand. The men—all ape-like specimens—turned and tried to catch a sight of us. They did.

'Shit!' Sand said, as he also had seen the trouble and pulled at me. We ran like beaten dogs, dodging people and horses and ended up near the harbor gates. We were both trying to see if there was anyone coming. I spotted one of the men, running and pushing men away from his path, craning his neck and we dodged away and ran on.

'I think we might want to stay away for a while,' I panted. 'They are sure to be there, hiding near the scaffolds. And around Bad Man's. They saw you, Sand, as well.'

'Yeah. I'm in trouble as well. That should teach you to rob the fun from the Lord of the Harbor, but I doubt it does,' Sand said.

'You should have kept your mouth shut!'

We walked and ran on nervously, staying where people were thick. 'Did Mir make anything from the shipwreck last week?' Sand eventually asked me as we both kept glancing back. No sight of the men. He called Mother by her first name, something that was strangely irritating. We had no last name, though.

I nodded. 'Some bastards brought her a chest of moderately fine loot. There were satin and silken women's clothing and nice noble's shoes as well. Expensive red leather and silver. A box of strange trappings of rank, gold, and emeralds. Some were bloody. Freshly bloodied.'

'Cutthroats,' Sand agreed with mild disgust. 'The guards should be faster when a ship gets wrecked down the coast, but then they usually get wrecked at night, anyway.' He began to hum a grating song.

> 'They were lured by the butchers and to the shoals they crash.
> In the murderous lot goes, to rob the jewels and the cash.
> The ships will be stripped, the goods snipped.
> The guards at the gates, cannot change the victims' fates.'

'Shut up,' I told him.

He looked hurt. 'It wasn't that bad.'

'Yes, it was. Was it a Sand original? Let us keep it like that, unique. Possibly even a one-time performance.'

He cursed and said nothing more about that. 'But she bought them?'

'Yeah. Mother sold them to an Atenian trader. Made good coin,' I told him as we pushed our way through a small crowd. Alrik had been liked in the Laughing Lamb, the local tavern known for the Trade, which meant anything illegal. He had been liked, even if he had connections to the major harbor gangs, which competed with the minor ones of the Bad Man's Haunt. We had a cellar shop below the Lamb, where we outwardly sold crabs and oysters to noble kitchens. It was named "The Shifty Crab", our business.

'I want my silver,' Sand sulked.

'Harbor? While we wait?' I asked him. He had neither talent for cutpursing nor the fingers for pocket picking, but I did. We would go there, mingle in the crowds, and pick someone to pickpocket, someone who was not paying attention. There were plenty of those around, but one had to be entirely preoccupied to qualify as a victim. That is why I nearly always picked off wealthy women's purses. They rarely noticed anything, being enamored by the many stalls full of treasures of the fabulous Harbor Side Market, and the wares of the Horned Brewery, a famous den of debauchery.

'Sure, harbor,' Sand said. 'Might as well. We were going to go there anyway, no?'

'Yes.'

He pointed back towards the scaffolds. 'Don't want to go up there. Might join Alrik, no? Harbor it is. I've got my knife.' He lifted his leather tunic. A white bone handle flickered in sight just for a second. Sand was there to make sure things settled down if any keener member of the many harbor gangs of criminals accosted us. 'Mir wanted you to go home after the hanging, no?' Sand said, having just remembered this bit of instruction we had been given that morning. 'But we cannot go now. Later. She will be—'

'Frantic with worry,' I said and rolled my eyes. 'She told me to stay near home to help her with some crates of stolen pewter mugs. Boring. Boring! I could do that, but I've got to make a living some other way than peddling shit. Can't be supported by her forever. Don't want to inherit the business either. Rifling through dead people's clothing and jewelry, haggling like a southerner? No, thank you. No, thank you indeed.'

'Shouldn't throw our silver away then. We will never get anywhere poor.' Sand spat. 'Father will need help in the evening. Let's hope we get back eventually.' He was his father's son, and Bear was one tough to catch criminal. Some called the Bear the Uncouth Lord, and none knew his name. He always left his victims tied to trees, most on their knees, robbed and poor. He was a fine father.

'I wish I had known mine,' I said with half a whisper.

'Eh?' Sand asked as I fingered a ring on my finger. It was a black metal thing with a precious yellow stone and gold etchings, and Mother had given it to me when I had been young, very young. It was tight, and I never removed it, and I sometimes wondered how it seemed to grow with my finger. I told Sand it was magical, and he laughed at me though not too harshly, for he too believed in magic. But the ring stayed, and I did not budge it. I had promised it to Mother. It was Father's seal of the family. I did not wish to remove it. Never had. Sand grunted as he saw what I was doing. 'I'm sure he was a fine nobleman, rich and spoiled, no doubt, but fine. The only thing I ever actually wanted was a noble house of my own. And I don't mean the title. I want a house. Up there on the hill.'

'It's an excellent goal,' I said.

'All I want,' he breathed softly, and I was surprised. He had dreams, just like me. 'You should change,' he said stiffly. 'Will help if they are about, though not me.'

I looked around and saw the crowds were left behind. Sand seemed nervous and gave me the slightest of nods. There was nobody in sight as we made for the harbor. I stopped behind a tall wall of crates, scowled at a cat, and concentrated. It was hard, always hard, but I managed it.

My face shifted and melted and settled to my own features. I felt drained.

Dark, long hair cascaded down my back, my beard disappeared and revealed a brooding, thick chin, and my eyes took on a golden brown hue. I was as sturdy of frame as Sand was, but I looked older than he did. Mother often told me I had suffered too much living in the Bad Man's Haunt.

'That is so damned creepy,' Sand complained. 'They would hang you for it, you know. I'll never forget the first time I saw you do that.'

'You should knock when you enter the restroom, Sand. That's why you found me out. But I'm happy you know. Even if you pummeled me first.'

'Didn't expect the moronic beggar from the gate to be squatting over my shit-bowl, in my own apartment, Maskan. If I hurt you, it was your own fault.'

'Didn't want to be drowned in my excrement, so I rather let you know.'

'Never imitate anyone in our home again,' he sighed. 'And please be careful out here as well. They will hang you if you get caught. They hang anyone with strange skills and curses and hints of old magic. Particularly in the south. Remember that only the kings are supposed to be godly, and no human I have heard of can do something like that. Sure, Phibs can conjure spirits, and she performs curses in the Squat Street, but this is too real. Kings are gods. Not commoner scums like you and I. And a king might open you up to find that magic.'

'They cannot catch me to hang me. I never trust anyone. Well. Only you.' I grinned.

It was a strange skill indeed. One that I had discovered at an early age. It took a lot of concentration to achieve such a change, and I felt there was something that resisted me, but I could change my face and my hair. Only Sand knew as he had caught me playing in the peace of the toilet ten years past where I had taken a face of a demented old man sleeping on the streets near the Lamb and the gate. Face Thief, he called me, and indeed I could adopt a face I had seen before.

It was a very useful skill for a thief. My name was Maskan.

## CHAPTER 2

The mighty harbor of Red Midgard spread out before us, and beyond the wharf there was the narrow seaway separating the north from the Verdant Lands. It was called the Arrow Straits, the waters where the western Callidorean Ocean and the Bay of Whales mixed turbulently. In the past, many a war had been waged in the narrow sea-lane. Pirates slipped through it during the night and smugglers as well. There were islands before the harbor, adorned by forts and towers manned by guards hired by merchant houses to warn them of pirates. You could see or at least imagine mountains and fortifications on the far, far landmass of the Verdant Lands stretching to the south, especially if the weather was totally clear of fog and clouds.

From the straight street we were following, you could see the fortified seawall and white towers guarding it, all adorned with the eagle's black talon on the red flag of the House Danegell and the fated words of a goddess and a sword scribbled on each flag. The brazen flags and thin pennants of the Ten Lords spread around the huge flag in the central tower, guarding the gap of the seawall leading to the harbor. That was the Fat Father, a flat-topped tower filled with ballista and catapults. There was a thick chain that ran from it to a slightly smaller tower across the opening to close the harbor entrance.

'I need food,' Sand complained. 'My innards are damned upset. There's something mean and small gnawing at them. That running caused it.'

'You're always starving. I'll get us something,' I told him cheerfully.

'Even the beggar children eat better than I do,' he said as he eyed a group of dirty-footed urchins with bags of colorful sweets. 'Your mother should cook. She never eats anything, just like Ann. They must live on air.'

I shook my head and pulled him along. 'Some say women never eat. Old Grinnon says his wife sucked all her nourishment from his soul.'

He laughed gruffly and eyed a group of people. 'You could lift some bread from that lot,' he said, pointing at a line of foreign travelers, all buying freshly baked bread from a stall.

'Bread is hard to snatch from someone's hand. Harder to hide. Try sticking a loaf in your pants while you run from a mob of hungry customers,' I told him. 'Especially if it's full of hot spices.'

I never stole food. Only coin and jewelry. And I did not wish to cause trouble for the local merchants, who would get a bad reputation for thievery. The peasants and merchants selling their wares in the harbor were living hand to mouth as it was. I forgot Sand's sour mood as we arrived at the gate in the port. The bustle and the fragrances of the vast area always made me happy. I anticipated the exciting thrill of seeing a hundred shady foreign merchants dealing with their customers in the shadows of the taverns and alleyways. There were even some honest ones out there, usually well-guarded. All of them made me daydream of faraway places.

I longed to see the south.

One day, I would, even if I would be one of the sell swords, who occasionally returned home with tons of stories, wondrous possessions, and a happy face, for they all claimed this was where the home was.

*Home.*

I squinted up the Dagger Hill. The Five Rings of walls and buildings climbed the high, broad hill of the peninsula. The military walls were red and thick and twenty feet tall, with ample, round towers of deadly design. Each gate was fitted with a silver bell that rang at every hour, starting from the gate of the first ring, where the bells were huge. The houses dotting the sides of the hill were larger and better made the higher you went. Terraces, groves of trees full of lemons and apples dotted the noble districts of the Second Ring. The Silk Lane merchant land of the Third Ring was a miracle of pastel-clouded roofs on one end of that Ring. The Blue Door's District of another side of Third Ring looked white and blue and clean. There, the lesser noble houses, middle-class officers, the non-noble officials had recently been the target for many thieving operations. There Alrik had been caught. The Fourth Ring? Land of the middle class, merchants, craftsmen. The houses were sturdy, wooden, well made of brick and thick lumber.

It was beautiful enough. It was home, perhaps. But it had a king I hated. Feared.

Sand read my mind and looked at me and nodded at the Tower of the Temple. 'He is growing erratic. You think he looks to start a war in the north?'

'The king?' I wondered aloud though everyone wondered if it was so. 'I told you. He has a tough job. He is a bastard, but he has one shitty job. Keeping all this governed.' *Murdering cur,* I thought, cursing myself for again standing up for the Danegell king.

Sand gave me a long look, knowing what I was thinking. He went on, 'But the alliance of the north is breaking. They say he has insulted Lord Tarx of Ygrin and demanded concessions on the border. Over some smuggling issue in the Bay of Whales? Over nothing, really. Nothing. A war looms where the north needs to keep together. The High King is restless.'

I shrugged. It was true the alliance of the north was wavering.

The three largest nations, Red Midgard, Ygrin, Falaris, and the smaller dukedoms had been allied and intermarried for hundreds of years, but no council had been held for five years. Indeed, rumors said the lords of our lands did not get along and that we had disgruntled traders and politicians whispering that Ygrin was trying to steal trade in the Bay of Whales.

If Balic, our nominal High King so wished, he could quickly take sides in these squabbles. *He would, if he thought Magor was not the lord to his tastes*, I thought. Times were dangerous, and I was not sure I would fight for Magor, should things take a turn for the worse.

*Home. Red Midgard.* A land one could not trust and one that was so hard to love.

A swarm of children hurried by, and I dodged and gave up my scrutiny of the city. Sand slapped my back. Sometimes I thought he could hear me thinking. If he did, he was not judging me. We arrived at the end of the street and waited as some rickety carts were being pulled up the street, filled with vegetables. The Harbor Side Market rippled with silken tents of green and red, and the bustle was so thick in places that we would have to push through. At the northern end of the harbor, there was the Horned Brewery, and there the crowd was the densest, like ants on a corpse. 'Go and find something by the walls?' Sand asked. 'Or by the ships? I think ships? I feel that is lucky.'

'Ships, waterside. Sure,' I told him with a grin, and I knew he knew there were salted mackerel sandwiches on sale there. He was a glutton yet gained no weight at all. I found a familiar stall, and there an old man gave us both servings of fresh bread filled with cheese and salty, peppery fish. It smelled heavenly, and I paid him and received a generous fistful of bronze in return, which I poured into Sand's pouch. We ambled on, seemingly careless for the brewery end of the harbor, though we were both looking for someone whose pouch looked enticing. The sea breeze brought fresh slaps of salty moistness from the Arrow Straits, and I could not help but smile as I happily looked at the crowds. So many people, wearing all the colors of the spectrum. Most all foreigners were happy, and only a few had the sullen face of Red Midgard. That was the thing with foreigners. They smiled. It was a beautiful day. I took an enormous bite of my sandwich and stopped as Sand pulled at me.

Everything changed.

He pointed his finger at a godly sight.

A young woman in white.

She was strangely familiar. And I could not draw my eyes away from her.

Despite my lack of interest in Ann, I flirted with other girls. Who does not? Sometimes they flirted back, and I dare say with my gifts I could bed quite a few of them by just taking the face of superior beauty if my own would not do the trick, and I could, of course, always take the features of their lover or husband. I'm sure many other men would use my skill for such a purpose, maliciously and without a second thought. I didn't because it was evil, and perhaps there was something pathetically romantic in my soul, something Sand would scoff at, yet agree with in silence. I yearned to love. To fall in love, head over heels.

And now I knew I could.

I had doubted myself, as Ann had not done the trick, but I could.

It is a strange thing, love, and has nothing to do with pure, burning lust. When you fall in love, lust feels shameful. All you want to do is to worship the goddess of your affection in a vain hope of being worshiped back. And this girl? My knees buckled as I contemplated on going to my knees, indeed, to worship her. She was a petite thing, not tiny, but not tall either. Her face was pale like Ann's, her eyes strangely iridescent in the light of Lifegiver. Her face was framed by lustrous, superbly thick blonde hair. There was a delicacy to her features that was delightful, and there was an easy, scoundrel-like quality to her smile, and I would never forget her face and that slightly crooked smile. I had dreamt of her. I was sure of it. It was there, behind my waking thoughts and hidden memories, the thought of this woman, a girl.

And I decided I could never love another as I did her.

I knew it then. Never.

Her white dress was cut low; the waist girdled with black leather belts, and her bottom swayed enticingly as she moved. I despised myself for looking at her rear and thought she was everything a man could want. She walked slowly and suggestively, skipping now and then over a puddle or trash and then—like a child—she would put a finger over her lip when she saw something interesting. She walked by a display of fine jewelry, running her hand across them. I yearned to see her face again and bumped into Sand.

Sand did not notice. His mouth was frozen in a wistful smirk, his mouth full of chewed fish as he did not budge, utterly mesmerized. I could swear his knees buckled as well. 'She is something else, no?' he breathed. 'I knew there would be something extraordinary here. I think we should rob her.'

'A goddess,' I sighed, though I gave him a jealous squint. Then I understood what else he had said. 'What? Rob her? Are you mad?'

He laughed. 'A goddess? She is but a girl. You will never marry a goddess. Or meet one, for that matter. But she is something else, no doubt. I just think we should rob her. I don't know why. Cut her purse.'

He had never paid attention to girls before. *Never*. I went on, 'I'll cut your nutsack, instead. She is a goddess. A divine thing, and one I intend to worship.'

'From afar, I hope,' he grumbled, and I knew he was thinking of Ann. He nodded as if to answer my thoughts. 'Ann would hate to hear that,' he mumbled.

'She never even speaks to me!' I told him. 'And I am sorry, but I don't think—'

He shoved me weakly. 'I think this one might enjoy a more manly man. Like your friend Sand. You take Ann, eh?'

'Ann is like a sister,' I said. 'Ann is not for me,' I breathed and endured Sand's withering look. At least he would not mug me in the street. 'There. Now you know.'

'She will be upset,' he whispered. 'You sorry bastard. Your lips can marry my fist.' He made a mocking punch my way.

I pushed him back. 'They won't marry any part of you. You smell of onions and fish, and your fist smells of grave,' I told him with mocking laughter as I watched the girl's hand run across some rubies under the watchful eye of a thick trader from the south and his bulging-eyed, burly guards.

'Oh ho!' Sand said, 'How will you make an impression on her, eh? You'll die single, young, and poor. I just know it. You will starve or hang. You cannot keep our coin safe, and one day they'll see what you do with your damned face. She needs a proper man who knows how to build up wealth. So I'll marry her, thank you very much.' He grinned. 'She alone? If we rob her, we can also give it back to her. She will appreciate an honest, good hearted and handsome rescuer. Not a crow's feast like you.'

'You'll hang with me, I'll make sure of it, and the crows will have to decide which tastes better,' I told him. 'No. Don't see any guards,' I whispered. 'But they could be there, anyway. If she is a noble.' That thought made our faces sour. If she were, neither would marry her. And if she were, she was sure to be in a company, it was true. There were so many people that she might at any time nudge someone and give them a familiar smile.

'Got a fat pouch too,' Sand smiled, and his face had a superbly disappointed look on it. 'Gotta be a noble.' She had a bulging sack on her belt, the strings hanging out haphazardly. 'She could be a merchant's daughter? Or a foreigner?' he whispered, clutching his forgotten sandwich.

'Could be, I suppose. What do we do?' I asked him. 'Truly rob her? I don't know.'

'What do we do?' he mimicked me with spite. 'We follow her. What do we usually do? As I say. Rob and give it back. It's a good plan.'

'Rob her,' I said slowly. 'Yes. I'll take it, the pouch,' I agreed, and stuffed my face with bread, wiping my hands discreetly on a silken tent cloth.

'Fine,' he stated, staring at me blankly. 'Shall we?'

'Be careful. See? She has a sword,' I said. There was a short sword with a jewel on the pommel on her side, the sheath half hidden in the folds of her white dress. I grinned. 'She is our target today. Then we decide what to do. Perhaps there are clues to her rank there, in the pouch? If it makes sense, we will return it and see how grateful she will be to get it back.'

'I agree. But we should wait to return it until she leaves the harbor. I feel there is something dangerous about her,' Sand said carefully, the lecherous, arrogant tone gone now that I had agreed. He often had animal like hunches one should not ignore. Yet, we would go ahead. We both knew it. The girl was intriguing. Beyond intriguing. He went on, 'Remember. I want to be the one who gives it back to her. No tricks. We flip a coin, fair?' I nodded and contemplated on failing to steal the pouch and then beg her for forgiveness immediately and that would eliminate Sand quickly, as the issue would be decided without delay. *No, I could hang.* Sand was right. She might not be a fool. *Better take the risk and let Sand compete with me,* I thought sullenly. She moved off from the jeweler, and I laughed hugely. 'What?' Sand asked.

'Yeah. She is our mark. She has it coming. She stole some rubies. Cannot be a noble.' I felt better for that reason.

'She didn't,' Sand breathed. 'Did she? No! Not her.'

'Eat up,' I told him and struggled with the food in my mouth. I ferociously brushed my teeth clear with my fingers as if I were about to go on a date. She had taken some of the precious things. I saw it. She had hid at least some in her palm and Lifegiver had betrayed her to my keen eyes, for there was a slight red glitter in the crack of her fingers. She was good. But I was better.

'You gonna ... you know?' Sand mumbled with a bit of fish sticking out of his mouth.

'Sure,' I told him, disgusted as he stuffed a springy, half charred fishtail into his carnivorous maw. I slipped behind a flapping tent and concentrated. I adopted a face. It was the face of the old man in the crowd, the one with blond and white hair.

'Why?' Sand asked with evident disapproval. 'That is so ugly. And your body looks young. You look like a monster.'

'I remembered it well,' I told him. 'And I'm just well-preserved.' It was hard to adopt a face unless you had stared at one recently. If I tried to mimic one I barely remembered, the result could prove to be misshapen and strange. 'Is it all right? Not really a monster, just ugly?'

'He was wrinkled, nasty, and old as shit, and so are you. Too ugly. Might draw attention and she might balk from you if she sees you are too close. She'll scream, and they will pummel you to mush. And poor Sand just after you. Don't like it.' He meant the whole thing, of course, no matter it was his idea, but I took after the girl without further discussion. He was right. But it was too late to change anything as she was moving away.

'Stop worrying like a tottering, grumpy grandmother and come on,' I told him as I walked, dodging men and women staggering with bales of wheat.

'You need to develop some form of imagination,' Sand grumbled nearby as he jogged after me. 'Always mimicking monsters, freaks, an official of the king and soon the king himself, no doubt. Ash-brained idiot. And what are you going to do if you get to take it back to her? You will stammer and blush like you do with Ann.'

'I stutter with Ann because I feel clumsy. But I am not really, am I? I'll rob her first and worry about it later.' I chuckled though I was sure I would make a mess of the whole return-the-loot part. I just wanted to do the part I knew and then figure the rest out. I have to admit, I was curious as to what was in her pouch. I advanced through the crowds, trying to look innocent and people barely glanced at me, despite the uncouth, old face. Sand was walking some ten paces away from me, apparently unconcerned and idle, but he was keeping an eye out for anyone who might not be a casual bystander.

Soon I was close to her and smelled a strange perfume. It left me confused for a moment. The flowery fragrance was suffocating all the other fragrances and stenches of the harbor that were usually so overwhelming. There was only this girl and her perfume.

The press of the people grew thicker. She had to push through two thin women, and as she muscled past them, she was smiling amicably. They got upset, for one had dropped a shawl, but then they were not upset, and her smile left them happy and apologetic. Her smile was perfect, even if a bit crooked, the eyes innocent and slightly tilted, perhaps, and I nearly fell as I tried to catch another look at her face. Then I had to dodge around a tent. There, I did fall over a crouched boy, who was cooing at a cat. I pushed up, grabbed at a stack of crates to balance myself and caused a small chorus of complaints from peddlers of ducks and red lizards that were the delicacy of many a fine tavern up the hill, as the crates fell with a terrible crash. I dodged the merchants without a word and noticed Sand was still following the girl on the crowded street. I dodged laborers, weaned through some scantily clad dancing girls, and ran as inconspicuously as I could to get ahead of her. She was easy to spot, even a tent row away. I kept glimpsing at the beautiful, pert nose, and the strange eyes seemed to notice everything. I rounded a corral of cows and two-legged milk lizards being auctioned to a group of unhappy servants of noble houses, sneaked silently through a tent of reverent buyers of some forbidden religious idols and resisted the urge to grab a fat pouch that was hanging from a thick belt of one of the men admiring the relics. I stopped at the door, gazing at the white-dressed girl that was about to pass the tent. I saw her figure through the silken walls and began counting.

Then she was there.

I drew in my breath, prepared. 'One,' I whispered, and moved.

I came out of the tent, brushed by her back, and a small knife flashed as I cut the strings of the pouch. I hid the bag inside my hand and disappeared into the crowd, not looking back, sure Sand was positioning himself between her and myself. Nothing happened. No one reacted. No shouts, no upset faces. I walked and dodged people and fingered the pouch, feeling rotten.

I had robbed her.

That had been the whole plan, but I was a rotten bastard anyway. Instead of complimenting the girl of my dreams, I had taken her coins. It was Sand's idea, wasn't it? Not my fault. *Gods, there was something dreadfully wrong with me, something much more twisted than defending the slayer of my father,* I thought.

I cursed the pouch in my hand and stopped to pummel my head on a tent post. I kept squeezing the pouch and felt the thing was full of thick coins. I hesitated and resisted as I fought the urge to see what kind. Sand should be here. That was the deal. We trusted each other but always shared the loot together, and never alone. The thrill of finding treasure was our shared joy, and discovering the contents of a pouch was exciting beyond anything else. I didn't want to rob him of the excitement, even if I was determined to snatch the girl from him. While I waited, I felt the rubies inside the pouch as well and grinned as I imagined her face when she sought the treasure that was no longer on her belt.

'What did we get?' Sand asked to my ear.

'Let's see,' I said, pretending not to having been startled. 'Did she notice at all?'

'No. But now we have to decide on the next step. And I still want to flip a coin with you on who gets to return it,' Sand said with a chuckle as his eyes sought my fist. 'But I guess we could take a peek? Even if we will return the money. Or some of it. Most?' I nodded, confused, and turned to an alleyway between two tents. We went there, crouched, and I fumbled with the bag, made of velvet that was slightly red hued, strung with strong silk cords.

'Let's see.' I emptied it.

On my palm were six huge golden coins. Thick as lips.

'Gods,' Sand whispered. They were so fat we drooled, and they were minted with a house insignia. I picked one up to squint at it as Sand was picking at the brilliant rubies.

There was a tower and two ravens circling it, and I knew the sign.

Sand grunted. 'Isn't that one of the Ten Lords? Blacktowers?'

'Blacktowers indeed,' I agreed. 'They are. I don't think they have any high lords or officers. Some old lady serves in the court? In the processions? And only some few hundred men-at-arms. Shit. The least of the ten? But still a formidable noble house.'

'They won't hang us if they cannot find us, no matter how high the lady is.' Sand grinned like a skull, the rubies in his palm. 'But the deal is off. She is beyond us, Maskan. If they do catch us with these coins,' he added, 'they will feed us to the sharks, wolves, or a sauk. Bit by bit. So, we might want to think twice about returning the pouch after all. She might scream murder no matter how chivalrous we appear to be, and then we are cooked.'

I shook my head remorsefully, feeling like a coward. 'She might. Don't worry. They won't find out. Mother can launder the coins. We will be filthy rich, so there is that!' Still, I felt miserable. She was beyond me. I fiddled with the coins and sighed. 'But why was this girl out here alone, anyway? With this hoard of coins? This is enough to buy you a small castle.'

'Shit, it's crazy,' Sand agreed. 'What's that?'

'That?' I asked and pocketed the coins as I hung on to a small piece of paper stuck between two of the coins. The silver bells of the guard towers of the first ring battlements rang midday; the other gate bells answered, and their hollow, clanging noise distant in the general commotion of the market. I fumbled with the piece of paper, neatly rolled up, and finally managed to pull it open.

*"As agreed, find the tavern called the End of the Road. Ask around and you shall find it. It is no secret. Bring the money. V."*

'The End of the Road?' Sand breathed. 'That's the haunt of the Grim Jesters?'

'Valkai,' I agreed, massaging my forehead. 'Valkai the Heavy, and she has business with the creature. They have some deal. The hanged idiot, Alrik worked for Valkai, they said.' I felt a hand of doom squeeze my heart. 'He was a Jester, they said.'

'Not our problem, is it?' Sand laughed, then shut up and looked down, distraught. 'We have her money.'

'We have her money,' I agreed. 'She is going there, into the lair of the dirt lizard to bargain, and she has nothing.'

'She had a sword?' Sand breathed unhappily, but shook his head. He cursed and struck a tent post so hard some birds took off from the top. 'Fine.'

'We going?' I asked him.

He nodded. 'I guess so. And then what? How will it look when we appear in some filthy, squalid back alley with her coin? She will know we are guilty. It was a fine game, but this—'

'Doesn't matter,' I told him. 'If we catch her before she enters, it will be worth it.'

'Damn, but you are an idiot,' Sand hissed. 'We should have some plan to save her if she puts her pretty little head in a noose, and we are too late.'

I nodded and thought about it. 'Try to find some rope.'

He stopped at that. 'Rope? Will you tie her up? You going to tame Valkai the Heavy and ride him around the harbor side?'

'No,' I said sadly. 'I have an idea. In case, we are too late.'

'Odin help us,' Sand cried and found some rope.

## CHAPTER 3

Dagnar has many dark places where few men should venture—at least without preparation and good company—and no decent woman should even think about it, company or not. The Gate District, the Bad Man's Haunt and the harbor has many such places, and while the Mad Watch guards were relatively thick in the harbor area and the gates to protect the customers and the merchants alike, there were corners of the harbor where even the Mad Watch did not venture without numbers and an element of surprise.

The shadowy maze of dirty alleys behind the bustling market was one such place, and while it had a few dead ends, there was only one *Dead End*.

That was the bloody land of Valkai's gang, the Grim Jesters. They specialized in break-ins, outright thievery and smuggling and were known to take the *Trade* very seriously. They housed themselves under the streets where the Old Town lay half forgotten, and there Valkai, a man of sinister and dark reputation, a former, disgraced captain of the army ran his business. They hired out at times if the price was right, and they knew how to keep their mouths shut. Usually we knew how to avoid them in the streets and didn't venture anywhere near the known rut of an establishment that served as a doorway to their nefarious underworld, the Dead End Tavern. There were great many entrances to the Old City, but this was their storefront.

'Never seen the shit-smelling tavern,' Sand complained. 'Never wanted to.'

'We cannot let her go there without the coin. They might sell her to the Tarmin slaves from the south. They might, if they have already performed their end of the deal and she cannot. They might just hurt her.' I said and kicked a stone so it clattered along the alley and scared a mottled cat into a panicky flight.

'Damned knight,' Sand spat, but he ran with me, nonetheless.

'I wish I was one,' I told him. 'At least I'd be armed. Sword, that would be nice.'

'You cannot use one, though.'

I spat. 'I could fall on it before they break my pretty face.'

'Well, you can always take a new one,' he said drolly, and but I was too scared to laugh. We dodged half-clean laundry stretched across the sooty streets. We kept slipping on what we hoped was mud. The stench of the alleys grew more pungent as we went on, the number of people grew fewer and most everyone had a look of poverty and desperation. It was the land of lawlessness, the part of the city you only moved when there was nothing else left. The bustling chorus of the harbor area abated as if even the sound was reluctant to visit the place.

Then we saw the infamous, a formerly grand alleyway with moldy lion statues on each side. They were staring ahead, once noble decorations as if ashamed of their current lot. Music wafted from behind the corner, a sad flute, and a ribald lute mixing in strangely, as if two musicians were waging a desperate battle between melancholy and merriment.

'Here we are,' I told Sand and peeked around the corner. 'I doubt she found her way—' But she had.

There stood our lady, her hands folded under her breasts. She looked bright and petite, and her hair cascaded down low behind her back. She was staring at two greasy men sitting in a table, set at a porch of a tavern, eating thick, blackened bits of mutton, taking no note of her. We did not budge. Sand was swallowing nervously. 'Should we … you just take it to her and tell she dropped it? Smile politely at the gents and bow out?'

'Yeah, I'll just explain the cut strings while I'm at it. That is just a great idea,' I said. 'She might tell them to clobber me.'

'But—'

And then Valkai the Heavy appeared.

He was heavy, there was no doubt about that, as he was one large, evil block of mischief, but the name came from his preferred execution method. He would jump on the victim until the ribs were broken. And then he would jump some more, just to make sure he didn't miss any. The man wore practical leather pants and a white shirt, stained yellow with ale, and his left ear was missing. It was only a lump of red-white scars and rumors said the king's Elder Judges had punished him right before he had been kicked out of the army. None knew the crime, but judging by the man's face, it could be anything. There was a manic gleam in his eyes, and everyone thought he was mad. There was also a sly look of cunning and a hint of brooding sorrow, brutality, and barely disguised civility. He was like a wolf in the disguise of a man.

'That's him?' Sand whistled. 'Big. Dangerous. I'll go home now.'

'Bear is bigger,' I whispered, but Sand's father did not have as ferocious a reputation.

'He is not here, you—'

'Shh,' I told him.

The woman bowed like the nobles did, quickly, as if the act was insulting. She knew him. Or of him. That's not usual for a noble female of one of the top ten houses. While women served the state, learnt arms and lore both, dealings with scum like Valkai were usually dealt thought contacts that could be found in the Brewery, and for a good reason.

'Lord? Am I on time?' she inquired.

The man chuckled crudely. 'Yes. And no. Do I look like a lord?' He turned around to show his disheveled condition and made a small mocking dance.

She waved her hand around the filthy, dark alleys and the tavern. 'There are no *noble* houses here in the shadows. But that does not mean there are no lords in the dark.'

'You are correct, small one.' He jumped down from the rotten platform, and the two thugs got up as well, wiping their greasy mouths. They all approached her, but she didn't flinch. Gods, she was brave. *Or stupid*, I thought. There had been a noble once, who tried to buy a murderous deal from Valkai, they said in the Lamb. That one had displeased the Jesters enough to be sliced into fist-sized chunks they fed to their dogs. I looked around to see if there were any around, but I only saw a dozen cats staring at us with their pitiless eyes. 'So,' he nodded at her. 'We are here, you are here, and shall we move forward with our business?'

'Have you found a way?' she asked imperiously. 'And please do not make a play out of this meeting. I hear you like to keep your clients hanging. We are desperate, as you know, but we need a way.'

'To the point, eh?' Valkai mused. 'Have we found a way to please the young lady?' he asked a man and I flinched, worried for the girl.

'Yes, perhaps,' the man to Valkai's right said with a vicious grin, and the prominent leader of the gang thumbed him.

'He found a man. This deed will be dangerous. Never done it before. Not that I can remember. It cannot take place in the Tower of the Temple. Up there, it is just too hard. Risky.'

*Tower of the Temple?* I thought. *The impregnable fortress of the king?* It had stood there—on top of the hill—for over two thousand years, guarding the ruins of the temple, the noble house of the Danegells, the hub of Dagnar. Survivors of the ancient wars built it, slowly, with purpose, fought to drive off pirates, ravaging savages, armies of conquering nobles. What business did the girl have with the place. Or the king?

She squinted at the thug. 'But is it possible? And I know it cannot take place in the Temple. *I* told you this. I hope you have not spent your time trying to find a way in. There is none.'

'I didn't,' Valkai said. 'But—'

She went on. 'I also told you where *we* think it might be possible.'

Valkai grunted like an animal. 'You did. Shut your face for a moment. I am not trying to sell you something you already know well enough.' He pointed a finger up the hill. 'There is a way. It will be very dangerous. It will be hard. But I think it is possible. Alrik, a rogue of mine, found a way as he stole in the house you told us about. He snooped around, asked questions, and did well. He sent me a missive and tried to find out more, but failed. What he got out of the household is enough. He hung today by the way, should you care.'

'I'll send his some flowers to his grave,' she stated emotionlessly.

'He ain't got a grave. He's a thief,' Valkai's eyes were burning as he took a long look at the slender female before him, his eyes running across her shapes. 'He succeeded. But as you know, one does not hand over the goods until one is paid.'

She laughed. It was a clear and high and happy voice and utterly inappropriate in the presence of the rogues. It was a show of bravery. Sand and I fell in love with her at that moment. Again. Except for Valkai. He frowned. She was apparently still chuckling as she addressed him. 'I wish to know the details. How will she die?'

*She? Die?* I thought and looked at Sand.

He shrugged, scratching his face. 'She's not a very nice girl, after all, is she? Bloody conspirator. Probably some business associate they want gone for good.'

'I—'

Valkai disrupted me. 'I've got the details,' he said harshly as a man ready to pounce, 'a way to kill the bitch. I'll give you all the details. And I'm not even asking why, though one hears things.'

'One does indeed,' she smiled, 'and I hear you have a family.'

They all froze. Valkai has a family? Was she threatening *him?*

Finally, Valkai shrugged. 'I see. Dangerous games you are playing. Whether I do, or I do not, is no business of yours. But I see there are other people you know in the shadows, and I shall remember that. That's surprising for a noble house of such a low rank.'

'Rank's got nothing to do with it,' she answered. 'And don't worry. We know little. But we can learn more.'

Valkai grinned, clearly impressed by the girl. 'I see you understand the game, but do you understand how far one goes before one goes too far? We shall see. I stand warned, of course, and this business will not spread beyond this alley. Jester's keep their traps shut.'

'Thank you,' she said sweetly. 'Please, go on with the details.'

'As I was saying,' Valkai growled, 'I have a way. It involves a doppelganger.'

'Really?'

'Yes,' Valkai said suspiciously, trying to read the girls face. As she didn't object, he went on, relieved she would let him speak. 'Alrik told us there is a man. The man is with *her*, serves her, in fact, and he will leave the house that day, for a while.'

'So you will switch?' she stated neutrally. 'You still need a man who looks *exactly*—'

He slapped his meaty thing forcefully. 'And I *do* have someone who looks just like him. I also know a discreet way to switch them up when he leaves the house for a few hours. Then our man goes in and does his thing.'

'What does the man do for her? What is his … thing?'

'Let's just say he is perfect for the job,' Valkai said with pride. 'He is just about perfect.'

'Just about? May I see this person?' she asked sweetly. 'I assume you have him or her at hand?'

'You may,' he agreed. He whistled, and a man in the red and black royal livery of *the king* appeared to stand on the tavern's porch. A red tabard covered his chest and hung to his knees. A dark eagle was imprinted on the chest, and it was the house Danegell insignia. A silver belt hung on his hips, and his boots were long and supple. Dark, thick, braided hair hung behind his back. He had thin cheeks and blue eyes. 'Meet …Asfal. I'll not call him by the name of the one he is supposed to mimic.'

She strode forward purposefully. Her white hem was dirtied as she carelessly stalked through a puddle of mud. She jumped effortlessly past the men and climbed some rotten stairs up to the tavern. Her face had a concentrated frown, and she seemed to ignore everything else around her as she went to stand on the terrace of the filthy tavern. She didn't even slap at the flies that escaped some bit of old rotten meat in the corner. She walked around the man, running a finger across his back. The man flinched. She stood there for a moment, frowning, and kept the finger there on the man's back, and didn't move. He did. He slithered out of her reach and she came to stare down at Valkai. 'I know who this man is to mimic. The idea is good. But he needs to be trained. In so many ways, they are alike, but then, in the critical ones, not so much. But he has … possibilities. He looks almost exactly like him.'

'He has been trained,' Valkai said darkly. 'Will be trained more. It is not your concern.'

'Not my concern? It is my damned concern, Valkai. He is skittish as a virgin before her wedding night,' she said with a nasty sneer that would have fit a queen of pirates. 'And the real thing can fight like a battle-loving barbarian. Which he used to be, in fact. Isn't that so?'

Valkai dismissed her concern with a snort. 'He will learn. He can fight. Probably won't need to, though. And as you said, he looks just like—'

'Yes,' she agreed. 'He does look like him. But—'

'*That* is the most important thing. Our actor here owes someone nasty a lot of money and will be paid well, and so he is motivated. And—'

She jumped down and walked to Valkai. 'How will you do the change?'

'You really want every detail?' Valkai despaired.

'Every single damned one.'

Valkai scratched his face for a while, struggling with his patience, that was not rumored to last for long periods of time. Perhaps he was counting the gold in his mind, and I cursed as I had it. He went on. 'Our man has vices. A vice, really. We will grasp an opportunity when he goes out to indulge in it. We have our ways and know his. That is why you pay us. Though you have yet to *show* the gold.'

'He is a slave,' she said with suspicion, not giving up. 'A trusted slave, true, but he never leaves her side. He is bound to her. He has to be, because—'

'No,' said Valkai. 'He is a trusted slave, as you said. And she does not need him *all* the time. He gets around. And in any case, he is always there when the bitch eats,' he grinned.

'She must die. It must not fail,' she said. 'Much depends on it.'

'I guess we know why she has to die,' Valkai grinned. 'To elevate you? Rumors say Morag fills his bed with you. And perhaps you aim to be the queen after the current one dies?'

*The queen?* Sand's eyes were huge as saucers, and we both regretted entering the alley. She wasn't plotting a murder alone. She was plotting a regicide. *And* she was the king's lover.

She stared at Valkai coldly, the beauty enhanced by the brief fury in her face. 'Now *you* are going too far. But I am indeed after Morag's ... heart.' She made it sound like it had nothing to do with love, only Morag's heart. And then I realized that's exactly what she was saying.

'Are they *also* after the king?' I whispered to Sand, who shook in terror. 'Look, she looks far less lovely now. I say—'

'Fuck us,' he whispered back. 'Can we go and get insensibly drunk and pretend this never took place?'

'No,' I said with some regret. 'No, I can't. I want to but can't. I still cannot leave her there, a murderess or not.'

'I can,' Sand whispered, but didn't move.

Valkai smiled hugely and bowed in a mockery of apology. 'So, let's agree you are happy and move on to the down payment. Gold. Or ... ' he spoke, but she interrupted him with a sigh.

'Favor?' she said tiredly. 'Yes, I heard the Jesters give their clients this choice. Gold or favor. We'll not owe you any favors. Gold it is. As agreed.'

'I'll give you a discount if you spend the night in my bed?' Valkai said crudely and smiled nastily.

She tapped her tooth with a finger. 'Will you be in it?'

'Yes, I—'

'Then I'll sleep in mine, thank you,' she said sweetly. Her eyes were judging Valkai as if someone had just offered her a plate of offal.

'Fine,' he grinned as she said nothing. 'Cough it up. Have you someone near holding it? Somewhere? Give me six now, twenty later. Or ten when Asfal here has begun his performance. Ten when she is dead.'

She shrugged. 'Six now, twenty when it is all over. I have the gold here,' she told him quickly and thinly as if loath to pay him anything.

'Where?' he frowned.

'Here,' she said and patted her side, and I swear I could see her fighting to hold her composure. Her hands were frantic for just a moment and then her shoulders relaxed.

Valkai was looking at his feet and then gestured at his thugs, who moved closer to her. Then he fixed a feral stare her way. 'Send a girl to deal with such important issues, and she fails.

Did you lose it? Spent it? Or have you not, you self-centered, isolated fool of a noble cow heard of thieves in the harbor?'

'I seem to have been robbed,' she agreed coolly. 'I will fetch the coins.'

'You will fetch the coins?' Valkai said slowly. 'No. We will take the favor instead.'

'No,' she said quietly.

'And you will spend the night here, after all,' Valkai laughed, and rage tugged at my guts. One of his brutes stepped forward as Valkai snapped his fingers. 'We will send word to your family. You will stay here until this deal is secure. Surely, you cannot expect to walk out of here after we explained what we are offering? We have no payment.'

Still she refused. Resolutely. She pulled the fabulous, glittering sword. 'I said I shall go and fetch the coin. Then I shall be back. That's all there is to it. I am a Blacktower, not some common merchant with a reputation for thievery.'

'Shit,' Sand said softly, fingering his knife. 'What will you do?'

'Alrik worked for them, no?' I said chokingly.

'So he said,' he agreed. 'They say it's so in the Lamb. You've heard 'em. Just take them the coin.'

'Valkai will kill me just to show he means business,' I told him. 'I need to scare him shitless.'

'Scare Valkai shitless?' Sand breathed. 'You hit your head or something? What are you—'

'Let's see how they take to meeting Alrik again,' I breathed.

Sand's eyes bulged. 'You wouldn't—'

In the alley ahead, the thugs had pulled long spears from where they had been hidden under the tavern floorboards and pointed them at the now obviously furious girl who was blocked by the chief of the criminals. Valkai was pulling a long skull-pommeled dirk. 'You know, it would be much easier if you just came along nicely. Might be you won't go home if you take this attitude.'

'I'm Shaduril Blacktower and no street wench, held against my will! I said I shall fetch the gold,' she took a step backwards, and then the thugs rushed forward, careful not to hurt her with the spear blades, but they prodded and pushed her, and her glittering short sword swished in the air as she tried to fight them off.

'You need to be humbled, girl,' Valkai said darkly. 'I'm sure that will be fine with your family. This is, after all, quite a delicate matter the king would love to hear about. And thank you for warning me in the matter of my family. As I said, I'll make sure they are safe.'

'You bastard, I—'

'I am a bastard, girl. Never knew my parents,' Valkai said happily and dodged under her blade and pushed her so hard she fell against a rotten wall. 'Ropes. Take her to my room.'

'Give me our rope,' I wheezed to Sand, my face twitched, and I nearly pissed myself from fear. It would have been perfect if I had, for my face flowed painfully, and soon it was Alrik's, who had indeed pissed his pants when he died. 'Get ready to run.'

'This is crazy!' Sand said and tried to grab me as I walked forward. I took the rope and left it on my shoulder and tied it around my neck. I bit my lip as hard as I could and felt the blood flow freely. I let it, and it trickled to my chin and chest. I hoped my face was as pallid as Alrik's had been at his death.

I took a deep breath, prayed to the Gloom Hand, and then shuffled forward.

They turned to look at me in alarm.

I was still swathed in shadows as I walked forward, and I heard Sand curse and then quaff behind me, despite the dangerous situation. I did not feel like laughing, for surely I was about to die.

'Who in Hel's rotten name is it? The tavern's closed,' Valkai said gruffly. The girl was staring at me with a frown.

I stepped into the light.

I saw them suck in their breath. I adopted a feral, snarling look and shuffled forward purposefully, if slowly and uncertainly, blood flowing down my chin, and the rope around my neck made me gag as I had pulled it too tight. The doppelganger, the man in king's colors, was blanching, taking steps away, and so were the two brutes. 'Alrik?' Valkai asked very softly, surprised, and there was a satisfactory shudder of animal like fear in his voice.

I gathered my bravery, fixed a dead eye on him, my hands coming up jerkily as if to embrace him.

'By Odin's ball hairs,' one of the brutes whimpered, and then he ran, tripping over chairs and a table, wine, and mutton went flying. The other one was taking steps away, shaking his head, and Valkai was struggling with his fear. *I was Alrik. I had died. Everyone knew this*, I assured myself. The girl was shuffling by the wall, inching her way past the dreaded criminal. I stopped to stare at Valkai with a confused frown. 'Alrik?' He breathed again, and then the girl ran. She stared at my face and I, the idiot, grinned and winked at her.

Next thing I remember was a stinging pain in my jaw and cheek and the kiss of cold mud on my lips.

'Freak,' Valkai said above me. 'What the Hel are you?' Then he kicked me, and I went to sleep for a while.

## CHAPTER 4

I came to in a dungeon with a sputtering torch on the wall. I noticed my rope was hanging right above me from a rusty hook. It looked ominous, to say the least. The ceiling was glistening with moisture, fungus, and rot, and there was a tunnel leading somewhere to my left. I quickly discovered I had iron and leather clamps on my wrists and ankles, and I was stretched out on a crude table that reeked of sweat, blood, and shit. All were alarming proof of the discomfort of the previous occupants of the dreadful thing. I also noticed my face was my own, and there was a cat staring at me from a dark shelf. I experimented with my chin and found I could speak.

'Frigg's milky tits,' I cursed and moaned.

A figure chuckled in the dark. I yelped and composed myself as best I could as I tried to see the face, but could not. 'Stop struggling, you idiot,' it said, and I could not decide if the voice was that of a man or a woman. 'Here, some wine? The best down under.'

'Yes, thank you. Don't have any coin to pay for it, though,' I croaked.

'You are a knight, are you not?' the figure chuckled. 'Hero of all the ladies in trouble, eh? They never pay their bills. Knights. Not the ladies, either, for that matter.'

'In that case, I'm a knight indeed,' I answered, and the figure stepped from the shadows. It was wearing long, tent-like robes of black, and on its face there was a simple, ominously horned mask of silver. It carried a silvery golden goblet and stopped next to me. 'Raise yourself a bit.'

'Do I need to be tied down like a pig carcass prepared for a roasting?' I asked.

'Yes,' the masked one said, and I decided I had better not give them any more ideas on how to kill me. 'Here,' it grunted and poured many mouthfuls of liquid down my throat. I gratefully swallowed all I could, though by the taste of it I should have taken the time to enjoy it. It was fruity, exotic, and sweet at the same time and likely very expensive. The figure pushed my face away and let drop the expensive cup. The clang on the moldy floor was gratingly loud, and I winced.

The figure came forward to wipe some residue off my lip. Its gloves were silken and dark. 'Quite a dramatic figure you cut, sir,' I told it.

'I'm not a sir. Nor a lady. I'm the Jester.'

'Ah, Valkai?' I asked, knowing it was not the brute. Valkai would have been jumping up and down on my ribs already instead of serving me tasty wine. Unless he had a sense of humor under the coarse, brute skin, which I was sure he did not.

'No,' it said with a dry chuckle. 'Valkai is not here, to your comfort. He is conducting our business elsewhere. I must say, it was very impressive what you did to distract my dear captain Valkai. But I'm not impressed by your thieving abilities.'

'She noticed nothing. Nothing, I tell you,' I blurted with pride. 'I whisked past her and took the pouch, and she came here, thinking she was still rich. And you—'

'Ah, Maskan,' the figure laughed, and I cursed for I just could not make out the sex of the thing addressing me. Not knowing that much left you curiously out of options. Flirting might help, if it was a woman, but if it were a man, the situation might get very uncomfortable. In many ways. Then again, if it were a woman, she might cut my balls off for such insolence. I told myself to be quiet. The masked one went on, running a finger across my forehead. 'Of course, you did splendidly with the pouch, yes. But you failed after that, though; despite Valkai's designs, the girl was in no true danger. Yet, a thief that felt responsible for her? The mark, the victim? Terrible business. Hardly professional. I'm sure you agree.'

'Yes, I agree. But she had a lovely smile. And ample buttocks,' I defended myself, cursing for I suddenly realized the creature had known my name.

'She is fair. Takes after her mother, I am sure,' the thing allowed, still not giving up its sex by agreeing or disagreeing with my brazen comments, not in any obvious way, and I felt it understood my game. The silver mask was hovering above me. 'But I have to admit your other skill gives me pleasure. It was something ... unexpected. And expected in some way.'

'I don't understand. What skill are we talking about? Any why is it both unexpected and expected?' I said dully, and the finger pressed on my forehead with such force I winced.

'The last man who lay on this bench cried. We thought him merely stubborn. So very, very stubborn. Couldn't understand why he would not speak. People came to see us play with him, and wagers were made widely in the guild on when he would eventually speak up. He was a bastard. He was a stubborn bastard, and one who did not pay his loans, and we hated him for it, for we knew he had hidden his gold and silver. But he wasn't stubborn, and perhaps not a bastard, either, just a mute. He had no tongue. As we broke him here on his very bench, we finally found out the truth when we tried to remove the tongue, which was not there. We had taken the toes and the fingers already, you see? We should have saved his hand so he could have written the whereabouts of the coin, but we lost him and the gold. Our silly mistake. And you can imagine all the grumbling after they found the bets were all for naught.' The thing went quiet, and I shrugged. It poked me once more. 'The lesson is: while we make mistakes, the suffering is usually done on this bench. We lost gold, he lost everything and went to Hel. Do not play dumb with us, Maskan.'

'No,' I agreed with a frightened smile I did not need to fake. 'I shall not. We are speaking of Alrik, then?'

'Your face looked like Alrik's, indeed. Your undead imitation left a lot to be desired, though, and the blood was a gross exaggeration, but certainly, nothing takes away the brilliance of what you did otherwise. The King would likely shut you in jail to be examined, and the One Eye priests would kill you should you do something like that in their presence in the south. You know magic is not only forbidden, but it is also denied. So tell us about this skill?'

'I've always had this skill,' I complained. 'Not my fault. Can hardly ignore it.'

'No, don't apologize. You have kept it a secret for such a long time.' The thing moved around me, and I could not see it.

'Who are you?' I asked, trying to keep calm.

'Who? Call me the Horns.' The Horns, I thought, is mad as shit, and I squirmed as I felt it was close to me, somewhere very close. 'I'm the head of this fine establishment and the gang.'

'Good. Yes, I guessed. Makes me feel important,' I said. 'Thank you.'

'You are most important, young Maskan. Most important,' it said. 'And do not worry, for you will walk out of here free. One day.'

'I will. Thank you,' I agreed, hating the last part of the promise. One day? Then there was silence for the longest of time. I was seething with impatience and lost the fight. 'I could leave right now and let the day be today?'

'No, not yet, young one,' the thing said. Then I saw movement, and something was placed on my chest. A ghastly head. It had thick braided hair, blue eyes, and thin cheeks. It had been handsome once. It was the man they had introduced to the girl and the one who had had a place in their common plans. It was bleeding on me, and I was swallowing in revulsion.

'Lovely present,' I said with a hint of panic in my voice, 'but I already ate. One of those sandwiches by the docks. I highly recommend them.'

The thing chuckled. 'You know what that is? And who it is?'

'I don't know its name.'

'Don't be coy. I just told you. We make mistakes, but you will do the suffering. You heard the discussion in the alley. Asfal. That was the name of this lost waif of the south, one I saved once from starvation and debt, and I did it for he looked like someone. I gave him gold; he gave me his allegiance,' the figure leaned over me, looking at me upside down. Dark eyeholes looked dead in the dark. 'You know the Blacktowers have an agenda. An extremely dangerous agenda.'

'Yes, they seem to be up to no good,' I agreed. 'Naughty.'

'Alrik was working for me after he was caught in the Blue Door Section. He managed to accomplish his mission, and so his death was no big deal, after all. He died swiftly, and they thought he was but a thief.'

'This ... the head seemed to be significant for your plans, no? Was the person to imitate someone? A ... bitch? Bitch, yes, who was to die as she visited her home from the Tower of the Temple. And this man was her companion?'

'He is not her companion. He works for her. Yes. And now this one is dead.' The mask stared at me.

'Why is he dead?' I asked, dreading the answer, and the head toppled away to roll on the ground. 'Is the deal off?' I asked after it had stopped rolling.

'Did you get a good look at his face?' it asked.

'Oh,' I breathed. 'You want me to—'

'Do it,' it coaxed me with a savagely poking finger.

I concentrated, resigned to my fate. I felt my face run like liquid, and then the thick hair grew around me. I felt the bones and skin writhe, and as I looked up at the silvery mask, I could nearly imagine it grinning. 'Happy?'

'The Blacktower girl was right,' it said. 'Our doppelganger was a coward. Sloppy. Useless, perhaps. But you will not be. No, you will not be useless. You are worth your weight in gold.'

'I work for my family,' I told it sourly, though the thought of my weight in gold made me stammer. 'And I have another rule. I do not abide suicide missions. What you are doing seems dangerous. Anything beyond the Third Ring is dangerous. Sometimes beyond the Fourth Ring.'

'It is dangerous. Tell me, do you hate the King?' the silver one asked.

I groaned. 'I'm not a noble. I am a commoner. I cut purses in the harbor. I care nothing—'

'But you do. Your father died at his hands. He, like so many others, was innocent. The King is going mad. Has been for decades. Danegells are a broken family of curs.'

'Ah, so it is not only the Blacktowers who have a cause,' I blurted, wondering how it knew of my family.

'No,' the Horns said. 'And yes, I know who your mother is. I have my ways. And I know about your father.'

I mulled it over, upgrading my opinion of the Horns. Mad, but brilliant. 'And why does a lord, or a lady, of such a well-to-do band of criminals care of the King's many intricate problems with his nobles?' I asked, brooding like a child, utterly unhappy.

The silver mask had no mouth, but I could see the person behind it get excited by the way it leaned back and then shot forth. I flinched as the mask's horns nearly poked my eyes out. 'We should all care. The alliance of the north is a fragile thing. We have the swords to fight the south when the so-called High King Balic eventually attempts to make slaves of us, but should the King be mad enough to topple without a fight, to attack our allies to the north over some damned insignificant trading port? He is insane and unable to lead us in the time of our great need. Such a time might come any day. That will not do. No. He is alienating the other kingdoms. The Fringe Lands are easy to gobble up by the south should our King fall to his madness and start wars that are totally useless. This is the Blacktower worry. And mine.'

I prayed and decided to argue. 'Still, I doubt a change of a king would alter many things for the thieves and the guilds of criminals. Surely, they would still thrive if the High King or some minion of his replaced this king. Like rats, they would adapt.'

The hand grasped my face. 'The High King burns thieves alive. And you are as much a rat as we are.'

'Ours hangs them slowly,' I said. 'Dead is dead. Rat or man.'

It nodded. 'More, Balic makes sure not a stone is left standing of the cities he takes in the east and the southwest of the Verdant Lands. His Hammer Legions are not like our armies. They take very few prisoners and rarely leave civilians untouched. And the priests will question the ones that hide and survive his wrath. The High King thinks himself the mantle-bearer of Odin. He thinks he *is* Odin. He brooks no challenges to his rule, and thus he hates the north as he hates any land that does not willingly bow down to his cult. No, they will not spare a rat here.'

'I see. And the solution?' I mumbled, and the Horns let go of my face.

'We need a new king,' it said quietly. 'We cannot replace the High King. But we can replace our Danegells.'

'And this is a task ... for ... me? A cutpurse.'

'Your task is to kill the Queen, to be specific,' the silvery one stated happily as if it were planning a breakfast meeting with the family. 'The Blacktowers are right. They hired us, but I would have helped them without a fortune in gold.'

'This is the bitch you were speaking of? The Queen. I see. I see,' I smiled, feeling an urgent need to shit my pants. 'You want me to take the place of someone in her entourage. Someone close to her.'

'Her slave,' the silver one said. 'The one who tastes her food before it is taken to her.'

'Her food and wine taster?' I asked, horrified.

'He is called Falg Hardhand. Formerly a fighter of the southern mountains, he tastes anything and everything they serve her.'

'He will have to die first before I take over his face. And she ... ' I babbled in panic.

The Horns smoothed my face for my voice had broken. 'Yes. Falg will die and then the Queen. They will both have to die, Falg preferably so that few witness the event. But that is not all. One more, the last one has to fall. The King. He has a lover. The lover could have killed him anytime this past year, but it serves no purpose if the Queen is alive. There will be a double murder, my sweet boy, for the sake of the nation. Valkai thought she was aiming to take the Queen's place, but she wants to kill him.'

'Who is his lover?' I asked, though I knew the answer.

'You know,' the thing said with a dry laugh, 'he has a fancy for our common acquaintance. Shaduril Blacktower. He is close to her. Every day, near every night. And she will slay our King, the Beast of the North, the moment we know the Queen is dead.'

'Shaduril …' I began, feeling foolish using her name, and I blushed, 'will kill the King in bed?'

'Ahh,' it said with amusement. 'I see. You are jealous. She does not love the King, no. She is doing all of this for the nation. She will be in terrible danger, and I don't know if the Blacktowers even plan for her to survive. But you will make it. Do not worry. You have unique talents. No worries at all.'

'No, of course not. Nothing to worry about,' I told the Horns carelessly. 'She will kill the Beast of the North? How?'

'Blade and poison,' the thing said seriously. 'It is possible. It will be very exciting.'

I nodded. 'Exciting. I'm so happy I met you.'

'So am I. Jubilant I met you,' it told me cheerfully. 'You simplify the plans. Your skill, it does simplify many things. Greatly. Our man,' it kicked the head on the floor, so it spun into the darkness and hit the goblet with a dull, clanging noise, 'would have been a constant, nervous risk.'

'What do you get out of this?' I asked the Horns. 'Other than the noble cause of securing your hunting grounds and your victims, the poor sods who will stay alive for you to maul and rob.'

It considered me carefully for a time. Then it took a deep breath and shrugged. 'If we are partners, then, of course, I shall share somewhat more of my thoughts with you. Are we?'

'We are!' I agreed enthusiastically.

The Horns nodded slowly and spoke. 'The King is rich.'

'We want his riches? An ordinary robbery?'

The Horns nodded vigorously. 'We will give old Balan Blacktower what he wants, and while he is taking it, we will rob the Tower of his old treasures. They are old as time. Perhaps magical treasures. With such treasures, we will no longer be a measly band of thieves, living in the dark.'

'I see,' I said, and I admit a seed of greed sneaked into my heart. 'Magical items? And I can take part in this looting orgy?' It was mad.

'You are not greedy, are you, boy?' it said suspiciously. 'Yes, you can have your part. It's only fair. But I shall set the terms of any such deal if we manage to secure this hoard before the Blacktowers. I know Balan Blacktower would love to see what the Danegells hoard from time immemorial.' I nodded as I breathed deep. I had no choice, anyway. It chuckled dryly at me. 'Perhaps I'm happy there is a greedy spot in your heart. Makes the trust that much more easy to come by. I trust the greedy over the meek. They have needs, and needs I can provide for. I do hate knights. But you are an artist. A true artist. And I shall sponsor you to greatness.'

'Yes,' I agreed with a grin. 'An artist. What is required of me? Now, that is.'

'You will be at readiness, boy,' the thing said. 'We have more spies looking into the royal family and the Tenginell house of the Queen. You will learn the ways of this slave and then take his place, at an opportune moment. We think there is one, months from now. He will leave the house for a moment.'

'Do be diligent in your investigations,' I stammered. 'Even if I have his face, there will be suspicious guards, terribly hard passphrases, deadly traps, hungry beasts. It is well guarded, no doubt. The house. The Queen!'

'Well guarded,' the Horns said. 'Very well guarded. But it is her home. She grew up in that Tenginell house. She feels safe there. Worry not. You are like a fish in the water, and all you need to do is learn how to kill the cow and how to act. I shall show you to your room, then.'

'My room?'

'I told you,' the Horns said with a hint of impatience. 'You will stay here. You shall be an honored, greedy guest, who shall not so much as fart without permission.'

I nodded. 'Yes, I can see the merits of this, and indeed I do fart a lot, but you see, my mother will get upset if I'm not home for dinner,' I said happily, fighting the ripping fear. 'I can come back?'

'Your mother will be happy when you get your due, no? Worth some heartaches and missed dinners. We will send her word not to worry and, of course, she will, but she won't be left in the dark.' It stopped to consider its words. 'Well, they will be in the dark. I'll give them candles and a good amount of food, of course. Of course, you understand that I will fetch them here. For us to be partners, I need some assurances. You understand this?'

*Would they take my family as a hostage?* I cursed under my breath while I was nodding.

The Horns clapped a hand on my shoulder. 'They are safe. So are you. Don't be so afraid. Understand you are ours for now. Obviously our deal with the Blacktower family has to be sealed,' the silver one said unhappily, 'but we will control you. They won't. They would never have controlled the doppelganger, anyway. They are nobles, and while such creatures are as decrepit as we are in many ways, they have no ways to manipulate the lower folk, and lesser folk will do well in killing a queen. The men who will kill the Queen are creatures of crude habits and have no sense of honor.'

'I see,' I breathed. 'And so I'm your guest now? With no access to the outside world?'

'Yes,' it said. 'And no access to the outside.'

I rubbed my head. 'If Shaduril fails to kill the King, assuming I kill the Queen, of course, will you and the Blacktowers take the Tower of the Temple? Surely, you won't just wait until he comes to fillet you in revenge? And if you do, how? I hear it is impregnable. The Tower. That there is only one access, and it is well guarded. And even an army would fail—'

'Do not worry about such plans. Worry about your part,' it said.

'But—'

'You are a Grim Jester now, Maskan,' the Horns told me and yanked at my chains. They opened up, the metal and leather were broken. I stared at the sight of torn fetters in shock That had been a clear message to end all further arguments, and I took note of it. My face shifted, and I retook my own face. 'Much better,' the silver one said with an approving voice. It leaned closer. 'Understand, my friend, that if you do not do this, we will murder your mother, your half-sister, and brother, your stepfather. And perhaps, now, even your Shaduril. It is not beyond us. Say, "thank you."'

'Thank you,' I said as I sat up, feeling rotten and beset by fear. My neck hurt and so did my face, where the brute had struck me. 'So.'

It waved its hands, pleased. 'We will train you. I shall give you some more information. Falg is a slave, and as a slave to the Queen, he has habits and arrogance of a king himself. He is also a warrior and occasionally sneaks off to fights in the Dark Sands events. He has a partner, and they do very well,' I was told as I got up. The figure and my new master or mistress—I still did not know which—was shorter than it seemed. 'He will fight the day we shall exchange him with you. Perfect opportunity, no? Alrik found this out, by the way. We know the date of the Queen's visit, and we learned there were wagers made for Falg in the Tenginell house by the guards. For that very day, she is there. He will leave her for a while. You will need to train, and the plans have to be perfect. Though, perhaps not all that accurate. People see your new face, and they have no reason to doubt there has been any change. All you have to do is to act the part. Shaduril Blacktower will be happy, so will her father. And brothers and sisters. They shall all be heroes! Perhaps even elevated in the ranks of the city. Royals, if they are ambitious, or close to it, after all.' There was a hint of amusement in the voice.

'Murderous family,' I told it. *Such a sweet thing a killer?*

'Yes, but that is the way of change. It takes place only through a hail of blood. The Brothers will be the problem. They have to die, all Danegell guards. Not sure how Balan Blacktower plans on taking care of them, and I can see why you worry. They will have to go. All the witnesses as well, of course,' the Horns chuckled dryly, and I decided I was a witness already.

*What the Hel am I doing?* I thought. *I'm dead.* 'Indeed,' I said with a grin, massaging my legs as I walked up the slope. To the left and right, there were cells. I did not turn to stare inside the musty-smelling holes, but I could hear scrapes and groans of people still living in there. *People, or something else*, I thought. Water was dripping from above as we passed halls of a formerly glorious make.

'The Old City. The oldest, the very oldest parts are positively ancient. It was burned in the Hel's War,' the masked master said. 'Thousands of years ago. Two thousand and five hundred or so ago. Perfect for our needs.' It leaned on me with cool familiarity. 'Valkai's men know the ways, and I'm learning to. I might lead them, but they are unpredictable. I hate unpredictable.'

'The guards never venture here?' I inquired. 'Truly?'

The Horns shrugged. 'Many are corrupt. Not all. They occasionally do. Sometimes we tend to go too far, and even coin in the hands of an official does not make a crime go away. They sometimes raid. Especially higher, up the hill where we have some bases. These lower tunnels are long and lonely and dark. Last year, they sent twenty trained men to clear us out up there. They found nothing. Two got lost. We found them.' The voice was casual and cruel, and I nodded unhappily as a burly, fat turnkey looked up from a meal he was enjoying in a dark corner. His eyes betrayed incredulity as if it were unlikely for anyone to leave the dreadful housing below.

Up we went, and there were underground streets we passed, some with scorched walls and ancient signposts. Up above, I heard the tumble of a barrel as someone was pushing one along the road, and I wondered what time it was.

'Night,' the voice behind me answered. 'It's nighttime.'

'I see,' I told the Horns as it pushed me past some villainous-looking men. A man was climbing down the stairs of what was formerly an inn, and then I witnessed a sight to shock me.

A troop of fifty men was marching by, holding blackened shields and spears, their steps in sync and a young, fierce-looking sergeant was marching next to them. 'You raising an army?'

'Why not?' the Horns answered, guiding me toward an official-looking building where great bustle was evident; men and women going in and out of the building that was likely some sort of a tavern under the streets of Dagnar. 'We get runaways from all the armies in the world. And those who have nothing to eat learn to wield weapons fast enough. There are a thousand people living down here. Few want to escape.'

I hardened myself. *They needed me,* I reminded myself. They won't kill me if I try. And so I decided I'd be brave. 'You sound like a real benefactor. Look here,' I said and pointed at the muddy tiles we were walking on. The Horn leaned closer; I grinned, prayed, and then I pummeled my elbow to the silver mask hovering over my shoulder.

The figure of my nemesis fell back, apparently surprised even if unhurt by the string of curses drifting from under the mask. I thanked the gods when I saw the Horns falling right amidst the marching men, many of them toppling over my jailer. I thrust forward and ran for the crowded building with the bustling crowd of a hundred or so. As I ran, my face flowed, and I took on Valkai's feral, stubble-marked face. Behind me, the troop of men was turning in confusion and some shouts rang out from the sergeant. I dodged and weaved my way inside the tavern. 'Hold!' I yelled, my voice guttural and mad. 'A prisoner is escaping. All of you, quick as you can, you mottled pigs! To the nearest exit!'

They stared at me for a moment. I feared I had failed, and they would laugh like jackdaws until I was clamped in irons. Likely, they would laugh during a necessary and deserved ass-kicking as well. I also feared Valkai would get up from a table, his quivering finger pointing at me.

But no. A one-eyed man got up instead, so did fifty others, all pulling weapons, and they ran out, toppling two armored men about to grab me. 'This way!' one of the women in the group screamed.

'He's a thin scoundrel! Dressed in silks!' I yelled, and they growled happily and ran on. I ran amidst them, not looking back. The mostly drunken troop went on, passing confused guards, all of whom I exhorted to join us.

Finally, in the dark corridors and in the midst of a press of sweaty bodies, we came to a thick, musty door well-lit by a dozen torches. The guards protested briefly; I growled at them as an animal, and they stepped back, their faces pale. The doors were pulled open, and so we pushed on. 'Up!' I screamed and rushed out to an alleyway. 'That way!' I screamed and noticed it was a dead end. 'No, this way!' I growled, cursing myself for an idiot and led them to the street. Forty men and women of the underworld charged to the Red Pennant Path, the main street running from the harbor to the Temple, and I saw we were in the Blue Door's district.

The angry group stopped in the middle of the street, making no noise, realizing they were in fact rats that were caught in the open. They stared at me suspiciously. I spotted a nobleman walking with another, not far, obviously drunk. I prayed for forgiveness from the gods, should there be any and pointed my finger at him. 'That one! Grab him! Take him to the dungeons!'

And they did. They lost their apprehensions and charged him like mad, skittering things of Hel. The man was knocked down so quickly I barely noticed. There were screams in the dark and some guards yelled challenges as they came to rescue the poor man.

I stayed in the back of the group. My face flowed, and I took the face of the beastly jailer and ran. I was running as fast as my legs could carry me. My face felt fat and bloated in my otherwise fit body, but overall the disguise served its purpose. I ran like a madman, dashed through the gates that were to close at midnight, leaving some dizzied Mad Watch guards gaping as they had been checking the papers of some drunken merchants. I ran and ran, weaving amidst the hovels and formerly excellent residencies of the Gate District until I saw the Crumbling Tower of Bad Man's Haunt. It was the remains of a guard tower, jutting upwards in sad ruination like a broken finger of the damned, and at its base, I took a right for the wall. There was the Laughing Lamb, a long, low building with thin slits for windows, and I dodged to the alleyway, taking the seedy steps down the piss-smelling side of the building and thrust open the familiar door to the Shifty Crab, our cellar apartment, and business.

Mir got up. A gigantic bald man turned to stare at me, the Bear. Sand was in the midst of beating his hand on a desk, and Ann was leaning on a doorframe, her face pallid.

'Who in Hel's name are you?' the Bear asked, pulling at a brutal maul the size of a small trunk. 'We are closed!'

I cursed and turned away, shedding the fat face and saw their eyes round in shock, save for Sand. 'I'll explain that bit of strangeness later. Right now, we should leave this place immediately.'

Mother was pale. 'That bit of strangeness? You explain it now! Who are you? I just came home after looking for my boy and—'

Sand echoed me. 'He is right, and it is Maskan, indeed. I told you. We should leave—'

'Why? We can defend our home,' the Bear said with a deep growl, not letting go of the maul. 'You sure you are Maskan?'

'I am Maskan. Of course I am. The Grim Jesters took me—'

'I know. Sand told me. I was about to go and bargain—'

'They won't bargain. I met their leader, and they are out to kill the King. And the Queen,' I said hysterically. 'And they think I'm crucial to their plans. In fact, they made it so there is none else who can help them. And they told me they would kill you.'

Bear hit his fist on the table. It cracked. 'I say we stay, and we fight. This is our home. It'd be the day of shame I let those sewer-dwelling dog-eaters kick me out of my own hall!'

Mir nodded at Ann. The blonde girl sighed and walked forward. Ann's voice was calm and soothing, and she spoke without any hesitation. 'I think Maskan is right.'

Sand growled. 'And me!'

Ann continued, 'They are too powerful; they have a great need, and Maskan here can fulfill it. It will end up badly for us. All of us.' The Bear stared at her; Mir was nodding reluctantly and so was Sand. Ann had a very sensible effect on people, and I regretted running after Shaduril. Ann was beautiful. *Sort of,* I thought and cursed myself for my shallowness, for I knew I only cared for Shaduril. Ann looked at me and smiled quickly, then looked away. Women. They can all read thoughts; I cursed in my head.

'Oh fine,' the Bear rumbled and looked at Mir. She shrugged and came to me. She wiped my face and then my lip and looked deep into my eyes.

'Maskan?' she asked.

'Mother?'

'If we go now, someone else will take up the business,' she told me. 'It will be hard to rebuild what I have done for nearly two decades. We will go, but at least tell us why. They want to kill the royals?'

I rubbed my face. 'I don't want to tell you more. I think I should not have told you that much. The less you know—'

Bear grunted. 'You'll tell me, at least. And I'll make sure Shakes don't close the business.'

'You cannot touch Shakes,' Ann told him, and she was right. Shakes was the owner of the Lamb and unofficial king of Bad Man's. 'But we must go.' Ann leaned on the Bear. He struggled, blushed with anger and resentment, but finally nodded at his wise daughter.

'I have a place out of the city,' the Bear growled. 'Ann found it a year ago. We go there. And then we try to settle this thing. Your skill. It is precious. Your face. If you can ... change it. I don't get it. How?'

'Doesn't matter, Father,' Ann told him.

'I can change faces,' I agreed. 'I don't know why.'

The Bear shook his head in confusion. 'Ann?' The blonde girl looked startled but nodded. 'Send word to Molun and Kallir. We are taking residence in the Green Hall. Pack up, you lot. We are leaving posthaste.'

# BOOK 2: MORAG'S FOES

*'Remember to kiss the girl. You kiss her. She will be happy. Grow bolder, fool.'*
**Ann to Maskan**

## CHAPTER 5

'Why didn't you tell me about it?' Mir asked me as we stared at Dagnar's walls, the Dagger Hill and the Five Rings rising majestically in the distance. It was not very far, just over some hills. It was chilly in the house they called Green Hall, and our guards, Bear's two hulking, bald men Molun and Kallir had made it as warm as it could get. It was a spacious old hall with an excellent, long fireplace, hidden on the side of a hill, and a strange, mountainous waterfall cascaded from craggy rocks high above us. It was a place Bear used to hide in when he had committed some crime that attracted too much attention in the city. A small river formed by the cascading water was just a stone's throw away from it. The water was bright as a star, the streams running from the craggy hills and mountains of the Wooded Blight, a hill, and a mountain range splitting the peninsula of Red Midgard far to the borders of Ygrin and beyond.

The place was peaceful, so peaceful I resented the fact we had not been here before.

'Maskan!' Mir chided and nudged me while I was sitting on a bench outside the hall. Sand was grinning at my discomfort on the side, toeing acorns. I turned to look at Mother. She had long, braided hair of dark and gray strands; she was thin and pale, and her well-formed, beautiful face was mysterious in some strange way, especially when she was furious. And now she was. 'You know what the priests do to those who tap into magical skills, especially in the south? The King might as well. It's so rare these days, you cannot afford to risk getting caught.'

'They claim there are no magical skills at all,' I brooded. 'And I've already had this discussion before with Sand.'

'Well, we know they lie,' she said mulishly and pushed me. 'There is magic. You know it. I know it. I always did.'

I began to ask her what she meant, but the master of the hut arrived and leaned over me. 'There are plenty of southern spies, even possibly some One Eyed priests in Dagnar, fool boy. I suspect I know of two, both working for the High King, no doubt,' the Bear said as he pulled me up. I dusted myself down and wondered how such a large man could move so silently. 'They are looking for you. Not the priests, but the Jesters. They visited the Lamb thirty minutes after we left and were watching it like a hawk. Shakes is neutral. Cannot afford the trouble. They have a bounty on your head. And ours. They hope to find one of us to flush you out. But they won't.'

'Should we leave Red?' I asked. 'For good?' Ann shook her head at me as she slid out of the house.

'No,' she said, and Bear nodded.

'And go where?' The Bear grunted in anger, and Ann made a small conciliatory gesture at her father, whose rage abated nearly that very instant. His tone was calmer, even if a vein in his forehead was throbbing. 'The shit of northern kingdoms? The Fringe? There is naught but chunks of ice out there and their rich are Red Midgard's equivalent to the poor. Shit hard to make a living there.'

'It's not exactly that bad, love,' Mir purred, 'but almost. I agree. But it is better than dying in here. We need a plan.'

'And the south?' I asked, for that is where I wanted to go. 'Take our leave and start anew across the straits?'

Bear rubbed his face tiredly. 'And risk the chaos of their wars and live in a rat-infested hovel somewhere? We would stick out like a sore thumb, at least for a time. Time enough for the Jesters to find us. And you can bet they are looking at ships leaving the port already. Some Jesters are in Aten, across the straits, you bet. And how the Hel am I supposed to work there, eh? I don't know the land. It would be extremely trying to carve a nice little operation while we know nothing of their customs, laws, and rival gangs.'

'We could—' I began.

'What?' he asked thickly.

'Abandon the Trade. Work? We could work,' I suggested and looked away as I saw his face darken.

'Work? Till the land? Carry bales for merchants? I ... ' he began shouting, and then Ann stepped to him and put her hand on his shoulder, and he went calm. 'I won't be a sell sword for some lord I care nothing for. I'm from the north, boy, and while I steal and make life miserable for some folks here, I don't want to leave home.'

'So, what do you suggest?' I asked with a sullen voice.

'I don't know!'

Ann tilted her head at him. 'Remember what you planned for, a year past?' He always confided in Ann of his business plans.

'What?' he asked.

'The heist none has accomplished?' she whispered with a small smile. 'In the city.'

'In the city?' he asked, and his eyes went dreamy for a moment. 'Oh, yes. I remember. I put it off because we are highwaymen, and there is a terrible risk, but ...' he shook his head. 'We don't need the gold, though. We need to find a way around the Grim Jesters.'

Ann leaned closer to him. 'Or over them. There are hundreds and hundreds of them. Those caves underneath the city have to be purged. Perhaps we could have the King scourge the bastard Jesters from the face of Midgard?' Ann suggested. 'Kill the lot off? His honor is at stake.'

'You damned fool, Ann,' the Bear said and froze mid-sentence. 'How do they connect?'

'Maskan can change his face,' she said with a small grin. 'He can get in.'

'I ... ' His eyes took on a glazed look and his full mouth turned into a lopsided grin.

'What?' Mir asked. 'Honey?'

'Ann is right.'

'In what?' Sand asked, astonished.

The Bear pulled at his beard, agitated. 'Yes. We cannot go and challenge them, that's for sure. We are a tiny operation, and even if we allied with some others in the Bad Man's, many others would take their side. They are just too powerful; we would be slaughtered. We will not leave and give up our home. No. Not just like that. So, we should make sure the King takes the time to finally kill the lot.' He looked at me meaningfully.

'What exactly are you thinking about?' I whispered. 'You look like that Horns now, sizing me up.'

He placed a meaty paw on my shoulder. 'You will have to do something. There is something me and the boys have been yearning to do since forever,' he said with a feral grin. 'Ann has been thinking about it, and I think you just solved the problem. Show me your Valkai again.'

I sighed and did. I felt the skill resisting me for a moment, but then my face flowed, and my family stared at me with astonished looks. Mother put a hand over her mouth and sighed, whether in astonishment or pride, I was not sure. 'Close enough?'

'Pretty damned close,' the Bear said with an uneasy smile. 'Ear gone and all. Nearly stabbed you. Listen.'

I did. Sand groaned. I did as well. The Bear clapped my shoulder. 'It will be okay. You will have Molun and Kallir doing the killing bit, and you just get them in. It will take some weeks before we can move, I think, but this will be splendid.' He looked happy, then embarrassed. 'Or messy. It's possible, of course.'

The following week, I sat in an excellent tavern situated in the Third Ring. I had been uneasy getting into the city, but Molun and Kallir had false papers and good disguises and mine, of course, was superior. Bear traded with a hunter in the Hall, a savagely handsome man with a mustache. I wore the face now.

The white and blue, near pristine housings, made me uncomfortable after living in woody hills of the Green Hall, but there was a sense of safety and peace in the better section of the city, one the harbor and the gate rarely granted a visitor. People were rough and strong as any northerner, yet well-dressed in leathers, sensibly dyed wool and linen, their disposition calm and far less dour, and one did not have to expect trouble, not actively, not all the time. I had rarely ventured up the hill, but perhaps I should have, I thought as I gazed at a pair of maidens, their long legs on show as they hiked up their skirts to jump over puddles. As they walked past, they flashed me a smile. I saluted them with a nod, self-conscious as I was wearing a wealthy tunic of red velvet and a doeskin vest. My pants were white and soft, and I felt uncomfortable with them, preferring the rougher styles of the Bad Man's Haunt, but they went a long way if one wanted to play a noble of Dagnar.

I sipped my ale, kept my manners mild and listened in on the discussion of two armored soldiers nearby. They were tall and wide, part of the Hawk's Talon, the first brigade of Red Midgard. Real army, not the Watch. Their helmets were swathed in chain, covering their necks and throat, their armor was partly mail, partly plate and thick leathers covering their arms and legs, all dark red and black. The nation had four such armies of three thousand men each, and the Hawk's were the most elite, holding the capital safe with the Mad Watch. Their fort was the Silver Spur, just outside the town, and they also manned the Navy and its galleys with a permanent troop of five hundred marines. They had some duties in the city, not many, but those important enough not to be given to lesser soldiers. These were the jobs reserved for real, disciplined fighters. I had been sitting there on that seat for days, staring at the two professional soldiers, who escorted a tall man with an expensive leather coat, elegant shoes, and oily hair. His name was Naram, and he was an important man.

"The Affront" was a tavern next to a huge, brick fountain of uncannily blue water. It was flowing from the mouths of strange beasts with antlers. The tavern specialized in spiced dishes from the far south, and the man the soldiers dutifully escorted had an appetite for them. He sat a few tables away, eating; his duty was forgotten as he stared at the cleavage of a sultry redhead sitting just across from him and chatting merrily. *That was his lover, a whore*, I thought. She looked expensive, sophisticated. This man, the King's Master of Coins, subject to the Lord of Harbor was always spending an hour of the early morning in the whorehouse disguised as a tavern.

'Lith, dear,' he drawled as he licked his fingers like a delicate cat. 'I'll be back tomorrow. Shall I bring you anything?' the man cooed and the woman purred, whispering something in his ear, nibbling it, and the man laughed. 'That is part of the deal, love. I never leave home without it. Never worry!' Then he kissed her hand, and I watched him go. The stoic guards stomped after him for the Cliffside Mint, the King's own mint, and the crucial business this man was supposed to be overseeing. I stayed put, and the woman walked over. She sat down and smiled at me voraciously. I sipped at the ale and smiled at her. There was something about her that made me nervous. A bit like Shaduril had, I decided. Or any girl, for that matter. But she was strange and odd, and there was intensity in her I did not understand.

'I don't get it,' she said bluntly. 'I usually get it, but not this.'

'The Bear gets it, Lithiana,' I told her with confidence I did not feel.

'Lith,' she whispered. Her low cleavage was overwhelmingly disturbing, and I fought to keep my eyes on hers. Where Shaduril had been like a goddess, she was different. She was brazen and confident and spoke bluntly. A whore, I reminded myself, is brazen. Yet there was more to her, a layer of intelligence and bravery I could not understand. I feared and admired her.

I shrugged arrogantly and waved my hand imperiously to the direction of the mint. 'It is our business, and you are paid. That is enough.' I hoped such a come-what-may attitude would make her stop the questions. She frowned, doggedly interested in our business. I went on, hoping to finish the business fast. 'Tomorrow, he will come up to your room, as is the norm. And we shall be there. It is time, the Bear says.'

She leaned on her hand, smiling demurely. 'But why? Did my Naram gamble down in the Brewery and then refuse to pay up?' the woman asked, tilting her head. 'He does that, I hear.' She scowled briefly as she saw I was indeed reluctant to lift the veils of mystery on the matter. Perhaps she was unused to not being able to sway a man, and she tapped her long fingernail on the table to get my full attention. 'He has been good to me. He has good manners, plenty of money, and he calls me pretty. He does not have to, but he does. It is nice. He is the sort of catch you don't easily let slip through your fingers. So yes, I am still wondering what you will do with him.'

I snorted and leaned forward. 'Catch? He is skinny, arrogant and should his wife die, and he would marry you, he would soon find another special whore,' I said and froze, for I did not know what had prompted such an outburst. 'Though you are most beautiful,' I added meekly. She stared at me with huge, shocked eyes.

'Am I?' she finally purred. 'The most beautiful thing you have ever seen?'

I stammered and for some reason, did not wish to lie. 'No.'

'What?' she asked me, cocking her head as if she had misheard. 'No?'

'I recently saw a girl,' I told her. 'A blonde girl I saved. I am hers. And she does not even know who I am.' I felt embarrassed, and I was sure she would not take well to my honesty. I had called her a whore and then placed another above her. I was terrible with women.

She did look upset. Very upset. Then her eyes softened, and something changed in her. Where she had been arrogant and demanding and flirting, now she seemed determined to make me relax. She clapped my hand and nodded at me kindly.

She smiled knowingly. 'I thank you for the compliment and laugh at the insult. My, my, but the lusty, drooling, silent man on the side table has claws after all,' she breathed and leaned closer. 'And he is a romantic. A true romantic.'

'I am not drooling!' I insisted.

'If I poked you with a dagger, a stream of molten lust would drip from the wound.' She giggled. 'And then you would hate yourself, for you wish to keep pure for your little woman.' I blushed deeply and shook my head in denial. She went on, 'You look like you are not entirely young anymore, sort of weather-beaten, but there is something boyish in you.' She was ticking her tooth with a nail.

'I'm not sure where you get this,' I insisted, still blushing. 'And we have an agreement. I can only assume you will not go back on your word.'

She nodded. 'We have a deal. I have one. With the Bear. He pays me well. At least promises to. Enough to make a difference, and as I know what Naram does for a living, it might be possible that I will be delivered such a bounty. Risky, but possible. Instant wealth. It is something one can never overlook. Naram is a dead one.'

'He is,' I told her nervously. 'As agreed! We will not fail. No.'

'Good,' she whispered and hesitated. She looked distraught, her eyes gleaming with some mysterious feeling, and finally she got up, strangely driven. 'So, come and I shall show you the room.' She got up, and I followed her. She was a friend of Kallir and apparently, Ann and the Bear had always been wondering how to take an advantage of the lust of the Master of Coin. Then I had come along, and it gave us a perfect opportunity to hurt the Grim Jesters. *Perhaps permanently*, I thought nervously. I'd go to the lion's den, and we would rob the place clean. Then I'd show Valkai's face to the onlookers. That would test the patience of King Magor beyond endurance. Beyond breaking point if we knew our business. I went in through the silken shades, dodged an old waiter carrying mugs of dark ale for the customers outside. The sound of the fountain faded as the people inside—sitting on cushy seats of dark wood and pillows—ate and made merry. Lith pulled me up the stairs to a wide staircase of redwood and up there, the corridor spread right and left. Her room was on the left, and it had a white marble door. Each door was of different color and unique to the harlot.

I stopped at the door, blushing once again.

She grinned at me from inside. 'Coming in?' She stretched her hand to me and tilted her head alluringly, a triangular earring twinkling in the light of the oil lamps.

I considered it. She was offering me something few men would easily refuse. But I thought of Shaduril, and Lith terrified me, for some reason. 'Ah! No, not right now. I know the place, and I'll be here tomorrow.'

She gave me a disbelieving look, and I did not blame her. 'You are jesting, no? Must be some woman to do that to a man.'

I opened my mouth and went silent. Finally, I decided to speak. 'I told you. She is beyond me, but I fell in love with her. I cannot—'

'Love?' she said coldly.

'Yes,' I told her.

'That is not love,' she said, looking away. 'It's just lies. I'll show you love. Go, and be here tomorrow.' She seethed and slammed the door in my face.

'I am sorry. I think you are stunning,' I stammered, rubbed my face at the idiotic comment, and turned and ran away. I dodged some customers downstairs, weaved my way past the waiter again, then a woman looking for the toilet. A thin noble nearly fell on his back as I thrust him aside.

'Hey! Is your wife looking for you? Why are you rushing like that?' he yelled at me, and I dodged to the street. I calmed my nerves, slowed my steps, looked around, and noticed nobody was running after me. I resisted the urge to glance up at the windows of the whorehouse and managed not to, but only barely. I dodged to a tiled alleyway where Bear's two bald men were waiting.

Kallir grabbed me and pulled me aside, his eyes seeking danger, hand on a short dagger. 'Well?' he said. 'Why are you rushing about like that?' They were both short, powerful men. Both were well suited to Bear's profession of robbing people out in the wide roads of the Red Midgard, but they were very much at ease in the streets of the city as well.

'I went up there,' I told him as if the world was about to end.

'Lith asked you? Never asked me. Lucky boy,' Kallir said with a leer. 'Of course, if she were to see how ugly you really are, she'd rather not.'

I stared at him, berating myself that I was blushing again. 'I did not—'

He sneered. 'You didn't do anything? Never mind. Makes no difference,' he breathed, and I cursed as they rolled eyes at each other.

'Something like that,' I told him and tried to change the subject. 'It is all set, then. Did you find out what you need?'

They nodded. Kallir pointed at the north side of the Third Ring. 'I followed him for a week. He has keys to the mint,' Kallir said.

Molun continued. 'In his belt. I know because I've seen them. But I also found out something more. From a doctor.' He leaned closer, and I resisted the urge to push him back. He stank of sweat and garlic. 'The keys are forged into a chain, and the chain is crafted to his bone. I paid silver for that bit of knowledge. This doctor once treated him and had to rummage around his rear end a bit. Saw the chain in the flesh.'

'Gruesome,' I breathed. 'Bone?'

'Gruesome? Really?' Kallir asked, looking very confused, and then shrugged. 'Bone, flesh? I don't care. Anyway, this is the process: we switch you up. He or you will walk up there, arrogant as shit. You will open the first door to the mint, and then you ask for the day's passphrase from the two guards. Then you'll go in and tell this phrase to some fool inside. The mint's never been robbed, and I know nothing about what's in there. But this is the way in anyway.'

'But I'll take his face and clothes …' My eyes went round with suspicion. 'And the key?'

'We will handle that,' Kallir said with a grin. 'It's just a bone. Or flesh.'

'But I don't want it to be stuck in mine, that chain,' I said, and half asked.

'Don't worry. We'll just tie the chain on your pants. Have to extract the chain first, of course,' Molun said happily. He had a broad, simple smile, and I had to remind myself we were talking about a murder.

'Won't it make a mess?' I asked and decided it did not matter as they looked at me blankly. I shrugged, and the rogues finally nodded, in full agreement that it was a meaningless fact. I leaned on them. 'She says she is worried about her payment. She has been making a lot of coin off him.'

Molun patted my back as if to calm me. It was somewhat insulting. 'We will pay her. Pay her very well. What has she got from him? A coin or two? This will make her rich. And don't worry about anything, the body included. It is a whorehouse. They sell corpses to strange people all the time. No questions asked, and some strange priest gets to experiment on an excellent, noble stiff. Lith will be happy,' Molun pushed me playfully, not unlike a horse would kick. After I had picked myself up, I smiled and nodded.

'Tomorrow, then,' Kallir said. 'Let us leave. Molun will stay and keep an eye on things. And an ear.'

'Fine,' I said, and so Kallir pulled a cowl over his face and hiked me to the gates, provided false documents to the utterly bored guards, and we left Dagnar. We walked to the Haybolt Stables, saddled the horses, and rode away to the west by the wide Broken Crown Road, and soon we were heading northwest, as the road followed the cliffs over the Arrow Straits. Then, after an hour of riding, we guided our horses off the main road, skirted a tavern and a way stop for coaches and took some animal trails for the higher country, making wild paths through wet, rocky forest, and found the Green Hall and Bear and Mir waiting. And Sand. The latter hailed me thinly, and my face melted to my own. I nearly fell as I dismounted. 'Rot-reared shit!' I yelled and pushed the horse. 'Old damned nag.'

'Maskan!' Mir chided me.

I laughed tiredly at Sand. 'We are about to murder a man, and she thinks of my manners.'

Bear appeared and pushed my bridle into Sand's hands. He smiled wickedly. 'It makes you less of a man, boy, to swear so. Makes you seem nervous as a virgin in a wedding bed,' the Bear said sternly. 'Only swear at your enemy's face as you fight him. Mock him after beating him. Or her. Never swear when you have lost or are in trouble. Obey your mother, at least when she is present. Kallir and Molun will do the killing bit; you stop swearing and just get us the King's gold. But … ' he began, and I said nothing, looking unhappy.

Yes, there was danger lurking, no matter who did the killing "bit", and anything could happen inside the mint itself. There, I'd be alone. The Bear hesitated, grunted, grabbed me and took me down a path towards the cascading waterfall and sat me down there on a flat rock. The noise of the waterfall was strangely soothing, and it was not all that loud, for some reason. He was walking up and down, back and forth in agitation until he finally sat down before me with a huff.

'How are you holding up?' he asked as sweetly as a man called the Bear can.

I nodded. 'I'm just fine,' I lied.

'Tomorrow, you will attempt a frightening deed. I'm not saying it will be easy. I don't want to lie to you, boy. It's a deed that will make the Jesters the most hunted fugitives in the land. But it can go wrong, and Jesters won't suffer, only us. You understand this. If you fail, they won't offer you supper and congratulate you for a worthy try. They will hurt you badly if you should trip and get caught,' he rumbled. 'I worry for you.'

'They'll not take me, sir,' I told him earnestly, gratefully, for I did like him.

'The guards stay out, you know this, no?'

'Yes, they will give me the passphrase and wait in the guardhouse just to the right of the gate to the mint,' I said. 'You said you had a way to take out the people inside.'

He rubbed his neck. 'I do. Hold on. Molun and Kallir will kill the guards in that room. You will have to handle the people inside, indeed, but ...' he said with some doubt, '... I am not sure how many there are or how well armed. I've heard a rumor they have a tunnel running up to the Tower of the Temple itself to bring in the gold and silver flans and also to take the coin back, and there is sure to be a guard out there. We've never seen anyone take any shipment out any other way. The Master of the Coin and the mint is utterly careful with his establishment and guards his special place with the King and the Lord of the Trade and Harbor. What does he do inside? I do not know. There will be a bunch of workers there, hitting dies together all day long. But we have a tool to take them all out. Ann has one.'

'I hope so,' I told the Bear with some concern. 'That key has me worried. What if I have to change clothes inside, and they see the chain is hanging free?'

'Perhaps we should weld the key on your skin, just to make it look authentic,' he said, and his wide, bearded face took on a speculative look.

'Thank you, no,' I said. 'So, you have it? This ... A tool?'

'Here,' he said heavily, and I stared at his hand. 'I hate it,' he said. 'It's cowardly. But I see what Ann is saying. Don't drop it. It breaks very easily. With a good reason.' There was no mighty weapon of power, no weapons at all. He handed me a clay bottle with a yellow stopper, and I took it in my two hands, for it was precious, despite my disappointment. It was to keep me alive, after all. The Bear leaned closer to me. 'Ann got it for us. She knows the ones to brew such evil things. Even I don't want to know. This here,' he said and shook the bottle in my face, 'will stop their breathing, almost. It will be, they say, a result that is seemingly deadly, taking one very near Hel's realm. They say you can mistake the victims for corpses. Yeah, if you fall and hit your head after you break this, it can kill them. They might choke on food. But otherwise, it should not kill them. Hurts terribly, Ann said, but leaves them alive. I don't want to kill the men inside, but it will be great if people think they died.'

'Should I pour this someplace?' I asked, terrified I should drop it. If I did, perhaps I did not have to go to the mint?

He smiled widely to encourage me. 'When you get to the mint, make sure they are all in the same room. All of them. Then smash that on the ground. Run to the shitter, cover your face, and wait. When it's over, you come out, and the lot will be out for a day. That's what Ann said. Then, find the key to the inner door. Open up, and the boys will be there. And they will take care of any remaining guards.'

'All right,' I told him. He pushed me. 'What?'

'You will need something to fight with,' he said, and I realized I would get a weapon after all. 'You see, the plan might turn into shit. There might be a military presence in the mint. A guard might happen by as we rob the place, no? The King might visit it? You have to prepare yourself for it. I once held up a wagon where sat a Brother Knight. We made it to the woods, but only barely. Molun lost a cousin that day.'

'I see,' I said, fiddling with the bottle. 'I need a weapon. Though I am not sure what I can do if things turn sour. Can't use one,' I sulked. 'Never did. Sand—'

He scowled, but not at me. He looked up to the hall, and I knew he blamed Mother. He voiced it. 'Sand is not to blame. Your mom never wanted you to learn how to fight. Gods know why! Sometimes I think she keeps you close to her tit on purpose. Sand does a lot of knuckle dragging for you both, but you are a damned big boy. Fast and smart. Brave too, as far as I can gather from the fact you went and stirred the hornet's nest for a girl.'

'But to kill—'

'Is hard, boy, very hard,' he smirked. 'Sometimes you stab and hack at someone, and they are still alive, where Gullinburst the Boar would have died. And then you have to finish it. Sometimes you stab someone so very briefly, and they die for it immediately. They fall lifeless like a log. But even that is hard. It changes you. Not gonna lie to you, boy. I never liked that, killing. I prefer other methods, but I have done it. Many times. Here.' He handed me a long, sheathed dirk. It was plain and simple and looked superbly deadly. I took it in my hands and eyed it with some hostility. It felt powerful. Somehow, strangely familiar.

'Honey?' Mir said above, coming down to us.

'Love?' the Bear asked sheepishly as if surprised. 'Look, he needs to be armed.'

'I know,' she told her man as she slid down to us and put a hand across my shoulders. She was gazing down at me, her thin face clearly worried, and then she wiped my lip gently. 'Leave us alone,' she told him, and he nodded. He eyed me uncertainly.

'You can do this,' he breathed, and I nodded. He scowled, got up and walked back up the path to the Green Hall.

Mir stretched and walked down to the water's edge. She picked up a pebble, threw it into the water and seemed absorbed by the ripples. Perhaps she was reading signs in the river, and then she finally nodded as if she had decided something. She turned to me and went to her knees before me. 'Love. You have grown so much.'

'You look as young as you always did,' I told her, and it was true. She grinned appreciatively at my words and tapped my hand.

'I had half hoped we would live our lives happily to the end. At least fairly happily. As happily as one can in the Bad Man's Hold, Maskan. We would grow rich, buy a better house outside the city, and we were actually close to that goal. Selling off stolen items, Maskan, it's a filthy job, love, but we have been doing well. Now, if this mint thing succeeds, we will get money to do anything we like.' She stopped at that, looking distraught. 'But what we are doing? This plan? It puts you in danger. I know you and Sand run in the harbor, and I know you steal. A cutpurse that's what you are. I blame myself. I can hardly tell you to straighten up your act, can I? I'm a thief as well. But that was not always the case. I wanted better for you, love. Your father—'

I looked at her and saw she was so morose. I grabbed her cold hand, and she squeezed mine forcefully. 'Tell me about Father,' I said.

She faltered and let go of my hand. 'He …' she began and let out a huge, haggard breath. 'It is a summer for changes. I am afraid. This plan of Ann's?'

'Bear's, surely,' I said.

She chuckled. 'Ann. Our serious, humorless girl is the thinker. Bear is wily, but she is the guiding light in their business. She almost controls him. A whisper, and he blinks. Be that as it may. This plan? It takes us perilously close to the King. I feel there's going to be a great struggle, and we are all in danger. I have a hunch we'll be very involved with the King and his lords soon, Maskan. Be careful, love, if you meet him. He killed your father. You know this.'

'Why?' I asked bluntly, though it had been a decade since I had done so before.

'Why?' she laughed dryly. 'Because the King desired me,' she whispered. 'He always has favorites with the noble women of the court. Some get hurt, especially if they have a virtuous streak in their souls. The Queen hates him. Always did, but she's a vicious bitch in her own right.

She gets people killed as quickly as he does, and if she ruled the land? It would be even worse. But the King? He is a goat.'

'And he—'

'And he tried to have me,' she said. 'He tried to rape me. I had told him "no" so many times, and he was drunk. He was drunk all the time then. It was not long after the Cataclysm and his son had died. But to try to rape a noble woman? I will never forget it.'

'Rape?' I breathed. 'He—'

'Your father was looking for me, and then he found me and stopped him. He gave his life for us. We escaped and hid. They looked for us, Maskan. They did. But we hid, and the Bear helped us. He had just lost his wife and saw a cause in us. I was grateful to him. I had little choice, but he was kind and never forced me into anything I did not want. He was patient. And eventually, the King forgot about us. I loved your father. He was an artist, a warrior, and a good man. The Bear is my man now, but not a night goes by I don't think about your father, who was named Tal Talin. You are Maskan Talin, love. Of the Seventh House. I was a commoner before Tal found me, but you will never be one. Not truly.'

Seventh House.

'Mother ... do I have relatives?' I asked her, mystified by her confessions.

'On my side? Distant,' she said with a smile. 'I come from the north, my love. From Ygrin, in fact.'

'Where in Ygrin?' I asked her, though I was anxious to hear about Father.

She waved her hand. 'A shitty hamlet in the mountains. Far past the border. But you have family still, living in the Second Ring. Your father's family supports the King even this very day. He had a brother, Gal Talin. He is the Merchant Lord of Red Midgard. Lord of the Harbor. Yeah, the one who mocked the crowds at the hanging.'

'What?' I asked her, disbelieving her words. 'He is one rotten piece of bone. He is a snake and—'

'He is,' she agreed. 'I never met him. We lived in the Tower, not with the family. Your father married ... beneath him, and his mother and brother never approved. Never even met them. Then your father died. Gal filled Tal's place after the King tried to ...' She went quiet and shook her head. 'But he is family, nonetheless. You are a noble boy, love. I am sorry all I could give you was Bad Man's,' she said. 'The gods made it so.'

'There are no gods, Mother, who approve of the King murdering his lord for defending his wife,' I said stiffly, enraged at the reason Father had died. My fists were tight as I thought about the Lord of Red Midgard with his hands around my mother. 'The Beast of the North,' I spat. 'But only a northern beast, really.'

'That title is old as time.' She smiled. 'I think it was meant to celebrate his family's prowess in battle, but he is a true beast under that skin of a man. He did not rape me,' she said softly. 'I was saved that ignominy. I cannot remember much of the night. I only remember grabbing you and running and Bear hiding me at the Lamb. And now, you will be involved with him again. In a very personal way, hurting him. Taking his coin will certainly draw eyes on—'

'Valkai,' I said resolutely. 'In Valkai the Heavy. And this Horns.'

'Let us hope so,' she said. 'But you are magical. I don't understand this skill you have. You can change your face, Maskan.' She frowned. 'I wonder if it comes from your father's family. Gal might know.'

'It is something I can do,' I said uncomfortably. 'It's not … magical. I don't know. It feels natural, though it is very hard. I don't want to share the secret with anyone but family,' I stammered. 'This family.'

'I agree,' she said. 'They might know about it, though. This skill or magic. But we have other business now, and let us think about that later. It is very much your power, love, and a magical one at that, and you decide. But your skill is not the only skill in Midgard that is magical.' She hesitated and opened her hand. 'I said I believe in magic. Here is why. This is what the King dropped the day your father saved me. He kept it close. Always. It is precious to him. He summoned it as your father attacked him but lost it in the battle. I grabbed it.' She opened her hand, and in it there was a piece of dark wood the size of a toothpick. 'This was his rod of office. His scepter.'

'Mother?' I said. 'The King. Did all of this happen while he was having dinner? And this toothpick a scepter—'

'No, Maskan,' she said with a soothing, patient voice. 'Or perhaps it did. I do not know. I don't remember a lot of that night; I told you. But I remember the King wielded this, and there was a fight.'

'He wielded that?' I asked, my eyes agog. 'Not a sword? He must be madder than we think. How did he manage to kill Father with a toothpick? I always imagined it would have been somewhat more heroic a struggle—'

She chuckled. 'Wait. He lost it as your father attacked him, and I grabbed it. He called it … Larkgrin.' She said the strange name with a whisper, and in her fist, there suddenly was a dark staff, taller than she was. It was full of strange runes burning with soft, white golden light, and a carving of a black singing bird was on top of it. She showed it to me, got up, and walked to a nearby oak. She grinned at me and whirled it around and hit the tree's trunk.

'Mother!' I screamed, for the oak shuddered, cracked, and the tree began to topple. Towards us.

I rushed as fast as lightning and pushed her away from the tangle of branches, and we rolled downhill amidst falling boughs and rolling boulders. The trunk crashed very near, bouncing madly. We ended sitting in a pool of mud, covered in light green moss, and she was laughing like a madwoman, holding her face. Then, tears were falling on her cheeks as she showed the strange artifact to me. 'Mother!' I chided her gently, for she looked totally miserable.

'Sorry, Maskan. I don't know why I am crying. I remember your father and I used to sail with their ships, and there was this storm, and the ship was demasted. We just barely got out of the way as it fell, and he saved us both. But this weapon … the thing also reminds me how your father died at the hands of a mad, evil king. They are all evil. High kings and small kings, all nothing but turds. I miss him. Don't tell that to Bear, though.'

'Mother!' I said once more, and she sobered and sat up. 'Larkgrin,' she whispered to me, very softly, apparently so the weapon would not hear it. 'A weapon of the old world. God-crafted? Dverg-made? And don't you dare to say they are not real, Maskan, the short smiths.' She hesitated and handed it to me. 'Call for it, and it will come and go, as you please. But look out. The King will want it back. Very much. You don't need the dirk. Just be careful with this weapon.'

'It is—'

She nodded. 'It is magical. The gods are real. So are the legends. And if, as I suspect you must, Maskan, you will fight the King; you have to be very careful. He has … I don't know what. Skills? He is not called the Beast of the North because he is ugly. He is powerful and strange. He has magic. So do his knights. I think it is time I let you live out the more dangerous life I hoped for you. Perhaps you will do well.'

I felt very uncomfortable as I gazed at Larkgrin. 'I'll try to avoid the King, Mother. I only want to get back to what was,' I told her earnestly and hesitated. She smiled knowingly and knew she had told me too much. *I wanted to kill the King,* I thought. And I wanted to see his suffering before he died.

'You are right. But this business with the Grim Jesters has to be dealt with first,' she said and got up.

'Mother, thank you,' I told her.

She shrugged, gave me a kiss on my forehead and began to walk up to the cabin. She stopped. 'Ann wanted to have a word with you.'

'Oh!' I said. 'I don't—'

She laughed teasingly. 'You hold a veritable miracle in your hand, and a mention of a silent, beautiful girl makes you forget all about the thing. Don't worry. I know you are not interested in her, not that way. You feel you should be, but I think you love another.'

'I saw this girl ...' I said, and realized I felt nothing for Ann, indeed. After Shaduril, everything else tasted ... common. I shook my head at myself. I was a right bastard.

Mother grinned. 'I know you are in love,' she chided me and laughed. 'Still. Ann. See her. She has some practical advice for you.' She walked up, and I heard her laughing with the Bear, who had apparently waited for her.

I stared at the staff and shook my head in wonder. 'Come out, Sand. What did you hear?'

'I came down after the tree fell. What in Hel's name is that thing?' he breathed from some bushes, not far.

'A magical weapon,' I told him. I held it, and it felt warm, but not uncomfortable. The strange runes glowed gently on the surface, but they felt just like the wood, smooth. They seemed strange, and I thought the thing would have been much fairer with only the wooden, supremely smooth shaft, and the bird figure on top. They felt ... wrong. I snorted. I had a magic staff in my hand, a real thing, and I found reasons to be unhappy about it. Sand inched into sight. I shifted the magnificently balanced staff in my hands and touched the surprisingly lifelike bird tentatively with the finger of my other hand. Nothing. 'Can I?' Sand asked and reached out for it. I snatched it away and felt very protective of the thing. 'I ...' I began and licked my lips.

'Oh! It's your toy, is it?' Sand said with humor, though there was a bit of envy there as well. 'Keep it. Just wanted to split some wood for the fireplace.'

'I don't know anything about it,' I told him apologetically, admiring the strange, dark wood with the weird etchings and runes. 'It might be dangerous. And it feels strangely familiar. As if it were mine already. That I should take ... care of it.'

'Fine,' he laughed harshly. 'You are the expert in ancient, magical weapons, after all.'

I twirled it in the air. It was supremely light; it trembled slightly as I moved it, and the symbols were strange. 'I'm no expert. But I don't want to give it up.'

Sand grunted. 'I'd love to have that in my pocket. Best give me the dirk, then.' I did. He was happily eyeing its sturdy pommel as I admired the weapon of the King. 'Maskan?'

'Yes,' I said, and he snapped his fingers under my nose.

He went on, 'We'll be there tomorrow,' he said and leaned forward. 'And be bloody careful, you damned nuisance. I'm not saying this is all your fault, but you sure did not help.'

'Sorry,' I told him irascibly. 'And if I had stayed with the Horns, they would have grabbed you to keep me in line, and I doubt they would have let us go, anyway, no matter how well I did. Now we have a chance.'

'You should have let the girl ...' Sand began and then rubbed his face. 'Forget it. I was there. I didn't tie you up. I even suggested we rob her.'

'Right,' I said while bowing my head. 'Let's share the blame. I should have forgotten the pouch and her. I could not.'

'Cursed idiots. Both of us,' he said darkly. 'I agreed to return it to her. That I did. I am not sure why, but I thought it was important.'

'It is strange,' I agreed. 'But she was special.'

'She is,' he agreed. 'Strangely unique. It's not like there are no other beautiful, petite girls out there. She did strike me as ... different? Yes. Enough to put our heads in the noose.'

'She changed everything,' I told him, and then Lith filtered through my mind. I frowned at the thought, and Sand misunderstood me.

'Ann,' he said. 'Don't break her heart. I know you don't care for her, you blind idiot, but at least think of her feelings. Act like you care. Or cared. Whatever. Make it up. She is smart as a goddess, but she is also wretched. Rarely smiles. Spare her heart. Or I'll break yours.'

'I don't know why,' I said. 'But I don't think you can, anymore.'

'Maybe,' he growled, eyeing the staff. 'Should something happen, Maskan, tomorrow? We finish it together. We have been friends this far. Be careful in that mint. I'll ... create a distraction up the street.'

'Oh? I didn't know about that.'

He chuckled. 'Ann's idea. Father didn't want you to, in case you get caught and spill your guts, and I am not talking about disembowelment. I'll set up a fire in a warehouse,' he grimaced. 'Terrible crime, that is. I'll roast if they catch me doing it. But I will be careful. You will have to be as well.'

'I will try,' I agreed.

Later we ate. It was a slow, tired affair, for it was late, and we didn't have much of an appetite. I rarely saw Mother eating at all, and Ann was always picky about her food. Bear often finished their plates. The next morning we would be up and about very early, and there was precious little anyone wanted to say. I sat at the end of the long table, staring at the fires. I ate a few bits of steaming venison, some frost-bitten potatoes, and one or two bitter tomatoes, but that's all. The women only sipped their ale and stared at the fires.

*Damned terrifying,* I thought, wondering if we would survive the coming day. The next day, men might die. At least the Master of Coin, Naram would. That much was likely. It was hard to imagine Kallir and Molun failing at that. The man was small and refined. If we succeeded, the Jesters would be at a war they could not win. The King would send thousands of soldiers down to the Old City, and there would be no mercy. If we failed, we might hang instead. With luck. Probably my skull would be strung up next to Father's, hanging in the Singing Gardens, ringing with bells. I rubbed my face. It did not matter. There was no backing out now. We would rob the King's gold, and I would carry it in plain sight of all the people of the Third Ring, and I'd be wearing Valkai's face. I chuckled at that, and the others froze for a moment as if I had committed a crime. The Bear snapped his fingers. I lifted my face to him. 'Know the plan now?'

'I'll be with this Lith tomorrow morning,' I told him.

He snorted. 'Lithiana. You'll go in and behave. And then this friend of ours will enter, he'll be very shocked by your presence, and my boys will do their thing, and that is when you step up and become the damned main actor in this tragedy. You'll dress up like this dandy, adopt … face, his face that is. You'll do your thing outside the door. Not inside, got it? Lith … Lithiana surely can be bought to be silent, but I don't want to pay her more than we will already.'

'OK,' I agreed. 'Then I'll go to the door, this gate—'

'Past the barracks, a street up from the Thin Way. Then to the gate. Open it up, talk to the guards. They will tell you the passphrase. Then Molun and Kallir will do them in at their guardhouse just outside the mint.'

'They are soldiers,' I whispered.

'What?' the Bear asked.

'They are soldiers. You sure Molun and Kallir can … do them in?'

'Yes!' he hooted. 'They'll use crossbows, and then swords, and those louts will be sitting or sleeping. They cannot find it in their hearts to suspect anyone would dare to do something like this.'

'And then, I'll just see what is inside and take 'em all out, right?' I said and giggled hysterically, and they stared at me glumly. 'Right,' I said and picked at the food on my plate.

'Yes. And may the Gloom Hand grant you luck,' Bear chanted, invoking the dark spirit of thievery.

'I got it,' I told him morosely.

Then Mir got up, gathered the plates, or rather kicked Sand up to do so and grabbed the Bear to follow her. He came reluctantly, and Ann was left with me. We sat there silently; so long, I nearly fell asleep amidst the crackle of the flames, but not quite, as Ann sighed. She tilted her fair head and leaned on the back of her hands. Her blue eyes regarded me strangely. 'You are an idiot.'

I opened my mouth in shock. She rarely spoke and always looked worried, but now she had a curious look on her face. I gathered myself. 'You were to give me some practical advice. That was not very practical. An idiot, eh?'

'Yes, you are,' she said darkly. 'Sand confessed you ran after this Shaduril because you both liked her. I tell you I am disappointed. You've known me for ages. So you are an idiot.'

'I have been told that previously,' I said with a somewhat hurt tone. 'But I like you.'

Her eyes enlarged as she stared at me, and then she giggled. She had beautiful laughter, and she shook her head at me. 'I have been staring at you like a lovesick dog for such a long time. I've seen you and Sand grow up into two handsome dolts. I have smiled back at you—'

'That is not true. You rarely smile. In fact, I just heard you laugh for the first time,' I said with rising anger, which I immediately regretted. I looked at her shocked face and prayed she would not walk away.

'I'm the daughter of the Bear. I don't make noise. I don't attract enemies. I think, I act, and then I survive, and so do those whom I love,' she said, sharp as a whip. 'And a daughter to the Bear, a bandit king does not simply run after a young boy. But had I done so, perhaps I would not have found he is smitten by someone else.'

'I am not …' I began and slumped.

'She was pretty. Shaduril?' she asked sweetly. 'Pert and blonde, and lips to swallow hearts?'

'She was pretty,' I told her, embarrassed. 'But most of all she was helpless as a doe—'

'She is hardly helpless,' she interrupted and bit her lip. 'I am sorry. I like her if you do. I missed my chance.'

'It was my fault,' I said simply, and it was the truth. 'I had to step in. And you are like a sister to me. An older sister.'

She was nodding stiffly. 'Old. A sister.'

I cursed myself under my breath. 'You are thirty? I cannot ever remember the time when you were growing up,' I said, and she nodded again.

'It is true. But you broke my heart,' she told me. She was nowhere near as beautiful as Shaduril, but there was something very becoming in her. 'I've been somber for years and years, Maskan. I've been hoping to die.'

'What?'

'Die, Maskan. I have been hoping to die,' she said seriously.

'And now I—'

She smiled. 'It's not your fault. You cannot change your heart.'

'Ann—' I whispered, feeling rotten. 'You must not—'

'I'll try to find something worth living for,' she whispered. 'I trust you. Give us a way out of this, and I will try. I promise.'

'Thank you,' I said weakly.

She got up, her tall body quivering. There was a strange look on her face. It was one of desire, and perhaps ... rebellion?

She pulled my face to her and kissed me with passion, murmuring sweetly, and I felt myself lift higher than the clouds over the mountains. She broke it off. 'That one was for me.' She lifted her head, and I saw Mir had entered the room and was looking at her with astonishment. 'At least I got a piece of you. And boy? Remember to kiss the girl. You kiss her. She will be happy. Grow bolder, fool.'

'Ann—' Mir began, but the girl walked off, angry as a cat whose tail had been stepped on.

'What is with her?' I asked Mother with confusion.

'She is unhappy, Maskan,' Mir said, scowling after her. 'She is strange. Bear says it was always so. Forget it. She was supposed to run through the plan with you a few times.'

'I know the plan,' I told her.

Mother leaned over me. 'Practice. Practice. Practice. Never think you are ready without practice. Come, let's do it again. As for Ann, I think our silent flower had more feelings for my boy than I thought possible. I feel sorry for her.'

So did I. And we practiced.

We should have practiced more.

## CHAPTER 6

It was very early in the morning, and Kallir and Molun were hunkered on a street leading to the fantastic fountain by "the Affront", staring at the alleyways, from where our man would soon emerge. He was fastidious and sharp as the gate's Silver Bells announcing the hours in Dagnar, and even if I half-hoped he would not appear, he would. 'Best get up there, boy. Just greet him, as he steps in. Say something nice to him, as it will be the last thing he hears. And don't scream when we do our thing.'

'Yes, and I won't,' I said and hopped up and down. Up and down. I was so tense. They stared at me incredulously; I stopped jumping, smoothed my mustache, and then I walked across the street, smiled at a vendor laying out fresh bread, and entered the tavern.

'Not a table this morning?' a brusque, sturdy girl asked me, and I shook my head, nodding upstairs. She smirked at me with barely disguised disgust. 'I see. Finally summoned up the courage to have something different for breakfast, have we? She's up there.'

I took to the stairs but hesitated as I mounted them; I thought of the mysterious anger of poor Ann, the enchanting Shaduril, and cursed myself for a damned fool as I feared opening Lith's door. I reached the upstairs, turned to the marble door, pushed it open and went in.

I stopped in shock.

She had just been squatting on an elaborately embroidered pot. She cursed me profusely as she pulled her skirt up. 'Ever seen that before?'

'No, can't say I have,' I said with a deep blush as she scowled at me. *Damnable idiot*, I thought, *why didn't I turn away?*

'Just ogling there like an owl,' she grumbled coldly. 'Nearly the time?'

'Yes, almost,' I said. She kicked the door closed and poured me some wine. I mulled it in my hand and went to recline on the windowsill that served as a bench as well. She was not her brazen self, not at all, but concentrated and careful. 'You OK?' I asked her while sampling the wine.

'I'm all right. But as I said yesterday, this had better be worth it,' she said.

A whistle. There were steps coming up the stairs. I got up, in panic. Lith stiffened and walked briskly over to me. She pulled me up, her face screwed in a determined scowl and then she devoured my lips. I dropped the cup of wine. She placed my hands on her breast and hips, and I did not fight her. *Again? First Ann, then her?* Then, I remembered the steps and realized they were now by the door, and the Master of the Mint stepped in, already removing his coat. His thin face changed from a leer into shocked silence as he saw us entwined in each other's arms, my hand rubbing Lith's eyes. He took an involuntary step forward, and then another, and then I saw Molun appear behind him. A truncheon went up and came down, and the man fell forward.

The door closed, and Kallir and Molun pushed in, kicking the twitching soon-to-be-corpse inside.

'Any trouble?' Molun asked, casting a speculative look at Lith, who was still pressed into me.

'No trouble,' I assured Molun and pushed Lith away. She was smiling dangerously at me, like a cat that let go of a mouse, but I tried to pay attention to the task at hand. 'Make sure the clothes do not tear.'

'Don't worry,' Kallir grinned. 'We have stripped nobles before. You want to help, Lith? You've done this often, no doubt.'

'You seem to be doing an okay job at it,' Lith said and made no move to help them, her eyes calculative. She stared at her former client with morbid fascination.

'Just be careful,' I whispered, feeling so nervous. They laughed and then tore the man around brutally, removed his long, dark jacket, then his shirt over his shoulders. There was a heavy pouch full of coins, bulging in fact, but Lith snapped her fingers and pointed at her desk. Molun hesitated, cursed, and left the bag with Lith. Finally, they removed one shoe; Molun fetched the other one from the hallway, and then the pants came off as Kallir jerked at them. And there, clinking to the floor was the key with a chain that had been crafted into the bone of the poor fool.

Molun grinned, and they took out a coin with cool familiarity. 'Sword or ship?' asked the bald man. 'Or do you still want to do this?'

'I want to do it. The ship,' Kallir said, and then the coin flipped and landed. Kallir grinned at Molun's sullen look. 'Give me the cutters.'

'Here,' Molun said and handed him something that was meant for thick hedges. He placed pliers and a saw on the side.

'Over the rags and the carpets, please,' Lith said with sudden concern. 'Don't want the stench to linger here for too long. I've heaped some thick ones on the floor, and that should do the trick. Please bind it after, the wound.'

'Hey,' Kallir said. 'He is alive.' He was poking at a piece of caved-in skull. Blood trickled to the top of the skin, and the man twitched. My belly heaved, and I turned away. Lith handed me the piss bucket, and I emptied my breakfast into her piss. While I was retching, I happily spared myself from seeing the spine-breaking coup de grace, though I heard it. Naram made a strange, moaning sound as he died. I decided to stare out of the window for the duration of the bloodletting. I sensed Lith also looked away, seemingly distressed, and I heard meat being cut. 'There, cut that strand!' Kallir said. 'Look out for my hands, for dark's sakes. Lok's hairy ass, he has so much of it. It's going to soak to the boards. He looks thin. Where does it all come from?'

'Just get it over with ... ' Lith said, and leaned on me.

There was a terrible grinding sound, followed by meaty, wet thuds, and curses. I heard saw grating on bone, and then bone cracking. There was a rattle of chain. 'I'll bind some of that,' Kallir stated. 'Wash the key.'

Molun grunted, and there was a trickling sound of water and clanking of chain. 'Here, boy, change,' he said, and I nodded, avoided looking at the corpse and began stripping as Kallir was pointing at the heap of clothing. I pulled on the clothes and tried on the shoes. The pants were very tight in the crotch.

'Eats too much. His ass is thick with fat,' Kallir noted with some worry as he looked at me with clear disapproval.

I cursed him. 'Not true! I'm fit!'

'He is just well endowed, Kallir,' Lith giggled.

Kallir sighed. 'Do not stretch them too much. Best not sit down.'

'How is he going to pass in?' Lith asked sharply, her mood swinging. 'He does not look like the man. And they have a very tight security in the establishment.'

'We know a way in,' Molun assured her and then looked a bit concerned as he mulled over the rest of her words. 'The security is the door. Why would they guard it inside? You said you didn't know anything about the inside.'

'I don't,' Lith told him softly. 'But it's filled with gold flans in the morning and gold coins in the evening. Of course they guard the inside of it.'

Molun nodded. 'He has something to deal with the people inside, eh?'

I did, I patted the bottle.

I glanced at the key held by Kallir. It was elaborate and made of black iron, and I wondered how they had managed to shackle it to the man's bone. The links were fine, thin, but supremely strong. 'Would take a long time to pry it off him on the street,' Kallir said and handed me the key. 'Hide it in your pocket. Make sure the whole chain never leaves it. Fake a limp. He had a slight one.'

'Fine,' I said and got ready to get up.

'Wait!' Kallir hissed, but it was too late. Struggling in the elegant leather shoes, I could not find my footing and nearly slipped. I windmilled, gripped at a table, and then sent one foot to the side, pushing myself up.

The pants ripped.

'Damned idiot.' Molun groaned.

'Wretched specimen, to be sure. You will keep your jacket closed,' Kallir said. 'You'll sweat like a pig, but you cannot take it off. Maybe it will cover your ass. It might, barely.'

'You lot are asking for trouble,' Lith said sadly. 'I won't even ask you how you will disguise his face. I doubt I will see you, boy, after you leave the room.'

'See me?' I asked, buttoning the thick leather coat, feeling heat and sweat pouring out immediately.

Kallir grunted. 'You are to bring her part of the payment here after we run and everyone has seen Valkai. I'll give you the sack, and then you will hide here for the night. And remember to keep quiet.'

'Not too quiet,' Molun said with a lecherous grin, and I prayed, for Lith nodded at me, her eyes gleaming with joy. Shaduril. There was only that girl in my heart. *I'd stay pure*, I thought, fearing the night with Lith almost more than the mint.

'Why can't I just leave the city?' I asked them.

'The city will be closed, and everyone searched,' Molun said with exasperation. 'Just let us handle this.'

Lith winked at me. 'Good luck, Naram.'

'Fine,' I growled and gathered all my bravery, wondering what we had forgotten. I walked out of the room, clutching the key like I would the last piece of bread in Midgard. I got downstairs, my confidence shattered by the fact I felt my underwear sticking out of the fresh tear in the pants, and I fought the urge to grope under the coat to adjust it. I prayed the coat would cover the damage. I walked to the door, stepped out and froze in terror.

I turned and walked back up the stairs, praying the soldiers had missed me. I concentrated, and my face flowed to adopt the thin face and silken hair of the poor man that had died upstairs. It felt right, and I screwed my lips into a ruthless, arrogant smile.

*Let me not make a mess out of it again, gods.* Showtime.

I went back down and exited the door, and the two brown-bearded guards shot up from the bench they had been sitting on, looking mildly surprised. I hesitated. Naram had only been up there for a short time, and they whispered some snide comments to each other about my longevity. I ignored the crude soldiers and walked forward towards the northern side of the Third Ring, passing blue doors decorated with white, wondering how the birds were singing so happily when I was actually risking my life. I prayed as I fingered the key and the yellow stoppered bottle and whistled a light tune as I walked. My mouth was dry with terror.

'She probably had a headache. Shouldn't wonder,' one of the guards still whispered to the other, but I heard him well enough. I turned my eyes his way, and his face straightened as if he had just been slapped on both ears. I got some brief satisfaction from that as we hiked on. There is power in this form. *Enough to make it through this Hel,* I thought. Ahead, we could see the guard barracks of the Third Tier, a pinkish white building with an iron fence. Riders in armor were going in and out, and I skirted them as I walked to the north side of the Third Ring, the hill face, or the Drop, as it was called. There, a seemingly bottomless, bird-infested rock face stood, and no walls were needed. The mint was standing at the very edge of it, a bit on top of it, in fact, and a major street went up and down the hill near it, the Griffon's Stride. Local merchants, hawkers of rarer products than those sold in the harbor, ringed it. We walked up it, and then I took to the northwest for the Thin Way, a narrow way with wealthy shops and some taverns.

My throat tightened as I saw the building.

It was made of dark stone, cumbersome and forbidding and had a single story. A light was shining from behind its colored glass windows, all barred and locked, and there was a doorway with an iron-bound gate and a lock my key would open. I went forward, slowly, but resolutely. I felt the urge to take a piss, and to vomit again, and to find shelter where I could just curl up, but I was committed. I reached the door, glanced back at the guards, scowled, and fumbled with the key. The two dolts were staring at me with some mockery. I inserted the key, twisted, and cursed, for it would not budge. Then I tried the other way, in a panic, nearly dropped the key and the lock just clicked. I ignored the guards calling out, saying something to my back, and entered. I locked the door. There, before me was a dark oaken door with a beast-headed knocker. I grabbed it, trying to calm my nerves. Then I froze.

I had forgotten to ask the guards for the password. The phrase.

I stood in shock for the longest time, cursing and shaking. Then I remembered Kallir and Molun were to silence the guards in their small guardhouse right about then, and I fumbled with my key. 'Odin's wrath, shit,' I cursed and opened the gate and rushed forward, looking at the whitewashed little guardhouse's doorway while sweating desperately. I reached the door and gazed inside.

I was too late.

Molun looked up, startled, and Kallir was there, his back turned to me. He was strangling the younger of the two guards and then, very suddenly, I saw he was done. The other one's chest had a crossbow bolt sticking from it and blood was seeping from the wound. 'What in Hel's rotten breath are you doing here?' Molun breathed. 'You should be inside. Yes?'

'Well, there is this thing. I forgot to ask for the passphrase.'

They stared at me in utter stupefaction. 'What?' Kallir asked with hysterical incredulity and despair, his voice growing thin as a child's. 'You have got to be kidding me.'

'Well, no,' I sulked. 'And you didn't have to kill them so fast!'

Molun snorted. 'They would never speak even if you tried to force them to, Maskan,' Kallir spat. 'They are proud like that, like idiots, they would not say a word. Some say they give dark oaths to the King, and they fall dead before betraying those oaths. Never been to the army, I dunno! And besides, we would have had to force both of them to speak. One of them knows only first part of the passphrase, and the second the other, and now it's too late. So, what do you propose?' Their looks told me they knew the answer.

I was quiet for a while, shaking in my awkward shoes. I croaked and shook my head. 'I go back and try to get in anyway?'

'You go back there and try to get in anyway. Shit!' Molun moaned. 'I cannot believe you messed this up. An ass would have done a better job!'

'Right,' I said and agreed with him. I turned on my heel, marched back, and opened the door. I took some brave steps forward and grasped the handle of the knocker. And then I banged it down.

A shriek could be heard from the other side. Then shuffling. 'God's vomit! Why did you do that? Just knock gently!'

'Let's get this over with,' I said thinly, preparing to bolt.

'Right. Go on, then,' the voice said and waited.

I was quiet, waiting and sweating.

There was no sound, none for the longest time until the voice could be heard muttering something. Finally it spoke, though tentatively. 'The answer to the puzzle, my lord?'

I shook my head. Puzzle. I had hope. 'Voice the puzzle.'

Silence. Then a curse. 'Why? That's just stupid. I know you, you know me, and why don't you just say the words so we can get on with this?'

I straightened my back. 'The Lord Commander has concerns, cur.'

'The Lord Commander Helstrom?' the voice asked with some puzzlement. 'Why would the Butcher be worried? And don't you work for Master of the Trade, Gal Talien?'

I gathered myself and bleated out an explanation. 'I do. But Lord Commander oversees the security of the King's works. He is worried about the mint. He made this abundantly clear. He wanted all our names, even.' I bit my lip, afraid I was going too far.

'He is worried?' the voice wondered. 'It is the mint. They make the coin here. There is a door. Guards out there and in here.' In there? I cursed. The voice went on with a happy tone. 'Nothing is safer unless it's the royal anus. Though I don't know anything about such matters. They say they are all drunk most of the time in the Tower, and so perhaps the royal anus is not–'

I tried to steady my nerves. My life suddenly felt like a rolling boulder; jumping wildly downhill with no constraints and no hope of a happy ending. 'Be that as it may, there have been many raids in the higher levels of Dagnar lately, and his is busily squeezing pimples.'

'I am not sure,' the voice said with some apprehension, 'why I would care for Crec Helstrom's pimples?'

I laughed roughly. 'We are the pimples. All of us. He is tightening the rules, breaking heads of those who ignore them. He got rid of his scribe, and the reason was that the scribe had no ink in his bottle when it was checked. Either he worked too hard, or not at all, or nobody cared to ask. Don't be like the scribe. We will do these things properly. You are supposed to tell me the puzzle, and I'm supposed to answer it, and that is the proper way of doing it.' Let it be so, I prayed.

There was a snort. 'And since when have you cared for proper ways, you noble wart? I bet he is squeezing the high, fine, and useless nasties as well as the low ones.'

'Do you wish to find work down in the harbor, perhaps in the Department of Streets and Cleanliness?' I asked him, not sure there was one. 'I like my job. I like being a lord.'

A snort. 'I'm just a guard! I can hardly be demoted … fine!' the voice said, deciding the job was too good to change into street sweeping duties after all. Then the man adopted a mocking, nasal, official tone. 'Today's puzzle, then. "They hide in a smelly house by day, at night they finally come out to play".'

I thought of Lith. 'Whores?'

'Your lordship would think so! But give me the answer, and I'll open the doors,' the voice giggled, a bit bored.

I was thinking furiously. 'Rats?' I said quickly, as I thought of Molun and Kallir.

The voice was losing its humor. 'You know, Lord Pimple, that if we go by the protocol, I should now ring the bells for an alarm. Then I shall get a raise, and you will be squeezed, and there will be a new Lord of Coin and Mint while you cry in the dungeons. They will run you down if you are a thief, stretch you and rip your balls off, hang you and before all of that, they will cut your toes—'

'Your toes,' I breathed and heard the voice cursing inside.

A latch could be heard moving. The door swung out, and a very small, bald, and wrinkled man scowled at me. 'Yes, your toes. But—'

'Shut up,' I breathed and pushed past him. 'Be happy I won't have you try the Drop. Now, let us get to work.'

'You have very little work, my lord. As usual,' the door guard said, holding out a leather apron to me.

'Coming from someone who opens the door twice a day, that is rich,' I dared to speculate and learned I was right for the small man's face soured. I stared around the room and ignored the apron. In the room, there were ten people and the guard, all staring at me. They were craftsmen the lot, all were burly, stoic and wore aprons over bared chests. So did the guard. I noticed there were cauldrons where the dies were heated and they gave off an acrid smell. 'All ready?' I asked the small man and cleared my throat to make myself heard.

'Your coat?' the door guard whined. 'Your apron awaits.' He shook it in my face.

'I'll keep my coat today. I'm feeling chilly. Must be catching a cold,' I said uncomfortably.

'Mustn't keep a coat in here, my lord,' he said stubbornly. 'King's laws. Prevents thievery.'

'Come, now,' I said. 'I said I am sick.'

He nodded, though he looked about to argue. Instead, he spat and laughed. 'You are diseased, Lord,' the man snickered. 'Twitch always told you to beware the women of questionable repute; he did.'

'Did you?' I asked him icily, disliking him greatly. He was eyeing the room. 'So, any problems?'

'No, no problems at all unless it be the Master of the Mint who is sick,' Twitch said. 'We are going to mint twenty thousand gold coins today. They have the anvil and hammer dies, though Gillan's set is not the best quality. Might break.'

I nodded and eyed the dies they would use to hammer on both sides of the gold coins. There were boxes of prepared gold flans by the several desks in the huge room, casks of ale and servings of food on large platters on the side table. At the far end, iron-barred windows were facing the northern mountains over the Drop and there, on the right side of the room, was a worn trapdoor where you could see scuff marks in the stone. That was where they brought the precious, official dies of Red Midgard and the flans to the mint and took out the coins as well for the Tower of the Temple. I shuddered and nodded at the lot. 'Begin? Go on!'

They all looked uncertain and morose.

'They should be allowed to break their fast first,' Twitch said softly and with some hostility. 'If we are now sticklers for the rules and all of that shit, they should eat. And you should inspect their dies as well.'

'I'll not bother, and you keep your mouth shut,' I told him and stood up higher to address the lot. 'Yes, eat away, and then to work!' I yelled. They twitched, but none moved. I walked around, keeping a stoic eye on everything and noticed a desk and a plush, huge chair on the side that was apparently mine. I sweated as I stared at the glittering boxes full of gold, pondered at the wealth it would grant one if one were free to use it as one pleased. I noticed the workers were still staring at me.

'Lord Naram,' Twitch said darkly. 'The bell.'

'The bell indeed,' I said, seeking one, desperately craning my neck around.

'Have you hit your head, Lord? Fell off the whore's bunk?' Twitch asked with suspicion. 'Your voice is sort of thick.'

'I said I am feeling sick, didn't I?' I pointed out and spotted a tiny silver bell Twitch was holding my way while scowling mightily.

I grabbed it, rang it, starting the day and decided I was not hungry. I eyed the fabulous fare set on the table. There was fowl, cuts of boar and venison, steaming amidst vegetables. 'Eat!' I said and pointed at the plates of food.

'Lord?' asked one of the artisans. 'That is your food. We eat the gruel.' He nodded at a vat of gray, featureless slop set near their desk. There was some ale there also, in a small barrel.

'Eat that then,' I told them with a nod, feeling like a rudderless ship. Twitch smelled the air, like a dog sensing trouble, his thick brow set in a permanent frown.

The men shuffled for the pot of gruel, and I sauntered over to the side after all. I smelled the delicate fragrances of the meats, a succulent fare that was apparently meant for me, and somewhat reluctantly I took some slices of meat, terrified I was making a mistake again. I poured some wine from a decanter and considered the men. They were whispering to each other as they ladled the strange pale porridge onto their cups, adding some butter and stealing envious glances at me. No, at my food, I decided. They were disappointed, and quite naturally so, suffering the shit while Naram ate like a king. They were avoiding my stare. I nodded. *Why not?* 'Come, take the rest. I will need to grow thinner. Take the wine as well.'

'You do look like you gained some weight, Lord,' Twitch said suspiciously. 'In the shoulders, even.'

'Eat, you mongrel,' I told him, haughtily as a lord would. 'Stop spewing nonsense.'

He frowned at me, shrugged at the artisans, grabbed a cup of his own and filled it with food and the others followed, nodding at me gratefully and with humility, their eyes cast down. They heaped meats and bread on top of their disgusting gruel and smiled like children. Apparently, Naram was not a gracious lord, and I felt some satisfaction at being able to give them some happiness. I nearly choked on a bit of a fowl, for I realized something. *Happiness, aye, before I would knock them out,* I thought and brushed the bottle in my pocket. Most were hunkered over their tables, and so, perhaps, none would die, after all. I ate in peace, the men enjoyed themselves, eating with wild gusto and relished the wine that was excellent. I eyed their ale with some desire but decided getting drunk was not a good idea. The artisans were thick around my wine, though, smiling happily.

I looked around, wondering what to do. Twitch had the key to the outer door. Overall, the job was not hard. I would have to find the place where they relieved themselves, break the bottle in the room, escape to the shitter, and hang onto the doorknob and wait.

I looked around.

I did not see any other rooms. None. There was a bucket in the corner.

I winked Twitch over. He was cursing under his breath as he had to lay his fare on the ground next to the door. He had a simple chair and no desk. 'What is it now?'

'I have to take a leak.'

He looked at me with deep confusion for a time and then visibly shook himself. He forced himself to delve deeper into the mystery. 'Yes?' he asked slowly. I stammered a bit, and his face turned into a mask of suspicion. 'I'm not going to hold it for you. That crosses the line. No matter how sick you feel. Lord or no, I—'

'Where should I take the leak? By myself,' I growled.

'The bucket, as always?' he pointed at a large vat by the window. 'You have grown too fine to squat on a bucket now? Even the kings squat on their bucket. Some do it in full daylight, before guests. But you cannot? There is a rule to the mint, Lord, and as you have recently grown fond of rules and proper ways of doing things, then surely you know the bucket is there so nobody can stick gold up their damned anus. It's a rule. Another one you have broken today. First, the coat. Then the bell. Then you give them beady wine and their work will be shitty.' *Gods,* I thought. *They were getting drunk.* 'And now you want to piss in peace? I will write a report. Or would if I could write.'

'I've got issues with my bowels,' I whispered to him. 'Can I just step outside to—'

He was shaking his head emphatically. 'Nobody leaves, Lord Pimple Warts. The door is locked, and I shall open it when the time is right. I do obey the protocol, you see.' He had a suspicious look on his wrinkled face.

'Fine,' I hissed, and then my eyes settled onto the hatch. There was no lock on it.

'And you have not asked for it yet,' Twitch whispered.

'What?' I asked.

He looked superbly shocked and shook his head. He went back to his chair and kept an eye on me, frowning. *He must think I am testing him,* I thought. He would have already called the guards otherwise.

The men eventually went to work, and I frowned as I tried to look official. Twitch was not eating, just glowering at me. The hypnotic clink of minting, the hammer's bang, the clank of a coin hitting a bucket filled the air. It was a strangely comforting sound. The anvil and the hammer dies cut the ship and the sword on the golden flans and the artisans eyed their freshly minted gold with critical eyes, though some had drunk too much wine, and I could see the result was not as good as it should be.

I had to do it. I had to. I nodded at Twitch and got up. I walked around the tables. It was getting unbearably hot with my coat, and then I walked around, slathered in terrified sweat. I picked up a coin to the silent resentment of the workers. One cursed, for apparently my prowling made him ruin a flan. That or the wine, which was apparently very strong. Naram was a drunk.

I wandered to the windows to stare out at the fine sights of the northern mountains, and I swear I could nearly see the cascading waters near our hut. Then I walked to stand right next to the hatch, which I prodded with my foot. It was not locked. Everyone was glancing at me with apprehension, and so I sighed, prayed to the gods I did not believe were listening and withdrew the clay bottle.

I accidentally dropped it.

It didn't break. I was frozen with shock and relief both.

It rolled crazily across the floor, and I rushed after it. It disappeared under a table; I went after it on all fours, and there was a confused silence as I grabbed the damned thing from the feet of two of the workers. I got up, smiled and turned for the hatch. I nearly screamed as I found Twitch was right there next to me. He scowled up at my face, his stubby nose near my belly, and he poked a finger at my chest. 'Your pants are ripped. We all saw it.'

'She was enthusiastic,' I told him. 'Ripped them off me, like she would peel an eel.'

'Bloody liar. They are too small for you. You are a fake; I knew it.'

'Knew what?' I asked him, circumventing his rotund body, nearly falling over the hatch.

'You are not him,' he said dangerously, hissing softly as an ugly cat stalking a fat rat. 'You have not told me how much your cut is today. You can make a mess of everything else, and I'd put that down to idiocy or being a drunk, feverish and having a bad rearing, but not that. You never forget your cut. No sir.'

'My cut? It is my cut, and I decide when I ask for it,' I stuttered in panic, for most of the artisans had turned to regard us. The clink of dies faltered.

Twitch chuckled. 'What is it? A mask?' he said and tried to grasp at my face. I slapped his fingers off. 'You never, ever forget to ask for your cut. It's as likely as my mother holding her gas. And she farts a lot. Loves it, you see.'

'Get off me!' I yelled. I pushed him away from me with surprising strength, for he rolled over a chair. I cursed the men in the room, all staring at me strangely. I prayed to the gods for deliverance, threw the clay jar high in the air and pulled open the hatch. It opened smoothly, chains rattling with some ingenious mechanism, and I nearly smashed my chin on it as it slid up. I dived into the hole, rolled on some stairs and saw there was a wooden cart on rails that led into darkness. There were lights burning inside, torches. I dimly noted there were screams upstairs, and I jumped up, groping my way up to a chain to pull the hatch closed. It closed swiftly with a high-pitched rattle of chain, and I swore I could see yellowish smoke billowing towards the hole.

It closed.

But not swiftly enough.

Twitch managed to make it through. He flew in and hit me before the hatch snapped shut, and we fell on the rails. He was over me, tearing at me crazily with a maniacal, surprising strength, and I could not get him to remove his hands from my throat. 'You excrement! I know you are not him, but it will give me satisfaction to tear the nasty mockery of a face from your skull!' He slapped his fingers on my face again, grasped my cheek and began to pull. It hurt like fire.

'I am not—' I wheezed, fighting to remove his hand from my throat.

'I said I know.' He giggled. 'And don't fight it. Die! And I'll get a raise!'

'I …' I tried to speak but could not, for the small man was puffing, and I found I could not draw a breath. I struggled and fought as best I could, trying to wrest his surprisingly powerful fingers off my throat, but could not. I began to see black dots, and then the small man flew away from me with such power he hit the hatch, which blew back open before Twitch rolled back down to me. I turned to see a booted foot in front of my face, and a plate and dark chain armored man was staring down at me, leaning on a fabulous, unblemished two-handed sword. His helmet was black, red horsehair was hanging in front of my face. Damned Brother. Red Brother, I despaired.

'You all right, Lord?' asked a young man's clear voice. 'What is going on up there?'

'Thievery! That … imp tried to murder me. He poisoned the crafters! Go and get help!' I panted at him, hoping to be rid of him. I stared up at the open hatch; sure we would fall unconscious.

We did not. It was silent as a grave up there.

The Red Brother chuckled and shook his head. He approached Twitch and leaned to grab him by his collar. He heaved powerfully, and while I was far from a weak man, this one was hugely savage. Twitch flew up through the hole into the room. The man climbed some stairs to gaze in. 'Who was trying to do this theft? That small one?' he asked with an amused voice, his huge butcher's sword dragging behind.

'That thing, yeah. Said he has help outside. I escaped … Can you breathe up there?'

The helmet went up and down. 'Yes, but it is an unfortunate sight. They are dead. Not breathing. Come up, then.' *Dead?* I cautiously followed the man to the room. It was true. All the artisans looked dead as poisoned mice. *But they were not, were they?* They had fallen into a strange stupor and done that so fast some were still holding the dies, and all their eyes were wide open, the whites showing. The Red Brother was grunting in rage, fingering his massive sword. He was nodding to himself and staring around, and then he bent to ruffle the clothing on Twitch. He came up with a key. 'You said this one claimed to have help outside? This key is for the outer door, and you got yours?'

*Shit,* I thought. 'Yes … but surely you must go and get more men? Guards? Your Brothers?'

'The Brothers are guarding the King and the Queen. The Mint is my duty today. I can handle this,' he said, almost happily. 'Help me with the other door. Use your key.'

'My key?' I said dubiously.

The dark helmet turned to regard me. 'I said I'll go out and see if there are any more out there,' he noted. 'I'll make sure they won't try again. And I'll take some for questioning.'

'But—'

'The key!' he yelled, his eyes smoldering behind his helmet's eyeholes.

'Here,' I said, gave him the key, cursed miserably under my breath, and hoped Molun and Kallir were ready.

He shuffled with the lock on the latch, kicked it open, then pulled my key, and deftly opened the door. He stepped outside, his sword at the ready; the baleful mask and armor were making him look very dangerous indeed. His huge sword came to the side, held with one steel-gauntleted hand.

Molun and Kallir were there, wearing the guards' uniforms. Their shock at seeing one of the Brothers was beyond comprehension.

'And who are you, I wonder?' the Red Brother said, staring at the two thieves. 'Surely not the men who brought you here?' This was addressed to me.

'They look like them,' I said, inching out to the yard. There were people stopping on the Thin Way to stare at the unusual confrontation. 'They wear armor and carry swords, and I don't really pay attention to them. Ever.'

Molun grunted and swiped his hand in a dismissive gesture. 'We are his guards. He is a drunk damned fool.'

'His guards?' the Brother said with amusement. He murmured something. The gauntlet glinted. His sword hand glowed; or so I thought. *Was it possible?* Then the air moved gently. He rocked and tilted his head at Molun. 'I think not. I know you lie.'

'I tell you ... ' Molun said, and Kallir shook his head, silencing him. I cursed myself as I grabbed Larkgrin. I shuffled to the side of the knight and tried to make up my mind.

Kallir made up his, spat, and drew his sword.

The knight roared and charged forward, the huge sword flashing in the air. Molun rolled away. Kallir did not, but tried to parry the deadly weapon. The impact was such the rogue bit his tongue through, fell as if a god had kicked him, rolled into the dust, hit his back on a wall, and I saw his arm was obviously broken, bent unnaturally to the side. The huge sword swished up and then came down and so died Kallir, the surprisingly fast weapon splitting him in half. I stared at the sight incredulously, the bloody meat and a mess of armor that had been a man just moments before. The monster of a knight tore the weapon out, and Molun was backpedaling from him. 'Surrender?' the beast asked, amused. 'Drop the steel. You have no hope.'

I whispered, 'Larkgrin.' The weapon flared up and grew from my hand, twisting out and the mysterious symbols glowed. The bird on top of the staff looked fragile, but I thought of the tree mother had felled and wanted to push the bird into the Brother's back. The onlookers stared at the spectacle in awe, but the masked Brother was herding Molun, unaware of the danger. He kicked Molun, and the thief flew to his rear, nearly unconscious. I prayed, cursed, and charged him.

At that time, the knight looked to his fist. There was my key dangling from it. And it was not attached to the bone.

I am not sure what saved me. Instinct? Luck? Instead of striking the Brother with the deadly staff, I fell onto my belly in the dust and the huge two-hander swished over me. I rolled away in panic as the man stalked closer. His eyes were fixed on the staff. 'What in Odin's name! That—' He concentrated, his hand glowed again. 'Ring? And his staff! Finally!'

'Is mine,' I hissed. 'Not Morag's!'

'Yours? A paltry Lord of the Coin?' he laughed, and then his helmet nodded. 'Thief? No. There is something else here. I cannot tell if you lie. Strange, strange! Surrender now. In fact, just pass out.' He rushed forth, terribly fast for an armored man, grabbed me by the coat, and smashed his helmet into my face. I swooned and tried to hit him with the powerful staff, but he blocked me and got ready to crush my face again, but with the hilt of the sword.

I changed my face to Valkai's. It flowed like wax and settled, and I leered at him, though I was terrified.

He hesitated, confused. 'What? Oh, Ymir's ice-cold ass! I know—'

And then Molun's blade entered his knee and he howled. The Red Brother lifted his sword and cursed, trying to turn, but Molun stabbed at him again, and his sword went through the shoulder armor and chinks in the chain. The Red Brother fell on Molun, and I fell with him. The warrior let go of me in the tangle of bloody armor, legs, and I fell to his chest on my knees. 'Get up, you lout.' Molun got up from under the large, armored body, hissed and kicked the Brother hard. The man didn't make a sound, nor did he move. Molun pulled me up. 'Stay here, growl at the bastards. Those. The ones looking on.' He nodded at the crowd of onlookers. 'Sand's going to torch a house up the street, Maskan. Make Valkai be seen here, and I'll fetch what we need. Shit luck with Kallir, but we have to carry all of the gold. The Bear will be happy.'

I turned to look at the dozen or so people in the crowd. My imitation of Valkai the Heavy was spot on, for I heard the name whispered in the crowds. 'Stay back, or the Jesters will slit your faces. Stay away, and you will do fine!' Then I waited for Molun.

It took forever, the people were whispering, and I grew restless. Finally, Molun rushed out, carrying two heavy sacks of gold flans and dropped one in front of me. He grinned at me, dipped into his sack, and threw an arch of gold to the crowds. Most of the onlookers forgot their apprehensions as they went on all fours, gathering riches. Shrieking happily, they smiled like children. 'Compliments of the Jesters! And Magor can hump a goat, our ugly king!' he yelled and pulled at me, whispering. 'Poor Kallir,' Molun lamented. 'He was my only friend, Maskan. I'll talk with the Bear tomorrow on how to honor him. Mix with the crowds, change the face, get to safety and good luck,' he said and indicated the sack with a heavy nod, then hefted it at me.

The bag burst asunder.

So had Molun.

He died, for the Brother was leaning on the wall, having just swung his blade one last time, and so Molun died at my feet, his ribcage peeking from the ruins of armor, his face a mask of terror as death took him. A sea of gold covered his crumpled corpse. I roared, growled, and charged the Red Brother. He saw me coming but did not lift his sword for some reason. His sword went down. I struck at the Gargoyle and Larkgrin whirred in the air as it hit the stubborn knight on the helmet. The hit was incredibly hard, the helmet spun off to the shadows, the man fell to the wall, and my weapon hovered over his face. 'Maskan? That is your name? And Bear? We don't know Bear's real name. We will. The White Brother knows a spell to find you, now that you have a name,' he grinned with bloodied gums, terribly hurt, and I cursed for Molun had given away my name. And Bear's. He was a beautiful, blond man with innocent blue eyes, and it was hard to believe he was so proficient and savage with a weapon. 'Valkai the Heavy? Naram? But in reality, Maskan. You are a strange creature. But perhaps not so strange. We will find you.'

'It is just gold,' I hissed. 'The Jesters covet it and should you come for us, we will kill the lot.'

'Jesters?' he said grinning. 'Oh, we will come for the Jesters. We must! After this, we have to purge them, so you get your wish. My brothers will do it happily. But you are no Jester. And we will find you. Listen. These friends of yours? You do not understand—'

I wanted to kill him.

But I would not.

Instead, I kicked his face, and his eyes rolled in his head. 'Larkgrin,' I whispered; the staff disappeared, and I grasped the gold and pushed my way through the crowd. I took the face of the hunter and nobody noticed in the frenzy. There was a group of guards running by, but I saw they were going uphill towards a terrible conflagration, just up the Griffon's Stride. People were now jostling and pushing each other, and they swarmed the mint to get rich. The Silver Bells rang in the walls, and I heard trumpets blaring in the tower. I ran, looked back and saw an old woman disappearing into the mint. Another was rifling through the Brother's body. *Hope she stabs him,* I thought and ran until I could not run anymore. I began to walk.

Then, someone tripped me into an alleyway. I fought him off, but I felt a blade rip my coat. I backpedaled away and saw Twitch's bruised face, his hand stabbing down with wicked steel. 'I still want my prize, Lord of Lies,' he hissed. 'And the gold.'

A spear hit him in his back; a thin point burst from his chest.

I was bleeding, and I saw three figures rushing forth. 'Here, get him!' It was Sand, his face covered in soot. 'Maskan?'

'Take the coin sack,' Lith said, and she retrieved the spear. She was wearing tight, practical leathers, her hair was wild around her face. And last came another girl, Shaduril, dressed like Lith. 'Maskan? We know Bear, but nice to meet you. Maskan is your name?'

'What is she doing here?' I asked Lith, stunned. 'Yes, that is my name.'

'The family owns the Affront, the tavern, Maskan. She is my … sister.' She did not seem happy about the fact. Shaduril looked away from her in disgust.

'What?' I whispered. 'How did you know it was us?'

Lith looked embarrassed. 'Sorry, we knew. Always did. Didn't want to lie, but we were ordered to play along by Balan, our father. The Jesters found your family. We knew as well.'

'Yes,' Shaduril said softly. 'I am sorry as well. Valkai sent a word to the family that they would use you to execute our plan, as soon as you were found. He named the Bear. When Kallir came to Lith, it was like the gods had sent you to us.'

'Why would you want the Jesters gone?' Sand asked. 'They worked with you.'

Lith shrugged. 'Valkai also demanded much more than they had previously. He asked for too much. We decided it was a good idea to be rid of Valkai after we figured out your plan. A brilliant plan. Sorry for the acting, Maskan. I knew who you were.'

'We succeeded,' I said. 'It was costly.'

'The Jesters will suffer,' Shaduril agreed. 'I think you managed that much. Now that they are gone, I hope you will work with us.'

'Killing royals? Look—' I began.

Shaduril shook her head. 'We are not Valkai. We are not forcing you. But we have common enemies, and we are here to help. And I think we did already. You can take your own face now,' she said. She was beautiful, and I obeyed her.

'Much more handsome than the other face. I dislike mustaches,' Lith said with a grin and Shaduril shuddered with brief anger. She controlled it and smiled, though it was visibly hard to do so. 'Allies?' Lith asked.

'I don't know,' I said.

'Look, you need—' Sand began, and then I clutched his hand.

'The family is in danger,' I told him in panic.

'How so?' Sand asked, looking strangely subdued by the two females prowling around us.

'The Brother said they will find me. Said they know who we are,' I hissed in pain. 'He overheard my name. Your father's title.'

'Shit,' Sand cursed and looked distraught. 'What now? We with the noble bitches?'

Shaduril was eyeing Sand unkindly. 'Your friend survived his crime, I see. An arsonist.'

'Barely survived,' Sand said defensively. 'There were guards looking for me, just after the house burned. Crawled out of the back window. It was an abandoned one. Nobody should die.'

Lith looked troubled as she waved Sand down. 'They know your name?'

'Yes,' I said and stood up.

Sand pushed at me. 'How do you know? The Red Brother is down. Hurt. Dead? I doubt he–'

Shaduril shook her head; her face was concerned. 'He was up just after the fight, pushing people out of the mint. We saw it. You should have killed him, Maskan. A Mad Watch officer was talking with him. They will burn the Old City, but they will leave no stone unturned to find Bear. And that likely means your family is in genuine danger. Right?'

'The family is not in the city,' I said while massaging my neck. 'He said White Brother has a way to find them, but how could he? They are well hidden. They are ... we are criminals, after all. They can hide their tracks. Nobody even knows Bear's real name. Though they do mine ...'

Shaduril leaned on me; her hair was brushing my face, and I saw Lith look away in disgust. 'But they have spies, Maskan, they will know someone who knows the Bear and where you are holed up. They are better at hunting than Valkai was, even. Believe it. They don't hunt all the vagabonds in the land, no, but they could catch the most. Someone will always speak up. And this business with the White Brother and your name is bad. You should stay with us. You are safe with us.'

'What about the White Brother?'

'He has strange ways,' Lith said softly. 'They did not lie. If they know enough about a person they wish to find, he can find them. The White Brother. He will find nearly anything. He has a talent, Maskan, for finding things. Or do you think that wondrous staff of yours is the only item of power? And your skill with face-changing the only magical skill in Midgard? They all have something, Danegells.'

'I thought I was unique, yes,' I said sullenly.

'No, it is not an unusual skill,' she said. 'We should hurry. Balan, Father, will tell you more about magic later, but your family? Let us go. We will hide you. All of you. They cannot find you while you are with us.' Lith tapped a finger on an amulet. 'Because we are well protected. Your family is not. I am sorry they are in danger. She leaned on me. 'I will, unfortunately, stay here to tie up some loose ends. Don't forget me, Maskan.'

I shook my head, and stone-faced Shaduril led us off, without a word to her sister. We tried to exit the city, but could not. The gates were closed, the walls crawling with men. Nor could we leave that evening. Nor that night. Very early in the morning, we inched for the gates. There were wagons rolling out of the city, filled with corpses. *The Grim Jesters*, I thought. The Bad Man's scaffolds were filled with hanging corpses, one with conical robes and a female's face and one vast man. *Valkai? The Horns?* While we stared at the endless number of corpses being taken out, Shaduril got a note, likely from Lith. By late morning, the gates were open again, though we had to disguise ourselves as Shaduril's servants to exit. Shaduril fingered the note and looked sadly at us.

'I am sorry,' she told us. 'The White Brother found your home.'

We rode like the damned for the Hall.

## CHAPTER 7

I stared at the burning Green Hall. It was no longer our haven, but a den of death. It was crackling fiercely; the timbers could only barely be seen amidst the smoke, soot, and flames. A small army of men stood in front of the hall. The Mad Watch, by their red cloaks.

Worse, there were corpses swinging in the haze of smoke and one, I was sure, was the Bear. The man's back was arched from the pain he no longer felt, for he had died. Then there was Mir, my mother. She was no longer the caring, practical woman I had known, but a sad, small corpse without shoes and she hung forlornly, her hooded face hanging on her chest. I was so happy I could not see her face, though I knew her by her clothing.

And Ann.

She was there as well. She was probably gazing up at the sky, her hands lax on her sides and she was gently swirling in the wind, also hooded.

Crows were hopping on Bear's corpse, but not on the women's. I was grateful for that as well. The killers were still down there.

Sand was sitting next to me, holding his head in his hands. He had not said a word, and I did not wish to know what he was thinking about. At least he had not rushed forward in a suicidal attack—so far, he hadn't—but I kept an eye on him. Shaduril was near us, looking grimly at the sight. 'Your sister is a whore? She slept with Naram,' I asked her, my mind dazed, and I realized I was blabbering. *Mother was dead. She was dead.*

'No,' Shaduril said simply and softly. 'Well. Not with him.'

'But …' I began but went quiet.

She crouched next to me. 'Naram and the Blacktowers were in a small business deal together. He would bring us a daily bag of stolen golden flans, and we would make them useful. We know the jewelry business. He was too lazy to make the connections by himself and likely too scared. He had a crush on Lith, flirted shamelessly with her, was jealous as any fool of her, of course, but they had nothing like that between them. I don't want to speak of her. Not now. But you must know that we are pretty much in the same business as you are, Maskan. Or were. I am sorry for your family. It was a risky endeavor.'

'Too dangerous,' Sand whispered.

Shaduril nodded in full agreement. 'Your success was Valkai's bane, and we are grateful for that. He was not trustworthy, and we were fools to work with him. But this is a terrible price to pay.' Her voice cracked with sorrow, and I nodded gratefully at her.

'They are dead,' Sand stated bluntly, in shock.

I grunted. It needed saying. It had to be said. I would not understand it otherwise. It was probably Mother's slight body swinging around in the wind. She was dead. No. Yes. 'Why?' I asked. 'Why are they dead? It makes no sense.'

'You robbed from the crown,' Shaduril said directly. 'They had your name, and someone knew Bear's business. He had associates. Likely, someone made a lot of silver for betraying him. The King has a surprising number of spies in Bad Man's. Or it was the White Brother who learned Bear's real name. There he is.'

There were Brothers down there on horses, hidden by the smoke. I did not see them right that moment, but Shaduril had seen the White one.

'No,' I breathed. 'I mean why did they hang them? Why not hold them? To get the gold back, to find me?' I wondered weakly, stunned as Mother's corpse swung around in the wind. I was numb. So numb. It did not feel real. None of it. A rider appeared from the smoke and Sand hissed. He was a Brother Knight. His tall helmet was glistening in the light of Lifegiver. A white horsehair tail was rustling in the wind. He was staring at the clearing as if unconcerned with the whole business.

'You said they went for Valkai?' Sand asked with a hollow voice. 'He was hung there this morning, no? I saw him, I think.'

Shaduril nodded and showed me the note she had received. 'They sent a thousand men, Hawk's Talon down there in the harbor yesterday and this night. They tore into the old city and butchered hundreds of criminals. You saw them being taken out of the city for burial in some hole. Most were Jesters, some others. They did a good job at making sure everyone saw the procession of the corpses being carried out. Then they sealed the tunnels, though I doubt that would keep a determined rat at bay. There are dozens of tunnels they will never find.'

'Valkai?' I asked her. 'It was him on the scaffold?'

'He fought well,' she said with a small, satisfied grin. 'The note said he holed up in some ancient tavern and killed six men trying to get in, but he was impaled and dragged out by his entrails. They hung him after.'

'The Horns?' I went on.

Shaduril hesitated. 'There was a southern woman there,' she said cautiously. 'They said she wore this strange mask. Perhaps it was this … Horns? She killed herself before being captured. They hung her anyway. The filth is gone, Maskan. Thank you.'

I nodded. 'He, she … was scheming. Just like you are. To kill Magor. Apparently, she was their leader. Valkai was just—'

'Yes, we guessed he was not the brains of the outfit. Shady and lucky and savage, but not smart enough,' Shaduril was wiping some stray hair from her mouth. I briefly admired her delicate features and then loathed myself. *Mother and Ann. And Sand's father. All dead. While I gawked at a woman.*

'As Maskan said, you and this Horns had similar interests,' Sand growled. 'You were going to use Maskan here to kill the royals, and now you are here, telling us you have no idea who betrayed us. You claim the king has spies, but you were onto our plan the whole time.'

She looked down in shame. 'Yes. Lith figured it out as Kallir came to her, asking for a favor.'

Sand spoke on. 'Someone let us down; that is true. Perhaps you did?' Sand's face was turned her way, rage playing on his features. 'That is my father over there. You played us for fools—'

Shaduril sighed and shook her head forlornly. 'You can blame everyone for what happened. I feel guilty, Sand, I do. My father will not. It was fate. Believe me; we had no interest in seeing your family hang. We wanted to see you succeed and could have done nothing more to aid you. We hoped to have Maskan help us after. It went wrong.'

'You wish to kill the King,' Sand stated with a low growl. 'And here we are. With no ties to anyone. We only have revenge left. But we cannot do it alone and you—'

She raised a finger and Sand went quiet. 'You are making quite a fantastic conspiracy theory out of this.' She laughed bitterly. 'I said, we couldn't have done anything more to help you. No. The Bear there had the plan to be rid of the Valkai, and it was a clever one, yes? We liked it. And yes, we helped you. And wanted you to help us after. Things went wrong. Shit happens. If we had wanted to use your family against you, we would have grabbed them and brought them to the Crimson Apex. That is our ancestral fort and home, the land of the High Hold. Now we only have trust. And we trust you. Remember,' she said and held my shoulder, 'we could have grabbed you yesterday in that alley like the Jesters did. But instead we are here, and I am at your mercy.' Sand was about to argue, but she shook her head at him, and my friend relented as Shaduril stared at him with pleading eyes. 'But can we trust you? You are now reckless, dangerous to you, dangerous to us, and gods know if we can manage to keep you alive. But we shall try. And yes, we shall need you. And you will need me. Us. He has to fall. Magor is merciless and mad. I see him daily and know he is evil.' She shuddered in hate and loathing, and I felt very sorry for her. She was right. It had been our plan.

The White Brother, the Knight, was joined by two more, both riding from the woods. One was the Black and the other the Red one. My hand twitched with hate. Red Brother. He had looked kind and brave but had led them to our home. *At least he had put them on the scent,* I thought. The Black Brother was gesturing at a soldier. The man twitched visibly, unsure of what was being asked of him and then, and he handed the King's flag to the knight. The Black Brother took it, drew a long dagger, and hacked off half the pole, leaving the end sharp like a stake. He guided his massive mount forward and stopped at the corpse of the Bear. The crows stared down at him balefully but thought better of making trouble with the large man and took off in a wild flurry of wings. The man heaved the pole forward, impaled the Bear with it, and left the King's flag there to be seen.

'Rancid cur,' Sand cried softly. 'You shit.'

'You will kill the Queen? And the King?' I asked darkly.

Shaduril shrugged. 'Yes, you know we will try. There are a hundred plots by the High King to discredit and even kill kings all around Midgard, but none by the nobles of the Red Midgard. I know Magor works hard to thwart the south, but he thinks the nobles of Dagnar are loyal. We have a chance, it is unexpected, hasn't been done before. And the Red Brother, Black and White, the evil Brothers, and famous knights down there? They will have to fall as well. I doubt they would serve another. Should you help Balan Blacktower execute regicide and help us bring new glory and stability for us all, perhaps you will see them hanging one day. Or just dead. Even that would comfort you, I think. I cannot promise you will kill them.'

'Balan. Your father?' Sand asked her without taking his eyes off the three knights now mustering their troops for a trip back home.

She sighed and turned to speak to me. 'He is. Balan is our father. This has been a family affair for this year, though, as you know, we had to ask for Valkai to help. They had the resources we do not have, though perhaps Maskan will change that now.'

'How many are there in your family?' I asked her.

She waved her hand east and west. 'Father. You know Lithiana, of course. My damned sister. There is Taram, our brother, but he should be kept at arm's length from this plot. He has trouble dealing with … with many things.' She shook her head slowly as if lost in her thoughts until she slapped her knee. 'But we don't have the army to fight the King. Some hundreds of men, mostly peasants. Our High Hold has a large population of villagers, but they are not fighters, no. We are training and arming all we can, of course, but that is barely enough. That's why Valkai's troop was a godsend. But he was greedy. Too greedy. Don't worry about that now. We will find men, and perhaps we will be happy to kill the royals alone, though that will be the death of me. I would love to see an army take the Tower after I slay the King, but I doubt that can take place.'

'I am sorry—' I began.

She interrupted me, looking somber. 'We will make a pact. If you just agree to do your best for us, we will do so for you. The result will be for the sake of the land and our revenge.'

Sand looked at me feverishly. *I owed him. More, I owed Mother.*

'Yes, we shall make one. I'll do what needs to be done. We shall … kill the Queen. Then you … will slay the King. I am sorry he is interested in you.'

'It is terrible,' she breathed. 'He is old but has been courting me for a while. He is in love. But it gives me the opportunity to kill him.'

I blushed. 'You are his mistress.' I cursed myself and looked away.

She shook her head, unwilling to discuss it. It was as if a dark cloud had descended over her, and I could swear there had been a tear in her eye. Finally, she nodded. 'We all make sacrifices for our family. And we will murder them and hope the blood washes away the shame and the pain.'

'How will I kill—'

'Not now,' she said.

'How will you kill the King?' Sand asked ferociously. 'I wish to know.'

'Sand—' I started, but Shaduril waved me down.

She sighed. 'I will poison him with a deadly hairpin. The Brothers are hovering over him, but not when …' She went quiet, and we nodded, embarrassed. She went on. 'When the Queen dies, I will try it. No matter if I am alone with him or not. Chances are he will not be alone with me. He doesn't last long in bed. If he is out of the bed, then I will likely die. But I will kill him, and we shall see what happens. If we fail, it doesn't matter for us any longer. If we succeed, we still have to figure out how to kill the Brothers and Danegell dependents. Father is thinking about the plan, but he will need allies, as we have none currently. So far, it is all pretty shaky. Let him work on that part. We should all do our best for our families and the country, and accept the price will be high. That way we won't be disappointed.' She steeled her voice. 'The Danegell family has to fall. All of them.'

'We shall see them die,' Sand added ferociously. 'I will see their guts hanging out.'

She was nodding, uncertain. 'I am not sure what you can do, Sand. But you are welcome in the Apex.'

'What do you mean?' he asked with a suspicious voice.

'Well,' Shaduril went on. 'You cannot change your face. You cannot get anywhere near our enemy. Nor can you tie people to our cause. You are a thief. A … thug.'

'So am I,' I said abrasively, and she lifted her hands, trying to calm us.

'You know what I mean,' she said. 'Sand does not fit comfortably into this plan. We are above him, and he resents nobles. Perhaps it would be best if he were hidden away.' She leaned on the shocked Sand. 'You will smile over the corpses of those men down there, one day. I promise you that.'

'You don't want me?' Sand asked, his face reddening with anger. 'I'll not stay out of it. No madam.'

'He should be there,' I said in his defense.

'There is no role for him,' Shaduril said with a soothing voice. 'He might put us at risk. If he is your friend, do him a favor and let us keep him safe. Far from you. I can hide him.'

They stared at each other. Finally, Sand shook his head. His face betrayed grief and hopelessness. 'It would have been convenient if those guards had caught me when I was burning the house.'

'No,' she said. 'You would have talked if they had taken you alive.'

Sand was fighting her words but seemed at a loss for what to say. I shook my head at her. 'Sand?' I said. He looked up at me, his face white with fatigue, sorrow, and disappointment. 'We will finish this together. You might not be able to join me in everything, but I want you to be there. It is our family that died. We shall finish it together. Always together. You won't take him anywhere. He wouldn't let you anyway. We go on together. Or not at all.' I hesitated as I said that. I did not wish to be parted from her.

'But—' Shaduril began.

I snapped my fingers, and her eyes grew large. 'No. He comes. And didn't you just say you need soldiers?'

Shaduril hesitated and then nodded her head. 'He might come to regret it. But yes. Balan asked to bring him along, so I guess I must agree. But remember I warned you.'

Sand ignored her warning and pulled at me. 'I swear on their blood, that the King and his Queen, the Brothers, and Lord Captain Helstrom, whose men are down there as well, they shall all die by our actions.'

'I swear it with you,' I said. 'On their blood.'

Shaduril said nothing.

We stared at the Brothers below. They were still speaking, gesturing, and looking around, confused.

'That one,' I asked her softly as I saw the White Brother shake his head. The Black Brother urged him to do something, and he shrugged and put his hands to his sides, concentrating. He sat there for a time. 'He can find people?'

'He can, sometimes,' she whispered. 'He did find your people. As you were told. But he will not find you while you are with us. Near us.' I looked at her carefully, up and down. She looked beautiful, but not magical.

'You have something to make it so?' I asked her, eyeing her. 'Some way to fend him off? That pendant?'

'The family has its ancient secrets,' she said, her finger tapping at an amulet of red, with a black tower and ravens. 'He won't see you while you are with us.'

'Useful skill,' Sand said, and Shaduril grunted in agreement.

'It would be,' she said, 'but it is not a skill. It is an artifact of past ages. Maskan shall speak with Father about things like that, no doubt. Now. Let us wait for them to leave. Then we can go.'

'What happens,' I asked her as we waited, 'if Valkai or the Horns told them about you?'

She shrugged. 'They found our coins. The ones you stole from me.'

'They did?' I asked, horrified.

She leaned on us and smiled. 'But there are so many houses who bought favors from them. Hard to blame us.'

'That was a fortune,' I said.

She nodded. 'It was. We have friends in high places, Maskan. Times are dark, but we have some few friends. The King won't hear of the coins.'

*They knew someone who matters*, I thought.

We waited in silence and stared as the riders finally led the men of the Mad Watch away. Their steel was bright in the light of the Lifebringer and tall spears were heaving above the troops. The three Brothers rode smoothly on their massive dark horses, apparently happy with the day's work. 'We go and bury them. Then we shall go to your place,' I said. 'This Crimson Apex.'

'Let us bury them,' Sand said and got up, and Shaduril grabbed his hand. 'What?' Sand asked incredulously. 'They left.'

'No, they did not leave. They have archers in the woods, and they will be there for weeks,' she explained softly, easing Sand's tensions. 'Of course, they expect you to go back there to cut them down and give them a proper pyre and perhaps even prayers, but it is not something we can do.'

I felt it was cruel, too cruel to fathom. 'I could take a face of a guard, and—'

'He could!' Sand insisted.

She smiled at him coldly. 'You would need more. Their gear. You would have to kill one first. Then you would go and find all the archers sitting in the wood, wondering why you are cutting the bodies down. And perhaps there is a Brother there. It is too risky. Believe me,' she told the enraged Sand, who calmed slowly. His frame shook as he fought the wisdom of her words. She whispered something to Sand, who looked at her rebelliously.

'She has a point, Sand,' I said softly.

'Fine. She is right,' Sand said unhappily and rubbed his face. 'I'll bury them later. When I can. First chance I get. Take us away, then. Let's go and hear your mad plans.'

'Yes. I will have to go back to Morag's court soon, but I have time to take you to Father to discuss our plight. This Horns had a beautiful plan, and we will use it, no doubt with fewer practical resources than the Jesters possessed, but still enough to try it. Trust us.' She nodded at three horses tied to a tree. 'Are you coming?'

'Lead on,' I said and turned my face from my dead family. And she did.

She led us through the thick, pristine woods and meadows of Red Midgard. The summer was old, but nearly unbearably hot and flowers seemed to cover most of the riverbanks. There were farmers and shepherds about, and we skirted sturdy walls set to separate the wealthy estates from each other. We hiked through rustic villages and saw pigs being chased by children. The tough, nearly black northern bread was being baked in huge outdoor bakeries. People might be dour, but they could be happy, especially out of the city. Most people we saw were healthy and stout, ready to take up spears for their country. For their King.

*I wanted to kill the King. So did Sand*, I thought. Mother had been worried about me. Ann had been so sad. I gazed at Shaduril. She was brave. And wise. I would follow her.

We slowly rode all day along the Broken Crown Way, then trailed the coastline northwest, and by late afternoon we reached a set of vibrant villages off the main way. We passed them, and beyond them, we found a land full of high cliffs falling into the sea below. She guided us to an unusually high hill and pointed to the northwest at a spot near the edge of a rough cliff, and on top of that, there was a white castle with red towers. It was not a large castle but boasted high plastered walls. The towers held gleaming ballista and catapults, and there was apparently a deep moat quarried across the cliffs, which to me seemed like an invitation to topple the whole thing to the sea.

'What is that?' Sand asked, groaning as his thighs were killing him. I was also so very sore. We were unused to riding for any length of time. I craned my neck to see what Sand was talking about and then took side steps as I glimpsed something above the castle. On the hillside, there was a ruin of a keep, its former glory still somewhat evident from the contours of the round towers, the still erect iron gate and a half spared central keep. I was not sure, but there were curtains in some windows and birds were flying around the structure.

'Is it yours? The ruin?' I asked Shaduril.

'It is,' she said. 'It's the High Hold, named after our land, and the new fort is called the Crimson Apex.'

'What happened?' I asked her.

She wiped her hand across her face and stayed quiet for a time. 'The Cataclysm.'

'That thing?' Sand asked. 'Some said it was a strange illness. Bear said Mother had fallen very sick during it. She died of it before Maskan's mother joined him. Of course.'

'No,' Shaduril said. 'Father said it was more than that. There were strange fires, earthquakes. It rained so hard the rivers flooded. The illness followed. It happened just after we were born. Thousands died, and we were not spared. Mother died. Servants. They are buried there. Come,' she told us, and we rode for the distant home of the Blacktowers.

'I would have built the new one somewhere else. Must be hard to see the ruin every day,' I said.

She grunted. 'That is true. Though we grew up not knowing its history,' she said wistfully as she hiked for the fort. Some guards were pointing at us now, and there was movement on the walls. 'An ill-chosen location or not, this one is a more sensible one. It should not leave daughters without mothers.'

'No, you just fall to the sea, and there will be no survivors,' Sand said brusquely.

'Yes, exactly,' she said with a small voice. 'Would be much better that way, I think. But we are all adults now. You are young, but you have lost people, we have lost people, and Red Midgard is full of people who will all lose more people they care about if we fail. We are all grown up, with grown-up goals. Maskan, do not show your power to people you don't know. Not to Taram, either, though you will know him. As I told you, we don't want to—'

'Your brother is to be kept in the dark, yes,' I said. 'We should avoid him?'

She shook her head. 'Hard to avoid him. He is curious as a squirrel. He is not a party to this ... *change* we are going to foment,' she said thinly. 'For now. We ... love our brother, but he is not the sort of a man you trust. But he will likely train you to fight. He'll pester you with questions. Give no answer to the bastard.'

'Bastard,' I echoed her.

'Fine. I hate him,' she said bitterly.

'Like you hate Lith,' Sand said.

Shaduril gazed at him coldly and shrugged. 'It's none of your business, boys.'

'I'll be careful,' I told her, put back by her vehemence. 'Though I am curious to hear more of this plan or yours with the Queen. It is sure to be better than our previous one.'

'You will,' she laughed. 'And it won't be any worse, at least. I promise. Valkai's gang likely had a good deal of it planned already, people they know, how they would make the switch. They probably knew Falg Hardhand inside out. We will do our best. One thing is sure, and only one! We will have a glorious adventure, my friends. Do not make trouble. Do not sneak around spying on us. We will be honest with you.'

We rode in silence until some birds began to sing forlornly high in the boughs. It was dark, but not too dark with the Three Sisters providing ghostly light. Near the Crimson Apex, there were many meadows that swayed in a gentle night breeze. I finally turned to Sand and whispered. 'Remember when we thought she would refuse us because she is a noble?'

Sand nodded and spoke softly. 'She refused me. Looks like I'm extra. Did she want to hide me? Where? In a grave?'

'She was thinking of your best interests, she said,' I noted, uncomfortable with saying anything evil about her.

Sand hesitated a bit and leaned on me. 'I see. You and her, eh?'

'I doubt it,' I said.

He nodded and did not believe a word I said. He went on. 'She is very persuasive. They have a weak plan. It's dangerous. But it's for the good of all of us. Perhaps so. She made a good case, and while she insulted me, I follow her. I don't know why, but I just nodded and got on the horse. But maybe we should just trust each other? Perhaps we should ride away? Or be prepared to do so if things turn out strange. If they plot for their sake, rather than that of Red Midgard? If they are no better than the Jesters?'

I hesitated. *We could.* But then Shaduril turned to me, and her eyes glowed in the light of the Sisters and she looked fair, sad, and she needed me. She was already carrying a heavy burden, and I felt like a coward when I considered leaving her alone to carry it. I looked away from Sand and spoke. 'They can offer us what we need. Let us stick around and see what it is they can do. And then, later, reconsider our course.'

'Might be hard to review our course much later on, friend,' Sand said sadly. 'She's got you. But fine. I'll stay with you until we get our vengeance.'

'We should also try to survive the vengeance,' I said. 'We have dreams beyond that, no? We are still brothers.'

Sand glanced at Shaduril and shrugged. 'You have a ... sister now, I think. And they will change everything for us.'

I began to refute him, but could not. 'She will change some things. She is sad. Alone. And beautiful.'

Sand growled a warning, and Shaduril looked back at us. How much she had heard, we could not guess, but enough, for she spoke. 'I'm a noble woman, Maskan,' she said sadly. 'You should be careful. Noble ladies have cruel streaks, and you will be hurt, no matter if your feelings should be answered.'

I stammered and nodded and spoke bravely. 'I cannot help getting hurt, then.'

She looked at me and shook her head in wonder. She looked stern, then happy and laughed brightly. 'Well said.' Her eyes went over mine, and there was a strange emotion there, one of gentle promise, then suddenly, of cruel anger. 'Lith.'

'Your sister,' I stated rather stupidly. 'What has she got to do with this discussion?'

She seemed to growl. 'I told you to beware of Taram. Beware of her as well. She will not be happy if you speak of me like that. Do not mention us, at all.'

'I did already,' I said softly. 'I spoke of … that day I returned your coins to you. And she knows. She knows.'

She was silent and resentful. 'I give you a fair warning. If you like me, do not touch her. I cannot forgive if you fail in that.'

'I will be careful,' I told her with a blush, thinking of the kiss Lith had given me. Sand was staring at her, frowning, fiddling with his saddle straps as if considering flight. I was strangely happy. She had made no promises, but she had not turned me down, either. I was so confused. *My family was dead. And yet I could feel happiness? I was mad.*

We rode on, and night came on entirely as the Three Sisters chased the Lifegiver's last rays from the sky. Evening birds awoke, and their clear chirping made the past horrors seem distant. Then, we passed a large village and saw the keep far ahead. And the ruin. I had been right; there were curtains fluttering in the windows. It looked sad and forlorn. Shaduril stared at it, her eyes still.

'Here we are,' Shaduril breathed as if a heavy duty would take over her life the moment she stepped through the gate. We rode up to it and saw the moat was rigged with iron stakes. A sturdy drawbridge spanned it. On top of the gatehouse, red flags with a white lily whipped in the slight breeze of the vast Callidorean Ocean. We walked past some alert guards, who wore very long capes, holding tall spears high in the air. They saluted Shaduril but stared at us with suspicion in their cold, dark eyes.

'Just guards, boys,' she whispered. 'But please make an excellent impression on Father. He trusts his first instincts, and he might reject you if you piss your pants.' She glanced at Sand. 'Or sulk overmuch.'

'Yes, lady,' I told her while Sand said nothing.

'Shad,' she smiled and then the smile disappeared, for we approached the central keep. A dense covering of berberis plants adorned the red walls, their scent soothing to our nerves. Then the smell of sweet cooking meat, whiff of rot, and a terrible stench of tanning vats replaced that smell. Sand nudged me and pointed to our right. By the wall, there was a blacksmith and a tannery and great activity was going on there.

'Looks like they are preparing for war,' I agreed with Sand's uplifted eyebrows. 'I guess you are serious about this business.'

'We have some men, but not enough for real war,' said a quiet voice of somewhat menacing quality. 'They need gear, nonetheless.' A man had stepped out of the doorway and looked at us with freezing, appraising eyes, and we saw little else of him but those eyes, as he stood there in the shadows. They were very bright and penetrating. 'But you know this, and you are here, to help us. Welcome.' He was a small man, about Shaduril's size, in fact. A man with a torch stepped up to illuminate us, and we saw Lord Balan Blacktower. His hair was dark like mine, but short and was held by a thick band of silver with dark stones set in it. His eyes were dark, and his complexion tanned as if he spent a lot of time outdoors, and his clothing reflected that. He had high cheekbones and a long neck. He had a leather tunic, scuffed doeskin pants, and well-used boots, and all were patched and dusty in places. 'And you are the famous Maskan.'

I bowed my head and decided he was the sort of a man one could see wearing the crown. *He was keen of mind, calm, and decisive*, I thought. Cold and emotionless as well, I decided, but he was a strong one. 'I am, Lord,' I said and bowed deep before Balan Blacktower, the lord of the Tenth House of Red Midgard. 'And I am grateful for the asylum.' His eyes went to slits as he regarded me. I decided to be a bit more assertive. 'Though, of course, you need my services as much as I need yours. I have innocent blood to pay back for.' I straightened my back and decided to act like a noble would. Which I was, I decided.

His face twitched slightly. 'Innocent? The Bear? The Uncouth Lord? Your mother, a peddler of stolen items. I suppose innocence has many layers. Yes. Unfortunate that your plans went awry, though not totally. It is good Valkai's gang is gone. It was a daring plan. But to face a Brother? You did not expect it. You should have. That mint is connected to the Tower of the Temple and is one of the few weak spots one might try to enter the heart of the kingdom.'

'I smashed him down,' I reminded him.

'But you did not kill him,' Balan noted. 'Amateurish. But ultimately,' he leaned toward me and whispered, 'ultimately, you are right about our King. Innocent or not, he had no right to hang the women. No one should hang without a proper trial. Just one of the symptoms of his madness, is it not?'

'We do not disagree, Lord Balan,' I said and bowed again. His smile was happy if fleeting.

He shrugged. 'I did not expect you to. Blood has been spilled; more will be spilled in the years to come if he is not stopped. Rest assured, young masters; we will act. And we don't have much time. We must act before the Yule celebration. Before this year's end.'

'Why is that, Lord?' Sand asked, and they all stared at him with incredulity, like a band of merciless wolves staring at a rabbit that got lost in their cave.

Balan nodded at Sand. 'Does your friend know of the plan?'

'I know of the scheme,' Sand said with tiny amount of respect, and there was a small silence with the Blacktower family as they gauged my morose friend. He noticed it and cleared his throat. 'You will replace the royals. Both of them. And she—' he nodded at Shaduril, but Balan interrupted him.

'She is a noble, and the court is a wicked place, my young friend. She is risking her life for our homes, families and she, like many others before her, will fight for what is right, just, moral, even if it means we are breaking the laws of the land. Laws are a beautiful thing but twisted to serve the evil. And yes, we are in a hurry. The Jester's plan was a fine one. And why must we act soon? Why, because the Queen visits her family once a year, and it will be just before the Yule feast. Next year might be too late for all of us, and we dare not try to kill her at the court, no. Too many people there. We will try it where she is at her most vulnerable, where she is relaxed, where there are few Brothers about and with a plan she surely won't expect. Her most trusted servant is her most dangerous enemy. Unprecedented! We will kill her in her home. Then the King. We must. War is looming. The south is quarrelsome.'

'How so?' I asked him.

He looked mysterious. 'They say,' he whispered, 'that Malingborg is empty of armies. That several Hammer Legions have disappeared, and Aten's Navy is unusually well fitted. And they say the King, our Danegell is not heeding the signs. That he will take our armies north with swords to punish our allies for trivial issues when he should send words of peace to them. No, next year will not do. Three months from now. Or we will all die.' His passion was invigorating. Both Sand and I were nodding, feeling the great danger as the lord spoke of it. His haste was catching on. His daughter was facing danger, his family was. And the whole Red Midgard could fall like our family had.

'Is there going to be war? With Ygrin?' Sand asked. 'Over some silly trade dispute with the Bay's fishing?'

Balan shook in momentary indecision, fidgeting with impatience. Shaduril nodded at Balan, ever so slightly, and the high lord deigned to answer my friend. 'I did tell my girls to save all who are close to Maskan, so I guess I should answer your questions, even if it is rude to address a lord with no respect and his title, Sand. As for the war, not only the two major allies of the Fringe—Ygrin and Falgrin—but the kings and dukes of Shalimar of Ice, Ollicas, Ranleigh, Kanninberg, and Urten have declined Danegell's invite to celebrate Yule with us. That is traditionally the time the alliance of the north is ratified. The northern kingdoms are meeting separately, and Red Midgard will be alone. Because Danegell is going mad. He thinks to take the north before the High King, but this will end in our destruction. He is playing dangerous games. Against Ygrin, against those he dislikes, and angering his people by approving this cult—'

'Of the One Man,' Shaduril added helpfully.

Her father nodded and shook his head towards distant Dagnar. 'In a way, I can understand him. It is because his son, the prince died twenty years ago during the Cataclysm, and I can understand such a thing might drive a man mad. But many others lost loved ones in the event.' His eyes wandered over the moat to the ruins of the old keep. 'In short, he no longer cares to govern Red Midgard and the alliance of the Fringe. But now, Maskan, you have a lot to learn. We will try our best to kill them all. I have some reluctant allies, and I am thinking about a plan on how to kill all of them, even the Brothers. There will be sacrifices—' his eyes settled on my ring, and he stammered. Self-consciously, I hid it. He went on, speaking thinly and he was apparently preoccupied with my treasure. 'Sacrifices. You will risk much, Maskan. Shaduril will as well. All my family will, in fact, if she fails. If you fail. I have given my daughter to the Beast of the North, a mad thing. Never forget that if you get cold feet.'

'I shall not, Lord,' I told him, my mind mulling over his words. *She is braver than I am,* I thought as I eyed the beautiful daughter of the Blacktowers. 'What do you require of me? Exactly.'

He clapped my back. 'The man you will replace, Falg Hardhand is the Queen's food taster.'

I nodded, uncertain if I enjoyed his hand on my shoulder. 'I know. So, shall I first learn how to eat?' I asked with some brevity.

'Yes,' he said sternly. 'Of course. You are an actor in a once in a lifetime role. You have to be perfect. You have to be proficient in so many things, and your attitude, young man, is the first thing you must change. Be perfect, not an amateur. You have been messing around for far too long, you thug. Our company, an elegant house of Red Midgard, the nobles and lords and ladies, will do you good. You will learn manners and discipline,' he said happily, ignoring Sand, who was standing on the side, forgotten. 'We will marinate you in nobility, boy. Falg will pale in comparison when we are done. You will have to learn Falg's ways, his manners, his faults, and his strengths. There is much more to this craft of subterfuge and lies than just taking a ... face. As you probably discovered in the mint. You made a mess of it.'

I nodded, blushing. 'I did.'

He smiled thinly. 'So you will have to be perfect. The Brothers are not to be fooled easily, as you know,' he added darkly. 'And there are sure to be some in the Queen's house, though why would they doubt Falg? We will see. We have a man, our butler Gray, who used to serve in the King's kitchens, and we know what Falg does and how. Of course, we don't know if the Queen has other uses for him. Some say he is her lover, perhaps as revenge for the King's addiction to beautiful faces. She might, Maskan, enjoy his brews.'

'But what if she requires …' I began, and my voice faltered. Sand was wheezing in soft amusement.

'If that is so, then you might want to consider killing her in bed,' Balan told me practically. 'Surely you know how to please a woman?'

'Sweet gods,' I sulked.

His eyes went large. 'You do not?'

'I am not comfortable with this subject,' I whispered, blushing deeply.

'Oh my,' Balan said, distressed. 'Surely you know how to take a piss, at least? Gods above and down, such a handsome boy and does not know his way around the bedchamber.'

Shaduril tittered brazenly, and I did not look at her, cursing the lord. 'I—'

'We will teach you,' he said heavily. 'I won't, but we will,' he added and looked at Shaduril. She shrugged.

'I can think of a solution to it,' she said, and I felt utterly left out of something that should be mine to decide. 'Lith might know a suitable one. Perhaps we can hire a girl or—'

'I'm sure I can manage this part on my own,' I interrupted.

Balan chuckled.

Sand spat, though not in my defense. He was seething with impatience, upset at being left out. 'Lord. Would you share …' he began, but Shaduril spun on him and shook her head furiously. He growled and went on. 'Would you share the plan with us? Let's say she dies, and even he. Let us assume it all goes well. What then? If we succeed, what shall we do next? Lord …' Shaduril was groaning, and Sand stared sullenly at Balan.

'Who will sit on the Rose Throne after we miraculously succeed in this plan?' I asked him in support of Sand. 'Is there such a plan?'

'Yes,' the lord said. 'But I'll share it with those I trust. Not with your friend. He should be happy there is a sanctuary like this for such as he.' Balan clapped his hands as if to signal an end to the discussion, and Shaduril looked down. I shut my mouth, sensing it was time to do so. Shivers of fear ran up and down my back. The thin man was swallowing and shaking his head. He had a sort of feverish look on his face. 'Rose Throne? I shall discuss that with you in a bit. As for the act of dealing with the Queen, I cannot give you a sheet of instructions to memorize, nor any pointers as to what you need to do and how. You will use the skills we give you, your wits if they fail, and you will be as prepared as you can be. In addition to the ways of the nobles, you will have to figure out how to fight. You have to know how to fight very well, indeed.'

'Why?' I asked. 'I'm to be a cake taster. Is this man grossly fat?'

Balan smiled, I think, but it was a fleeting smile. 'He does not gobble up the Queen's foods, boy. He tastes them. But he is fit and healthy and ready to fight for the Danegells as well as keep the Queen safe from poisoning. And so will you. You will learn how to fight and how to kill. Not only will you take Falg's face, but you will also take his savage reputation. He will attend a fight in the Dark Sands that fateful afternoon, and he will do well. He always does, though few know him, or his real name when he escapes to have this fun for a while. Lith, you, my men will deal with him. But you will need to know how to do even a portion of what he does, for you will take his sword and ax, and you cannot drop them with foolish incompetence. You must swagger as you walk, hold your hands over your weapons with cold familiarity. You have to play the part, as I said. And who knows; perhaps you have to fight while serving the Queen. Briefly, but still.'

'What if he dies in the Dark Sands?' Sand asked him with incredulity. 'What if Falg dies? No matter how well you think he does?' There was a dangerous edge to Sand's words, and Lord Balan did not even look his way. My friend went on, 'Is it a death match? One versus one?'

'No,' Balan said drily. 'It's a special event. There will be some eighty men and women in there. Teams. And beasts. If he dies, we go ahead with the plan. Perhaps the news won't travel fast enough to the Queen. But it will mean we will have to kill another man in the streets. I'll explain that later. We are all in, boy.'

'Why would this Falg do this kind of a battle?' I asked with curiosity. 'That sort of thing gets a man killed.'

Shaduril shrugged. 'He is from the Shadowed Rocks, far to the south of Verdant Lands. They all fight there, all the time and here, in the north? Despite the King's madness, laws still rule the land. Falg is a silk-covered beast and has few opportunities to enjoy a good fight. Dark Sands is his playground. A home far from home. He has a partner and a superb team so that he will be with the winners. But as Father says, it won't matter. Understood?' she asked and looked around. 'Our weapons master will train you.'

'And who is that?' I asked. 'This—'

'A very, very good fighter,' Balan said with some dry humor. 'But you will keep your trap shut about our business. All aspects of it. And here comes the little monster,' Balan laughed softly, eyeing a figure that was striding for us from what looked like a stable. 'Not one word.'

'Greetings,' said the young man who was lathered in sweat, and he bowed to us. The most memorable part of him was his grin and wide neck, which belied bullish strength, despite the fact he was short. His eyes were large and full of mirth, though a cunning flash in them told me he was curious about us. His hair was curly and brown, and his eyebrows were strange and lively. He seemed the sort of a man who would smile when surrounded by enemies. 'Taram. Taram Blacktower at your service.' Balan turned to his son, and Shaduril looked away from him. *Lith and Taram. At least she spoke with her father*, I thought. Balan gazed at me, and I nodded. I would say nothing.

'You are at their service,' Balan chortled maliciously.

The man looked startled, though only for a second, but he rose to the occasion. 'In their service, eh? And what kind of a lord are you? I have not seen you two before. In disguise, are you not? You look and smell like peasants. Clever! From the north, perhaps?' Sand was shuffling nervously. I felt sorry for him.

'I'm a nobody, Lord,' I said, though that was not true. I had been as noble as they were, and my family still was. I kept that to myself and noticed Balan was staring at my ring again, raising his eyebrow. 'We are both peasants, and we thank you for your service.'

He looked shocked and finally laughed, though the laughter was forced. 'Gods laugh! Peasants! And what shall I serve you with? Shall I make your beds?'

'You will teach them to fight, Taram,' Shaduril said softly. 'To fight. You shall not maim nor kill them. You will teach them to defend themselves as a soldier. Nothing shady or shitty, just basic fighting skills.'

Taram's eyes took on Shaduril as he gauged her reactions. She stared back until he flinched. 'What shall they fight with? Pitchforks?'

Balan clapped his hands together, and Taram bowed. The lord took the man aside and had a long discussion with the young lord, whose face was an unreadable mask, with a hint of arrogance and contempt.

'They are weird,' Sand whispered, and I nodded. They were. 'And thanks for lowering yourself to my level.'

'I'm not a noble, Sand. No matter what Mother told me,' I said. 'And they are no better than we are. Either one of us.'

'They sure act very nobly about this Morag business,' Sand whispered and went silent as the young Blacktower strode towards us.

Taram saluted us. 'So, my peasant friends. I am literally at your service, or my allowance is cut.'

'Taram!' Balan admonished him, and the man raised both hands to indicate his willingness to cooperate.

He went on. 'I will teach you how to fight as my dear father requested. I am not sure for what cause I am to suffer this indignity, but I know it is an eminently good one. That will suffice. As long as my debts are getting paid, I have no saying in the matter,' he grinned and clapped my back so hard dust flew. Sand scowled at him as he was about to do the same to him, and he raised his hands to show he would not. Taram nodded at the keep. 'Every morning, from sunrise to noon, I shall teach you to fight with weapons suited for you.'

'Staff and sword for Maskan,' Balan said. 'Show him how to use and carry the sword, but teach him how to fight with a staff.' I stared at him. *Did he know about Larkgrin?* He saw my face and shrugged. 'Staff. I know it is not the most famous weapon in the old stories of wars and heroes, but it is a very useful one. My father taught me so. Sometimes you have to improvise; sometimes you must fight well with a piece of wood. Spear, broken shaft?'

'I'd love to learn two-handed sword,' I said softly, feeling foolish as I remembered the martial weapon of the Red Brother.

'Staff,' Balan said sternly. 'And you shall learn long sword on the side. First, you learn how to walk, then to run, boy.'

'My esteemed father is right,' Taram said with a hint of mockery, which he hid with a small bow. 'You seem fast and big, so do not worry. Perhaps we have time to find what else you are proficient at. Speaking of which. How much time do we have anyway?'

'Three months,' Shaduril said coldly, and Taram's eyes went to slits.

'I'll be finished before Yule,' he said slowly, thinking, and Balan scowled. Taram was dangerous, I decided. In more ways than with weapons. 'We will see what I manage,' Taram added, brightening. 'Your simple friend will learn sword and shield, perhaps spear. I'll train him as well, though I will concentrate on this man here.' Sand held his tongue admirably, partly because Shaduril stared at him with a steely look. 'See you in the morning, boys!' He went off and was soon instructing a group of men carrying planks in torchlight.

Balan smiled coldly at Taram's back. 'My boy is the rebel in the family. Did you notice he did not even greet his poor, old father or dutiful sister? He dug into the fresh meat and tried to gobble it up, he did. He is an arrogant liar, but he is a Blacktower no matter how different he is from most of us. He despised you two, but it is ironic, for he is a simple thing, really, and enjoys pleasure over morals and duty. Your face. Keep it that way. Secret. Your face, which I will see now in my office. Come and accompany me. Shaduril will see your … friend is settled in.' He turned and disappeared through an enormous set of thick doors, both braced by steel and iron, and Shaduril followed him, chatting politely if not amicably with Sand, despite her obvious disdain for him.

I sneaked after Lord Balan, who was taking a long stairway to the right, up for the second and third floors. The sconces were alight with flaming torches; the keep was decorated with tasteful dark velvet drapes mixed with brazen reds and fragile, cozy furniture. There was art in the form of statues and even paintings, some enormous and enthralling. I gazed down the stairs and saw Sand seated alone at a table in a long hall. Beyond him, there was a busy official handing out orders while chatting with Shaduril. An old lady was seated near a window, where candles fluttered. She was a gray-haired old woman, bent over her desk, poring over texts, and she would write furiously now and then.

Balan smiled. 'The family owl. She hardly sleeps at all. Illastria. My aunt. Always reading, always delving deep in the old lore. She is likely the best scholar in Red Midgard. Though she doesn't speak much.'

'In what subject?' I dared ask him.

He snorted. 'In myths. The past. I am the one looking at the future. One day Shaduril will take over both duties.'

'I see, Lord. Your daughter,' I began and saw his eyes gauging me. I stammered and cursed myself and went on. 'She seems to be a capable one.'

'She is a most dutiful girl. We owe her for so much,' the thin lord said. 'I could use her in the house, but she must keep Morag interested. So she is rarely here.' He was climbing, his hands behind his back, and he gazed at me now and then. He nodded at my scrutiny of the art. 'A good thief knows his art and his mark. Make sure not to sneak around the hall, my friend, and keep your hands off the old treasures. In any case, we shall keep an eye on you. And your friend should be careful as well.' He said that with an emphasis, and I got the message. Playing face-changing games might get Sand in trouble as well. 'And,' he continued. 'I will have to sell it all. We need mercenaries.'

'Yes, my lord. I want what you want,' I agreed with him meekly though I could not help but admire a golden-edged vase of ancient making. 'Won't your Taram see soldiers preparing for battle?'

He chortled as he heard this. 'He will. Perhaps he thinks the Crown has asked for men. That is what I will tell him, anyway. What I want, boy, is to stand before the Rose Throne and see the Danegells gone. I wish to run my finger across the throne's contours and sit on it. Once. I would like to be—'

'King,' I stated coldly.

He shook his head. 'No. I will not be a king of anything. I just wish to sit on the throne. Always did. I will gladly vacate it later. I cannot explain it to you, Maskan. Then I want justice for Red Midgard. A strong nation. Please make sure not to make a mess of things. You have been warned. We beheaded two thieves in one of my villages the other week, and not even your fine skill with faces can change the way things cut through flesh. But you are a unique thief and with some patience, we shall make you pass as a royal slave. What a great leap forward in life, eh?'

'Getting beheaded is certainly better than getting hung, my lord. Were they starving, the thieves?' I asked him sweetly.

He laughed briefly. 'They were thieves, boy. Makes no difference why they stole. Beheading is a kinder way to go, but make no mistake; you shall piss your pants in either case. Make sure your pants stay dry.'

'Did they stand on trial?' I asked him. 'Or did they go without one, as my family?'

'I judged them, Maskan,' Balan said tartly. 'Do not accuse me of the same I just did our King.'

'Of course, Lord,' I said sweetly and disliked him. I was a noble; I reminded myself. A noble like him. 'But a damned poor one,' I whispered and chuckled. Balan did as well, as if he knew what I had said.

We climbed up to the third floor, passed servants and guards and splendor and came to a white door with a thick locking bar, which he pushed up, hung on the wall and nudged the door open. He stomped in and waded through a thick carpet of southern make, colorful, red and yellow. It was surprisingly bright considering his dour demeanor. There were fine books, most expensively bound, a chandelier of gilded silver and pictures of times long forgotten; the art of the past by some fabulous artist. I turned to stare at them. They tugged at me, hung on the walls, and I could not tear myself away from them.

He grunted as he sat down behind a long desk. 'You are no peasant. A thief, yes, but you could have been something else. You are Tal's son, no?'

I whirled on him and looked at him with alarm. I groped for Larkgrin but did not call it forth. 'I am a thief.'

'Tal's thieving son, no?' he asked me. 'The age fits. And you are arrogant as he was.'

'How do you know this? I only learned—'

'I know he was a bit strange, Maskan. Tal,' he said dryly. 'I collect information. Illastria delves into myths, and I use that information, and some of that information claimed Tal had strange skills. And we all know Morag never found your mother and you. I doubt he knew her name, and you had not been named yet. There were no records of either of you, really. Lax of the scribes. White Brother's spells could not locate you. Morag likely thought you had fled the land and managed to hide yourself. But Tal had one unique thing everyone in the court knew about. And it's that ring. Isn't it? It's in one of Illastria's books. Risky to wear it. Perilous. But I suppose it is a sentimental thing.'

I rubbed the thing briefly, trying to hide it. His eyes were feverish as he regarded it.

'Perhaps I am of that house, yes,' I agreed softly.

He roused himself. 'You see, I am not entirely foolish. Your face-changing trick is a great one, and it will serve us well. I thought I'd meet criminals. You would have been very well rewarded, indeed, even if you were like your Sand. A lowborn. But now I see you might be much more useful.'

'In what way?' I asked, fuming at his low opinion of my friend.

He chuckled. 'I did not tell you of what is supposed to take place after the murders. Not ten minutes ago, I needed a solution to your question. What after? What after, indeed? There are problems we are facing. While I have one powerful ally who listens to me, he doesn't like my plans. But now he might. I need to find a way—'

'How to get to the Tower to save Shaduril,' I said.

'Yes,' he smiled. 'And to kill the Brothers. I have a man who would take the throne, yes.'

'You do?' I asked, shocked. 'This ally of yours?'

'Yes. One man would take it. He has listened to my lamentations. He has answered them, and we still live, so he has not betrayed us. He hid the coins they found with Valkai. And the note from Valkai. But he is cautious. He would slay the tyrant, but he does not wish to risk his neck. He loves his life more than this land. And so you are more valuable than you think, Maskan Talin, a thief and a lord,' he chuckled. 'And in truth, despite our high airs, do not worry about being a thief. Did you not see what kind of business my girls run? Just like your mother did, only more profitable. Much more. The Affront is a great business and—'

'But they are not in danger of being beheaded for thievery,' I said and grinned. 'The King would pardon Shaduril, no doubt, and Lith as well if he has Shaduril to warm his ... bed.'

He waved his hand tiredly. 'Ah, that bothers you. It bothers me, even if I fight to hide it. Every day my girls suffer him. He might pardon them for thievery, for Shaduril is his lover,' he allowed. 'Of course, he will not if we get caught with the flans you stole and if we fail in killing both of the royals and if my ally betrays me. Then we will all die. We are all thieves, most everyone in the Ten Houses.'

'Hypocrisy is the mark of the great houses,' I whispered, but he heard me.

He scowled. 'I have a need of you, hypocrite or not. And perhaps, since you are Tal's boy, I shall learn to tolerate your arrogance. Mind you, our Tenth and your Seventh House were in a good enough relationship before Tal died. Had been for ages. Gal, your uncle, is the Merchant Lord now, Master of the Harbor and we occasionally do business together.'

'Gal, I don't know him,' I told him.

'But gods love us, for Gal is perfect and will make everything right. I always thought we needed Gal in this but never had a way to get to him. If he joins this conspiracy, we have a way to kill the Danegells and to take the Tower. You see, that is the issue. There is no need for us to smuggle an army all the way up to the Tower of the Temple. No need to fight through the wall and then to dismantle the gate, for that gate is too hard to break with ... conventional methods. Gal is the answer. Do you know why?'

'No. And the Mad Watch would stop you anyway,' I said.

'Not if the king-to-be is their commander,' he laughed.

'Crec Helstrom?' I breathed. *The Butcher. The man we had sworn to kill.* I struggled with the thought. To deny Balan my help for this fact would surely ruin everything. But I did not want to see him as the king. Sand would not understand. 'Go on,' I said hollowly.

'Crec will join if we have a way inside the tower. The Mad Watch doesn't guard it, you see. Danegells do. Gal can take the tower,' he laughed. 'There is a way. And you have seen it. By chance, you have.'

I sat there and thought carefully. Then it came to me. 'The mint?'

'Indeed. Gal can open the mint to us,' he cackled. 'That way we can march an army under the hill and inside the Tower and surprise the Danegells after the King is dead. Gal is the key. And you might be the key to Gal. Let me think about it. I need just a day to plan this. Less! You are gods sent. With you, we might survive. All of us. Shaduril as well. Now, I am done explaining myself to a noble who has lived like a pig all his life. Show me.'

I nodded, angered by his insult. My face flowed and hair thinned and took on his features. My eyes and hair were dark, my neck thin and mouth arrogant, and I instinctively stooped to make myself shorter. I tilted my head, snorted with dry sarcasm and spoke: 'It is a miracle I have such handsome sons and daughters, considering my obvious handicaps.' I screwed my face into a disapproving grimace and stalked before him, my hands behind my back. Then I stiffened with terror. *Gods, what did I say?* I expected him to explode. Yet, his face did not twitch as he regarded me coldly, and I kept my head as I stared at him, cursing my idiocy, but perhaps I was tired of being pushed around, and Lord Balan was nothing like Shaduril. They needed me.

'You are obscene and rude,' he stated as he stared at his own face. He smiled at the irony of his statement for a moment and chuckled, but the joy passed quickly.

I shrugged and sat down and accosted him. 'Had Lith told us she was no whore, but a Blacktower, there might be fewer dead loved ones now. Though, of course, you would hold them as ransom to get me dancing to your tune.'

He grunted and slammed his hand on his desk. 'Do not blame us for your misshapen plan. We owed you nothing, and are you not a grown up, despite being a virgin? Your family died at the hands of the King, and we but helped you along with your plans,' Balan snorted. 'Abandon my face, boy.'

I did, and my thick, dark hair ran down my back, and my brooding face replaced his weak features. 'Do I pass?'

'I'm not the judge. The Queen is. And the King.' He leaned forward. 'We are planning a regicide, son. To save the realm. You are of the ancient blood. I would have given you gold and silver as a reward, but I shall offer you an alliance now.'

I nodded. 'To save the realm. You know, the Horns wanted to loot his treasures. The King's. You are not so interested in the treasures he has accumulated?' I asked him, raising my eyebrow at him.

He leaned back, his eyes flashed what I thought was greed, and finally he spoke. 'Maskan, Maskan. If we succeed? Yes, I'll take his treasures. I know, and you know and anyone would. There is enough treasure in the Temple of the Tower to make us all fabulously wealthy. But I will reward you with better than treasure.'

'I was not looking for treasure as reward.'

He waved me down. 'I know. But deliver me the Queen and the King, and I promise you will find out what happened to your father. It's in Illastria's book.' His hand rapped a massive dark tome on his desk. 'And since I know who you are now, I shall make you a lord. One of us. Would that please you? Silver and gold shall follow the title and the house.'

I hesitated and bowed to him stiffly. *A lord? How would Sand react to that, then? But I could make Sand one, no?* 'Yes, Lord. I agree.' He nodded, snapped his fingers and a black-liveried, bald servant with a cropped beard appeared and smiled at me, indicating the door. I felt Lord Balan's dark eyes on my back as I left, and I vowed to be careful. Very careful.

'Maskan?' Balan asked stiffly as he saw I was not paying attention.

'Lord?' I turned towards him.

'Can you change anything else than your face?' he asked with curiosity. 'Or do you feel strange, sometimes?'

'No, Lord,' I told him. 'Why?'

'Does not matter,' he told me happily and waved me away. 'I shall make plans for the after part now, Maskan. Thank you. And do not tell Sand anything about this discussion. That is critical.'

'Why, my lord?'

He leaned forward. 'Because you will prove to me you have discipline. And I do not trust him. Neither should you. Not after his family died. It changes people. Say nothing or the deal is off.'

I hesitated. Then I nodded. 'Yes, my lord.'

I left him to his plans and fingered the ring in my hand. I would one day know the truth of Father. And be a lord. A noble. Like Shaduril. But the price would be the reign of Crec Helstrom. And Sand's trust, perhaps.

Gods help us.

## CHAPTER 8

Our room was cozy, plain, but functional. There was a pair of sturdy beds, a red rug and table by a small window overlooking the Callidorean Ocean. I slept the rest of the night, though not very well. When I woke, it was very early morning. There were already people running around the keep. I got up stiffly, looked out of the window and found myself looking at the vast, beautiful sight. The ocean. I gazed at the smaller islands very near the coast, most bereft of woods. That was a clear hint the ocean was far from calm most of the time, but right then I enjoyed the sight of sturdy ships racing back and forth, many heading for Ygrin, others yet for Dagnar, some going for Aten, the port city of the Verdant Lands and Malingborg beyond the Arrow Straits. Beautiful white and blue waves rolled for the coast. I sat by the window and stared out of the excellent glass panes, and pushed the window open. A freezing wind whipped in the room, and I embraced the biting cold. Yet, it did not offer me any solution to the nightmares that had plagued me that night.

I had been offered lordship. And the truth of Father, even if I had mocked our host in his study, unwisely.

*But Crec was to rule?*

I brooded and hated the thought. *Should I take Sand and leave?* Or stay and hope Crec would not be part of the plan, after all? The Mad Watch would take the city. Gal and Blacktowers would take the Tower. No, he needed Crec. And I wanted to spoil that plan. I did. I decided Shaduril was right. I was dangerous. To myself. To them. Balan was right not to trust us. I wanted the King dead but also Balan's ally. And worse, a small part of me began to justify Crec.

*Mother was dead. Was it not my fault and not Crec's?*

I banged my head to clear it.

No. It was his fault as well. Unjust tortures, no trials. It happened to our family. They hung like geese.

I was numb when I thought of Mir. I felt strangely unattached. I had seen my family hang. They were corpses. I owed them. I had been a boy with dreams of travel. Now I was trying to kill the King. No, the Queen. I felt small, foolish, like a child out to fight a bull. I would kill the Queen, and Crec would reign.

*No.*

I could not do it to Sand. To myself. Crec as a king? I would not have a part in that. Perhaps we would leave and find a way to hurt those who hurt us. On our own, if we must.

There was a constant roll of thunder as the water crashed itself against the rocks below. I hoped to freeze to death rather than decide such important matters, but the cold did not bother me at all. Then I rubbed my face. I heard teeth chattering, for Sand was asleep, shaking with the cold. He was snoring lightly, like a baby, in fact. I pushed the window closed and turned to regard him. He was scratching his belly, which annoyed me. His tongue was lolling on his cheek, like a dog's.

*He was real.*

Everything else was just promises and memories. He was worth fighting for. We would leave. I spied a fat spider spinning down from the roof and grinned. Our family was gone, but we had each other. That was something. And there was no reason to waste a perfectly good spider. I groped for the thin strand of the industrious thing and found it and resolutely moved over to Sand.

'You wouldn't,' Shaduril breathed from the door. She was wearing a knee-length dress of white and her blonde hair was in a braid on her chest. She was carrying clothes, expensive and elegant ones. They were well-crafted leathers and animal skins. I noticed Sand already wore his. He looked like a young gentleman. 'He has to shave. He might be presentable then.'

'He is really into boys, you know,' I said mischievously, and Shaduril giggled.

She shook her head. 'Don't worry. He is not for a daughter of the Blacktowers. Dress up. I'm taking you to the beach below and shall explain what you will be doing here. I can even give you some hints on the fine art of tasting food in court. Gray will teach you, but I can begin.'

'How hard can it damned well be?' I complained, staring at the fat spider, which getting worried as it scuttled up the line now. 'You chomp it up in your mouth, and they wait to see if you die. Is this thing poisonous, do you know?' I asked, looking at the spider.

She sighed. 'It's not. It's just a sorry little dust spinner. Harmless unless you choke on it. As for the job you are to fill, it is all done according to the etiquette.' She frowned. 'And the Queen is a big one for etiquette. You cannot just slurp some of the soup like an animal, no. You have to do it in public and with grace as people will observe you. Of course, they wish to see you choke from some exotic poison, but still, you have to have manners. I think you should have them even if you died of poison. Crawl into a petite ball of misery and smile as you die. She would smile, the Queen.'

'With grace? My gods,' I complained. 'This Falg is a damned southern fighter from the Shadowed Rocks. Some of them fight with their ass bared, nude! And you say this one wears silks and linen and shoes, and he likely bows before he tastes each and every food she is to eat?'

She gave me a long-suffering stare. 'Yes. He is a barbarian, but also a slave and can adapt. So can you.'

'Odin's balls,' I complained and dropped the spider in Sand's mouth. 'Come,' I said and ran out, pulling her after.

'This way!' she giggled, and we passed the other way. Sand was sitting up, his face screwed up in a look of utter disgust, and our laughter echoed in the hallways and the spiraling stairway. 'His father just died, and you feed him spiders?' she breathed as we dashed past some frowning servants and a young guard.

'I lost a mother. I needed the laugh. And he is my friend,' I said with a grin as we reached the great hall downstairs. I loved her laughter. *But we would still leave,* I thought, my heart breaking. 'Everything's changed. But I don't think I wish to forget our ways. I pranked him often, in the past. It will do him good. Keep his feet on the ground.'

'Dangerous, are you?' she smirked. 'Taram will train you in an hour. In the meantime, let's chat a bit. This way.' She led us to the doorway, the one leading to the western wall. Then she took nearly imperceptible stairways down a winding, oppressive path with thick, stale air. After ages of clambering down them, my calves began to ache. I fought the impulse to ask her how far we would go, and I was rewarded for my patience as we reached an iron doorway and she fumbled with something. She struggled with a ring full of keys, picking off one after another until she found a red key, which she inserted into the lock. 'Took Father's keys. Hope he won't miss them,' she said. She pushed the door open, kicked off her shoes and ran to the beach. I gazed up to the keep towering above us and wondered at the tall cliff. Then I walked for Shaduril. She was tottering on some very loose sand and nearly fell, and she laughed. Fat, black birds looked at her in terror and took off for the cliffs, complaining with high-pitched calls to each other, but Shaduril Blacktower did not care. She ran to the water's edge and waded in until her dress was wet, and spread her hands to the sides, trying to keep her balance as the waves pushed and pulled at her. She was beautiful, beyond beautiful indeed. Her smile was competing with the Lifegiver's rays in brightness and warmth.

I walked to sit down on the beach. I laid down my new clothing on a white rock and stared at the girl whooping as a fish nibbled her calf. I called out: 'You challenged Valkai with a pig sticker and run from a fish?'

'He wasn't trying to eat me!' she complained and ran to the shore. 'I think,' she added and ran out of the waves. A horde of small fish was following her, obviously attracted to her. She plopped down next to me. I saw she had tears in her eyes.

'Can I help—'

'No!' she said and wiped her face. 'It is nothing. A fading memory, of the past. I loved to run here on the beach. With Lith and …' She went quiet.

'Taram?'

She shook her head. 'No, not Taram. Someone else. Never mind. It is the past and what is time but a dream?' She smiled, her eyes still teared over and poked me. 'That pig sticker belonged to Mother, by the way. It has killed evil men before. You have that strange staff somewhere? I saw it when you hit Red Brother with it. I was proud of you when you did.'

'You saw that?' I asked her, fidgeting uncomfortably.

'I saw you, yes. You were very brave,' she whispered.

'Yes, I have it,' I told her, blushing for her compliment. 'It is strange, isn't it? Mother gave it to me. Something from the night Father died.' I shook my head, wondering why I spoke so freely of that to her.

'Truly?' she asked. 'Father told me about your father last night. Seems you are born high.' She smiled at that and shook her head. 'It is good.'

'You think so?'

She nodded. 'We have our traditions, Maskan. It's just so. I wouldn't sit here with Sand. I am sorry. And that staff fits you. The whole of Dagnar is filled with rumors about it. Father knows about it, just like the ring. He knows it belonged to the King. It was his mark of rank. But it's a weapon, and he finds them boring. I doubt he will ask you about it. But it is clearly magical, and the One Eyed priests, who were looking for trouble in the shadows city will want to know more about it. And they say the King has sent a hundred spies to find it. They lie, these rumors.'

'Why?'

'He sent two hundred,' she grinned. 'It might be true it belonged to him. He needs it, it seems.'

'It's mine now,' I growled. 'And I'll keep it. Besides, our King has no use of it when you are finished with him, no?' I eyed her sourly. 'I cannot understand you are his lover.'

'You jealous?' she laughed softly and pushed me hard. 'I don't want to talk about it. But I tell you this much. I give him wine. He often falls asleep before he can have me.' She shook her head. *But not always*, I thought and cursed softly. She nodded at my obvious thoughts. 'Three months is a lifetime.'

'Can't you be sick or something?' I asked her, miserable.

She chuckled and rubbed my hair affectionately, looking sad. After a while, she went on. 'No. He'll take another. You know it. We likely won't survive the whole ordeal. The Brothers will have to be dealt with, no matter who takes over. As long as the King and the Queen die, then we should all be happy. You have to motivate yourself, Maskan, with duty. Red Midgard. Our people's well-being. Forget my discomfort. And accept Father's plans. He said you looked dubious as he outlined his ideas to you.'

*Crec*, I thought. *I cannot.*

'I don't hate my land,' I told her, unsure if I was telling the truth. 'But neither do I love it. I will figure it out, I am sure,' I stated with more confidence than I felt. 'But I hate the thought of the beast laying his hands on you. It's wrong. You should be able to choose.'

'I'm honored you like me.' She looked troubled. 'I'm afraid to like you.'

'Why?' I asked her. 'I mean, I am only the most handsome man you have ever seen? I can make it so, at least.'

She giggled. 'You certainly can. But ... life. It is merciless. It's almost natural to be the lover of the rancid, old King. You have to beware of the Queen, yes, but otherwise, you know what you get. You hate it, and you will hate it the next day. But if a man comes along and takes your heart? Everything is risky. Life changes. You will be miserable, but not like you were. Happiness is a terrible affair. You are always afraid of losing it. And you will. You always will.'

'That, Shaduril, Lady Shaduril,' I said, feeling like a ship lost at sea, 'is a terrible way of living your life. I'd rather be terrified of losing you, than just miserable.'

'Losing me?' she said with a smile, though there was a small flutter of nervousness in the smile.

'I ...' I stammered. 'I've never lost anyone before. Save for Father, but I was not even born. I lost them yesterday. Or the night before. You know what I mean. Mir was my mother. Ann, sister, half-sister. Or not at all. And Bear. He was an excellent man. A highwayman, but just a fine man. But I think losing you might hurt more than I was hurt yesterday. It is a terrible thing to say.' And it was. 'But I don't know why, but seeing you, there, surrounded by Valkai and his bodyguards? I didn't think twice.'

'Gods help you,' she said sadly. 'You are in love. You were not supposed to be here. Or in love.'

I stared at her. 'What?'

'Never mind,' she answered.

'I am not sure, but I think I have known you since forever,' I said gallantly.

She sighed. She looked at the waves crashing down on the beach and did not speak. It was torturous. I had reached for the moon, one of the Three Sisters high up in the sky, and what else could a man expect but to tumble down to the hard, rocky ground and splatter there like an egg? She would refuse me. She would deny me. She would, perhaps, laugh at me.

Then she spoke. 'I am fond of you. Fonder than you might guess. When you grinned at me with that rogue Alrik's face? I didn't know you then. Not your real face. I think you are very handsome, Maskan, the real you, and I trust this face is truly yours. Lith would think about that, your looks, the way you move. You would be an ornament to her. Especially if I wanted you. But with you, it was that smile. It was real, honest, love by a complete stranger. That crooked smile when we were all in danger of dying and it filled me with warmth. I could not stop thinking about it. Had you been a nobody? Valkai would have killed you and I would miss you. Tell me this. Would you have done it had I not been so beautiful? A girl of your dreams?' She wiped hair off her face and hid any emotion there might be playing there, but there was curiosity in her voice, somewhat intense. She wanted to know.

'Let us be fair, Shaduril,' I said, afraid, terrified. 'There are plenty of truly beautiful women out there in the world.'

'Why you—' she began with a small, bitter laugh.

I stopped her with an upraised hand. 'But I would not have done the same for them.'

'You would not have tried to save them?' she asked, surprised.

'I might have if they had been in trouble. I told you, I am a terrible thief. But I would not have stolen their pouch in the first place and planned to give it back to them,' I said with shame. 'I wanted to give it back to you, to get to know you. I wanted to see you smile. The gold, the fortune in gold? It mattered not in the least when all I wanted was to be your hero.'

She smiled. 'How romantic.'

'I think I only wanted to find a reason to speak to you. I'm terrible with girls,' I said miserably.

'It was romantic, really.' She giggled and went silent for a time. She wiped her hair from her eyes and shrugged. 'I loved someone once. I'm not sure I'll ever love again.'

My heart fell, and I was nodding like an idiot. I felt the dark hand of fate grasp at me. 'I see. Who was it?'

'A boy. A fool,' she laughed bitterly. 'You are a fool as well, but not a fool like he was. Is. You are a thief; he was a nobleman, but you are more honest.'

'He betrayed you?' I asked her, and she leaned on me, which startled me.

'He was to marry me. He took another, and I found it out from her,' she said. 'It's a deep wound. Give me time to heal. Just a bit. Who knows how things will go?'

'I'm …' I began and nodded. 'Honored. Exhilarated.'

'Give yourself time,' she said. 'I'm not a dream girl anymore. Perhaps you will love another?'

'Never,' I whispered, and she squeezed my hand. 'Do not speak of this to Father. Do not. And get to know me. Know the true Shaduril, not a dream and a smile. Do you have anyone else? A girl? A lover of past life?'

'I love Sand,' I told her.

'Is he a good kisser?' she mocked.

I choked. 'Like a brother. We are all on a perilous path, but I'll never put the dead before the living.'

'A good, immensely wise principle,' she said softly, looking at the horizon. 'You should never trust the dead. They are unreasonable. They make you do things you should not. Memories make you forget the living. I'm happy you are so wise.'

'You make me happy, Shaduril, even if you give me little hope,' I said and pulled off my shirt to dress in the one she had provided. 'Fancy clothing.' I fondled the fine, expensive leathers.

She smiled and stroked the sleeve of the leather shirt. 'Not really. It's well made, but we wear rustic gear here,' she said with a wistful smile. 'In the court, I wear finer things, but here? Simple and practical and it is … home.' She slapped me playfully. 'As for your upcoming trials. We think you need to learn the basics of good manners.'

'I'll not bed anyone to learn … you know,' I interrupted her.

'Thank you for saving yourself for me.' She giggled and sobered. 'Relax. I trust you can make things work if it comes to that with the Queen.'

'Thank you, but I—'

She put a finger to my lips. 'Listen. There is a servant in the Crimson Apex, a butler called Gray, who used to serve the Danegell kitchens. He is a superb servant and a very patient man. He managed hundreds of people, and here his skills go to waste, to be honest.' She leaned on me again, and my heart sang. 'He managed to teach Taram proper table manners. *That* is an accomplishment. You will shine under his tutelage. He will teach you everything.' She was very close to me, whispering. 'You and I both know Father will never approve of you, not really, no matter where you were born and by whom. You are a noble, but not really. Everything we will teach you will seem weird, very odd to you. You will feel an outsider. And that is how Father will think of you, no matter how useful you will be, no matter his words. Whatever his plans, if he manages to pull this off, he will let us down one way or another. So let us make a deal. I think I will have earned something after I am done with the King business. You will take me out that day. Riding?' Her eyes were suddenly desperate, and her hands were clutching her dress. She was terrified.

'I cannot ride very well,' I said and banged my head with my fist. 'But I'll learn. Of course, we go riding.'

'We can take your Sand, perhaps, and we go and we travel,' she said. She did not mean to come back. She wanted to go. Balan had promised me riches, she promised me love. *Perhaps we could get both?* She saw my hesitation and tapped my hand, trying to calm me down. 'We will see, Maskan.'

'Yes, we shall. I'll not hurt you,' I told her, and she smiled gratefully. Crec was to rule. It was intolerable. But Shaduril was there. She needed me. She was brave and alone. I was confused, stuttering, and then I remembered Ann. Ann had told me to kiss her. She had. And so I did. It felt right. I leaned down to her and kissed her cool lips. It was a long kiss full of promise, and I smelled her perfume, which was like a dizzying whirl of flowery fragrances. I swooned as the kiss went on until I had to break it off. 'You can hold your breath for a long time,' I told her and nodded. 'We will ride that day.'

She looked so happy. 'I believe you. I'll ride with you, Maskan, that day,' she said after she pulled out of my embrace, and I loved her. It was so simple. I would have tried to catch a black shark with my teeth if she had asked me to. I nearly giggled. *Killing the Queen of Red Midgard was probably harder, though.*

'Good,' I added like an idiot and looked to the sea. Sand would have to endure Crec. I would. And we would not leave. I was fully, unconditionally in love.

'Now,' she told me, bringing me down from the clouds. 'As to the fabulous art of tasting potentially dangerous dishes. The few times the family have dined with the royals we have seen how they do this on public occasions. Gray tells us when it is unofficial, and she is eating alone; you will just simply taste the food under the nose of the Brother Knight in attendance. He will then take it out. If it is official, Falg comes to the feast hall from the kitchens, escorted by guards and a boy. The latter carries the food the Queen will eat. She does not take anything from the feast but only eats that one plate. Same with the King. They fear murderers. They should. The boy then sets it down near her and bows to her. She will give him permission to go on. At some point. She might be engaged in a discussion, after all.'

'How very bureaucratic even dining can be,' I said drily. 'I used to munch on bread while picking my ear,' I teased her and resisted the temptation of kissing her again. She pressed a finger to my chest.

'She will not expect you to simper and act like a virgin girl before a lusty lord. You don't have to be afraid, nor do you need to turn your eyes down out of modesty. Falg is like you in the basic manners. Rugged, tough and to the point. Be a man, look handsome, and be patient, but efficient. Back straight, eyes focused. Gray will show you. Then, when she gives you the permission, you will use a fork set for you, mind you, the least fancy, plain one, and you will taste the food in one go!'

'One go? So I cannot taste this and then that?' I asked her. 'She thinks I have a disease?'

'Of course she does! You are a slave and a man,' she chided. 'There, under her scrutiny, take a bit of each and swallow or chew, depending on what the cook has prepared for her and then, take some wine. She has only one cup, so pour some to the cup the boy will carry, again the plain one. Do not drink much. Do not gurgle the drink in your mouth. Do not burp or comment on the taste. Then wait. Do so for many long minutes until you are dismissed. Sometimes she is hungry and does not care to see if you die, other times she might keep you there for ten minutes. Then, walk back to the kitchen. And escape.'

'One question,' I asked her. 'How will I poison the food?'

She chuckled and flipped her hair to cascade behind her back. 'Good point. Happy you asked. We will use poison from a fish. Deadly and rare. Will kill her in minutes,' she said somewhat uncomfortably. 'I know people who know people knowledgeable in these unfortunate matters.'

'OK. But how will I poison the fish? The food I mean?' I asked, utterly nervous.

She made a vague motion with her hand. 'That's when your deft fingers will be useful. You will have some of the dried poison pellets in your hand when you bend down to taste the food. You will crush and let them fall into the food as you pick up some of it. Make sure you don't drop any to the part that goes to your mouth. You will have to practice. Practice. You must not swallow any of it.'

I sniffled, insulted. 'I stole your pouch, and you never noticed a thing. If anything, I can work miracles with my fingers.'

She shook her head and teased me with a smile. 'I was distracted.'

'By the shine of the rubies you stole,' I whispered mischievously.

'Ah, you saw it!' She giggled. 'I also am deft with my hands. Hopefully enough to stab the King with a poisoned hair needle and get away from angry Brother Knights unless Father's plans make it unnecessary to run. He hinted that he might have a way to secure us all a great victory.' She eyed me curiously, and I nodded, hating the plan.

'Will they engage me in a discussion? The Queen and her family?' I asked her, not liking her part of the plan one bit. Nor mine, as I thought more of it. 'This is a terrible plan. Horrid.'

She shrugged. 'I don't know. Keep it simple. Be sullen like a mule, but answer if they ask you something. Might you have a bad day? Do not blush! And yes, this is a brazen, terrible plan. But it's the only way. You could stab her in the heart as well, but that would leave you no option for an escape other than to die from torture. You have seen them deal with—'

'Thieves,' I growled. 'Then again, your father told me how he likes to hang people like me.'

'We behead them,' she corrected me. 'I didn't know we also hang them. That is so common. I mean—'

'Yes, beheading is the Blacktower way of dealing with vagrants,' I agreed. 'I am so sorry. My mistake.'

She tapped my hand to get my concentration back. 'All the kings hang thieves. Even you would, were you one,' she told me and pushed me gently. 'If Maskan were the Beast of the North, he would let them swing to keep the balance, and none would tell you to be merciful. Yeah, starvation drives men to evil, but then there are those who are too lazy to work like most. Don't be a fool.'

'I don't like the idea of killing a woman,' I said.

'Would you like to get humped by the King instead? I'll change you your queen for a king. Take my face and bend over for him. No, wait, that would—' She giggled and rubbed her face but could not contain her giggle any longer as she saw my shocked face. 'Too bad you cannot change, you know, that.'

'You are not as severe as you claimed to be,' I told her, blushed to my ears.

'I used to be fun,' she agreed and went silent. 'Will you try it?' This thing? Even if I see, you hate parts of it.'

'I'll do it,' I whispered. 'And try to survive it. For my family. And ... for you.' *Sand would hate me,* I thought and groaned.

'Gods, this will be terribly hard,' she whispered, and I was not sure what she meant. The deed we were to try, or what was between us. 'Try hard. It will have to do,' she whispered. 'I'll be in the court of Dagnar, seducing the King, but might drop by, now and then. Practice every afternoon. Practice the act of poisoning, hiding the poison, practice looking indifferent, march around nobly. We will have our man training you.' She held onto my hand and thumbed my ring. She was anxious, looked indecisive and nervous. She gripped my hand, and her finger pressed down. There was a sharp sound. Then she looked terrified. 'Oh! I am sorry!' I looked down to see my ring was indeed broken. Her nail had moved the stone, and it was loose. 'Such a beautiful thing! I can fix it. Have it fixed!'

'It's nothing,' I insisted though I was shocked. The stone moved, and I worried it might come off.

'If you say so,' she said and smiled at me. 'Let us give love a chance. We will be Morag's bane, Maskan, and then we shall, perhaps, be free.'

'I love you,' I said without hesitation. Even enough to let Crec sit on the throne and Sand suffer.

She kissed me gently. 'And I love you. You make me feel alive.'

# BOOK 3: THE BLACKTOWERS

*'While men cannot use magic, we can use magical items.'*
**Balan to Maskan.**

## CHAPTER 9

'I don't understand it. Not one bit,' Taram Blacktower said an hour later, his eyebrows raised. 'Why am I training you?' He was wearing a dark open shirt, his lean muscles glistened with sweat. 'You know nothing of fighting, and Father told me to make you proficient at least. To make you look like one, a fighter. He has so many strange plans, and I never know anything about them.'

'It's your father's plan so ask him,' Sand said and held his side, experimentally twisting his torso as he poked at his sore ribs. I cursed, as my friend did not really know the full plan, the part Crec was to play in it. He didn't even know I was related to Gal. It bothered me, but the memory of Shaduril's smile and kiss overwhelmed the remorse. Sand nodded at me. No bones were broken, and Taram wiped his hair from his eyes as he prepared to pummel Sand again with the staff. We were standing in the middle of a circular chamber, and it was empty, save for racks of wooden weapons on the side. The Lifegiver was shedding its light through holes on the top, illuminating the room, though it left parts in deceitful shadows. Taram was just about done testing our abilities, and he was not impressed.

'I know it is my father's plan, thank you,' he said irascibly, swirling the man-length staff wildly about him, his balance, and skill perfect. 'And asking won't do any good. But I don't enjoy being on the outside. Especially if I have to spend my precious playtime on this useless crappy joke. I could be courting rich women in Dagnar. I could bed some, if not most. I could be gambling in the Brewery and sailing the Straits. But I cannot make you a fighter in a few months. Not with you displaying such utter lack of skill. I promised Father, but perhaps I should not have done so. The simple, clumsy movements. Predictable, girly arms, weak strikes and thrusts. I could beat you with my legs broken. This training is as likely to succeed as it would be to teach a starving beggar to dance.'

'Now wait right there …' I began, and he launched an attack at Sand. My rough-faced friend had not expected it at all. He dodged aside, awkwardly, holding his own staff up with a shoddy, weak block, his arms straight, and Taram's staff danced down, then under the block and ended up on Sand's cheek with a meaty swat. I charged forward, pushing at Taram's apparently unguarded back, but the young man sprung away and lithely landed on the ball of his foot. I fell over his other, outstretched leg, landed heavily, and bruised my shoulder. I saw his staff coming down, cursed and tried to shield my face. I yelped as the staff bit into my midsection instead of my face. I yelled from the pain, and Taram stepped away, swishing the end of the staff at a speck of dust as if terribly bored. I cursed and climbed to my feet and together with the wobbly-footed Sand we clambered around, searching for the staffs. Taram laughed softly and waited for us to come at him. He looked deadly, his face hidden in shadows, and I was not sure how we could earn any speck of respect from the man.

'Right,' Sand whispered. 'I say I just tackle the bastard, and you pummel the Hel out of his hide. The way we would do it at Bad Man's. None of this pretty dancing shit.'

'Go,' I agreed.

Sand charged forward; I followed and Taram grinned, danced aside, kept Sand at bay with a whirling slap on the shoulder that made my friend cry out with pain. The young Blacktower was turning and running from us, positioning his body so we could not tag team him. Then he stepped forward to poke at us with the staff, playing cruelly with his victims, unconcerned and superior. 'Inexperienced? Inept? Clumsy as an old whore?' he chortled. 'Which shall I put in my report of you two?'

'Tyr's beard!' Sand hollered and threw the staff at Taram, who was surprised enough to stumble back a step, blinking his eyes. Sand charged in, roaring, rolled on the floor under the poke that Taram threw his way and just managed to grasp Taram's foot.

The young man fell on his rear, his grin gone.

Sand was dragging Taram to him, grasping at his waist, and I got there, using the staff like a spear and thrust down. It connected.

With the floor.

Taram had managed to squirm aside, and gone was the near eternal, foolish smile on his handsome face. He kneed Sand so hard blood flew across the floor from a cut lip, and he pulled himself up. I cursed and slapped the staff at him from the side, and he blocked, then poked ahead for my face. It connected, and I fell back and saw red dots of pain. He was coming for me again, fast as a snake, the staff whirling in the air, and I rolled aside, only to feel stabbing pain in my back, then again and a well-aimed kick in my rear. I groaned and saw him aiming another kick for my face. 'For Shaduril,' he hissed. 'Keep your grubby hands off my sister.'

His foot hit hard, and I was sure I would not get up. *Shaduril? He was beating me for his sister?* He had seen us.

Then I felt the rage.

It was lingering at first. It throbbed in the edges of my consciousness, hammered at my lobes. Another kick connected with my face, and I barely felt it for the rage ripped through me. My ring burned on my finger; I felt it resist the rage, but I beat the resistance, as I wanted to unleash the anger. It came on fully and filled me with savage strength. The anger felt like molten fire, and it made me see things. I saw brief images of laughing, old faces. A bitter wind whipped across a wintry landscape, and a bear growled with a bloody maw. The rage was tearing at my heart, and a snarl escaped my lips. I saw the vision of the bear, its neck snapped. I laughed at that terrible image, and other blurry visions of inhuman carnage. I screamed and began to get up. Even the stone under my hand felt fragile. I ripped at it, and to my astonishment a slab of it moved and crumbled under my grip. I felt another wild swing by Taram's staff connect with my back; I heard him curse, tell me to go down, and then I got up, fast as a cat.

In my hands, there was a hefty piece of rock which I tossed in Taram's direction. His eyes were round with surprise, and he fell aside with a yelp. I leapt over Sand, so fast, quick as a fox, and I could not fathom my speed. Despite my fox-like speed, my steps were heavy as if a tree trunk was pounding the stone. Chips of stone flew around, and I tried to catch Taram. His stabs kept stinging at my chest and my face, but I laughed ferally at the pain and his surprised, terrified face. I feigned a move to the left, but then I bounded at him—like a bear. He tried to dodge away, but he was cornered.

'Maskan!' he screamed and thrust his staff at me and hit my chest. The weapon broke in splinters, and what remained drew blood from my chest and shoulder. Taram was looking shocked, and I felt very little pain, only more anger, ripping rage and hate. I hated like I had never hated before. I punched his face, launched him into the air, and he fell onto his back in the corner. I ripped a large splinter off my chest, viewed the wound, and licked the blood off my hand.

He was alive though dazed. 'Taram! It is I! Taram!' he explained with a high-pitched voice and shook his head desperately, looking for a way out. I stalked closer, fighting the urge to rip his head off. I stopped, knowing something was wrong and tried to calm myself. It was hard, very hard, and then I suddenly felt a bursting pain go through me as Sand smashed his staff across my scalp. I tottered and went down on my knees. Then on all fours as my friend jumped on me. And finally, I went all the way to the ground as I resisted the urge to fight back. I wanted to rip the floor apart, my muscles were on fire, but Sand sat on my back, spitting blood, and I did not wish to hurt him.

'Lost a tooth,' he complained thickly, apparently pulling at one, for something hot fell on my neck. He addressed Taram, who was getting up painfully. 'What in Lok's rotten heart went into you. Cannot lose, eh?'

Taram was shaken, still shocked. 'I don't like to lose, no. And you should learn that attitude if you are to survive a proper fight. What the Hel went into him?'

'You were beating him like you would a mangy dog,' Sand said darkly. 'Kicking him, you filthy piece of shit. And what was that about Shaduril?'

Taram snorted, and I lifted my head at him. 'I don't like you two staring at her as you do. She is my sister. She will marry high, not low. It's filthy to have you bastards drool over her.' He flinched and rifled through the remains of his staff and stared at me. 'You should just calm down. I might have overstepped it a bit. He needs a doctor?'

'I'm bleeding, but I don't need a doctor.'

'Some of the staff went into your chest,' Taram said suspiciously. 'And you are fine?'

'Doesn't hurt much. I think it's just some splinters,' I told him morosely, avoiding looking at him.

Sand looked down at me, and I shook my head tiredly. 'Nope, no doctor,' Sand said and tapped my head. 'He will be fine. Just hungry. Gets like that when you don't feed him. And you didn't. Dragging us here before breakfast.'

'Indeed,' Taram said carefully. 'Have you fought like that before? Maskan?'

I sighed and got to my elbows, toppling Sand off. 'No, never. Just got really angry.'

He grinned. 'Such anger can grant you a victory, boy, but you should be careful. You could have impaled yourself. You have to fight with control, not like a damned maniac. You looked strange as Hel. Bestial. Not like a wolf or a bear, but bulky and dangerous. And I've seen something like that before.'

'You have?' I asked him, feeling the extraordinary strength ebb from my arms. The ring throbbed and went cool.

He had a casual grin on his face. 'Ask Father. He dabbles in magic and lore. I'll tell him to talk to you about it, in fact. Don't want to get killed because we don't understand you. But for now, let us bind ourselves up.' He spat out a glob of blood and whimpered as he touched his jaw gingerly. 'With that strength, I think you might do very well in Dark Sands.'

'Dark Sands?' I asked, shocked. Did he know?

'Fighting pit,' he explained, holding his hip painfully. 'I sponsor a team there with a dozen other nobles. The Red Sashes. You could try it after I've trained you and Father is done with you. Would make some gold to sate my gambling habit. You'd do well.'

'Or be entertaining, at least,' I agreed.

'That can be superb business as well.' He laughed. 'There are bets made on who wins the fight, but also on who slays how many and who makes a fool of himself. Sky's the limit with betting.'

'I'll pass,' I told him. 'I disdain people dying for no reason.'

He looked shocked, and then his eyes went to slits. 'Father is making a mistake if he trusts a man who cannot kill. No matter what he is doing.'

I snorted. 'Careful, Lord, or that other person might come visiting, and he is not like Maskan.'

Taram nodded at me slowly, pulled his hair into a ponytail and walked to the door, which he pushed open angrily. 'The main room, breakfast is served there,' he said and walked out unsteadily. Sand was smiling at him, and as soon as he disappeared, Sand turned his face to me.

'What the Hel was that?' he asked me with a whisper. 'I was to be the brawn of the outfit. Show me the wounds.'

I turned, and he lifted my shirt. He was clucking his tongue as he was picking wooden slivers out of the shallow wounds. 'I don't know, Sand. The rock was there, I lifted it, and it was so damned easy. I just ... ripped it out, and I wanted to kill Taram.' I rubbed my face. 'Just got so unreasonably angry. I was thinking of Ann earlier. And Mother. And how Black and White hung them. The King? And my Father?' *And of Crec*, I thought but did not voice it. I spat and groaned as Sand shook his head at me. And Shaduril. He wanted to deny me Shaduril and that had been the real reason. 'Perhaps I don't want people standing between me and my ... goals.'

Sand nodded. 'Goals. That's a funny way of putting it. You and that noble bitch? The one that disdains me? I know.'

I looked at him. 'I kissed her. She said maybe.'

'Maybe?' he asked, hammering at his head. 'Really?' He looked astonished.

'Thank you for the vote of confidence,' I growled.

He slapped my head. 'Didn't think it possible. This is getting complicated. They don't want you to court her.'

'She is sad, but also lovely,' I told him. 'And she makes me happy. While I worry about our vengeance, she is there, at the end of the road. And so are we. You and I. Let's remain positive, Sand.'

'I said she will change things,' he grumbled. 'She will never accept me. It won't be like it was with Father and your mother. She would not accept me under her roof.'

'She might yet, and who knows what our roof looks like? Give her time. For me,' I pleaded with him as I eyed the scratches on my chest. 'Strange how little this hurts.'

'Skin mostly,' he said and took a deep breath. 'I am sorry. I will try.'

'Thank you,' I told him and looked away. 'It might change things. But not our friendship. They will mock us both, and they will ignore you as best they can. Remember it is not me, who—'

He slapped my head again. 'Look, I'm your friend. I am,' he said uncertainly as if unused to speaking of such matters and he was. He poked me roughly as if to make sure I understood he was still thoroughly dangerous. 'I'm the Bear's son. He, like the others, despises me; I can see it in his face.' He nodded at the door and Taram. 'I have no place in this world of nobles, other than making a living off their hides. That is my function. Thieving and robbing. I have no family left, but you.' He bit his tongue as he said that, and there was a hint of moistness in his hard eyes. He looked away and then back, discreetly wiping his eye as if making sure no hint of his weakness remained. 'I don't really care about the high politics and even Red Midgard. I will fight for you, and I will fight for me and damn the rest. I'm of the low. But you and I shall bring down the mighty. Don't mess it up. You have been messing up a lot in the recent past; whatever it is that made that thing come out just now? Keep it closed and locked. And I shall endure my humiliation and loss and their damned high airs.'

'Yes, Sand,' I told him sadly, feeling terrible for I had not told him everything.

He went on. 'The Queen is the key, and then Shaduril will do her bit, and we will figure out how to go on from there. She will be hurt,' Sand said sadly. 'And you know it. Do not try to stop her. Remember why we are here.'

'I will trust her. And respect her. She is determined to do this, no matter if I wish someone else killed the King,' I whispered. Gal was the key. And I could secure the key. And I would.

'Right,' Sand said and slapped his thigh. 'Well. Don't feel sorry for me,' he whispered as I heard Taram speaking in the hallway. 'I'll do that part.' Then he fixed an eye on me. 'When she goes to the King, do not mess up. She will go there, and you will let her.'

'I will,' I told him bitterly. 'I will.' He glanced at the door, and Taram was there.

'Maskan?' he said.

'Yeah?' I nodded and got up.

'I told my Lord Father about you, and he wishes a word with you,' Taram said. 'Be careful with him. He has high ambitions. He might not smack you with a staff and kick you around, but that does not make him docile.'

I snorted. 'Everyone is giving me advice today. I only have your father, my lord, I will not risk the Blacktowers and their plans. Never. I will obey him in this most crucial mission.' He hesitated, and I slapped my forehead. 'Oh, I forgot. You know nothing of these things. But thank you for the advice.' I turned my back on him, looked at Sand, and he nodded.

Taram laughed with a booming voice. 'If you weren't a peasant thief who is protected, I'd show you how to talk to the Blacktowers. Come, you ugly monkey,' he said with a clipped angry voice and nodded at Sand, who reluctantly followed him.

I pushed past him, went up the tall stairway, and witnessed Sand walk to the central hall where bread and eggs were being served with butter and mead. There was porridge and meats, and my belly rumbled. Sand grinned up at me as I stared down at him enviously. Taram snapped out a chair for himself and sat down to see Sand eat. He made no noise other than thrumming his hand on a dirk at his side, but Sand ignored him and smiled at a serving girl. 'Bounces back fast, my Sand,' I whispered. 'Soon he will be married.'

I got up and took a stairway to the third floor, and guards nodded at me in their cumbersome, gleaming chain mails. I got to the door of Balan Blacktower, slightly winded, and knocked.

'Enter,' Balan said.

I did. There, a sumptuous breakfast was laid out on a table, and Lord Balan looked up at me. The room was nearly dark; silken drapes had been drawn to cover the windows, and only the sound of gulls and flying lizards could be heard outside. Balan nodded at the table before him, and I was startled to see Illastria, the old lady leaving the room. She stared at me, her red-rimmed eyes huge, and I stepped back, involuntarily. The old lord waved at her as she hesitated, and she passed by me, looking down. Her hair was pearly white and covered most of her face. 'Eat,' he said and nodded at the seat opposite him.

'Will you eat, Lord Blacktower?' I asked him tentatively as the old lady left, hoping he would. I would not be able to swallow if he sneered over my breakfast.

'No, I never do,' he grimaced as if disgusted by the thought. 'Taram gave you a beating? He will do that for months. I think he is protective of his sisters and the family name.' He smiled briefly at that and adopted his usual stoic look. 'Though he did mention something unusual happened, and you would fill me in. Said it is important. Oh, Illastria and I spent the night plotting and have a plan for the "after part" we discussed. Gal. And more.'

'You do?' I asked.

'Sit.' I did. 'Yes, we have a plan, and I'll talk to you about it. First. What happened down there? Taram said it was something strange and mythical, and he also said he kicked the Hel out of you,' he said, leaning forward. He is always intrigued by mysteries and by the unknown, I decided.

'I gave him one as well,' I told him. He did not blink, and I filled the gap. 'A beating. I nearly killed him, in fact. There was something strange inside me, or perhaps it was this ring?'

'Something inside you?' he whispered, fiddling with a pen. 'Like a power? Evil spirit? Some disease? Gas?'

I hesitated as I fidgeted there. 'No. I mean I don't know. It was like … like I would imagine magic. It was a strange, rippling feeling. I felt ferocious, and it was somewhat familiar. Like a dream, but I was awake. I was very mad, so unyielding, and Taram is only alive thanks to Sand.' His eyebrows rose in surprise. 'I know. I'm also baffled.'

He sat back, his eyes gleaming curiously in the dark. 'I knew your father, as I said. The ring? Possibly it has something to do with it, indeed. Tell me, boy, do you know much about artifacts? I saw Taram was shocked to his core about the fight. He is used to being the superior being in that practice room of his. He is the house master-at-arms. He trains men to kill. Has done since he was sixteen. And what I smelled in him? Saw in his eyes? Fear. Shock. It bothers me. You have no idea what happened?'

'I …' I began while lifting pork and dark bread onto a golden plate. 'Would rather not speculate…' I shook my head. 'I've been changing my face, but what just took place? It felt very strange. Yet also very natural. I know little about artifacts, to answer your question.'

'I see,' he said, eyeing me carefully, and finally his eyes settled on my ring. 'Do you know what an artifact is? And what do you know of the past?'

'Past?' I said, hiding my black metal ring with the yellow stone under my thumb. 'About Hel's War?'

'Yes. Indeed. That, and time beyond,' he nodded. 'Hear me. There were Eight Gates in Midgard before that war of Hel's. They led to worlds the gods chose in the beginning for themselves. Odin's Aesir and the Vanir, who became allied, drove the other gods away, and the Nine Worlds were chosen by them for their kingdoms, many well shaped and formed worlds and all crafted and perfected by the beings. They claimed these worlds, and two of those worlds stood out.'

'Indeed?' I asked, intrigued.

He smiled at my eager tone. 'Yes. Two of these worlds are more than the fine wonders the gods made the others into. They were there in the beginning, before the First Born and from them—the nine rivers of Niflheim, the fiery infernos of Muspelheim—were all things are born from. Gods were cradled in the Filling Void, where the celestial heat and the fierce ice mixed up, there were born many races, some of which no longer exist. We? The humans? Odin made us later. Perhaps we are the only race that does not possess the gift of hearing and seeing the mixing of the ancient ice and fierce fire. That is what magic comes from. That skill ... a sense, really, of having access to the old power of creation. We cannot see or hear the power. Humans. It was never given to us. Magic.'

'Magic?' I asked him, mystified.

His brow was sweaty as his hand trembled. 'Magic. We do not hear and see the great power. Most races can, at least some can. I am not sure if every single elf hears the call, but—'

'Elf?' I asked him, bemused.

'Keep an open mind, boy,' he scowled. 'Other old races in the old books, they are close to magic, others far from it and yet others are connected to it directly. Gods are part of it. Some beings only hear and see the ice part of magical power, others the fire part. This is in the books of Illastria.' He leaned forward, clearly excited. 'They say it can ... one can ... see it? Hear it? In your mind. It's like a sense as I told you. Then you can grasp these powers, pull and combine strands of heat and icy winds, chunks of ice and fire, ever so gently learning millions of ways of using this power. You can create spells of destruction. Spells that can lay low armies. Or you might create more subtle spells, helpful, even entertaining spells. The sky's the limit. That's what they say.' He slumped and waved his hand around lazily. 'This world is just very, very boring.'

'I can imagine such spells being very interesting,' I told him dreamily.

His eyes were wide, thin face shaking with slight anger. 'Interesting! I've spent my life finding such magic. It can make and break this world, Maskan. You see,' he said, his eyes feverish and mad, 'Hel's war changed the world. There were kingdoms here. Human kingdoms. We governed each other, and Odin kept the world safe from marauders. But a war is an unpredictable matter, and his attentions were taken elsewhere. Hel sent her armies—'

'Why did she do this?' I interrupted him.

He looked shocked for a moment. 'I forget; you have never been tutored.' There was a mild look of disgust on his face, and I thought Shaduril might be right to think he would not approve of me, not ever. He went on. 'Why? Because the bastard Odin had taken her, Hel, a maiden of joy and threw her to Niflheim, condemning her to rule Helheim, the realm of the dead souls. He did this to punish Lok, his kin, and a demi-god and Hel's father. She was robbed of half her beauty, her home, her father Lok, her sisters and brothers and set to judge and guard the dead. Many wept for her, many rumbled in the dark shadows against the heavy-handedness of Odin. She had friends.'

'And?'

'And, Baldr died,' he said gleefully. 'Lok, using Hodur the Blind's stupidity, poisoned him, and since Baldr died of poison, his soul went to Hel. Odin wanted him back, of course, but they schemed and made it so, Hel and her father, that there was hope, but no true hope of his release. It was a cruel torture for Odin; it was, and when he was denied? Rage.'

'It was called Hel's War, though,' I stated.

His eyes glinted shrewdly. 'Yes, and that is a good observation. It was. She lost her left eye after Baldr's death. That tipped her over. She longed for her old life. Hag's Eye, her left eye, and some called it the Crow's Orb allowed her to scry the lands she once loved, the pastures she had once danced in, people of all the races and the First Born she loved. It was the one thing keeping her even remotely sane in Helheim, on her Thorne of Bones. And it was stolen.'

'By Odin?'

He shrugged. 'I am not sure. Neither is Illastria. Aldheim was involved; elven nations. Illastria's books are all speculative on that matter. I know there were many races fighting for her. First Born and dukes of Hel as well. What followed was a terrible war. Hel held a speech to the Jotuns, most of whom hated the gods. She spoke to the rogue First Born, some dragons of great power, beasts and generals of many races. Many joined her. Legions of fighters and mages. She robbed the dead of the gold, she bought mercenaries and then? She released the armies. In all the Nine Worlds, the lands and followers of the gods were assaulted. Lands burned, Hel's kingdom welcomed the dead, and she sought her eye mercilessly. In Aldheim, she finally failed. Elves threw her back. They threatened Niflheim, even Helheim. Some lord called Timmerion won that war. She had her steward Ganglieri steal the fine horn of Heimdall, the Lax Guardian. The great horn was taken indeed, an incredible, heroic feat. It was rung on all the gates, for that artifact is the key to the gates. They all closed. Gods in Asgard and Vanaheim could no longer find their Nine Worlds, and thus it stands today, even today. But Midgard? It was in the war. It was a brilliant move by Hel to shut the worlds from the gods.'

'What happened?'

'Hel's troops took much of the land,' he said sadly. 'She surprised the south, the east, and the west and in here, where Dagger Hill, Hill of Fangs stood,' he nodded for Dagnar, 'there was a great battle.'

'Fangs?'

'Few know it by that name. It is Dagnar. Dagnar is the name our Danegell kings gave the city, survivors of the battle. It means "Mauled Hill" in some old language, and it is an apt name. Men won that day, Hel's armies were beaten, finally. They had their base up there, but they fell.'

'You know a lot of this,' I noted, my food cold.

He sighed. 'I have ever sought out items of power. Illastria helps me. Hel's armies brought magic to Midgard. They had powerful spells, weapons of fame, armies and—'

'Were there dragons here?' I asked him with utter wonder.

'Dragons?' he asked. 'I suppose so? But I,' he said empathetically, 'have ever collected lore of magic. Especially lore of those items made by the dverg.'

'The short folk?' I asked him.

'The smiths of Svartalfheim,' he told me reverently. 'While men cannot use magic, we can use magical items. Hel's armies had plenty. Now the Danegells hold a hoard of them and the highest, oldest houses hold many as well. Most of them fought in that war for the humans. And that is how White Brother can track men, if he knows their names, sometimes. It is an artifact, no doubt, he is using.'

'But not you,' I said, eyeing his amulet. 'They cannot find you.'

'Not us, the Blacktowers nor anyone near us,' he agreed, sitting back in his lush seat. He tapped a finger proudly on his chest, and the familiar amulet of towers and ravens clinked. It was heavier than the one Shaduril had, thicker and had a golden rim. 'Old. We fought in the Fang, our family. Same as the Danegells. These are from Hel's army, and we adopted the figure as our house symbol. We used to be the Blackships. I prefer the tower, though.' His eyes gazed at the figure of tower and ravens with admiration, and I waited patiently for him to focus on the matter again. 'Gods know whom they belonged to. We have many of them. They have power we cannot even understand.'

'How do you know so much about the history. Surely this is all speculation—'

He rapped a thick, red-leathered volume on the desk. 'This is Moragorium. Annals of the King. Our family upholds it for the King. It is Illastria's job, to be exact. While most of the Ten Houses have a special duty to fill for the land, ours have been performed in the shadows. There are many more powerful houses than ours when it comes to men and might and riches, but we are the Tenth for we remember the past. We uphold the memory of the past for those living in the present and record the stories of the land. We remember. It's all here.'

'Oh!' I said, chewing on a tasty piece of pork. A thought came to me. 'And if the High King has been pressing for Morag to bury the past, to worship the High King, to change everything? It must be risky for your house.'

'Yes. The High King wants Morag to forget the past and replace it with his mad lust for power and legacy as a god, but how could we?'

'And is this why you are trying to kill him? To save yourselves?'

He shrugged and rubbed his face. 'We fear him. Illastria spends a lot of time in the Tower of the Temple and these past ten years, the King has demanded we change history. He wants Moragorium in his rooms. But, of course, we would not survive long if he decides he wishes to change the history entirely.'

'But as you said,' I told him sarcastically, 'you are also doing this for Red Midgard.'

'Yes,' he said, irritated by my tone. 'Enough about us. Your ring was your father's and no doubt, it too was from Hel's war. As is the staff.' I nodded carefully, and he waved his hand. 'That weapon you used. Yeah, I know of it. Probably stolen by your mother? That, Illastria thinks, is the Larkgrin. It has been the King's scepter.'

'It is,' I said.

'Don't worry, keep it,' he said with a forced smile, and I knew it was hard for him to let go of such a thing. He went on, 'But the ring's name. It is the Sorrowspinner. A sad, unfortunate name. I do not know why it is named thus. But probably it helped your father fight Morag that night he died.'

I eyed the ring carefully.

He wrung his hands. 'It gives you the power to change your face, of that Illastria is certain,' he told me and saw I frowned in disappointment. He laughed mockingly. 'Ah, you thought yourself very special? Yes, yes. I see it. But that ring, I think, is the cause of the skill.' His hands rapped Moragorium. 'There are hints of it in these old books. Some say it was used for spying, to avert evil, but perhaps your father, like we, knew too much of the past. Perhaps the King desired it, feared it? It was the treasure of Tal Talin, taken from a great lord of Hel, and it cannot be removed. To do so, it would slay you. You cannot remove it. Try!'

I fingered it. 'I have never tried. Mother made me promise.'

'She knew it would stay on, I think. She wanted you to have it. How nice.' He smiled with contempt. Likely he cursed the fact it could not be removed and given to a more reliable man to help him with his quest.

'She didn't know about my skill,' I told him with some doubt.

'She might not have known the exact powers,' Balan said happily as if he were exploring some ancient, forgotten ruin for the first time in millennia. 'But we know it gives you the ability to shift faces. Let me see it.' Reluctantly, I gave him my hand. His eyes went to slits as he poked at it with his finger. He was humming, happy, and then his eyes grew huge. He noticed the stone was moving. 'It's broken!'

'It was—' I began but decided against telling him of Shaduril.

'You have broken an artifact,' he hissed and let go of the thing. There was a manic intensity in his look as he scowled at me.

'It is mine,' I stated carefully. 'And if I did break it? It's not your business. And,' I growled, 'perhaps it is not such a mighty artifact if one can break it so easily. Cannot remove it, but one can break it. Ridiculous.'

He slouched and rubbed his eyes, gathering his composure. 'It is old. Gods know how old. It might be malfunctioning, boy, and perhaps this strange battle rage was caused by it being broken. I ... dabble in such items. I might try to fix it. I'll think about it. But you,' he said and leaned forward, 'are a risk. You must keep calm. As calm as you can. You cannot let that power break free of the ring. Understand? You might kill people you should not kill. And you might lose your ability and then? We are all doomed.'

'I understand,' I told him sullenly. 'I will keep to the plan.'

He hesitated and finally nodded. 'Yes, we keep to the plan. Poison it is. The name of the artifact had better not be prophetic.' I nodded and ate the cold food, deep in my thoughts. Sorrowspinner? Artifact? I tried to resist it, but I did thumb the ring. It was dangerous now. Broken. But it didn't budge. I didn't have to look up at Balan to know he was smirking dreamily. 'Finish your fare,' Balan said as he sat there, thinking.

I nodded and ate. It was a long uncomfortable breakfast, swathed in silence, and finally I could not bear it any longer. 'Where is Shaduril?' I asked him innocently as I struggled not to lick my fingers after sweet bread dipped in honey.

He snorted as he saw my struggle and then waved his hand towards Dagnar. 'Taram told me you met her. And more. He was enraged, as you probably guessed. Felt you are slighting our house by dreaming of her. She is meant for the King, boy. You know this. That means she has to be there where he can see her, and she suffers his presence. She is my daughter,' he said, looking down at his hands that were trembling. I felt sorry for him. I did. I did not think it was possible, but I did. He sighed and waved his hand for Dagnar. 'Magor Danegell is probably staring at her as we speak. There, in the throne room, he dreams of war and Shaduril's warm embrace. She holds up, but I cannot understand why he is not into Lith, for she is a rare harlot, but no, it is Shaduril. He writes to her, you know? Of love. Of heirs, if you can imagine. To his lover? He has no heirs since the Cataclysm, and his Queen while still beautiful, and is too old to squeeze any out. And Morag would have to touch the Queen, of course, to get any, but he rather enjoys his lovers. Shaduril is his favorite. Let us hope that lasts until Yule.'

'How old is he?' I asked him. 'Morag?'

He smirked. 'Old as Hel's milk. But not old enough to let her be at nights.'

I choked and nodded in agreement, rage playing inside. 'Yes, Lord. We can only hope for better days?'

He nodded. 'Hold that rage in check. We will do more than hope. For Red Midgard, we will. For my family, also. Now, if you will kill the Queen and make your escape, it might even be that Magor hopes to marry Shaduril. He will rip his tunic to show some proper anguish for the Queen, and then he will have the Lord of Life bless them. He has promised Shaduril this.'

'The King has promised ...' I said chokingly. 'To make her queen? What if he sails away with her and marries her elsewhere? What if—'

'Yes,' Balan told me glumly, his feral smile uncannily white in the semi-dark. 'I see what you are saying. Of course, I do. Nevertheless, he will die. Here or out there and if not, then we need not worry about it. We will all hang, together or separate, and Red Midgard will sink with us. But the place where he holds his power is his throne room. That is where kings marry. That is the custom. And he makes some promises he keeps. Especially if he stands to gain something from them. Gaining Shaduril as a queen is something, he greatly desires. I thought you should know this.' I said nothing and wondered if he tried to make me feel inadequate. I munched on some cold eggs that tasted spicy and splendid and tried to concentrate on Balan's words as he spoke on. 'Also, he has told me I shall get a position in his court, should the Queen die one day. The Queen has blocked all our ambitions for years since he began looking at Shaduril. Of course, he has no idea what kind of position in the court I desire.'

'Black and White,' I said darkly. 'And the Red Brother. Sand and I. We have business with them.'

'Black and White and the damned Red and the rest of them,' he sneered, 'are but simple henchmen. You are a crucial piece in the whole plan, Maskan. Your actions will bring the man to justice. The King. And we must move quickly. The Yule is here before we know it. And now for the plan.'

'Yes, Lord,' I told him angrily. 'But I cannot help but rue not seeing them die. These ... simple henchmen. Shaduril said we will see it take place.'

'The Brothers will fall with the King,' Balan said. His eyes flashed. 'You might or might not see it. Depends on how this will play out. I have plans yet that need to be tied together for the eventuality of a royal death, and Rose Throne has to find a sturdy ass to fill it. The remaining houses have to work together. Danegells have ruled for thousands of years, and that brings me to the issue I wanted to discuss. Do not interrupt me again.'

'Why don't you take the throne, oh keeper of secrets?' I asked very unwisely.

He laughed. 'No, our house is not illustrious enough for the throne. Lord Captain Crec Helstrom will take it. I told you.'

'The Butcher,' I grumbled.

'The Butcher and the Lord of the Mad Watch,' he agreed. 'I see. You hate him. You despise him. So do I. But some things cannot be had. It must be Crec of the Second House, which, of course, will be the first house after the coup, who will take the crown. He will marry my Lith, and we will all be rewarded as that marriage is surely going to be profitable. Hate Crec, but do not dare to touch him.'

'Lith?' I asked him, stunned.

'Yes, Lith,' he agreed dryly. 'She has charmed him and is probably part of the reason Crec works with us. I said I had an ally. And my girls are all doing their part. What? Don't tell me you are laying a claim on her as well?'

'No Lord,' I said, blushing.

He looked at me incredulously. 'Ah, to be young again. Stay far from Lith, boy. Perhaps from Shaduril as well. She is not ... well in the matters of the heart. Don't risk this by falling in love with her.'

'My friend Sand said the same thing to me,' I told him.

'Ah, he has the practical wisdom of the peasant, he does. But yes, Lith. Crec is a man to enjoy a girl like her. I'm sure they will be very happy. She will drive him mad. Utterly mad. But she will be a queen, won't she? But that is not enough.'

'Crec the Butcher is surely enough? He commands the Mad Watch,' I said and regretted it, as Balan looked at me with pity.

'Are you a politician?' he asked. 'A wise one? Elder? Or a scoundrel from Bad Man's?'

'A scoundrel from Bad Man's Haunt, Lord,' I told him angrily.

'We need three houses to cooperate. I hold the secrets of the past. I will do the deed. Crec will make sure things don't get out of hand during and after. He will take care of the Brothers that might be out of the Tower. He will keep the Mad Watch and the Hawk's Talon in check. And Gal will get us into the tower. The door to the Tower of the Temple is an artifact, by the way. Only usable by the Danegells. So we need Gal.'

'I see,' I said unhappily. 'I figured this out already. But why will he help us?'

'Because he can gain power?' Balan asked with a smile. 'Our gratitude?'

'More likely to lose power,' I growled. 'He is already very mighty.'

'Come, think!' he chided me. 'Oh, scion of his house.'

And I did. And then it came to me. 'Because you can use me to supplant him? I am ... the heir?'

'You are,' he said happily. 'Well done. Very much so. We have him by his wrinkled ball sack, Maskan. All we need. The army, a way in, and royal deaths.'

I squirmed in my seat. 'So you will promise him what, exactly?'

'He is predictable and will want peace, assurance, Maskan,' Balan said. 'And this is crucial. You must trust me. He will ask for you.'

'My life?'

'Yes,' he laughed.

'And you will promise it?' I asked him, fiddling with a fork.

'I will give him a solemn promise that you will enter his house the day the Queen dies. He will want your ring as well, won't he? Tal's mark of rulership over his house.'

I stared at him, hoping he would go on. He did not, but looked at me with a mocking smile. 'Just tell me this, Lord Balan. What words of yours am I to trust?'

'The ones I give you,' he hissed.

I shook my head. 'What if Gal asks you to give over your family as a hostage until the matter is settled? My death that is. I don't like it.'

Balan leaned over the table. 'What do you want, Maskan? You wish to have assurances? I have nothing I would not sacrifice, boy, for this home of ours, but I am here and freely admit what I am planning for. I do so solemnly. You could just run away, could you not? You could disappear easily with your skill! You would only have to leave Sand behind.' And there was the threat, and I knew why they had let Sand come, why Shaduril had wanted to hide him, and why Balan had asked for him. He was a hostage.

'You would threaten him?' I hissed.

He looked disappointed. 'You are not very subtle. Yes! But you could destroy us if you decided to leave him. I trust you. I trust in your love for your Sand. I trust you, and you will have to trust me. But if you must have an oath,' he said conspiratorially, 'I can swear to you on my soul we are allied. Don't break up the alliance, Maskan, and remember your dear dead mother.'

I snorted and rubbed my face. 'I see. If I had my father's skull, you could swear over it, but I don't even know which one it is. It's in the Singing Garden.'

'Which skull is his, you asked,' he said while I sipped mead. I stared at the thin man, who was scuttling over to fetch a thick tome. He came back, utterly oblivious of me as he skimmed the book. His fingers were running up and down the pages. He slammed the book aside, got up to fetch another one, and again skimmed the pages until I was done eating and drinking. Minutes passed, and he did not move as he mumbled over words.

I cleared my throat and placed the empty goblet on the desk with a clang. 'Lord? You had some other business? Something to do with Gal?'

His eyes snapped to me. He looked supremely reluctant as he abandoned the tome and turned his attention back to me. 'Quite. I can do this later. There has to be information on which skull belongs to whom. I am sure of it.'

'It does not matter, really,' I told him. 'I was being sarcastic.'

He looked supremely bothered as he struggled with his thoughts. 'I will find it, nonetheless. So, you are the Trade Master's nephew and as we were discussing the what after part of the plan.' His fingers were twitching agilely. 'And of trust. We will make a deal with him, and he will supposedly receive you in payment for his help with the Tower. But in the meantime, he will want something more. You are right. Trust, like with you, is hard to come to Gal.'

'Trust is an issue, yes,' I agreed.

'So I will give him Taram,' he said. 'As a hostage. I sent Lith a message by bird last night. It came back not hours after. He agrees. He wants someone. I'll give him Taram.'

'It makes sense,' I whispered, suspicious. 'The least loved child would make a perfect hostage.'

'I love Taram, Maskan, and he will survive Gal. He has skills. It all comes down to getting you to the Tenginell household and you doing your bit.'

'I will do it,' I said, feeling uncomfortable.

'As for your reward,' he smiled.

'I need none,' I answered. 'Only your true word.'

'No?' he asked with a bemused voice. 'Gal is a man of ... few political aspirations. He is a trader of the first degree, of course, and keeps Red Midgard fed and loves his position and easy life. But you are a Talin.'

'What are you thinking about, exactly?' I asked him, for I thought he looked a bit nervous. 'You said you would make me a noble.'

He nodded sagely. 'Since you are your father's heir, perhaps you should take Gal's place?'

'Is he going to die?' I asked, feeling very uncomfortable about the discussion.

'Yes,' Balan said. 'Since we are being honest, he must. He already extorts us. Lith will tie the King. But Gal? He is rich. And so shall you be. After he falls. He has not done an exceptional job, you know. You can do it. Just have to learn how to read and write.'

'I can read!'

He waved his hand lazily. 'There. All set for lordship. Scribes can do the rest. You will have deserved it. And you are the true, the legal heir of the dead lord of the house.'

That stopped me. Heir to the Seventh House? Sixth if the Danegells fall. 'I surely have no heritance,' I smirked uncertainly, sure I did not. 'As my father was a traitor.'

'Not currently you don't,' he smiled. 'Gal was made the head of the house and his children if he had any, are legally the heirs. But such heritance can be restored when the criminal King is dead.'

'I see,' I said and nodded. 'And now, you will set this up?'

He rapped his fingers on the desk. 'You will do your bit with the Queen. Then, later, you will support the crown in the unstable times that are sure to follow,' he stated bluntly. 'So be it.' He swept his arms aside as if he had nothing to hide. 'We will deal with the details and meet here to discuss it. Play the fool with Gal when you see him. It's a splendid plan and a smooth one. Perhaps even so smooth that Shaduril will survive.'

'I would love that very much,' I said softly. 'She needs hope to survive. Surely she is terrified.'

'She is dead, Maskan,' he laughed bitterly. 'She will go through with it, but she is dead. With Gal and Crec, we will perhaps save her from the Brothers. Just act with us. And trust me.'

'I will help in any way with Gal,' I told him hollowly, feeling uncertain by his feverish plans and scared by the devious schemes. 'And what of her?'

'Her?'

'After,' I hissed. 'You say Lith will become queen. But what of Shaduril?'

He stared at me coldly. He struggled with his words, his thoughts and sat there, looking feverish. 'So. Are you now making demands to me? I offered you a high house of much wealth and power. But you are looking at also securing her. Is that so? Answer.'

'Yes,' I said, 'I am. You hate the thought of me having her for my own, but I want to make her happy.'

He sat there, mulling it over for a while, and then he said, 'I will think of a useful, calm occupation for her. She deserves a holiday after the coup,' he said, thrumming his fingers on the desk. I thought there was a hint of some long lost emotion on his face. Sorrow? Love? Finally, he nodded. 'She will decide such matters. There is a past you know nothing of, Maskan. You bargain hard, but I know you do so for love. Let her decide for herself; I shall also, and perhaps you will make her happy again.'

'I thank you, Lord,' I said.

He thrummed his fingers on the desk again, this time very hard. Then he snorted. 'But you did not thank me for the House of Talien. Never mind, you value what you value. I like a man who knows his cards are unbeatable. Ask me for a mound of gold, and I would procure it. And you are asking for such a mound, for I do love all my girls dearly. Yes. You will have your own House. The Sixth House. You will be groomed to nobility, you will be rich as a Master Thief, and life will be boring for you. So you will need a good wife.'

I nodded.

'A marriage to Shaduril is a great thing to ask,' he said with a displeased voice. 'Not sure I enjoy the thought of giving her to someone who has been thieving all his life, but she might do worse. She decides, but I agree.'

I blushed. 'Thank you, again. I want this in writing.'

He blinked and shuddered in shock. 'Writing?'

'Writing,' I growled. 'Everything we discussed. With your signature and seal and witnesses. And I can read, as I said.'

He was nodding and did for so long I thought he had broken his neck. Finally, he said yes. 'I will deliver it to you. An insult, but I shall.'

'Thank you,' I said with a polite smile.

'Now, I have business to attend to.' He waved his hand across a stack of papers, and as he did, one flew to the stone floor.

I grabbed it and saw it was a bill of sales for The Dead End Tavern. He scowled at me. 'It's being auctioned, as Valkai no longer uses it. The King sells it, and I want it.'

'Going to turn into a criminal?' I asked him smoothly.

'We were ever in the Trade. You know it.' He laughed softly. 'Now don't look at me like that. Coin is coin, and I'd be a fool not to prepare to make some money out of all this. I am in this for Red Midgard. And our family.'

'And for the King's artifacts,' I whispered, and he heard me.

He glowered at me and shrugged. 'No word to Sand.'

'No, Lord,' I said miserably.

'It's for his own good,' he added and tapped the table. 'Make sure not to speak to Illastria, either. She likes it in that corner of the main hall. Makes her feel safe. Let her be. Sand should as well.'

'Safe from what?' I asked him.

'Go,' he breathed, his face twitching.

And I went. He aimed to rob the nation of its royals and its magic.

We trained for three months.

## CHAPTER 10

Living in the Crimson Apex was a curious affair. In the evenings, the main hall filled with mild-mannered soldiers. They sat there, sipping mead and ale and spoke gently amidst long tables while warming flames from the huge fireplace lit the room. They were rarely the same men, but often new faces. Some were like us, blond and tall, others stout and short, all apparently warriors by their hardened looks, scars, and their weapons. 'Mercenaries, I am sure of it,' Sand said one night. 'He is buying men for Yule. He said their army is too small, but I guess coin can buy you anything.'

'But they keep changing,' I told him.

'He sends them somewhere, bit by bit,' Sand agreed.

To assault the tower, and Balan was hiding them indeed, I thought. In the Old City. There would be a thousand men there, perhaps. It would ruin the Blacktowers. I chuckled. Money was the least of their concerns.

Then there were the Blacktower men, who sat by themselves in the corners. They were hundreds strong, for I had seen Balan address them all in the yard; all wore house colors of the white lily on red, but the chain mail and leather armor they used was dark. They were a curious lot. Others were happy and young, farmer and herdsmen of High Hold, others sullen and scowling. Their wives and children would visit them during the days while they trained, and many stayed in the nearby villages.

There was always soft singing in the hall as a bard sang of past wars and lost treasures. There were many legends of the past, of the gods, of creatures that had tried to take the land. Of beasts and giants, dragons, and even elves. Men listened, nodded, and some of the young farmers sang with the bards, but the mood was ever drowsy, almost like a dream. Balan never joined the celebration, but old Illastria would gaze at the singers, sometimes, afraid, her white hair a halo around her head as she sat on the side, hunched over her desk. What was she afraid of?

We had a hard time sitting still.

We were sore. So very sore. Every day, every evening.

We swam in the mornings, as Taram forced us down to the beach. He would jog on the fine-grained sand while we waddled in the cold water for an inordinate amount of time, back and forth until we nearly drowned. I dragged Sand out one day, another day he had to punch me in the gut to force out all the saltwater I had swallowed. Taram would snicker at our sorry states, and then he would run us up an obscure track that led to the fort. This involved a hefty amount of climbing. Sweltered by the morning's heat, lathered in sweat, we managed it each time, but our arms and muscles were trembling madly as we struggled with the last strides up the hill. Those last fifty yards were especially grueling. Taram did not break a sweat. Often, as we re-entered the

Apex, we saw wagons stop by the old keep of High Hold, unloading great bundles of gear. 'Weapons, no doubt,' Sand always noted.

We cursed Taram, and then we ate breakfast. The few hundred Blacktower men were being drilled, and they joined us in the breaking of fast. The mercenaries had always marched off. By the fall, the Blacktower clients were unhappy. There were archers in their light leathers and helmets. There were men-at-arms with halberds and men with shields and spear. They looked splendid, but it was clear by their whispered cursing that they thought they should be reaping their harvests. The north was always on the brink of famine, so I could understand them.

Then, in the afternoon, the training commenced.

The first day had been brutal.

The following were nearly dull. That second day of training, Taram stared at me as he was picking out a staff for me. 'I know he told you to give me skills with a sword, and mainly staff, but I would still prefer the longer sword.'

'Father insisted you train with a staff,' he said with a shrug. 'It's best we obey, no? He gives me my coins, and I can hardly live without them, and so you get to learn the staff.'

*Larkgrin*, I thought. Balan wanted to make me proficient with that weapon, despite his words about his own training. I scowled, for while the weapon was an artifact of power, it felt somewhat disappointing. It was not heroic. Of course, it was, but it also was not. I gazed at Sand looking at some fine chain armor and a scimitar of a beautiful make. 'Slightly shorter than you, I think ... this one,' Taram was murmuring. He picked out a sturdy brown staff that was not very tall. 'Don't mope. It can kill a man easily if you know how. You will learn some sword, yes, but not a two-hander as you liked. The staff is a deadly thing. Put a point on it, and it's a spear. Learn to strike with it, and it's good for two-hander sword training as well. I'll teach you. I had a master who taught me many things. I cannot claim I'd prefer it myself, but you will not feel inadequate after you learn to love it.'

'I'll try,' I said darkly.

He snorted and turned a reluctant eye to my friend's direction. 'And you, Sand? Daggers? Thieves love knives when they cut purses and murder in the dark.'

'I've never cut a bag,' Sand said, and I realized it was the truth. I had. He had guarded me. 'I've only carried loot. And I haven't killed anyone, either.'

'All right,' Taram said dubiously. 'I was joking about the daggers. Good for a back alley and perhaps a fight in the shieldwall, but in war you also have to have something taller to put inside the man before you.'

'Shit,' Sand whispered. 'I'll take this scimitar, then.'

'And a chain. You will train in chain mail, gauntlets, and pauldrons and chin guards. A helmet as well. Will shed some of that extra fat. We will make you into proper little soldiers. For some reason.' He kicked at some rubble and cursed profusely. 'A few months is hardly enough to do this, so it will be terribly cruel to you. No holiday for you in the Crimson Apex, boys. You'll learn a skill that can make you rich. Then you will join my father's war. I don't understand what all the men being recruited are for, and so I suffer. That is my lot. Ignorance and servitude.'

'Yes,' I told him patiently. 'That's your lot.'

'Take the scimitar, that sword. That one,' Taram pointed at a heavy wooden sword that was curved, 'and that shield,' he nodded at a huge, round iron thing. 'Go and start stabbing at the target. I'll show you how, in a bit. Get used to it, my peasant friend.' Sand bit his teeth together, growled, and went, not looking back.

'You have a way to charm my friend, Taram,' I said with ambiguity. He was not fooled.

'He hates me; I hate you.' He grinned. 'Usually I get along with soldiers just fine, but not you.' There was strange intensity in his eyes, and I wondered if he would attack me. I thumbed my ring, preparing, but he turned away.

'But I hate others as well,' he stated. 'It is not unusual. You are just one of the many, Maskan. We shall train and see if that head of yours can take it. I'll find out your secrets, Maskan, one day when I have no more duties with you.'

It was a chilling threat, delivered like a fact. I shook my head at him. 'Don't you have any other plans for your life, my lord? You gamble, you fight, and you enjoy women, no doubt. And plot revenge for imagined insults and things that do not concern you. Is there something you will be when you finally grow up?' I asked him.

He hesitated and tilted his head at me. He shrugged. 'I used to read stories when I was very young.'

'You are young still,' I snorted.

'Very young.' He chuckled and went on, 'Stories of heroes and kings and wars. I wish nothing more than to be in a book.'

'Then you are in the right family,' I smiled. 'Ask Illastria to pen you in some tome. That Moragorium for example.'

'Oh! You know our lot? Yes, I'll get into some book, I'm sure. Yes. We all do. Father and Illastria will pen the stories down. Father will do so until he dies. Then Shad will take over, no doubt. Poor girl.' His face went lax, and he breathed deep, in sorrow, I thought. Then he went on. 'But I do not wish to be mentioned a drunkard and a fool. I would like to do a great deed, one day. Kill a king in battle? Or a god, even! I can. I'm that good.'

'Kings and gods,' I said. 'A fine plan, Taram. I just wanted happiness and a home.'

'Not with Shaduril, you won't.' He grinned like a dead thing. 'Enough of dreams.' I was not sure if he meant his or mine. 'Pick up the staff. And keep calm. I won't let you go madman on me again.'

And so, he trained me. He taught me to stand, cursing me profusely for my lack of skill even with the most basic of stances. There was a horse stance, very balanced, suitable for changing into an offensive and defensive position. There was a cat stance, perfect for the uppercut hit. Standing and gliding from one stand to another was all I did for weeks, and one might not think it is so, but it actually tires you out quickly. Not unlike dancing, it built my stamina. When I did these steps over and over again, he trained Sand. Stab, stab, shield up, legs spread. It seemed simple, but there was nothing simple about it. It was an art form to stand and fight properly.

Only when I showed some more grace at the basics, he began to teach me to strike. There was the overhead strike, and he showed me how to bring up the knee and execute it with power and grace. There was an up-to-the-side thrust from the horse stance. I immediately excelled in a rib strike and slowly begun to understand how to transition from defensive stance to an offensive one when Taram changed his. I learned for Taram did not give me any mercy. I would often train against a padded dummy in the semi-dark room, meticulously working my screaming muscles next to Sand, who was thrusting, ever blocking with the shield, and only slowly learning slashes and longer maneuvers. But most of all I learned fighting with Taram. By the end of the second month, I managed to keep him at bay and launch somewhat dangerous counterattacks. Sand was growing better as well.

In the late afternoons, I was waiting in a pantry, where Gray, who was a gray-haired, stooped figure of a man would train me with my stance, again, with my walk, which was ridiculous and painful both, as my muscles were screaming in pain. He was patient and of mild manners, yet as authoritative as a god as he forced me to dress in tight finery, expensive clothing of embroidery and tight leathers. He taught me how to carry a tray filled with food, how to do it while armed, how not to make sudden, fatal movements, how to keep my face, in what he called the Mask of Stone. He taught me how to eat properly with grace, and how to drink my drink without slurping, taking only sips. I actually began to enjoy that part of the training, for he would make me deliberately drunk to make sure I could perform the noble acts even then. Eventually, I could.

## CHAPTER 11

We grew stronger as the months rolled on. But we were not happy. We had trouble sleeping, and I thought it was due to the Yule feast that was soon to come. In a month's time, it would be our time or at least mine. Sand would often lie on the bed, awake, sweaty, and I would ask him what was wrong, but he would not say. Not specifically. Then one morning, I did not let go of the matter. 'Come, tell me. Are you having nightmares?'

'No,' he whispered and wiped his face.

'What then?' I asked him. 'You are not saying anything. We barely speak.'

'I'm a statist,' he stated. 'The least of the actors. But I knew that, didn't I? And yes, I dream. Terrible dreams, Maskan. You will betray me.'

I gawked at him. 'No. Why would you think so? For a damned dream? I once dreamed you tried to eat me. Will you?'

'Only if there are a good mint sauce and taters involved,' he said miserably and swung his legs over to the floor. He rubbed his face. 'Yeah. I see strange dreams. I have not slept well lately. Not at all. I keep seeing you, and you have left me. You lie to me, all the time, in that dream. I'm alone in the dark, and then I die. It is very uncomfortable.'

'No, I wouldn't,' I told him and felt miserable. 'And I also have nightmares. It's only natural with Yule so close. I dream of her. Shaduril. She is a queen. And marries Morag. I dreamt, just now, that she could not remember my name as I was introduced to her up there in the Rose Throne.'

'What does it look like?' he asked me with a small grin.

'What? The Rose Throne? It was a large chair with roses engraved all around it. Dark red. Why?'

'Just wanted to know,' he said tiredly. 'Never seen it. Few have. Especially if you grew up in the Bad Man's. Incredible what you can do in a dream.'

I hesitated and shrugged. And felt sorry for him. 'You up to training?'

'Got nothing else to do, right?' he said weakly. 'I hope the skills will be useful one day.'

'No, you will not train today,' said a thin voice from the door. Balan stood there. He eyed Sand, and I stared at him, refusing to ask my friend to leave, which was obviously what Balan desired. He noted my mulish mood and shrugged. 'You will rest this day, my friends. In the evening, Maskan, you will sit down with the family. Lith will be here.'

'And my uncle?' I asked and froze. *Gods, I was a fool.*

Balan's face was unreadable, and then he nodded. 'And your uncle. He will agree to our deal. And this letter is for you.' He held an official-looking document up in the air.

'I see,' I said. Sand perked up as he understood what I had said.

'You have a family?' he asked.

Balan was rubbing his forehead. 'I am sorry, Sand. We agreed not to speak about this before everything is settled. We,' he nodded at me, 'thought you might be safer not to know more about it.' Lying bastard, he did not trust Sand.

'I agreed,' I said and shrugged at Sand. He scowled at me, deeply hurt.

'What is this part of the plan?' he asked. 'Last I remember we agreed to help them kill the Queen and then the other murderers. There's a plan now?'

'We are trying to survive a regicide,' I told him softly. 'It is more complicated than our oath.'

'Well, will you not tell me more?' he growled. 'Or do you think I don't understand these complicated plans? I have been patient.'

Balan hesitated. 'There will be people coming and going this night. Stay out of sight, Sand, if you can. Deal with this issue, Maskan.' He bowed to me and left me the letter. I took it and fiddled with it. I put it down, not wishing to open it. It was a written agreement by Balan on our deal.

I nodded at Sand and sighed. 'Sorry, it's likely a dreary affair, this dinner,' I told him. I looked at him as he did not answer and saw he was staring ahead, not reacting. 'Sand?' I said, and he looked up, slowly, his mouth open.

'Who is your relative?' he asked me with a thin voice. 'And what is this plan?'

'The plan involves my relative,' I told him softly.

'And who is it?' he insisted. 'I know your mother told you something that day you got Larkgrin. I didn't hear it, but she was crying. I know it's some noble. Always did. So?'

I shrugged. 'Gal Talin.'

His eyes were wide open, and he froze and stammered. 'Gal Talin. The bastard who oversees the executions and robs the dead? The Lord of the Harbor?'

'My father was his brother,' I told him sorely. 'He is my uncle.'

He held his head. 'I know what an uncle is, Maskan! And he will be here? You will join him?'

'I will join the dinner,' I affirmed, playing with the letter.

'Why?' he asked. 'That means there is an alliance being built, no?'

'Yes. And no. It is complicated,' I said, looking away. *Gal would die.* I felt filthy for all the lies.

'Look at me!' he yelled and slammed his fist on the desk so hard the chain mail draped over it slid to the ground with a jarring, clinking sound. 'What exactly have they promised you?'

'I cannot tell you. I promised—'

'Cannot tell your brother?' he hissed. 'But then, I am not. Not really. They will make you a noble? In his house? Gal Talin's house? In return for aid?'

'Yes,' I said with a small voice. 'But—'

'And?' he asked. I said nothing, and he just stared at me. Then he got an idea. He leaned forward. 'I have been wondering about something. You see, an idiot like me sometimes has thoughts inside his thick skull. Who will be the king? If Morag dies, that is.'

I waved my hand and rubbed my face. 'Crec Helstrom. He will marry Lith.'

'What?' he breathed. 'The man who ordered the executions of our family?'

'Yes,' I said resolutely, determined to have it out.

He stammered and stared at me, waiting for me to go on. I did not and so he shouted at me. 'It was Mad Watch standing there at the Green Hall. And you said yes to this? Even if we swore

… And you said nothing?' He went quiet and held his head. 'You are moving on. To a new family. Probably won't even spit in Bad Man's direction. You should have told me.'

'It's not a small matter to share information on a treason. If things go wrong, they will question us—'

He laughed with a mocking voice. 'They will kill the lot and ask no questions. At all. No matter what they know or find out. Doesn't matter. Stop lying.'

'There is more to it,' I said defensively. 'It's not as simple as you think. But I promise you, I have not forgotten our enemy. Not Crec. Not the Brothers.'

'You heard?' Taram asked from the doorway, and we froze. 'I hear there is no training today.' He stopped to stare at our stupefied faces. 'What is wrong?'

'Nothing. No training today,' I confirmed.

He hesitated, bowed, and left.

'Think he heard?' I asked Sand with a whisper.

'Don't really care if he did,' he answered. 'We swore on their blood. An oath.'

'It makes no sense, Sand, to curse Crec. He likely did what the King told him to do,' I said, hoping Sand would calm down. 'Should we also go after the soldiers?'

'And now you defend him?' he breathed. 'You are doing this for your reward.'

'My reward, Sand, is to see Shaduril survive.'

'I told you to let her do her bit!' he yelled.

'I am letting her do her bit. But I don't want to lose her. I want to see her survive and thrive! She might if Balan manages to pull together an alliance. Crec is needed for the Mad Watch and so that he can be the king. He is high enough to be accepted by the Houses. Gal is needed to enter the Tower. Shaduril will be in there. We swore an oath, Sand, but we have to keep focused on the real goal. And that's all about the King. He is the rooster we must pluck, not the others.'

'And the Brothers? What if they choose to join Crec?' he asked me, cocking his head. 'Surely, Crec might invite them to his house? Balan does not command Crec, does he? What if Crec decides to hang the lot of us?'

I opened my mouth to refute him, but could not. 'We cross that bridge when we come to it.'

'And you will be rich?' he laughed. 'You'll have a beautiful house and riches. Just what I wanted. And Shaduril?'

'I was going to share with you. I'm still a thief. I will share everything but her. We always have. And she has not decided anything as far as I go. She says she has feelings, but who knows? She is frightened.'

He snorted. 'You would have shared with me? But you didn't tell me the good news any more than you did the bad news. I wish I had ignored you lot and buried my father. Here I am. Useless. A silly little puppet.'

I whispered. 'I worry for you. Shaduril was right. You should not have come. But not because you are useless. I am sorry for my mistakes. Balan keeps you here, Sand because he knows I care for you. You are a hostage,' I said, hoping he would understand, not at all sure he would.

He shook his head and sneered. 'And you let them? Another thing you should have told me.' I opened my mouth, but could not. He was right. He turned on his heel and pushed past me. 'You have changed, friend. I think my dreams were wise.'

'What is wrong with change, Sand? Eh? We have to think about ourselves as well as the dead. Compromises have to be made. I'm trying to make one. Attempting to make it right for everyone. Why can't you see that and forgive me?' I walked after him to the hallway as he walked down a staircase. 'What is wrong with that? Huh?'

'Nothing,' he called out. 'Nothing at all. Go and enjoy yourself this evening. I doubt you could stomach a piece of bread down at the harbor anymore.'

'I've not changed that much!'

'Remember Ann? My sister? Bear and that one lady, Mir?' he called out. 'And our dull lives? But I guess you were robbed at birth and now, it's time to reclaim what was yours. After the Queen is dead, Maskan,' he said with a grating voice as he reached the downstairs, 'we should both reclaim what was ours, once. Perhaps sooner.'

'I'll choose the living over the dead, Sand, any day!' I yelled so that the Crimson Apex echoed. 'I told you this once. And that includes you and Shaduril both! How could you demand it is you alone? I'd love your woman like I love you!'

'I want respect and answers, instead of mirrors and smoke,' he yelled back up at me. 'I might be a prisoner, but I am not happy. I need air that's not sullied by the stink of shit and lies.'

I went back to the room and stared at the ceiling. I writhed in agony, cursed him and tried to convince myself I had not forgotten him. There were plenty of reasons to keep him in the dark, but the truth was I had left him in the dark because it gave me Shaduril and riches, and he would have made it harder. He was never one to make compromises. He was like his father, quick to anger. And yet, I felt like a rotten bastard, even if I knew it was not that simple. I did not give him a chance to change. And perhaps he was right. Perhaps he should not have changed. Had I not thought of running away with him before Shaduril gave me hope? For Crec? Finally, I fell asleep and suffered nightmares until the evening.

'Lord?' said a voice at the door, and the butler Gray was there, bowing. I got up, totally at a loss as to what the time was.

'Is it ...' I began, and the butler gave me a ghost of a smile.

'This way, Lord.' He helped me up, guided me through the door and showed me to the corner chamber, a round room with a high ceiling where we bathed every day.

A very beautiful servant gave me dark leather pants and a pearl-white shirt at the door, but I barely noticed their excellent quality, as Sand's parting words bothered me. He needed air. He had not returned to the room.

I went in, saw a steaming bath, undressed, and slid in. It was heavenly, warm and perhaps nearly scalding. The scent of the water was strange, the room calm and relaxing, with shadows and light in perfect balance and birds were chirping away outside. Despite having slept most of the day, I felt drowsy. Soon, I felt like I drifted away, and I decided I had never been as relaxed, not for a long time at least.

Then, something splashed into the bath with a wild shriek, and I nearly had a heart attack.

'Maskan!' Shaduril shrieked and smiled at me, her sultry smile beaming at me. She had nothing on, and her bared bosom made me yelp.

'What are you doing?' I asked her, holding my chest while trying to look at her eyes. 'And when did you arrive? And you know—'

'Just this morning,' she said with a grin, playing with their house symbol that was enticingly having a bubble bath between her breasts. 'Things have been moving along rather nicely. And I've missed you. I am sorry.'

I stared at her, and she tilted her head at me. I dared to speak after a while. 'You seem much happier. A lot happier, in fact.'

She nodded and looked down, demurely. 'Things are much clearer. Time is almost up. It's a relief. And I have been thinking about you.'

'And Morag?' I asked her.

She waved her hand. 'I don't want to talk about him. Could you not, either?'

I nodded at her. Her ice cold feet were brushing against mine under the water. 'I hear Crec will be here. For Lith?' I stated the obvious.

'He will,' she agreed with a somewhat subdued voice. 'I ask you not to speak of Morag, but you will speak of Crec and Lith. Thank you. But yes, the Lord Commander will be here. Gods, he is a bore. Utter, total windmill. Lith will yawn when she has to endure him again. Looks tall and handsome, but only does one or two things. Broods and plots. But he does bring new blood to this conspiracy. Many things might happen, Maskan. The future is ours to mold.'

'I never thanked Lith …' I stammered. 'After the mint episode.'

'For saving you from a short, murderous guard of the mint?' She quaffed, and I did chuckle at that. She dipped her head underwater and rubbed it vigorously. 'You are welcome, I am sure,' she told me under her breath. She had a most beautiful earring dangling from her lobe, a thing of silver and pearls.

'Thank you on her behalf, Shaduril,' I said with gratitude.

'Welcome.' She grinned, and I was glad she was so brilliantly happy, though her nakedness made me very nervous.

'Why are you here?' I asked her to distract myself from her nipples.

She shrugged. 'Morag is busy. I had some time. I wanted to see you. Are you complaining?'

'No. You were supposed to help me get ready?' I repeated. 'Will you dress me, then?' I said with a smile.

She splashed water on my face. 'I am no maid, Maskan. I'm just having a bath with you. But you can massage my foot.' She arched her neck, her foot snaked into my lap, and I nearly shrieked. She grinned again, and I decided I either had to escape or play along. In the end, I let her leg rest there, and she, quite maliciously, did not budge it. 'No?'

'I don't know how,' I told her and grabbed her foot while pressing it here and there.

'That is really sad,' she decided, and I nodded. I had no idea what I was doing. She smiled suggestively, and I groaned with desire. Yet, there was a part of me that was wary. She spoke softly. 'You know, I'm just jubilant right now. You don't have to be an expert. Just press there … right there and move your fingers gently. There! You see. You can.'

'You are different. A bit like a—'

'Slut?' she said, her eyes hardening.

I cursed myself. 'Perhaps, no, definitely not. But I am not saying—'

She leaned forward and her leg brushed at me very suggestively. I enjoyed the excitement of the seduction; I feared it. She seemed strange. 'Yes, you are saying just that. It is fine. I am enjoying myself tonight because soon I might be dead. Indulge me. Let me be the old Shaduril, just for a moment. In a bit, this very evening, Father will introduce you to Gal Talien and that pompous ass and future king of the land, Crec Helstrom,' she said flatly. 'Perhaps I should marry Morag before killing him, and I would be the Beastess of the North,' she laughed and a feral look flashed on her face, clawing at the air. 'I'd have Crec hung.'

'I see,' I breathed, totally at a loss with her mood. 'I am happy to help you forget,' I told her. 'I am pleased it is no longer a suicide attack on the crown.'

'Our plan, dear, is mad as a bat in daylight.' She grinned. 'But it has a speck of hope. I rather like … living. Right this moment.'

'Will you tell me what you think about our future? You still interested in … seeing what lies further afield?' I asked her, thinking about Sand and our plans together.

'I want to see what is under the water, right now,' she purred, and her leg came to rest in a very inappropriate place.

'Not now,' I said in a panic, for it was strange, and I was suddenly not in the mood. Her mouth smiled, but I saw she had lost her patience. Her foot pushed me very forcefully, and I winced.

'Fine,' she said after a while. 'The mood is gone. You damned fool,' she hissed. 'My last night.'

I groaned. 'I am sorry. I did not mean to ruin this for you. I worry. I always worry. That's what I do.' She nodded and sighed, and leaned her head back.

'I forgive you for turning me down.' Her eyes flashed as she looked at me, and I flinched for her foot dug in my side. 'Just remember this. We are all driven by goals and desires in this family. Much more so than other families. We obey Father, but only so long as we get what we want in the end. I want you. I cannot understand how you keep resisting me.'

'I have not! I'm very much yours! I'm just confused. You have me,' I said with some panic. 'I told you I am sorry.' She got up—a glorious sight—and got us towels, and I could only stare at her. She threw one to me, and I grabbed it from the air, barely in time before it hit the water.

I pleaded with her. 'Can we start over? We can. Right?' She snorted, and there was a sound of dogged anger in her voice. 'Forgive me. This evening is remarkable, and I am an ass. Let me make it up to you. I care for you. And we can go … riding the day when it is all over. I'm committed to that. My friend might think it is a good idea, as well. Start anew. Your father has promised a lot, but you did warn me not to—'

'Riding?' she asked me. 'Why riding?' She waved me down and took some deep breaths. Her sodden blonde hair was curling wetly across her back to her buttocks, and I stared at her, hoping she would forgive me and not take the future away from us. She had sounded cruel. She stood there for a long time. I had heard women can make a storm seem docile, and she was truly brewing with rage. Finally, almost visibly, she relaxed. 'Yes,' she said and nodded at me. 'We can start anew. Forgive me my anger. But you ruined it, very nearly at least.' She pulled me up and took the towel from my hand. I instinctively covered myself, but she giggled, her mood swinging fast. She slapped my hands aside and began to dry off my face and chest. She sang softly, and her voice was like silk on skin. 'Shall I dress?' I asked her weakly, not covered in the least, and I was also naturally interested in anything but dressing.

'I'll do it after all,' she told me with a whisper. I nearly slipped on the wet floor, but she balanced me. She smiled at my clumsiness and rubbed the towel across my belly. Then she did the same with my neck and shoulders. She nodded at me and made me sit down on a desk. 'Help me.' She nodded at her towel, draped over her shoulder, and I hesitated, then took it. I wiped her belly and moved it gently across her hips. She stepped between my legs, a bit forcibly as I resisted and pressed her chest on my chest. She tiptoed, and her breasts were caressing my throat, and she looked down at me. I tried to kiss her, but she retreated. She looked puzzled but smiled. 'No kisses. It solves nothing and leads to trouble. One day, perhaps, but I am happy with the rest. For now.' Her words bothered me for some reason, but I forgot it as she moved herself so that her nipple brushed my cheek, then my face, and I opened my mouth to kiss it, gently, very gently, and she pressed it deeper. I put my hand on her hip, and slid it to her buttock, her firm flesh trembling under the touch. I pulled her to me as I kissed those breasts, her shoulders, and her neck. I was consumed with lust, and she climbed to sit over me. I felt her hands grope between my legs, and she smiled as she teased me for a moment. I begged gods for mercy, but they were not there, and then she finally slid it inside her. She sat on me with all her weight, slowly, and pushed me on my back to the desk. I let her move, tried to find a rhythm to make it better for her, managed it, as she seemed to enjoy a short, powerful thrust. It was all very wonderful, and I did not want it to end. She was patient as she guided me to our climax. 'Don't be a screamer, Maskan.' She giggled over me as I came, right after her, and I bit my lip to keep silent. But she was not done so quickly and pulled me up, leaned on me and guided me to renew the pleasure.

In the end, we were late for dinner, but no maid appeared to hurry us up.

Soon after, she was dressed. She smiled coyly at me, and I smiled back at her, though I was ashamed. 'Remember, Maskan, what I just gave you.'

'You are my first, Shaduril ...' I began but stopped as I stared at her.

She wiped her hair into a bun. There was a moment of fury on her face, but it disappeared. She nodded, apparently having decided something. There was a soft glow as her earring changed to a simple silver thing. And so did her face. The blonde hair grew into red, the body a bit taller, and Lith smiled at me furiously. I stared back at her and looked away. 'Funny,' she said. 'I thought you might have been more shocked.'

'I am shocked,' I said, and I was, but I did not wish to give her the satisfaction. 'What artifact is this?'

'I have my secrets, my love,' she said and tapped her earring. 'Father's toy. But only useful for a female. He does not need it.'

I opened my mouth to refute the claim she was laying on me, but could not. Love? Lies. I was a fool.

She shook her head. 'Let's not upset poor Shaduril. She and I? We have past issues with men.'

'You took a man of hers before?' I asked her, enraged inside, but I forced myself to stay calm. Shaduril had told me to be careful. To be faithful to her.

'We had a conflicting interest,' she murmured. 'Don't judge me. She is not a perfect angel nor am I the incarnation of evil. I gave you something to think about and you are safe and sated. For now. But you won't forget this. I was set on having you because you are ravenously handsome. And because Shaduril wants you. Now I have a foot inside the door.'

'If you can change your face,' I said with budding rage, 'then why do you need me?'

She touched her earring. 'It can only take the face of a female and a female must use it. You are still irreplaceable. Valkai could not find a woman that got close to the Queen. Not one. She hates women, you see. We could use it to kill the King, but the Queen would still be making trouble for us. So, we had to try to find a man. And we did. Better than a doppelganger. A real man.' She smiled lecherously, and I shook my head.

'Why don't you take her place with the King? You can fight, no?' I asked her darkly.

She hesitated. 'You would rather risk me than her? She can fight as well.'

'You are more ...' I told her and hesitated. 'You are dangerous. She is not.'

'You are wrong,' she said with a smile. 'Wait. And if you still insist on being with her, I shall keep this a secret. But I will ask for something later. And you will be mine when I ask for you.

For Shaduril.' *Bitch,* I thought. She looked at me carefully and saw my struggle and relished it. 'Say yes.'

'Yes,' I hissed.

She slapped her hip. 'Good boy. Let us be careful, love, and enjoy the dinner,' she stated, and we dressed. She pulled on her shoes and got up. She walked to me and kissed my cheek, and I struggled to remain still. 'Time will make our heads clear, and our problems will disappear like fog in the morning. Wait. Forgive me for this, and what I will ask of you later on.'

I escorted Lith to the main hall.

Shaduril was not there. Lith was wearing a black gown; no jewelry save the earring, and her hair was silky and set with red ribbons. Red ribbons on thick red hair, she looked stunning. She smiled demurely at the crowd, and I fell behind her in step. *Gods,* I thought, *she had made a mess of things.* Or I had. I should have known better. I felt awkward in the beautiful clothing, now complemented by tall leather boots. We reached the middle of the hall, lit by the usual fire in the fireplace, and the lords got up as we arrived.

Both were apparently high lords. They wore house colors, yellow and silver for Crec, who was the Lord Commander of the Mad Watch and also wore dark pauldrons with the Watch insignia of skull and sword. He was a balding, hard man of the second house and in his eyes, there was definite interest as he eyed us. He bowed his head at Lith, who curtsied at him, and her smile was one to turn a dead man into an amorous youth. It worked for the dour Crec quickly enough. The man the thieves called the Butcher was smiling widely and not brooding like Lith had predicted. Then I gazed at the man that was bound to be Gal. He looked the same as he had on the day of Alrik's hanging. He was tall and gaunt and dark, but now with a recent short beard, and he wore an expensive red silk rope. I saw Balan swirling a mug of wine as he looked at us, and he gave Gal a nod towards me. 'Your nephew, Lord of Trade,' Balan said with small satisfaction as the man shuddered with surprise. 'He was in some serious trouble, but we managed to fish him out of it. The King killed your brother's wife not long ago.'

'Why,' said Gal, staring at my ring, 'did not your mother bring you to us? Why did she not flee to us?'

I stopped as Lith slid onto a seat next to Crec, who was all smiles. It was clear his face was unused to such smiles, but he was trying. 'She was pregnant with me. She did not trust anyone? I know not, Uncle. You knew her, undoubtedly.'

He considered it. 'You have Tal's eyes. His bearing. And his speech. And our house ring.' He could not take his eyes off the ring. His eyes were glazed. *Was it greed? Or suspicion? Did he desire it?* Finally, he went on. 'It's been twenty years since I last saw it. The ring. I had forgotten what it looks like, I think. But I believe Balan now. Do you know what happened to Tal? Did your mother tell you? And yes, she likely did not trust us. She had not even met the family, well, only briefly. Your father lived in the Temple, not with our household in the Second Ring. He had married her the year past. For not taking the effort to know your mother, I am to blame.' He bowed his head slightly, and I mirrored him. 'We did not get along with Tal.'

'Uncle. He tried to take my mother by force.'

'Did he?' Gal wondered. 'There are rumors of the man. Beast of the North is truly just a beast.' His voice was calculating as he still stared at the ring.

'He is an honest boy, a good boy,' Balan said, nodding at me. 'And yes, Shaduril knows the Beast. Too well. She suffers for all of us. She will do this deed, brave girl that she is. And he?' Balan nodded at me. 'He will marry Shaduril if they both survive. Our houses will be allied through the marriage, Lord Gal.' Lith looked at me and raised her eyebrows as she was nodding at something Crec was whispering.

'If she survives this attempt,' Gal said glumly. 'In fact, I still have grave misgivings about the whole matter,' he stammered, his brow lathered in sweat as if he were struggling with something. Balan scowled at him and nodded at him to go on, but he shrugged.

Crec snorted and toasted Gal. 'You know Balan is right. The Fringe is alienated from us. You have seen the King. The Pearl Terrace, every morning. He stares over to the north, seeing enemies where there used to be allies. He is making us look weak. All four brigades are less than enthusiastic about the King. Hawk's Talon had twenty men deserting last year. Unheard of. I am not one for rebellion or breaking thousands of years of tradition, but the past two decades have changed us. Both the High King and ours have been going mad for years and years. You know this. We need a sane king, nothing less.'

Gal mulled his wine and nodded. 'And the Brothers? His uncle and relatives and the Ministry? Lord of Light? Everyone in power?'

'They will be shut in the Tower of the Temple by Crec's men,' Balan said softly, and Gal was nodding slowly. Balan went on. 'And you will give us a way to get inside. Through the mint. You will lead them there personally or appoint a Master of Coin you can trust. Then, once the battle rages, they will all have to choose. They will choose. Everyone has to choose. Except for the Brothers. Formidable as they are, they cannot beat a determined attack by our men, and I don't want them. And you know the guards do not trust them, no. They are strange. They have … magic.' They all looked at my ring.

'The Four Armies will not bother us,' Crec said calmly, apparently hoping to see my face change. 'The Mad Watch has three thousand men. Granted, they are not soldiers like the Hawk's Talon outside the city, but they will be enough to defend the Temple after the business is concluded. They will slaughter the King's relatives and men out of the Temple and yes, even the Brothers they will find. And your money, Gal, will buy us allies in the Houses. We need you for more than the mint and the Tower business. You will make sure the trade goes on, and food gets sold and distributed and people will remain happy.'

'A question,' I whispered.

'Yes?' Balan asked, worried I should have one.

'If Lord Gal,' I said and could not entirely hide the hate in my voice, 'has a way to the Tower, then why don't Lord Crec's men just use it and throw the King off the Pearl Terrace? Now? And kill the Queen at the same time?'

The Lord Commander sat back in his seat. 'Because that is treason, young Maskan. Because I do not wish to stain my honor with the shame. Because a king must be seen as a good man, not a tyrant. Because,' he said coldly as he leaned closer, 'it is a filthy thing to do. And risky. The Mad Watch is mine, but the King might make them theirs easily. He must be dead before we kill the rest of his family.'

'But Lord Balan will carry the shame?' I asked. 'And as for the honor you are so concerned about, condemning people to hang without a trial is not dishonorable? You do that, Lord.'

His eyes flickered with annoyance. 'Balan's daughter will take the blame,' Crec said mulishly. 'Did he not mention it? Your wife will bear the shame. And what comes to criminals, the Elder Judges are not efficient. It takes them ages to condemn a thief to hang. The King does not care as long as they die, and the judges are grateful they don't have to hear every sorry tale. So yes, I am called the Butcher by the vermin for a reason. Don't lecture me, boy.'

'Shaduril is to be blamed,' Balan told me cautiously, hoping to calm me down. 'She will retire. As I said, Maskan. She will disappear. And someone less important will … take her place in the scaffold. Few know Shaduril's face. We will find someone suitable.'

Crec laughed. 'Balan is as much a butcher as I am.'

'I see,' I said coldly. They would hang some poor fool girl in her stead.

'Shaduril will take the blame, and ultimately we shall blame the Brothers for the coup,' Crec said happily. 'They had her do it. Problem solved. People will believe it. I will be legitimate. A right great king.'

'But only on the surface,' I whispered, though loud enough to be heard. Crec was about to comment, but Gal raised his hand.

'If the King does not die,' Gal said coldly to Balan, 'and it might very well go like that, if your girl fails, my house must survive. Mine. As we discussed. If I have a man show your army the way inside,' he said, apparently having decided not to do it personally, 'I will want assurances.'

'Come, Gal!' Balan cried. 'Not one of us will survive the war with the north and the south both. Be brave!'

'Stop being a fool,' Gal breathed, waving his hand around. 'No house will die willingly for Red Midgard that yet stands firm. You see phantoms.'

'No—' Balan said, for his would die willingly.

'Yes,' Gal interrupted Balan. 'If she fails,' Gal said empathetically, 'if that happens, we will purge you. I want your son, Taram,' he pointed a finger at the Blacktower, 'to stay with me during the coup. If it succeeds, we will go to the Temple together. If not? I will hand him over to the King myself. He will be released when we are all happy.'

'Yes,' Balan said tiredly. 'As we agreed.' He gave me a warning look, and I shrugged. As we had planned. I'd be delivered to Gal next, but I was not supposed to know that.

Gal opened his mouth and spoke. 'And you.' He nodded at Balan, who stiffened. Gal flashed a small, evil smile at Balan. 'You will come to my house with Taram. Should he,' he nodded at me, 'fail in his job, I will alert the King.'

Balan smiled at him carefully. 'We had not agreed thus.'

Crec was nodding, eyeing Gal with no surprise at all. Lith looked down, and I realized the two guests had already decided on this. The Lord Commander drawled an explanation. 'We do have to be careful, Balan. Many things can go wrong, and I agree with Gal. My house comes before the land.' Balan was looking at them, smiling thinly.

'If you and Taram do not come to visit the day after tomorrow, my lord,' Gal said sternly, 'the Brothers will be warned, and they will stop your king killing. Your house will fall. We have to have this assurance, heavier than you might have expected. And if we do, we have a deal.'

'Deal?' Balan chortled, fiddling with his rings. 'I said yes. Your Highness,' he bowed to Crec, who grinned. 'The Beast of the North,' Balan saluted them with a rough voice and Lith smiled wildly, grasping Crec's bicep, which pleased him immensely.

Gal raised his glass. 'The alliance of the three,' he said softly, his eyes never leaving me. 'You will have a home with the family, nephew. It will take time, but we will figure out a place for you.' *Or rather, where the grave shall be*, I thought. I nodded at him, and we did not speak again that evening. He was a relative, but I felt no kinship with him. I would not survive his hospitality, but I was committed. Would Balan and Taram? I doubted it. So did Balan, by the look on his face.

Balan got up. 'Rooms have been prepared for you in the inn of a village beyond the wood. It's just ten minutes away from here. You will be comfortable there.'

Lith grinned. 'I will accompany you,' she said and gave Crec a smile to melt an iceberg. They ate and drank and finally got up and went out in a merry mood. Gal nodded at me and I to him. His eyes never left the ring.

Balan was sitting still on his seat. He turned his eyes on me. 'Yes, Maskan. We must be very careful. And we will be. As I said, you will get your heritance. Though perhaps not as Gal planned it. Greed and lack of trust were ever the banes of lords. That he asked for me? That changes things a bit. Do not worry. We can deal with it.'

'Lith has an artifact, then,' I told him.

He raised his eyebrows and stammered. 'You … seen it?'

'I've seen it,' I told him. 'Not going to go into details.'

'She showed it to you?' he asked me. 'She is reckless.'

'Female faces only, it seems,' I said. 'But we appear to have things in common.'

'It is true.' He smiled. 'It's been very useful for us, that artifact. For spying. What face did she take?'

'Doesn't matter,' I said. 'So, some innocent will die, wearing Shaduril's face?'

'Yes,' he said heavily. 'We have time aplenty, later, to restore law to the land. There will be sacrifices, Maskan, to reach that goal. Perhaps we shall hang a real female criminal in her stead. I am sure we will find one.'

'Life is cheap, Lord. We are no better, then,' I said, my mouth sour. 'No better. We will see Crec on the throne, and there is no justice in that. And we will hang people who have not been judged.'

He squinted at me. 'Are you saying I am like Morag Danegell? Evil?'

I stood there and did not know what to say. 'I do not know. But Crec is. And Gal. And—'

'You will be head of one of the Nine Houses. You will have great power. You will be the Lord of the Harbor and master of merchants, and you will oversee executions. You can show your mettle then, and I hope you keep your innocence, boy.'

He was right, I had not thought of that. 'I—'

'Doubts are healthy, Maskan, for any man,' he told me. 'I will deal with this Gal's situation now. It will be difficult. Risky even. I am not sure if it will ruin everything, what they just did, and what I must do now. But I won't let him take my head after the King is gone. I'll act. And it will be well. Trust me.' He got up. 'Now, I will have the house locked up. Stay inside this night. There is something afoot later.'

'I'm always inside here, Lord,' I told him.

'Be so this night especially,' he said grimly.

'Yes, Lord,' I said. He had another plan. Gal and Crec had made a mistake.

He got up and nodded at me sagely. 'Here, to our future, boy.' He poured me red wine. 'One week, Maskan. Be ready,' he said and walked up the stairs. 'Kill the bitch.'

'Your mercenaries in place?' I asked him.

He hesitated. 'They are. They cost me a great deal,' he said. 'But it will all be repaid.'

'How many are there?'

He shrugged. 'Some two thousand? Half are already in the city. Disguised and hidden. You know where.' He walked off, calling for a guard to lock the doors as he pulled his keys and handed them to him.

I drank down my wine and brooded in the dark.
The butler Gray appeared and looked troubled.
'Yes?' I asked him as he stood there, his eyes glinting in the simmering light of the fire pit.
'Lord Taram. And your Lord Sand,' he said softly.
'What of them?'
'They are gone,' he said.

## CHAPTER 12

'What happened?' I asked him as we walked into the room.
'Lord Sand. I saw him speaking with old lady Illastria.' His voice was disapproving. 'Few speak to the lady. It's forbidden, even. And after this? He left the hall. He sneaked after some men heading for the beach entrance, and he did not come back. They said he ran past them, and they let him go, for they were not sure if he was allowed to leave. I know he is your friend, Lord, and I was wondering if you know where he went?'

I shook my head. 'Did he have anything with him?'

'Odd, Lord, but he had a shovel,' Gray informed me. 'They are renovating in one of the wings, and he grabbed a tool from there.'

'A shovel?' I asked and then cursed. He was going to bury our family.

'And Lord Taram,' the butler said, even more distressed. 'Was reading a letter in your room.' The letter. I had left it on the bed.

I rushed to the second floor, dashed into our room, and saw it was empty. I saw the letter, now stained, and crumpled in the corner. I rushed to it and picked it up. Then I read it. It was an official letter and in it, Balan listed all the terms of our deal. The coup of Seventh House, Shaduril. And what we were doing with whom. 'I've risked all. Even Shaduril.'

The butler grunted. 'I have known her all my life,' he said sadly. 'Lady Lith? I disdain of her. And what she did to you, just now, Lord. You will suffer for it. But sir, you must find your friend. Lord Taram looked furious. And he knows Sand left. He will want to hurt you. To punish you. And your friend is out there alone. I will tell Lord Balan, but perhaps you should find him?'

'Taram would risk his father's plans?' I asked, terrified.

'He ... like the family, all obey Lord Balan. But occasionally, when Lord Balan is not present, they do not. I cannot explain it.' He looked supremely bothered, his loyalty stretched.

'Why are you helping me?'

'Shaduril,' he said. 'She is like a child to me. I've known her for forty years.'

'I have to leave,' I said, my mind whirling.

'I would say that is accurate. You have to get your friend.' He looked anxious, which was unusual for the man.

'Should I trust any one of them? Balan?' I asked him. 'He might be able to help with Taram.'

He hesitated and said nothing. I nodded, and he looked visibly relieved as he did not have to betray his master. 'I can tell you the doors are all locked,' he reminded me.

I cursed. I could take Balan's face, perhaps, but dared not. 'Who has the keys?'

'Lord Balan,' he said softly. 'They are with him, and he is outside, dealing with the people who would leave. He has spares in his room.'

'You cannot—'

'No sir,' he said, regretfully. 'I will tell him everything later, but you have to—'

'Stay here for thirty minutes.'

'Why, sir?' he asked me.

'Do you have the keys to Balan's work and bedchamber? For Shaduril. I am asking for her.'

He shuddered and shook his head. 'The door is open. But there is something ... worked into the heavy bar ...' he began and went quiet. 'Only a Blacktower can ...'

I nodded at him, thinking. 'I'll be careful. Sit down while I tie you up. Just to make it look good. Is there a guard there?'

He nodded and gave a small smile. 'There is one. And sir. You need not worry about him. The guard. His life does not matter. Ask him to lift that bar.'

'No good?' I asked, surprised by his lack of compassion.

'He is beyond redemption. A thief and a murderer,' Gray said, and I accepted it. Sacrifices, as Balan said, had to be made.

'I'll tie you up now. Undress,' I said.

After a few minutes, I walked out. I wore the butler's leather shirt and woolen pants. And his face. I walked up the steps, stiff, arrogant as if I belonged there. My hand was bandaged, and I held it up, awkwardly. I went up the stairs and heard a clamor on the yard from the window. The guests were leaving. I walked up the steps and past the guard, a young man who was sniffling with cold. He nodded at me, his halberd dark in the shadows above him. The man's eyes were glittering as he followed me. *Let him be truly beyond redemption,* I thought.

I got to Balan's door and hesitated. It was indeed barred. There was the thick wooden bar blocking it, and I sensed not all was right with it. I held my hand awkwardly and hesitated. 'You there.'

The guard nodded at me. 'Yes, Gray?'

'Can you help me with the door and the bar? My hand, you see,' I indicated the heavy door. I looked and sounded bothered as if unused to asking for help.

'Lord Balan does not like anyone in his rooms when he is not around, Gray,' he said suspiciously, shifting from one foot to another.

'I am not a thief, fool,' I told him impatiently. 'He waits in the yard, don't you see? I am to fetch him a paper.'

'But—'

I hissed in anger and turned to leave. My steps were clicking on the tiles, and I walked toward the staircase. 'I'll go ask him to fetch it himself, then.'

'Wait, I'll do it,' the man said, his voice nervous. 'Yeah, I'll do it!' he added as I did not show any signs of stopping. I sighed, turned, and waved for the door.

'The bar, if you please. I'll take the responsibility,' I told him and felt terribly sad for him.

He nodded, set his halberd aside, and walked to the door, his armor clanking. I watched him reach for the bar. 'Better not get into trouble for this, Gray.'

'We'll see,' I said, and he arched an eyebrow at me as he lifted the bar. 'The little lord of ours makes it look so easy. Says only Blacktowers should do it, but this is not so heavy, is it? Í–'

There was no flash. No explosion. Nothing you might expect from a magical trap. I was not sure what kind of magic was placed on the wood, but it was deadly enough.

The guard shuddered. Then he fell on his back. He was still clutching the bar, but his armor was smoking, and I smelled burned flesh. I looked around to see if anyone had seen, but none had. I felt terribly sorry for the man and hesitated. I swallowed. 'Murderer and a thief,' I whispered to myself, hardening my soul. I stepped in and grabbed the handle to the room. I shuddered with fear, as I had not asked if there were other traps in there, but the handle felt normal, and the door opened up.

I turned and grabbed the guard's feet, careful not to disturb the bar, and dragged the man as I went in. I entered the room, left the guard in the doorway, and pulled the door closed. I looked around, smelled the air, and it was musty. I walked around the room, wondering at the shadows and the books all the while keeping an eye on the famous book, which was still on the table. All the secrets of the past? I'd read it, should I have the time. I popped my head into Balan's bedchamber. It was still as if frozen in time. Old flowers were hanging from a vase; remains of a dinner were forgotten on the table. The bed was dusty and the sheets stained. He did not sleep there.

I walked to his desk and opened up the drawers. There was clutter. I saw simple silver coins, some small crystals, bits of iron, and some strange gummy substance. It was like a pocket of a child. Then I found the drawer, which clinked and clanked as I drew it open. There, keys. Lots and lots of keys. Old and new keys, black and white, and … red. There was the key to the downstairs door; the route Sand had taken. I grabbed it, gathering determination. I noticed some of the Blacktower pendants at the end of the drawer, and took one, thanking the gods for small favors. Then I hesitated as I looked at the ancient book. I grabbed it, prayed to the gods again, and took it. No traps. I was alive, and I was a thief again. I dropped the thing in a leather bag set on the floor next to the table and walked out, calmly. I walked to my room, smiled at Gray, who did not ask questions and thanked him with a bow. 'For your teaching and kindness, I thank you.'

'I have a heart, no matter what you will think,' he answered and went on his way after I let him go.

I let my face change again, this time to Taram's. I felt revulsion as I touched it, but it would have to do. I went to the downstairs door, smiled at the guards, walked down the dark stairway, and looked around. None challenged me. I opened the door and walked to the beach. I heard commotion and bustle as far above the party was leaving slowly. I ran down the beach and climbed our usual route of misery. I dodged from shadow to shadow, wondering what to do next. I needed a horse. I could not get one in the Crimson Apex. I saw the lights of the larger village, named Kintarra, of High Hold, near the Broken Crown Way, and ran that way. It took half an hour, and I was lathered with sweat as I got there. I looked around, saw the large tavern and a stable next to it. I gathered myself and lifted my chin, walked to the stables and noticed men who came out to meet me. One hesitated, his eyes grew large. He grabbed his felt hat and bowed deep. 'My lord!'

'Saddle a horse, boy,' I told a mop-haired stable hand. 'I will return it later.'

'Lord, you passed this way not long ago. What happened to the other one?' he asked and blanched, as I looked at him furiously. 'Yes, my lord.'

I waited while they made a horse ready and noticed there was a lot of commotion in the tavern. People were running inside; maids were asking for instructions. 'What is going on in there?' I asked them.

'Ah! Lords Helstrom and Talin will stay in the tavern for the night. There is a storm brewing and the Maiden's Moon is famous for good ale and entertainment. Lord Balan, your father, paid for the whole establishment.' I grunted and fingered Larkgrin, which was in my pocket.

'Storm brewing?' I asked.

'I do not know,' said the felt hat. 'That is what she told me. Your sister.'

'Lith?' I half wondered.

'No,' he answered, looking confused.

So did I, no doubt, but I decided I had no time to think about it. I shook my head. 'Hurry up.' And they did. I was not an expert rider, but I doubted anyone would pay attention to me in the night. I mounted the horse, adjusted the stirrups, and whipped the beast. I dodged men at the village gates and did not look back.

*Damned idiot*, I told myself repeatedly, though I was unsure if I meant Sand or myself. I should have told him everything. But Shaduril and perhaps Balan's promises had made me forget him. Sand had undoubtedly gone to bury our family. Perhaps he was on foot.

I rode into the darkness and left Kintarra behind. The horse was uncertain of the way, but I saw a glimpse of someone riding the Broken Crown Way, which was not too far to the east, and I whipped the horse through the fields and small wooded hills to get there. I found it and took the way to the east. The Three Sisters were shining high in the sky, lighting the land enough to see the way. I dared not leave the road, rode through a smaller village, dodged some corrals full of startled poultry and the fox that had been slavering over them, passed a white façade of a local tavern where men were bustling and rode for the east without looking back. A road sign showed the direction of Dagnar, and I kept on the road and whipped the horse like crazy.

After two hours of this, I saw the lights of the Dagger Hill, Dagnar's many splendid towers and walls, and then I saw the familiar game trails that led north. There was the usual way stop with spare horses as well. I began to find my way towards the Wooded Blight, tentatively, for I did not wish to get lost. Surely, I would get to the Green Hall before Sand. Unless he had stolen a horse.

I found the remains of the Green Hall. It was a burnt down husk of past glories, the many-roomed cozy hall of a robber baron. It was our hideout, but only a memory now. With apprehension, I saw there was a lathered horse in the corner of the hall, tied to a burnt timber. I rode that way, cursing softly, calming my horse with gentle strokes, and I hoped it would not make a sound. I dismounted, left the beast there and rounded the corner carefully, holding Larkgrin in my palm.

The tree was empty. There were ropes hanging down it. All had been cut.

And Sand was on his knee before a large mound, sobbing.

I approached and stepped on a twig, and he twirled around and pulled his scimitar. He saw me and stared at my face, and I cursed and took my own. He nodded carefully, unsure if I was welcome, but I walked over anyway. We stared at the mound for a long time. A stench wafted up from it, rotten meat mixing with mud and grit. 'Gods. He never smelled like roses,' Sand whispered. 'But this is just terrible.'

I snorted, and he did as well. We chuckled and wiped our faces as we took steps back. I pushed him. 'I am sorry.'

'You should be sorry,' he whispered. 'You treated me like vermin.'

'I should have told you about the deal I made with Balan. He did not trust you. But I should have. And I did. Sort of. I did not think. I failed.'

'You have grown proud as shit,' he told me. 'They dangled this new life before your eyes like a piece of fresh meat for a starving wolf, and you jumped.'

'I jumped,' I agreed. 'I mainly jumped for Shaduril. I will jump still, to kill the King and to save her, as well as to keep our oath. But I won't forget us. Not again. Nor will I abandon you. I don't know what my future holds. But you are part of it.'

'We won't be thieving together again, not ever,' he lamented. 'I will miss that.'

I shrugged. 'I think nobles are far worse thieves than we ever were, Sand. And perhaps I shall be a thieving noble as they are. And maybe we can figure something out.'

'Perhaps we can,' he whispered. 'He was buried, after all. They were.'

'They were?' I asked him.

He shook his head, his face white with a strange emotion. 'Yes. Someone cut them down and put him to the ground, though burning him would have been kinder. Gods would have—'

'It would have,' I agreed.

'We should leave,' he said. I hesitated, and he saw it and shook his head.

I went on. 'Balan is making his plans, but he tells me not to worry, that he will deal with the issues, but I am not sure it will be that simple,' I told him. 'I will try this anyway. But I have an idea.'

'It's high time you started to think on your own,' Sand growled. 'We should go away. Listen–'

I interrupted him and grabbed his arms. 'I must go back. But I think you should not come back to the Crimson Apex.'

'I was going to tell you. I won't,' he said. 'Look—'

'I think you should disappear. Find Shakes. The Lamb. Until I call for you. Hold onto this.' I thrust the book at him.

He took it and stared at it with confusion. 'What is it?'

'A book. Famous book. I'll explain it later, but it's collateral against Balan's treachery.'

'So I am basically out of the picture,' he whispered. 'I'd have to hide with this book. While you ... No. You come with me.'

'I don't know exactly what is in that book, but it tells the history of Midgard. There is bound to be a hoard of delicate information that might hurt any of the high houses. It's a goldmine. Keep it. It has a lot of worth. It might even have enough information to punish Crec and Gal if Balan does not. If I die, figure out what to do with it. They cannot find you, not easily if Shakes helps you out of town. And they have to wonder, always wonder what might happen if I am betrayed. If I die. I will have to see this through. We made a pact to punish the bastards. We swore to avenge our family. I will try it, but I need you to hide for both of us.'

He chuckled. 'A beautiful plan. But it is far too late.'

'Take this,' I told him and pulled at my stolen pendant. 'It will keep you safe from the King as well.'

'No,' he said. 'Look. I am going to the King.'

I stared at him in total stupefaction. 'The King?'

'The King, yes,' he said. 'I spoke to Illastria. And their old keep? I peeked in. Listen.'

And he died.

A whip-like voice rang through the woods. We turned to look up the hillside. 'Fire! Fire at them!' we heard a man yell imperiously.

'No! Hold!' another answered. It was a Brother's deep voice, and the archers he had told to stand down had already acted and released their missiles. Arrows rained down on us. Some hit the grave mound, others the muddy yard, some went through shrubs, and one pierced Sand's face. He fell howling, shuddered and then he went very silent, his eyes open and bloodshot. I turned in horror to look up to the wooded hill. The White Brother Knight was up there, holding the dreaded whip and the sword, gazing down at us. His archers were spreading out. I hesitated and pulled at Sand. An arrow hit the mud before me, and I let go of him. 'Stop firing, you dog-faced mongrels!' the Brother hollered. I grabbed the bag with the book, cursed and wept and ran away, looking back at the terrible Brother, who was now mounting a horse. His hand glowed, and I heard him calling a name. Mine. My hair stood upright on my neck.

I vaulted on my horse. Despite the order, arrows flew around me again, and one struck Sand's horse and the beast fell, whinnying, the sound strangely like that of a child. I whipped my horse for the darkness. I rode like a madman and heard some of the King's men ride after me. I heard a deep thrumming noise, a horse heavier than the others beating the ground with its dreadful hooves, and so I knew the Brother was leading them. I stroked the amulet, knowing he could not find me, not quickly if I did manage to escape.

I rode to the south, crossed the Broken Crown Road, took to the cliffs and meadows before the Arrow Straits, and turned to the west. I rode carelessly, then waited. And rode again. I was soon breathing hard, but still I went on, riding and stopping every ten minutes. There were no sounds that I could hear from the men pursuing me, the houses I passed were asleep. I hesitated for a moment as I considered my situation. Sand was dead. It was my fault. *Should I go back? Yes.* Where else could I go? Shaduril needed me. I considered the bag. I spied a branch on a curiously twisted tree, one that was dead and sturdy. It was by a stream of silvery water, and there were mossy boulders around it. I sighed and hefted the bag. Then I threw it. It spun in the air, twisted as it flew and got caught on a sturdy branch. It was swinging there, apparently well stuck. I nodded. I would never find it again, I was sure.

I shook my head as I tried to memorize the place. A stream led south, and there I heard the noise of the waves of the Arrow Straits. The sea was hitting the cliffs. The land was open there, and I hesitated, and then I forced myself forward. I had lost them, had I not?

I rode on, slowly believing I had made it. I had to get back to the Crimson Apex and face Balan. I stopped at the cliff's side. The Straits were below me, and there was series of dagger-like boulders down there. I turned to squint up to the woods and saw the twisted tree. I might find it again.

Then, from behind me, came the neigh of a horse.

*Shit.*

I turned to look that way, the impending doom pressing heavily on my heart. There, three shadowy archers were riding forward, their bows held comfortably on their sides. A dark knight sat on his horse, his hand glowing gently, and the dreaded whip uncoiled as he rode forward. 'Take him. Alive,' he rumbled. Birds flew from the woods around me, startled by the armored men. They were very careful and spread to right and left. 'Come smoothly, Maskan,' the Brother said.

I shook my head and held onto Larkgrin. 'You killed my friend.'

'I've killed a lot of friends to someone, boy,' he said. 'But this one was a mistake. One I didn't make. I didn't give the order. You heard me.'

'It's my mistake,' I whispered, for I should have done something a long time ago to get them buried. *Sand would be alive*, I thought.

'Whom are you staying with, boy?' he asked as they spread out around me. 'We need to know. It's crucial.'

'Torture me if you like,' I said defiantly. 'I'll not talk otherwise.'

He laughed so hard inside his helmet that his white horsehair crest flew to his chest and face. He pushed it away from the helm's eyeholes. 'I don't have to torture you, you ridiculous fool. Morag will make you sing, easily he will,' he laughed some more. 'He will be euphoric.'

I got ready to die. My horse was suddenly nervous as the men guided their horses around us. It whinnied, and more birds flew out of the branches.

White Brother raised his head in alarm.

A small army of men charged out of those woods. They wore dark leathers, no insignia on them, and they were fast and looked deadly. They carried long spears and axes, and their faces were covered. An archer turned and fired his arrow at one, sending the man face down to the ground. Another shot his arrow, but it went wide.

It made no difference. There were easily fifty of them.

One sat on a horse, a dark beast of noble bearing. While the newcomers swarmed around me to chop at the hapless archers, this figure was pointing a finger at the White Brother.

The beastly Knight was pulling at a sword, his white horsehair flying around him wildly as his horse reared. The dark mass of warriors stabbed and ripped at the archers and their animals and soon formed a spear bristling crescent around the fearless Brother.

'Kill him,' whispered the rider, and I knew it was Taram. He was not supposed to know about our business. But yes, of course, he did, having read my letter. But where did the men come from? Balan's men? Was he there to save me for Balan, or to kill me for his pleasure, later?

The mass of men charged. The White Brother rumbled something, and I felt a wonderful tug of power fluttering around me in the air, but the result was not as pleasant. All of us fell to our knees as a wickedly fiery storm of fire whipped up amidst this mass of charging men. Cinders flew; flames danced in a whirlwind of death. A dozen men fell in blazing flames and made no sound as they died. Others fell down, dazed, but most went forward. They were no longer organized, and the knight charged the mass. The whip went up, came down and ripped a man nearly in two. A sword stabbed down at one man, then another, and both fell on their backs, shuddering. Spears emerged from the shadows to stab the knight, and then I felt another tug of power. The Danegell Brother was using mighty artifacts, as the fierce enemy covered himself with dull, gray stone skin. I could not believe it. He looked like stone, and probably it was rock, for the deadly spears shattered on him like icicles. The knight was moving slowly now as if the spell was hampering him, but he let the enemy come to him. The whip went up repeatedly, the enemy swarmed him and tried to pull him down, but could not. It was like ants trying to tear down a mountain. The sword stabbed, it backed up, then stabbed, and the horse carried the deadly thing around.

Some twenty men were left, a ragged band of silent warriors. They hesitated.

Taram cursed softly. He shuddered and swayed, and I realized he was also doing something with magic. 'How—' I began.

'Silence!' he hissed and released the power. I felt it. Dark vines grew from under the Brother's horse, and there were thorns in them. They entwined the beast and the men around it and tightened around the Brother and his mount. A line of fire left the knight's hands, rushed near me for Taram, who pulled his horse away. He shook his head and uttered a curse. He charged forward and dragged me on top of his horse. 'Kill him!' he yelled at his remaining men. 'Die rather than get caught!' he added as I dangled before him, rather ignobly as his horse swerved too close to the Brother. The whip went up and reached for us. Taram howled as it ripped at his back. The knight screamed in anger as he tried to release himself from the vines; masked men died as the sword came down again and again, but we were riding to the night.

I struggled in his lap, but he slapped a hand across my neck. He leaned over. 'Silence, I said it once.'

'Let go of me, Taram,' I hissed.

'You saw what he did,' he spat. 'They have powerful artifacts. I could not touch him, not even with what I have.'

'What artifact do you have?' I snapped. 'Everyone has something. I thought your father did not trust you.'

'He had none else when we found out Sand was gone,' he said dourly. 'Before that I was curious and read your letter. And learned of his plans at the same time. I heard from a guard Sand had left. I rode out, but Father sent those men to find me. They did. Don't ask how. They told me to obey him. Now I am in, no matter what.'

'You read my letter,' I said.

He said nothing, but the grip on my neck was constricting. 'I did. I read it. I don't approve. Not at all. I knew he was plotting, but I had no idea how high ambitions he has. But now he has to trust me. And I'll face you when it's done. I'll fight to keep you far from Shaduril.'

'Fight me now,' I said.

He hummed. 'Later. Where is Sand? I tried to find him before Father's men found me.'

'Why?'

He leered and shrugged.

*To kill him,* I thought.

He went on, with a bored voice. 'I'm happy I found you, though. Had no damned idea you would be this stupid. It cost the house a lot of men, just when we need them the most. Best hope they won't recognize any of them. But they won't talk. That is for sure.'

'Sand is dead. That Brother killed him. Like he did our family,' I said, and I thought of my poor friend. 'You wanted to kill Sand.'

He chuckled. 'I might have been tempted. But I was given the men to keep me in line.'

'They are not here now,' I taunted.

He didn't reply and rode for a time. He led the animal deeper to the wooded hills, rode around villages and houses and seemed to know the ways very well. Finally, he stopped to sit on his horse, steadily, listening. He pushed me off the horse and nodded for northwest. 'That way.'

'How far are we from the Crimson Apex?' I asked.

'An hour, two, depending on if there will be unfortunate accidents on the way,' he said darkly. 'Your friend got us into some serious trouble.'

'Your father has enough trouble with Crec and Gal,' I whispered.

'They are no trouble,' he spat. 'If the Brothers guess it is the Blacktower family plotting against the crown? There will be armies marching our way. Happily, there are hundreds of noble families along the road, and some are much more likely suspects that the Tenth House.'

'He followed me. That knight.'

'He did,' Taram agreed. 'I trained those men for five months. Your Sand deserved a bigger punishment than death. And they called me reckless.'

'My medallion should have stopped the White Brother from finding me,' I told him. 'But he did. Perhaps he still can.'

'Perhaps he was following your horse?' Taram snickered. 'Did he know its name?'

'Sand is dead, and you are joking?' I spat at him with spite.

'I'm always having some fun, Maskan. Life is dreadfully short without pleasure. But I will help Father from now on, and you relax. The Brother won't find us now. Perhaps Father's craft with his books and artifacts is not so keen after all. Perhaps it only works for our family. I don't know how he builds them. I know not.'

'Balan said they were looted from Hel's armies,' I said.

'And perhaps they were,' he told me impatiently, thinking me tedious.

'Where is Lith? If she was not available to go after me?'

He chuckled. 'Lith and Shaduril. How you all vex me. I really hate the thought of you buzzing around them. And Shaduril seems to love you. Gods know what you thought when you reached for her, peasant, but that letter was pretty indicative why Father wanted to keep me in the dark. He agrees. Incredible. Shaduril and you. I cannot fathom it.'

I cursed, turned, and ripped him from his horse. His eyes betrayed incredulity as I slammed him onto the leaves and grass. His hand moved for his dagger, and I suddenly remembered the magic he had wielded, but I was beyond caring. Sand was dead. He mocked Sand. And me. 'Balan promised me Shaduril. And she loves me more than anything. And I love her. Nothing can change that.'

'Really?' he chuckled. His face flared in a hideous grin. I blinked a few times, but when I looked at him again, he had calmed himself. His eyes were cold and calculative. 'Does she?' Taram hissed and ripped himself off me. 'We will see.' He pushed past me and mounted his horse. We traveled through the night and came to the Broken Crown road. We traveled hills and meadows near the road, avoiding it. There were riders on it, mostly peasants working very late, or early, depending on the point of view. They were hauling food and drink for Dagnar, which was preparing for Yule feasts. Finally, we arrived at the end of the road and went past the familiar village. Taram stopped suddenly in front of the whitewashed tavern where I had gotten the horse from. He guided his horse aside and gazed at the stables by the tavern. They were full of horses. He dismounted, tied his horse to a pillar and walked into the tavern. He turned to look at me. 'Come then. Let us go apologize for your lost beast.' He laughed and went in. I hesitated and followed him.

Inside, there had been a massacre.

Lith raised her face to look at me, in shock. Shaduril turned, equally shocked. Both were spattered in blood, and so were their men, a gloomy band of Blacktower men. There were dead everywhere. On the stairs, the tables and the floors. Many had been wrapped up for removal and burial.

Taram snickered. 'Is this the Shaduril you love?'

'You bastard,' Shaduril said and looked from Taram to me.

She had slain men. It was clear. Her beautiful sword was stained with blood. At her feet, were the bodies of the mop-haired boy and a woman. Others had been pages and servants of Crec and Gal. Blacktower warriors stood in silent ranks on the walls, eyeing her, waiting for her reaction. I took a horrified, hesitant step forward. Lith had been bent over Gal, whose face and chest was one ragged wound. 'Maskan?' Shaduril whispered.

'What in Hel's rotten tit is going on in here?' Taram asked her with mocking laughter. 'Excuse me, our friend has quite forgotten his voice.'

She straightened and glowered at Taram. 'Get out!'

'Oh, don't think you need to explain yourself to him,' he told Shaduril. 'Lith had him this day. I heard it. They were at it for an hour. But I am going to be fair. She took your face. I doubt that matters to you, eh?' The man laughed and bowed at her and went out.

Lith wiped her face on the back of her hand and adopted a stern look. She nodded at the guards, some of whom hauled still living men aside, some five villagers. They had not killed everyone yet. 'It is not true, Shaduril,' she said with a worried voice. I felt half grateful to her, but then I remembered she had planned on extorting me and now she could not. I looked at Shaduril's face. The girl that had sat on the beach with me was gone. In her place, there was a hopeless thing whose eyes glowed with anger. She turned from me, her explanations banished, and walked to the side, where she sat down and stared at me and Lith. Lith looked at her carefully and then turned to me. 'I don't know if that can be fixed. She will want us dead. So. You have seen this. What now?'

'Are you not supposed to be in Dagnar?' I asked Shaduril while ignoring Lith. 'Why did you kill these—'

'She was needed here,' Lith said softly. 'Forget it.'

'Yes, I see you were needed here,' I told her and looked around the room. I blanched as I spied two very young boys amidst the corpses. And a maid. The floor was awash with sticky blood. I shook my head in shock when I spied Crec amidst the dead. 'There are your people. The village is yours,' I whispered. 'And how will you deal with the quest now? You killed your allies.'

'It was necessary,' she whispered. 'This was the ideal place to ambush them. But the villagers must not expose us.' Lith sighed, and I fixed my eyes away from her. She pointed a finger at the dead. 'This is part of the war. Murdering and killing in the dark are a means to an end. You knew we were capable of it,' she said. 'They made a mistake.'

'How will you achieve anything without them?' I despaired. 'The two lords.'

'Balan has a plan for that,' she said. 'I agree it is desperate. But we have you. We will use your face.'

'I cannot …' I began, but yes, perhaps I could. I went quiet and she nodded. *Murderers.* There were children.

'It will be perilous and hard, and much will be asked of you,' she whispered. 'And I am sorry Taram screwed up you two.' She nodded at her sister.

'She will want to die now,' I said, looking at Shaduril.

'She will want to kill us first, I said. And if she does want to die,' Lith said softly, 'you have me.'

'Gods laugh,' I said and spat at her feet.

She frowned at that but went on, 'Taram was cruel to bring you here. Love, you need not worry. One day all this will be over. You will smile again. Dreams are born of nightmares.'

I did not listen to her. I only stared at Shaduril. Something had died in the girl I loved. I saw it. She shook her head and went to stand in the corner, in the shadows. I looked at her and felt miserable. No matter the reasons, no matter what had happened, she was hurt. It was my fault, no matter if I had been fooled.

'Gal was an ally we needed,' I whispered. 'He had a way to the Tower. I am not sure I can change that with a simple face trick. Keys and passphrases will be needed.'

'There is a lot to learn, but we will do well. Crec is an issue, and the Brothers will have to be dealt with, but we will do our best. We have to think about it. Do not worry. Please. We have an excellent chance to change many things.'

'I see,' I told her, thinking how strange she was. She had been a loving, even vulnerable creature in my arms, not so long ago. Now, she was a practical killer who did not flinch standing over a child's corpse. Like Shaduril.

'Sand?' she asked me. 'Taram was sent men and then to find you.'

'Sand died,' I told her. 'This amulet did not work. We were ambushed by the White Brother.'

'I am sorry,' she said softly. 'I knew he would be in danger eventually. He was not really useful for the plan, other than to keep you in check. And he felt left out, no doubt. You were showered with promises, he was forgotten.'

'Yes,' I whispered. 'It is my fault.'

She saw I was heartbroken. Distraught, hurt. Terrified of the scene and the murdering things before me. She stood there, swaying for a long time, wondering, thinking and finally, she sighed. 'Go to Balan. It will be all right. In the end, all will be well. Even Sand. I promise you this.'

'You cannot speak for Hel,' I told her.

'I can try,' she grinned.

'Shaduril?'

She turned to look at me. There was despair in her eyes, but also a desire. And she voiced the desire. 'I really want to see you die, Maskan, painfully. Just to make you feel what I feel right now.'

'But—'

'Go away, Maskan,' Lith said with a whisper. 'It's over.'

I cursed and walked away. I went out and saw Taram sitting on his horse. I hesitated. I should run, I thought. But I would not. They are all mad, evil. Taram winked. 'I did not have to show you this, did I? But I wanted to. Grows you up. It is over. There was nothing real with Lith and you. And now there is nothing with Shaduril.'

I spat at his horse's feet. 'Truly you cannot hurt me any worse.'

He hesitated. 'I can't? Let me think about that for a moment. 'His face twitched and his eyes gleamed dangerously. I walked past him for the Crimson Apex. He turned to ride before me. He rode ahead of me the whole way, not saying anything. When we arrived at the Crimson Apex, I stared at the old keep, but it looked dead. As dead as Shaduril had. The bastard Taram. The fool Maskan.

Balan met us at the doorway. He was scowling at Taram and then pointed a finger at me. 'You killed a guard.'

'He killed himself,' I told him, feeling sorry for the man. 'And you killed a village.'

'What?' he breathed. 'Who—'

'Taram took me to visit the village in question,' I grimaced as I stared at the man.

He nodded, rubbing his face. 'It has to be a secret Crec and Gal died. You see? The villagers would know.'

'No,' I said spitefully.

'And you took my book,' he accused me with a quivering voice. 'Why?'

I laughed. 'And that's it for the village? Why? You kill left, you kill right, and you promise away family and friends and allies so fast you probably cannot even remember what you have agreed and with whom. That book is filled with shit I can burn you with. Or anyone,' I told him bitterly. 'I'll never return it. I'll use it to make sure you will not become a ruler of the land. Oh, we will kill the royals, but that book is mine now.'

Balan's eyes turned to Taram, who smiled smugly. 'I knew you were a mistake,' Balan told him. 'You are mad.'

'I am,' Taram agreed. 'But I will help you now. Want me to kill him?'

Balan cursed us both softly. 'No. I don't like this.'

'I don't like many things,' I told him. 'You are one manipulative bastard. Who will be the king? Not you.'

'We will find a king, boy,' he told me softly. 'Crec has a son, I think. He might grow into our man. But you? You are risking our endeavor. You are ruining us. You stole our most excellent book, the ancient chunk of history. You were very nearly caught. Get clear, boy,' he told Taram, who bowed stiffly.

We heard a rumbling noise.

'Come inside,' he hissed and pulled at me. I poked a finger at him and pushed him back. I turned to look at the old keep. From it, an army emerged. There were dozens, then hundreds of well-armored men marching out. Hundreds. Spear points bristled, shields clanked and cowled men looked ahead in the dark. There was one leading them, larger than the others, and he was not cowled. 'Valkai?' I whispered.

'Valkai,' Balan agreed. 'He did not die of the hanging. We spared his life. He is impossible to kill. I have armed all my own men and bought hundreds of others, lots, and lots, and Valkai there will lead the last of them to Dagnar for the day of reckoning. There are ways in and he knows them all. He knows the Old City. There are a thousand there already, and these will make a formidable army.'

'Shaduril is in much worse danger now,' I said darkly. 'You expect me to fill the shoes of those two men?'

Balan turned me around. The pupils of his eyes were tiny, his face drawn. 'Grec and Gal betrayed me. They would have disposed of me. And you. And Shaduril. The whole family. The Mad Watch would have blamed us for the crime and off to hang we would have gone while they enjoyed the fruits of our work and sacrifices. No. You will take Gal's place after the Queen dies. We will use Valkai's tunnels of the Old City to hide the men and sneak them near the Thin Way. You will get them in. It will be messy. But it will be done.'

'I see,' I told him. 'And when Crec and Gal don't return home?'

'I will send letters signed by them to the families,' he said with a small, ferret-like grin. I have their seals as well. They are busy and out of town for a week. Don't worry about the details. Soon, things will be back to normal. What you will need to do, Maskan, is to kill the Queen, and then meet the new lord of the mint wearing Gal's face. You will lead them in. Later, you will be Crec and command the troops to purge the enemy from the city.'

I looked at the marching, ominous army. They would take the route to the city and stage an assault into the Tower of the Temple. People would die. There were a thousand of them now, some were not armored but apparently peasants. Others were young, others old.

'I'm taking all my people to war,' Balan said softly.

'Fine.'

He scowled and hesitated. 'Fine. I am sorry for your friend. I am. But I am not happy about the theft.'

'Behead me, Lord,' I told him.

'Funny,' he whispered. Balan looked at the figure of Taram. 'For good or for bad, he is now in.'

'He was going to kill me,' I told him. 'And Sand.'

'I cannot guard you against him. Be careful. I will have Lith with you until the business is concluded. Taram is unstable.'

'I'd rather not—'

He laughed but then looked sober and sad. 'I see. She broke you and Shaduril, then. Perhaps for the better. Think of your dead family, Maskan. Think of the glory of nobility and Gal's house. Your father's house. Go and do us proud. Later on? Who knows if things will change for the better for you and her.'

'Who knows?' I echoed him. 'As for you. You will give me another letter.'

'I—'

I pushed him, and he stared at me in astonishment. 'In that letter, you will confess the murder of the village. I have the book. I want this as well. You will not be the king.'

He hesitated and shuddered with indecision. Then, after a long while, he nodded. 'You will have it,' he said and went in. I hesitated and followed him, and I noticed Illastria was not in her usual spot at the end of the main hall. Her desk had been cleared.

Our room was silent and empty. So was the keep. All the men and even the servants had marched off.

# BOOK 4: QUEEN'S BANE

*'I despise him too much. And he did dare me. He said I cannot hurt him any worse than I did. I think I can.'*
**Taram to Lith**

## CHAPTER 13

It was the day before the Yule feast. Something akin to snow was falling from the sky in a wet, freezing drizzle. We were standing in the shadows of an alley near House Tenginell, where the Queen was supposed to make an entrance. The alley held no warmth, and the wind was blowing through it. Lord Balan was on a horse. The Lord of the Harbor was dead, and I was unsure how it would play out when the King had to fall. They had men, yes, hidden in the city, but likely not enough to take the wall of the Tower of the Temple, and should they get in through the mint with me leading as Gal, perhaps the Brothers would fight very well. I had not seen Shaduril after that evening, but I knew she hated me. Sand was dead.

And I was about to begin my part in the show.

The Tenginell house was located in the Third Ring, not far from the mint or the Affront, in fact, and it was a very well-guarded affair. There was a dark gray wall and then a gatehouse built of white and pinkish stones. The stones were lined with green moss. The house itself had seen better times I decided while I shivered with the damned weather. I stared at the strange circular main building with four stories and a crenelated roof with the house flags. There was a red snowflake on a white field on the flag, a delicate symbol and strangely peaceful. Tenginell was the Ninth House, not an overly powerful house.

But they had the Queen.

'When will she appear?' a man whispered.

'They will be here,' Lith whispered from the shadows, not far. 'Patience, dolts. Patience. And keep alert.'

'What if they use some underground tunnel?' I asked her. 'The city is full of them, as you know.'

'That is her,' a hulking soldier told us and nodded towards the mouth of a smaller street some hundreds of yards away. 'I'm sure of it.' There was movement there, indeed. A procession of savage armored men on horses surrounded a tall figure, riding on a sleek, white horse. There were seven Brothers riding before them.

'Hardly subtle. Didn't they say they would be subtle as she visits her house?' I asked. 'That she would sneak to her family? That is as secretive as a dozen roaring drunk sailors trying to attend a wedding.'

'Shh,' Lith said. 'Perhaps the late events have made them value security over everything else. Does not matter. That is her.' She nodded at the tall figure, and I saw it was she. Her face was covered with dark clothing, leaving her hair and eyes free, and those eyes were brilliant blue as she was nodding at the men around her. The gate to the Tenginell house was opened, and a slight man peered out of it, then nodded back inside and they filed in. Balan guided his horse near us and sat in silence as the parade came closer.

'Falg is the one at the end of the procession,' he whispered. Indeed, there rode a wide-shouldered man with thick, braided hair, and a sword and an ax on his silvery belt. 'Take a good look at him.' And I did. Most of all, his eyes were grim and cold, dull and full of life's misery. He was a slave, a warrior, and a man who lived his life serving until death. He had no love in his soul, no fear, no hope.

'Why would they have someone like that serving the Queen?' I whispered. 'He looks homicidal.'

'He's from the Shadowed Mountains,' Lith whispered. 'They swear a life oath if captured. They are wonderfully loyal, get by with very little, and no matter what they think about their masters, they will fight for them until their oaths are fulfilled. He, like any man, hopes to see home one day, but he won't.'

'I see,' I told her and eyed the wealthy procession trotting inside the gates and to the yard. There were horses neighing beyond the gates, orders were barked, and some laughter could be heard.

'The poor pale Queen,' Lith said spitefully. 'Very pale, very dangerous. But soon, much more white.'

I nodded, unhappy with my doubts. They were criminals. Deadly, dangerous killers. Our royals should die, indeed. It was my oath with Sand. Balan said they wanted to destroy the world of Red Midgard. *He was right, was he not?* Rumors of war were everywhere. And the King had killed my family. He had ordered them hung. And Sand had died to them.

But I did not know the Queen. And I would poison her. How could I?

'Do you have the poison?' Balan asked me as if he had read my thoughts.

I patted my chest. There, in a yellow bottle were three pebbles of gray color right next to Balan's two letters. 'Yes. I have it.'

'Good,' he said. 'I know this is hard. But think of your mother and your family, your father, even. They hung. They begged, cried, perhaps, and paid the ultimate price. No matter how much you distrust me, this will be good for the people. Do not hesitate. Never hesitate. Or you will die. And so shall we.'

'I will do my best,' I told him morosely, afraid. He was glowering at me, and I scowled at him. 'I will do more than my best! I will exceed all expectations, even.'

'You had better, thief,' he said. 'The Dark Sands event begins in a few hours. Falg will likely leave very soon to prepare for it. The Queen will eat in a bit, and perhaps an hour from now, we shall move.'

'Yes, Lord,' I told him.

'For Shaduril, do not fail,' he added. 'I know Lith made her wretched, but she is still there. I don't want you in the family, Maskan, but I don't want to see her unhappy, either.'

'We will see,' I whispered, avoiding Lith's long looks. 'And if I get her back, you won't get the letter back, nor the book.'

He hesitated at that and shook his head slowly, his eyes resentful. He nodded at his daughter. 'Lith will tell you where to go after the killing. We must go to the mint, as soon as we can, so please hurry. Shaduril's life depends on it. Gal's treachery cost us time, at least. Follow her instructions, then and later. All of them. To the dot,' he said and rode away.

'In there,' Lith said, and nodded at a house on the corner of the alley. There was a door, we entered it and found a former tavern. Men remained on the streets to look at the Tenginell house. Lith walked the shadows to sit by the window and showed me a seat across from her. She nodded at some of her men, who disappeared. She was beautiful, her smile wide, if nervous, and she was mad enough to think I'd let her back into my life, for she lifted her foot on my lap as soon as I sat down. I resisted the urge to break it. She saw my face and sighed. 'Come now! It was Taram who hurt you. Not I. I only made both of us happy, briefly, and I am not even done with you. I would and will get you later, for Shaduril is a sad, dull specimen, and no man could love such a morose girl forever. Am I not desirable? Worth your time?'

'I do not deny,' I told her morosely, 'that you are beautiful. But so is a poisonous flower. Fine. You kept your promise to keep our … mistake a secret. But I love her. And I do not find her boring. I have seen her whooping in the surf, happy as the sun.'

She hesitated at that and rubbed her forehead as if fighting a memory. 'She was happy once. I remember that as well. But we loved the same man, and she has not been the same since. I loved the boy. I won. Now? It's all happening again. Except you claim you love her over me! It is beyond my understanding. You don't know the first damned thing about love. Massage. Calf.'

I hesitated. She kicked my shin. I cursed and pulled her foot up and removed her short, fur-lined boot and massaged her calf, as instructed. Her skin was cold, but then, we were all freezing. She moaned in pleasure, and I looked away. 'This good?' I asked her. 'Better than in the tub?'

'It is excellent, Maskan,' she groaned. 'I knew you would get the hang of it. You took Father's book,' she murmured.

'I did,' I said. 'He'll not rule. That book will make sure of it.'

'He will need it back,' she said softly, eyeing me.

'Why?' I asked spitefully. 'A murderer like him won't dictate anything to me. There will be a king, and I'll make sure it won't be someone he controls. No.'

'He won't,' she agreed. 'Crec returns.'

'Huh?'

She smiled. 'Perhaps you will keep Crec's face and live your life as him? Gal will die off, and you will be the king. Then I'd have you! I'll be the queen. And you can let him have the book back. You have his letter, no? Surely enough?'

'What?' I asked, still distracted by her suggestion.

'It's possible,' she said, and I shuddered with anger. 'Crec's son cannot wipe his rear on his own, little less rule the other houses. But you can.'

'You seem very sure you can slay Falg,' I stated, my mind whirling with her words. *King? Living as Crec? Never.* 'He looks like a capable fighter. And he had a partner as well, no?'

'We can kill one or two men, yes, no matter their worth. We have these men here, and you saw the army yesterday. Some will be at hand,' she grinned and poked me with her other foot, demanding I employ a more vigorous approach to her toes, and I did my best.

'What,' I asked her, 'is her name? The Queen's?'

'Name?' she said, staring at me in exasperation. 'You people of the Bad Man's don't even know the names of your royals? It is fine, perhaps. Don't ask the name of someone you aim to kill. We call her the Pale Lady.'

'Very well,' I said miserably. 'But I'm not like you. I will do this only once. And try to live with it on my conscience.'

She stared at me in astonishment. 'Didn't you kill our guard? Pray, tell me what I am like?'

I regretted saying anything but shrugged away my apprehensions. 'Vivacious. Beautiful. But I don't think you care about anything. Except a foot rub, of course,' I added to take away the edge of my claim. But I could not. I looked away from her. 'You are murderers. Did you help kill those villagers?'

She sighed. 'Really? Did I? Yes. It's war, Maskan. And I used to care,' she said with a soft voice. Yet, her eyes were hard as stone as she yanked her leg off my lap. 'You know nothing of my hardships. And I care for many things. You as well.'

'I don't think I will ever be as casual about it as you are. Or ... Shaduril.'

'It's in my nature, Maskan, to enjoy occasional bloodshed, same as Shaduril, but you need not worry. You'll perform just fine. Just do this one deed and then play Gal and Crec. Imagine it is sugar you pour on her dinner and then go.'

'Alert,' a man said from the doorway. 'Look out!' We jumped up. Lith pulled on her boot while jumping with one foot, cursing. We moved out carefully. We saw there was something happening at a side gate, a small, red door on a side street.

'Damn, he is early. I wonder if the Queen skipped her lunch,' Lith growled.

Men came out. A Brother, the White one rode out of it. He was whipping his horse; the horsehair tail was flying from his helmet. He passed by quickly, riding his horse through the higher parts of the city. Then, more men came out, some to look around cautiously. We saw a man whispering to the tallest of the men, and there was some altercation going on between them. Then the gate opened fully with a sudden creak. A shrouded man left the gate. He was wearing a long, dark red cape; his arms were gauntleted with leather gloves. They were laced with iron strips and a chain mail glinted from under his tunic. A silver belt was evident under the shadows of the cape. His eyes were wide and savage, and Lith pulled me into the alleyway. 'It's time indeed. That's Falg. Our slave is sneaking out to have some fun.'

'Where did the Brother go?' I asked.

'Doesn't matter,' Lith said. 'Come.' She nodded at me, and a burly Blacktower guard watched me as she went in. There were sounds of preparation in the tavern; men were talking as Lith whistled at them. They filed out.

'Now,' she said with apparent excitement. 'We join him,' she nodded, and we walked to the street. I could see Falg, walking quickly. Some men were following the fighter from a distance, flashing hand signals to each other in the alleys, and our main troop tromped after. 'We will go and enjoy the show. You saw his face?'

'I did,' I told her, resisting the urge to change my face. 'What is the plan?'

'We will take him out in the Pit's Edge, the dressing rooms. They all have their own. We know which one he will use. He belongs to the Silver Fingers, and they always use one near our booth. Or, if it is impossible to do the job in the Edge, then we shall shoot him full of arrows in a maze of alleys near the Dark Sands,' she said and glanced at me. 'You see; harsh, cold. Calculating.'

'I'm sorry it is so,' I agreed.

'Bah!' she spat, and we marched on. We passed fabulous taverns of high rock facades, outdoor eateries, now near abandoned for the winter. The sky was a billowing front of gray clouds, and they looked heavily ominous, promising rain.

We passed the gates to the Second Ring and came to the main road of the area, a red-bricked road, rich with statues, pine trees, and strange yellow house facades. 'I always imagined this is what our whorehouse should look like,' Lith said, eyeing a tall building with velvety red drapes and some sort of a party going on inside.

'I've lived in a basement all my life,' I told her. 'Not sure I could live in something like this.' We walked on for fifteen minutes and passed a small market, now empty. Then, the alleys Lith had mentioned. They were full of people, dark with shadows and filled with opportunities. I could see how one could murder someone easily there and escape.

'Ware,' she said, and we stopped. I gawked at the sight. Beyond the alleys, the small streets widened and finally combined into a spacious road where thousands of people were slowly moving ahead. On top, a huge structure of white and yellow marble spread to left and right, curving out of sight. 'Dark Sands,' she told us, and up ahead, house Blacktower scouts were following Falg to the crowds. 'Come on. We have permanent seats near the Sun Entrance.'

We waited in the line for an hour, slowly shuffling forward. People were swathed in leathers and cloaks, chatting merrily. The dampness and the light snow did nothing to douse the festive mood, not even when the snow finally turned into a drizzle. The façade of the massive structure was littered with small alcoves holding burning lamps and candles, and a tune of flutes was playing high in the air, its source unknown. The Blacktower men were pushing resolutely forward, the people around us were scowling at us until Lith smiled at them, apologizing, charming them. Finally, we made it to the gateway, where a pale sun was painted on top of the doorway. 'Tens of thousands?' I asked her. 'People I mean.'

'Twenty,' she agreed. 'Blood and adventure, Maskan. Spill blood, and they remember it. Acts and plays pale in comparison.'

'What is going to be taking place? Some kind of a group event? Was it eighty men and beasts?' I asked her as we pushed up a stone staircase. Our voices and steps were echoing strangely. Up ahead, I could see huge spine-like supports arching across a vast, circular, gray ceiling.

Lith pushed me to the side. 'Yes. They have a team event in the afternoon. There are four teams fighting in a maze, and they release a stak into the fray.'

'A stak?' I wondered as she pushed us to a small booth of simple stone and pillows. The vast chamber was echoing with voices; people were bustling all over the place like ants over their hill. 'What is that?'

'Stak?' she grinned. 'You peasant. It's a lizard. Not terrifyingly huge like it might be, but still large, ferocious, and stealthy. Southern thing. Like most deadly creatures, it is imported.'

We sat there, waiting, and a harried servant in a blue tunic brought us mead. Lith toasted me, and the crowds dispersed, settling down very slowly. A buzz of voices made it hard to hear Lith, and she gave up talking soon enough. There were yells and screams as families sought each other, and I could only wonder at the circular building with rows and rows of seats and booths, some very elaborate with house or business crests.

Only then, did I look down.

You could see the rectangular bottom easily from everywhere, but the closer you were, the better you could see the finer details of it. Teams of muscular men were working, erecting some last wooden walls with the aid of cumbersome lizards and clever pulleys. There was a large middle room and several corridors led out of it, and I guessed the teams were going to enter through the four corners.

'Falg will fight with the Silver Fingers,' Lith said as she leaned on me. 'They are some ten strong each, there are four teams allowed, only the best teams, and so it's forty such expert men and women down there. In the evening, they will have famous duels and archery competitions. Most root for the Silver Fingers team. It's noble sponsored and likely will do very well. Hammar Moonchild is their trainer, and he has rarely trained a losing team—'

'Surely putting your money on surprise winners might make you rich? What are there? Red? Silver?'

'Gold Helms and the Feathered Sisters.' She grinned. 'Feathers replaced the Blue Blades. It's some southern outfit. They say they burned the trainers of the Blue alive and bought their arena contract from the owner who had seen it all take place.'

'I'd wager gold on them,' I decided, childishly excited about the whole affair.

One of the Blacktower men stood by our booth and held a foaming goblet of some juice nectar, his beard bristling angrily. 'Won't matter.'

'What?' I asked him, confused. 'What do you mean?'

He leaned down to me. 'A Brother, the White one is with the Silver team. I'm sure it's him. He leads them, and he is not armored as a Danegell, of course, but I am certain it is him. You saw him leaving the house just now. Coincidence? Hardly.'

'White Brother? A Brother Knight?' I asked him, confused.

'They are happy when there is a scuffle, those knights.' He smiled. 'That Falg is his guard. They all fight in teams of ten, but all teams have a spear and a shield tactic for pairs. Falg is the shield to the White Brother. He guards his partner. I've seen them before. Very evil duo.'

I sat there, stupefied. I leaned on Lith. 'What if the Brother escorts Falg home?'

'Then we will kill him,' she whispered. 'Like I told you. In the alleys.'

'He killed fifty men the other night,' I pointed out.

'Only because he was given a chance to fight,' she said. 'We will not make that mistake. I have men looking at the dressing rooms at the Pit's Edge. We will soon hear if we can take Falg alone down there. You saw how they moved separately, the Brother and he. He has to keep his distance from the slave. We have a hundred men looking at both of them. We won't fail. Have faith.'

'There are forty men down there. Thirty will go after him. How can you think—'

The man beside me grunted. 'More than forty. Remember? Eighty total. There will be the fools as well.' He looked at me and saw I was not comprehending. 'Volunteers. The rabble.'

'Volunteers? What does that mean—' I asked, but choked as I spied the teams entering their starting areas. There was huge applause and whistling as men and women entered the four corners. There were forty in all. I spied the Feathered Sisters, ten females in leathers and chains, a gorgeous feather ornament on their headbands, their faces painted white and red. They were swarthy and albino, half and half, all hosting tall spears, and small shields. Then there was the Red team, red sashes on their hips and all sturdy fighters, chanting their battle calls, showing their weapons to the crowds who either cheered or mocked them. Then there was the Gold Helm team, their helmets glittering with the metal, and black horsehair reached their calves.

'Dangerous,' Lith grinned at me. 'That hair has gotten many of them killed. You should never have hair or horns on your helmet. Perfect way to get yourself killed, eh?'

'Yes,' I agreed, and then the Blacktower man nudged me.

The Silver Fingers team was entering.

And in the front, there was an enormous man with bright white hair, pale, tattooed skin, and a feral-looking chain-swathed helmet on his head. He raised a whip and a long sword in the air, and I winced as my ears ached for the screams of approval. Men and women were standing up, holding pieces of paper, probably those who bet on the Silver team, and the man in the helmet grinned mightily, showing his tremendous physique and white teeth to the masses. He was taller than I was, broad and powerful. So were the others of the Silver Fingers team, all sturdy men, and there was not a single female amongst them. And there was Falg, his ax and sword out as he lazily spun them in the air, standing very close to the White Brother. *It was him*, I thought, looking at the leader, the whip was the same, studded with razor-sharp bits of metal.

They yelled some sort of scream of defiance, clashed their weapons together, and the clanging sound echoed even through the noise of the crowds cheering the teams. Then, each team hoisted a spear with a pennant and drums sounded all around the vast place.

The drums quit beating. Silence reigned.

A thin woman in a simple white robe appeared on a balcony that I had overlooked. It was built half over the pit, adorned with gilded pillars and silver leaves. She raised her arms high up to the air.

'Blood cravings of Dagnar!' she yelled, 'will be sated here this evening! Hail the brave!'

Curiously, none screamed in answer. People thrummed their feet. I leaned on Lith. 'I am pretty sure most people in the Fourth Ring and the Fifth have no idea there are such strange rituals in this city.'

Lith leaned on me. 'Not supposed to speak. It's an old ritual, one to celebrate bloodletting with respect. It's almost like a sacrifice.'

'Forty volunteers for the battle!' the thin woman yelled. 'To represent the innocent and the weak!'

'What is this?' I asked Lith. 'Where are they?'

'Having mercenaries fight each other would be quick, boring butchery,' she grinned ferociously. 'So there are forty volunteers.'

And then I noticed Taram. And so did Lith.

'What is he about?' she murmured.

Taram was walking our way. He looked quite pleased with himself. He halted before our guard, who stopped him while glancing at Lith uncertainly. Lith nodded, and the guard stepped away and Taram leaned over. 'Well. Father was right.'

'Was right?' Lith asked him. 'What do you mean? He has a message for us?'

'No message from him. Only from me. He was right in that I cannot control my urges,' he chuckled. 'I despise him too much. And he did dare me. He said I cannot hurt him any worse than I did. I think I can.' He nodded at me.

'What have you done?' Lith hissed.

'I took away your present, sister,' he laughed.

'No!' she said softly, furious.

Taram nodded, near apologetically. 'I did. Look carefully at the volunteers, boy. And suffer.' He got up and ignored Lith, who shouted something after him. I got up to follow Taram, but Lith pulled me down.

There was a drumbeat. It was ominous, deep.

A hole appeared in the middle of the central room. Others opened in the corridors. Dust billowed up into the air. 'Take him away,' Lith told the guard who grabbed me. I pushed him off me.

Haphazardly armored and armed people appeared from those holes down below.

The elaborately dressed woman yelled, 'Wish them luck! Let the real fighters win. Be they of the warriors or the innocents. And let there be a force of nature to make it much more interesting.' She pointed reverently at the ceiling.

'The sauk!' someone said too loudly a few rows from us and held his mouth as people glowered at him. On the roof, a hole appeared. Misty smoke billowed from the hole, and then a thick chain rattled into sight. I didn't see the thing at first. I stared at the hugely thick chain coming down, but then I did spot it. What I had thought an abnormally thick part of the chain, moved. People gasped. There was a dark, sleek lizard twelve feet long, with an elongated neck and a thick, scaled tail. It was entwined on the chain, and it eyed the masses of people staring at it and hissed audibly.

'Begin!' the woman shrieked; drums rolled and went silent.

The chain began to descend faster.

In the middle room, the volunteers, some ten of them turned against each other at first, but then they looked up at the descending sauk and all blanched. They ran off for the corridors. The teams bunched together under their colored or feathered pennants, and then I saw Sand.

It was Sand.

It was impossible, but it was he, and he was running from the central room. Lith saw him as well and got up. She was clutching at the railing, her face a mask of shock.

I stood up and whispered. 'He died.'

'He didn't, though. Taram ...' she began. 'The bastard. You have to think, Maskan. Think.'

I was thinking. And I decided what to do.

Down in the arena, some of the volunteers ran into others of their kind, who instinctively ganged up on the newcomers. A man stumbled into a savage ax cut and flopped to the floor, nearly lifeless. A burly woman speared another in the face and left the victim howling on the ground. People were throwing down dark flowers, celebrating the kills, and I knew then how the arena got its name.

I cursed, for Sand skidded into another room, where three men were waiting. They hesitated; Sand lifted his shield and backed off, his scimitar out. He even had his weapon. The crowd heckled him, but one of the three men gestured for Sand, and he joined them, though cautiously. Overall, the volunteers were trying to come up with bigger groups, someone always pushing them to cooperate. The Reds were now marching down a corridor, the Silvers were standing under their banner, in no hurry, and the Golds were etching very slowly forward in a big column. And the Feathers? The females? They ran wildly to the corridors and there, the first real battle took place. The ten deadly girls found six men locking shields, bunched up. The girls chanted, and with their spears overlapping they went ahead, and their spears snaked for the shields, rapping against them. A deadly shriek was heard, and I realized some of the spears were wicked razor-sharp hooks. Flesh and shields were pulled aside, spears flashed, and two men bled on the sand that turned dark with blood. The rest ran.

'Those girls will give the Silver Fingers trouble. I think Maskan is right,' the Blacktower man snorted, not noticing the tension Lith and I felt. I watched Sand nudge at a man; they moved off, and I knew I would have to help him. The sauk's chain reached the floor, and the slithering thing got off, immediately hugging a shadow by a wall. It was a thing of claws and spear-like teeth, and it blended with the darkness. A woman ran past it, the thing let go a thrilling high shriek and jumped on the back of the runner. They rolled in a ball of scales and red, torn flesh.

The Silver team chanted and moved.

I turned Lith to me. 'He will die.'

She did not look at me. 'He might. I'm not blind. I am sorry.'

'I'll not let him die alone,' I told her darkly.

'No, you will,' she said with a clipped tone. Lith eyed me carefully, gauging my reaction to her words and saw I did not care for her orders. She pulled at me. 'No! He was always ... not really part of this. There are bigger things at stake here, Maskan, than one scummy thief.'

'Scummy thief?' I stated coldly.

She took a deep breath. 'You were raised in the gutters, Maskan. But you are better than that. Sand is a simple thing, a simple creature, and a crude boy. We are thinking about the whole nation here. And perhaps he shall be a hero? And win? Be logical!'

'I'm no better than he is,' I hissed. 'He is not going to be a victim of the Blacktowers logic that murders villagers and children.'

'You cannot risk everything we are doing here,' she hissed, her face losing color. 'Taram did something evil, Maskan. Again. But it cannot be undone. Leave him.'

'No,' I said quietly.

'Why is Sand more important to you than we are? Me. The cause. Shaduril!' she pleaded with me. 'Why?'

I got up, and she grabbed my hand. I looked down at her. 'You cared nothing for the cause when you fooled me. Nor for Shaduril. Let go,' I told her.

She squeezed my hand, uncannily hard, and her eyes burned with purpose. 'I am sorry, but you will not intrude in this.'

'The living—' I began.

'Go before the dead! Yes, I've heard you say that. And you are making a mistake now,' she shouted at me. People around us were shuffling, uncomfortable at the whole scene. 'You are so wrong. And you cannot go down there. Not like this. You'll ruin everything.'

'Shut up,' I told her. The familiar rage returned. It was boiling inside me, burning like fire, rolling like a molten stone inside my gut, and I felt the tug of resistance in the ring. I pushed at the resistance, pushed it away with an inhuman growl. Dangerous, Balan had said, for the ring was broken. I did not care. I needed the rage. No matter the price. 'Let ... go,' I articulated to her and saw her face go slack as I lifted her off of her feet. I grabbed her hand and squeezed. There was a sound of crackling bones, and she flinched. Only flinched. She let go of my hand. I grunted like an animal and tossed her across benches, toppling people. There were screams, but they were mostly aimed at the battle raging below. The Gold Helm team had rounded a corner and faced off against the Red Sashes; both sides were running at each other, shields, swords, spears, and axes held high. They did not see it, but the Silver Fingers were very close.

I turned to look at the Blacktower man. The burly man who had been with us blanched and took steps away as I exited the booth. I passed him, turned and lifted his cloak. A sword was there, long and broad, and I raised my eyebrow at him. He smiled sheepishly and nodded. I tore the weapon away so hard the belt came off, and he was left grasping his pants.

Then I ran downstairs.

I was going to save Sand, and the Queen be damned.

## CHAPTER 14

I ran down the stairs, holding the sword. It felt weightless in my hands. I was not really nervous because the rage made everything clearer. Do or die. Sand could die any moment. I had left him there at the Green Hall, assuming him dead. He had had an arrow buried in his skull. Could anyone survive that? I shrugged; it was possible. It was, as he was here, fighting. I came to the bottom of the stairs, looked around frantically and noticed a way down, not far. I walked that way briskly and pushed open a door. There was a small, circular room where there were men standing around. They were two members of the Mad Watch, both holding spears. Both wore helmets of conical style, skull and sword symbols painted on their shields and pauldrons. I spied the corridor behind them, and it led down. They eyed me curiously. 'What is ailing you? Drunk?' one of them asked me.

'No,' I growled and nodded downstairs. 'I wish to go that way. Where does it lead?'

'It leads to the fighters' pits. The Pit's Edge,' the other one said with some doubt, eyeing my sword. 'Silver Fingers' Pit's Edge. Their kingdom. What do you want with that place? Go take a piss elsewhere, boy.'

'I volunteer,' I spat.

They looked confused, and one stepped forward, holding his spear laxly. 'It's too late. Forty is all they take,' the first one chided me. 'They chose the fools hours ago. And the volunteers don't go this way, anyway. You go, and try again next month.'

'Don't have time to come back later,' I said and stepped closer. 'I'll be going in.' Their spears came down to point lazily in my direction.

'Get going, you drunken fool,' the first guard said. 'Or you will bleed. Don't want to stench up the place. Go on.'

I stepped closer, and their eyes went round. 'What are you—' the other one blurted, but I was not listening. I smashed their spears aside with the sheathed blade and charged forward. I pushed one guard onto the other, and they fell in a heap. I stomped on the leg of one, and it broke. I blinked as I saw that, but the other guard was getting up. I grabbed his helmet and crushed it on the floor so hard it left a dent, and the man was throwing up, shocked, then unconscious. I gathered their spears and ran down the stairs. The first guard was howling in pain. I was powerful as a bear, and as mad.

I found an elaborate iron gate leading to the Pit's Edge of the Silver team. It was locked, and I cursed. I hesitated, tried to break the gate, but I was nowhere near strong enough to do that. I cursed again, and I ran back up. There I saw a chain of keys on the unconscious guard's belt. The other one was holding his broken leg, his eyes huge with terror. He stopped sobbing as he spied me. He was probably in shock. 'Just keep your trap closed and you might walk one day again. Scream, and I'll take it right off.'

'Have fun down there,' he whispered in his terrible pain and gave me a pale smile. 'Too bad I can't go bet on you.'

'Thanks,' I said, ran back down, and opened the gate. I gazed around and heard the people screaming with wonder at something that was happening in the arena. There were doors to the right and left, tables and armory, and beyond the room, there was a doorway. A richly dressed man was leaning on the iron grill, humming, and beyond him, there was the arena. He turned to look at me and froze. 'Who in the blazes are you?'

'You Hammar?' I asked him. 'The owner of the team?'

'Tergil!' he yelled, and a tall, gaunt man came out of one of the rooms, holding a dirk. 'Tergil is the trainer of the team, and you should leave now,' Hammar explained confidently.

I twisted the spear in my hand, grunted as I threw it, and Tergil shrieked as the spear impaled him to the door. The spear shaft shattered with the power of the throw. I turned my face to Hammar. 'Where,' I began, 'is the Silver Brother's gear?'

'What? You would not dare touch it!' he breathed and saw I would indeed. He pointed his finger towards a large door to my right. I started that way, hesitated and walked to Hammar.

'Open it up,' I told him and indicated the door to the arena.

'Never! You will not go in there! They will blame me if you ruin this event! I'll lose my commission!' I grabbed him and thrust him at the grill so hard he made a huffing sound as his ribs broke. The gate swung open; the lock was broken.

I walked over to the dressing rooms, saw Falg's robes and cloak on a peg and heaped on the side was the fabulous armor of the White Brother, the horsehair long and winding. I grunted happily and pulled the door closed. I locked it with the keys, and then I turned and eyed the open door, heard the screams and yells of the crowd, the tumultuous echoes of excited howls and disappointed booing of those who lost money. I stared at the face of the trainer who was bleeding on the door, dead. I had killed him. It had been easy. And I didn't care. The rage changed me. My face melted and broke into his angular looks, my nose flattened, my eyes grew thinner.

Then I walked to the table, hefted a discarded chainmail and pulled it on with difficulty, cursing as my hair caught on the chain links. I pulled on thick gauntlets and stopped to consider Larkgrin. I placed it on my palm, under the gauntlet, grabbed the sword and the spear, and took a deep breath.

And stepped out.

I heard the crowds take note of me. I ignored them and tried to remember how the maze had been placed. I ran forward, heard the tumult of the battle ahead and came face to face with five members of the Red Sashes. They were pushing their swords and spears at a Golden Helm and a volunteer pair of women. One Red Sash charged the Golden Helm soldier, thrusting with his spear, but stumbled on the sand, and the Golden helmeted warrior hacked down with his scimitar, carving at the neck of the enemy. The two volunteer women pulled one Red forward by his careless spear and stabbed him in his gut, but it cost them dearly, for the three remaining Red Sashes ran forward, brandishing tall spears, and should anyone think a spear is an inferior weapon to a sword, then they are wrong. The women dodged, danced away, but got punctured and wounded and herded into a corner. One died with a spear in her heart, the other one was pleading with a raised hand.

And so I charged.

My remaining spear flew in the air. The Golden Helmet turned to stare at the specter of death, and then it pierced his chest, and he fell away. The crowds went wild, and I felt a mix of glee and rage as I happily charged to attack the three reds. The sword's blade came off the sheath easily; I loped their way, balanced on my toes and carved one of the men to the neck so savagely his head flew to the wall. I roared and raged and pummeled into the two others, both of whom were turning. I grabbed one's sash as I pulled him to the blade so hard his spine broke. I blocked a spear thrust with his corpse and pushed the dead man on the Red team's remaining member. They fell hard in a jumble of limbs, and I jumped after, landing next to the last thrashing man. I had few skills with the sword, but I needed none, for the weapon was weightless in my hand, and as I slashed it at the man's face, the weapon split his helmet with a jarring sound. It was like carving bread. It was so natural. There was more to it than Taram's training. I felt born to use a sword. Any weapon, in fact.

The crowds screamed. The dome rippled with cries of joy, and then I received accolades. Black flowers rained down on me. I spat and felt like a small god. I pulled the spear from the chest of the Golden Helm, spattering myself with gore, and held onto the notched sword. The one surviving volunteer female was holding a hand up in supplication. 'I needed the money. Please,' she begged, and I doused the red voice of an evil spirit whispering to me of her death. With difficulty, I nodded at her and went on.

I ran forward to the next room and found a man sitting in a corner, waiting to ambush anyone passing by, but not from my direction. I rushed him, he turned, and I kicked him through the wall. His neck broke, and he died in an eye blink, but the wall behind him fell with a rumble.

The main room opened up before me.

The huge melee in the next room paused for a moment as they all considered the unexpected event of a falling wall and the dead man plastered on it.

I stepped on the corpse and looked around frantically.

I breathed a sigh of relief.

Sand was alive. He and three volunteers were fighting near a corner of the main hall, and there were two Golden Helms dying at their feet. Sand's scimitar was dark with blood, and he was eyeing the ring of the Silver Fingers team surrounding them. On the side, the Feathered Sisters had butchered the last of the Red Sashes, but there were only six of the sisters left. Their spears turned towards the other two groups.

Falg was alive. White Brother as well.

They turned and saw my face, and their eyes enlarged with surprise. 'Tergil?' Falg asked, utterly mystified. 'You are not allowed here! You'll ruin this!'

'Forget him,' the White Brother said, his chin tight. 'Kill the lot, then ask questions.'

And they did. The Silver Fingers tightened ranks and turned towards Sand's group. The Silvers linked three huge shields, their metal was gleaming red and they went forward. The White Brother flicked his whip up and brought it down. 'No!' I screamed, but it was hopeless. The whip was aimed at one of the remaining volunteers, who blocked it with his shield. The deadly whip went through the shield, of course, and tore open his shoulder and neck. He fell wordlessly as the White Brother retrieved his whip with a savage pull. Sand and the two others charged forward, aiming at the huge man, blades coming from all directions, hammering at the shieldwall desperately. They were held easily. Falg danced to the side and ran a man through expertly. The White Brother's blade dug into the chest of his enemy as Sand pushed past a shield of one man. His brawling madness, his wild swings, his enraged strikes drew blood, and a man fell, holding a hole in his side. Falg appeared in front of Sand, his ax and sword blocking my friend's hits, sparing White Brother a wound. A man blocked Sand with a shield and kicked him down on his face.

This all happened so fast I could barely move.

But there was more.

The Feathered Sisters charged, their extra-long spears and hooks probing ahead, the crowds roared, and it was because they had seen something we could not.

The sauk sprung up from behind me, having hidden in the shadows.

I felt a hot intake of breath, saw movement and fell flat on the corpse. Seemingly endless sets of claws tore at the rock around me, one claw caught on my chain mail and dragged me along as the bellowing, enraged creature sprung to the back of the Silver Finger group. The man carrying their pennant went down under the savage claws and fangs; the Feathered Sisters stopped their charge just shy of the Silver Fingers, but the beast rolled through the Silver group and stopped before the women. The crowds roared as the sauk's jaws clamped down on one of the hesitating Feathered Sisters and threw her remains into the wall. 'Kill it! All together!' The White Brother screamed, and his men turned to fight it. They charged the beast as I got up. The Feathered Sisters did as well, and the sauk banked and reared. Its claws were slashing in the air, its teeth chomped savagely, turning a man into red ribbons. Then its tail slashed a woman in half. It ran around and scrambled for Sand. He saw me coming as he was getting up. I waved him back and pushed him away as the sauk's tail sailed by his face.

He snarled at me and pushed his scimitar to my side, his eyes wide with fear.

He didn't know it was I.

I rolled away from the hit, my face melting to my own. His eyes grew wide in shock, and he bent down to grasp me. There were surprised screams as people witnessed the change. 'Sorry! Maskan! I didn't know!'

'My fault,' I spat, feeling blood trickling to my side. The sauk bleated in pain. It was stamping in rage, and a Silver Finger fell on our side, his head gone. I glanced at the beast that was missing two of its legs and part of its snout. It was having trouble maneuvering as two Feathered Sisters had impaled it to keep it still. 'There is a door. It's open. We can escape from it,' I told him, as I got up.

'I won't leave until he is gone. He killed my father,' Sand said sadly. 'I won't. I have nothing left.'

'You died,' I whispered and did not see the arrow wound in his face. 'How—'

'I am here now,' he growled and pointed at the White Brother. 'We cannot go before he is gone. We must not!' he yelled, and there was mad intensity in his eyes.

'Gods cursed fool,' I yelled at him as I pulled him away from the thrashing sauk and the last three Silver Fingers, all hacking at the beast. The two Feathered Sisters were meaning to keep the beast still, but they were struggling with fatigue. The whip went up, then came down and blood flew high; the sauk shrieked. The crowds cheered as the sauk shuddered in pain as one of the Feathered Sisters tore her spear out and stabbed it repeatedly.

'They will win, Maskan,' he spat. 'We should act!'

'Wait,' I told him desperately but saw he was right. 'Fine. We will try it.'

Falg bashed his ax on the head of the lizard, and it finally died very slowly, shuddering and still dangerous as its claws raked the sand. The Sisters pulled out their tall spear and turned to look at us. White Brother lifted his eyes at me and saw my face. His eyes grew huge. 'You? You are free!' he yelled. 'Listen—'

And then, the Sisters attacked. They came at Falg and the Brothers with a savage charge. One was red-headed under her high feathers and tall and lithe, the other one was short, sturdy, and blonde and the two beautiful creatures were still fully able to fight, even after the terrible battle with the sauk. Falg pulled the White Brother around as the women came to them. The feathers waved, Falg blocked one hooked spear, but the other spear came at him. The White Brother cursed and charged, but Sand ran at him at the same time and the Brother lost a precious second as he glanced at Sand. I grabbed my friend as a whip slapped where he had stood and the Brother kept moving for Falg, but it was too late. The spear pierced Falg's belly, and he hung on to the spear shaft desperately as the White Brother went into the attack. He snorted and grumbled like a mountain as the whip went up again. 'Pretty. But not so pretty in a bit!' he yelled and went at the women. The tall one, whose spear was lodged in Falg's belly cursed bitterly and fell back, but the deadly whip came down and ribbons of blood and feathers flew high in the air, mixing with the dark flowers raining down from the spectators. Then, the sword stabbed at the dying red mass. The other's hook got ripped from Falg's grip, and then it was coming for the White Brother. She had jumped forward to gain momentum, and the sharp blade tried to lodge itself under White Brother's helmet. The Knight moved like a wraith; the hooked blade turned red as a wound opened up in the man's chest, but his sword snaked in under the hook, and the short woman was impaled brutally. The crowds cheered wildly, enjoying the kill. More and more dark flowers rained down on us.

Sand cursed, pushed me off, and tore off in a canter for the man.

'Sand!' I shrieked and ran after him. He was dodging the twitching tail of the sauk, vaulted over some of the dead Silver Fingers, and charged the White Brother, his scimitar held low. The Brother turned, saw him coming, smiled and the whip struck Sand's shield.

Then it curled around it, around his hand and arm, and the man tore the whip off, ripped off skin, meat, and Sand's shield. Sand fell on his face.

I roared and the White Brother stared at me strangely. He shook his head and raised his sword. 'Wait. Maskan? You have to—'

But I didn't listen. I roared again and made my way forward, struck the blade on his blade, and we both grimaced as the lumps of steel shuddered in our hands. 'My family. Sand.'

'Your family?' He laughed gutturally, dropped his whip and grabbed my throat. He pulled me close. 'You care for your family? You should. But—'

I let go of the sword. I grabbed his temples.

'Larkgrin,' I whispered, and the staff grew into my hand, ripping through the gauntlet. The weapon glowed wildly, the runes glittered and then turned into a red hued shade, as the end of the staff—the bird—was inside White Brother's thick skull, then past it. 'Larkgrin,' I whispered, and the weapon shrunk as we fell. There were screams of despair and shrieks of triumph, many more dark flowers rained down on us, blocking the light. I pushed at the White Brother's shattered helmet and saw a look on his broken face that was very surprised by his grizzly death. I spat, felt my rage disappear, replaced by fatigue, and I ran to Sand. He was conscious, his eyes wide. There were bones showing in the mess of flesh of his arm, nasty abrasions running up and down his side. He was pale and sickly looking; the arrow wound showed in his face, dark red and polluted. He was severely injured. I cursed and grabbed the whip and the Brother's splendid sword, picked up Sand and ran amidst falling flowers for the doorway. It took time; I could not see very well, and my ears were thrumming as the crowds cheered us wildly. I passed the wounded woman, who blanched as she saw me approaching.

'Go and take a bow. You won,' I told her and walked over Hammar and disappeared into the doorway.

## CHAPTER 15

Lith greeted me at the door of the Pit's Edge. She scowled as she eyed Sand and shook her head as she turned to me. I looked around and saw she was not alone. There were a dozen Blacktower men there, all with weapons drawn. 'What now?' I asked her with a growl.

She shrugged back, eying me thoughtfully. 'You are hurt.'

I looked down to my side. I was bleeding from Sand's sword thrust. There was a distant yell echoing around the Dark Sands stadium, and I did not know what to tell her. 'He is hurt worse.'

'He is,' she said, and her eyes softened. 'I am sorry.'

'I'll need him healed,' I told her and saw she was shaking her head. 'No?'

'You don't understand, Maskan,' she answered. 'You have a job to do. We will take it from here.'

'You?' I said incredulously. 'I will not leave him.'

Regret was playing on her face. 'I am sorry. But we will take him. We will care for him. And you shall have to hurry to do your duty. The joke has gone on for long enough. If you do not obey us …' she said softly, and I understood the threat. They would kill us both. She softened the threat with a small curtsy. 'We will heal him. You will see him up in the Tower when it is all over. We don't have time, Maskan,' she told me and touched my face, but at the same time the men in the room took a step forward. I flinched away from her, and her face bubbled with rage. 'I said, we do not have time.'

'He is alive. If I do not see him alive again, I shall kill you,' I told her.

She nodded at me. 'I understand. Nothing's changed, Maskan,' she said, hugging herself. 'Nothing. We still have something to do, something important, and the guilty ones must perish. They must. You agreed to this, no?'

'I did. But I've lost my appetite for murder, especially the death of someone I have no real knowledge of. Only your words, actually. And they have all been twisted and filthy.'

'Red Midgard needs this, Maskan,' she explained and put a hand on mine. Her touch was cold, but there was desperation in her eyes, and I found it hard to turn away from them. 'Look,' she said and showed me her hand. It was hale. Her fingers were dexterous, the joints moved. 'You broke it. If you care nothing for Red Midgard and a house of your own, then do this for him. I will heal him. He will need you to obey.'

'You are a bitch,' I said as I stared at her hand. I laid Sand on the ground and threw the whip aside. 'Yes,' I said with a sigh. 'Now, I have a date with the Queen.'

She nodded, nervously. 'Falg is dead, right?'

'He died. Made a mistake,' I said. 'I didn't kill him.'

'It will be risky going as him,' she said, listening to people complaining to Blacktower guards on the top. 'They want to know where you went and if the woman you left alive honestly won. There is a Helheim up there with all the bets going awry.' She grinned. 'I lost some gold as well.' She turned to look up, listening to the sounds. 'I do hope they won't take the news of Falg's death out there too fast.'

'Won't matter. Take Sand and spare his life,' I told her, 'and I will bring you news of the Queen's death.'

'Where are you going?' she asked me as I walked past her. I pushed some Blacktower guards away from me, walked to the door to Falg's and White Brother's dressing room. I opened it up and tore off my chain with a wince as the wound throbbed angrily and headed for the magnificent gear of the White Brother.

'Help me with this,' I told her with a grin as she gawked at the door.

'What about the poison?' she said weakly, joining me. 'No. We must stick to the plan!'

'I'm bringing the Queen sad news of Falg,' I grumbled and grabbed the helmet. 'He died.'

'No! This is too risky. Dangerous! We had a plan and …' she began but saw I was not listening. I tossed the bottle of poison to her, and she grabbed it from the air. The pellets rattled inside. The rage was still throbbing in my head, and I felt dangerous, uncaring. She shook her head, and helped me pull on black chain mail, black boots with greaves, pauldrons and cuirass, gauntlets and a gorget and finally, the helmet. There were many other parts, and I didn't even know what to call them, but Lith was expertly making me look presentable. She smiled weakly. 'Can you walk around in it? You will waddle like a duck.'

Surprisingly, the armor felt like I had been born to it. 'It feels incredible. The damned whip? And the sword.' She nodded and fetched them.

She bowed to me. 'Good luck, savior of Red Midgard.'

'Queen killer,' I corrected her, feeling wretched with the whole business. 'And if Sand dies, prepare to join him.'

She laughed merrily for some reason, and I went out.

I found the White Brother's horse readied in the stable; the boy in charge of the establishment was bowing with confusion, and I ignored him. He had probably heard the man owning the armor and the horse was dead, but there I was, mounting the unfamiliar beast. I guided the creature downhill and then for the alleys. Sand. Sand was alive. Still. I'd keep him that way. I rode to dark alleyways and people gave way. Most looked scared, alarmed, and I thought of a King whose men made such an impression on his subjects. The Queen was no better. That I told myself as I rode on. The horse was skittish, probably because it knew there was a wrong man inside the armor. It tried to pull my grip off the bridle, and I felt foolish for fighting with it in plain sight of the commoners and nobles of the city. 'Easy, you damned thing. Be a good boy, please,' I pleaded, and it seemed to listen to me, for it settled down a bit. I made my way through the lanes, praying for the gods to have mercy on me for what I was about to do. Murder. I would murder. For Sand, as well as my family. I would. Though had I not already done so? I made it past the Second Ring's gates without any questions from the Mad Watch and wound my way for the Third Ring. I went past the street where the mint was, passed the Thin Way, entered the main street and headed for the Tenginell house.

I pushed the horse forward and rode for the Tenginell house. The guards were closing the gate after some carts had rolled out, but spied me and stopped. They eyed me nervously, and I clutched the deadly whip in my fist. They stared up at me, one nudged the other and they began to crank open the doors. 'Congratulations, Lord. You won again. Will your partner be coming back soon?' one chatted with me amicably.

I shook my head and nodded at the main house and said nothing. They bowed, confused, and let me through. *One obstacle behind,* I thought. The mush and slush on the ground was white and gray, and I noticed my blood was dripping to the snow from the horse's flank. It hurt, but I had business to finish. Larkgrin was again clutched in my gauntlet. The Queen would not have a chance in Hel to survive it. I looked around and hoped to figure out a way to escape the place. In armor, I realized, it would be very hard.

For Sand, I would try.

I rode in through the gate, and slaves ran out of the house and the stable area. There was one lanky man with a thin beard and a girl of twelve gawking up at me. I dismounted heavily and cursed, as the wound hurt desperately. I held onto the horse for a moment, gathering my resolve. It moved away from me.

'Shh, pretty one. Galisan,' the man told the horse. 'She is upset, Lord, but I will take care of her.'

Her, I chuckled.

'May I ask how your event went, Lord?' the man asked me.

I waved my hand at the dripping blood. 'Well. It is nothing. Nothing, really. I'd see the Queen. Falg is dead.'

'The Queen?' asked the young girl, very confused.

'I'd see the Queen. Alone. Her servant has died,' I told her slowly, trying to mimic the voice of the White Brother.

'I see,' the girl said and hesitated. Then she brightened and nodded my way. 'She is praying. Alone,' she said meekly. 'She is in the crypts. Not sure you wish to disturb her there?'

I could not wait. I'd get caught. 'This is important. I will bother her only for a moment.'

'Yes, Lord,' the girl said with some hesitation and curtsied. 'This way.'

'Thank you,' I grunted. 'Keep the horse here. I will leave momentarily for the Tower of the Temple.' I was shivering with fear but headed for the main doors, arrogant and superior.

'May I show you the way?' the girl asked as she ran past me.

'By all means, do,' I agreed and waited as she skittered for the door. I nearly kicked myself, for surely the real White Brother would need no guide. She was not suspicious, however, and bowed to the guards at the door, hustled through to a round roofed portico and held the door open for me. There was a footman in a rich, silver-threaded coat and his eyes followed me as I walked past him. He cast his eyes down, and the girl showed me the way forward. In the middle, there was a central room with a cold fireplace, couches and armchairs scattered around and a circular wooden stairway to the higher floors. There were many guards up there, and I wondered how I would get away, for I saw several Brother Knights in the rooms above, laughing at a joke. I started for the stairway, but the girl gingerly pulled me to the left. There, at the shadowy end of a hallway, was a pillared marble stairway leading down. There was something forlorn about it, and there was a smell of violets in the air. *Crypts,* I thought. The Queen was visiting her dead family as well as the living ones. The girl stopped there, at the door and nodded that way. 'She is there, now. Praying.'

I nodded and stood on top of the stairway. She eyed me curiously, probably wondering at my timidity, and I was not sure I could go through with what I had planned to do. I walked down the stairs, the armor clanking on the stone steps. There were oil lamps fluttering on the walls, held by iron claws. There was an ominous feeling in the air, thick, strange, and I smelled the incense.

Below, at the end of the stairway, was a black doorway that was ajar. Inside, fires were burning. Torches were fluttering, a small wind was playing with cobwebs. I looked up the stairway, and saw the girl, following me. She stopped as I stopped. She smiled and waved me onwards.

*Gods, I would have to murder the Queen with her watching. I would have to think about what to do,* I despaired.

'Go back,' I told her. 'I know the way.' I noticed she was smiling. And her hand glowed briefly. So did my ring. And my gauntlet. 'What are you doing?'

She did not answer. Not to me. 'He has that evil ring. And your staff, my Lord. That is all.'

'What—'

'Come in,' said a regal female voice.

I turned around, then faced the girl who looked at me with encouragement. She winked and pointed a steady finger down to the door. 'Are you not going to heed her call?'

'I—'

'Won't kill her. Trust me. You can breathe easily now!' she told me. 'And you won't die, either. Probably. You are safe and it is all over. In a good way. You failed and the draugr did as well.'

*Draugr?* I hesitated. *Sand. Sand was with the Blacktowers. He was far from safe.*

I took a deep breath and walked down unsteadily. I pushed at the door and hesitated. There were no Tenginells there. She was alone. There was only the Queen. She was lounging on a throne on top of a curious looking mound full of carved stones. She was draped in an attire of red velvet, seemed fragile and pale, and her blonde hair was shimmering in the dark. Behind her, there were a dozen fires burning in small cauldrons. The mound was twenty feet across and ten high. The slabs that made up its sides were subtly differently colored, all gray and black or nearly white. There were runes on the rocks, and I noticed they were all inscribed with a strange, undecipherable language that was oddly familiar. I nodded at the Queen, then cursed myself and bowed low. Her eyes flickered with amusement, but then her mood changed to a somber one.

'You killed him?' she asked me gently. 'Borlein.'

I stared at her. I clutched the whip and breathed hard. 'Yes. If Borlein is the White Brother, who hung my family. I did it. With your—'

'Staff. My staff,' she said. 'It is sad I ever lost it. It was a surprising night. We lost many things then. I'll miss Borlein. We grow few.'

I shrugged. I had killed him indeed, and he had murdered my family. 'Your staff?' I asked her. 'The King lost it the day he tried to rape my mother.'

She rubbed her face, and I noticed there was a brief look of relief mixed with sorrow in her eyes. 'Take off Borlein's helmet,' she told me. 'I wish to see your face.' Her face was pale as snow, hair blonde and long, and she looked very young. There was something strange in her voice, a thrumming, inhuman rhythm, and I felt my hair stand up all over my body. 'Never mind. Allow me.'

My helmet lifted into the air and fell behind me with a clatter.

I stared at it. I heard a giggle behind me, and the girl was standing there, leaning on the wall. 'It is him. So lost.'

'Maskan, I hear they named you,' the Queen said, standing up. She flicked her hand, and the helmet flew to the girl, who grabbed it from the air. 'We never got the chance.'

'You know me, your highness?' I choked. *Your highness,* I groaned to myself. *I was there to murder her.*

She grinned, wringing her hands. She hesitated and gestured to the side of the mound, where a great slab of stone stood. 'Go ahead,' she said. I took a hesitant step forward and then walked forward slowly, trying to keep an eye on every shadow. *She had lifted my helmet*, I thought. Artifact?

She grinned as I reached the slab of stone. It was white and black, with veins of gray running across its surface. 'What is it, Maskan?' she asked from her throne. 'That stone?'

'It is a rock?' I asked her, looking up at her face. She smiled and waited. I looked at the stone carefully. It felt strange ... honorable, sacred. The incense made me feel a bit weird, and I thought I could read the text, though only for a moment.

'Struggle, Maskan. Try. You can. It's that thing on your finger that is stopping you,' the Queen said with a hint of loathing in her voice. 'Show it to me.'

I hesitated but pulled off my gauntlet. She leaned forward. 'Sorrowspinner.'

'It is,' I agreed.

'Tal Talien's cursed ring. His family found it long ago in a battle—'

'So I've been told,' I grunted.

'It cannot be removed unless your heart stops and you die, and they thought it appropriately ghoulish to mark their lord like that throughout the generations,' she chuckled. 'It is just another thing that was lost that fateful night when we killed Tal and his ... people. In reality, it dampens most all magic. Not all, but most all. A strong one can resist it somewhat. And I sense you have. Resisted it.'

'It gives me my face changing ability,' I said, uncomfortable with speaking to the tall lady I was supposed to kill.

She leaned forward, smiling. 'Truly fascinating to hear their lies through your lips. Fine. But fight now. Look at the rock. And read it. Fight through the haze.'

'What—' I began but hesitated. And then I tried. I felt the rage return, the ring throb in my hand. I looked at the rock, furious and determined and fought as hard as I could. My head throbbed, my eyes burned with salty sweat and then, I made out the words, though only for a second.

> *'Here lies Queen Mellina Tenginell the Good.*
> *A gentle soul, face hidden by a dark hood.*
> *Slain by the Night.*
> *Eaten by the Blight.'*

The Queen nodded at me, and I fell on my knees, holding my head. She sighed. 'How they shackled you, boy. How they made you something so strange to us. They took everything you were given as a gift at birth. But it is all there. Still. Under the lies. And spells.'

'I don't understand,' I said miserably.

'You have your skills, boy,' she said evenly, nodding at the thing. 'A shackle makes you weak. We will have to think about it.'

'It is an artifact,' I insisted. 'My father's artifact!'

She snickered. 'No, it is not. I—'

'Who is Mellina Tenginell?' I interrupted her. 'Your relative? And why could I read that text?'

'Oh, yes. She was related to me by marriage,' she grinned. 'She looked like this,' she said and indicated herself.

'I don't understand,' I told her, frowning. 'Are you mocking me? First, your husband killed my father, and then my mother, and my … half family, and now you are here, making fun of me. I came here to slay you, and perhaps I shall.' I heard the girl shift behind me, but the woman raised her hand at her.

Her eyes fixed on mine. Her face went solemn. 'No, dear boy, I am not mocking you,' she said sadly. 'As for the woman you speak of? This so-called mother of yours? She never gave birth to you. She was not your mother, Maskan. Mellina was your mother. What you know are lies. All lies. Their kind … lives to plot. They embrace risks, they create elaborate shows and enjoy complications and hardships and failures. They can work on a plan for decades, slowly nurturing it into its final steps, as they did with you, though they failed. They are driven by their desires, often conflicting, they obey their lords only when they must, and they will kill us all if they can.'

'But you all lie and—'

She shook her head heavily and interrupted me. 'Though, of course, we also lie, yes. Royals do. We have fought your recent acquaintances for decades, their lies, and fended off their attacks after that terrible first one, where they took so much from us, including you. We have bowed to the south, tried to keep the north together. All sides tell lies. Yet, this is the truth. Once we were the enemies of the people of Midgard. Then, when we lost the war, we made peace with men. We have governed the city and the land for well over two thousand years.'

And so she changed.

Her form blurred and thickened, she grew large, tall, imposing. And it was not a she, it was a he, a fourteen-foot man, whose hair brushed the ceiling. An icy white beard replaced her smooth chin, a thick hank of hair changed from blonde to dark and heavy, a brooding face with strong bones bulged out of the formerly beautiful face. He wore the magnificent dark armor of the Danegells, though no helmet. He had massive, wide shoulders, and his thick gauntlets glittered with silver and gold, and the creature looked down at me. It's face was bluish and nearly white, and its eyes were bright as crystals. 'Yes. We are shape-changers. It is what we are, ancient and skillful. Welcome home, Maskan,' it rumbled. 'Son.'

I stared at the thing. I took a step back, fell over a small precious vase, and sat in the dust as I tried to understand what I saw. 'What in Hel's name—'

'Do not utter that name here, Maskan,' the creature said. 'We have forsaken Hel, thousands of years ago. We lost the war in Midgard and instead settled in and took over Red Midgard, eventually. But she is a persistent mad goddess, isn't she? It was Hel's spell that changed our lives near two decades ago. We lost your mother that night. Others died. You disappeared. Many treasures—one we truly need in these desperate times—was taken as Mellina died. She guarded it. Tal Talin led a rebellion that night, and we fought hard. They were not really skillful, and had no plan but to try to surprise us with numbers. And they did, to a degree.'

'I don't understand,' I told him, feeling weak. 'Anything. They? Son?'

'We lost you that night, Maskan,' he grinned. 'I am King Magor Danegell. She was my wife.' He nodded at the grave. 'Mellina Tenginell. The Danegell and Tenginell houses, son, are not from Midgard. I am the Beast of the North, and my father was a king of a different world.' I shook my head in denial. I turned to look at the girl, who grinned and fell on all fours as he, for it was a he, changed. He grew into a humanoid as wide as the King, though not quite as tall. The face was still boyish and happy, if blue tinged. It was the Red Brother, the man I had fought in the mint, and he was no man. His armor glittered in the dark, and his massive sword was on his back. He bowed to me. The King nodded at him. 'Our armor and weapons are dverg-made, magical. They change with us. When we take a figure of a girl, the armor is still there. This one is of our clan. One of the few survivors. You nearly killed him once. Bjornag he is called.'

'Prince,' the Red Brother said with mirth and bowed deep. 'An honor.'

'What is this?' I asked them, not really expecting an answer. 'You call me son,' I told him. 'Yet, my father died at your hands. My mother did. Or are you going to explain this before I go mad?'

'I told you,' he growled, 'lies have been told indeed. To you. All your life. And all for this moment. They groomed you, created fantastic lies, and hoped my son would kill me and that I would not know him. Bah! Borlein fell, that is a terrible loss, but you know me. In your heart you do. I am your kin. And what am I? I am a jotun.'

'You are a giant,' I whispered. 'A Jotun.'

'Jotun,' he sighed. 'Strangers from Nifleheim. A shape-changer, a spell lord, a warrior. That we are. Near as strong in spells as many gods, we are one of the old races. We are god foes, the ones they nearly destroyed when they made some of the Nine Worlds. We live in Jotunheim, in Muspelheim, in Niflheim and we are no lumbering beasts. We have some treasures, magical armor, and our weapons. The rest were stolen.' He glowered at that. 'Like my scepter and that ring, that disappeared from slain Tal's hand that night long ago. And that one thing I told you about. What Mellina guarded.'

'You use magic,' I insisted. 'Don't you? It's not an artifact that you use.'

'Yes, we use magic. We hear and see the ancient streams of ice and the molten power of fire. It's a sense, Maskan, one granted to the mighty races by something that was before the gods. We Stir the Cauldron, as the Jotuns call it. We are part of the weave, and see and hear the grind of the ancient ice, running down the Nine Rivers, Gjöll, and the others. We see the cascades of ice and winds when they go roaring down to mix with the fierce fires of Muspelheim. We can draw from that power; we can make spells out of it. It takes time to find ways to make right weaves and to figure out how to release the power. Some die learning; many, in fact. There are more spells than stars in the sky. Our magical shapeshifting skill is part of our race, and we all do it without thinking, but most jotuns have their own special spells. Red one here, Bjornag, knows a spell to detect magic. Borlein, the Jotun you killed, knew how to find people if he knew their name. Alas, his spell was useless, as long as you were with them.'

I shook my head, staring at the wondrous creatures. 'This is impossible to believe.'

The giant laughed so hard the walls shook. 'You see me, no?'

'Yes,' I said mulishly.

'Indeed. But it is true, nonetheless. Your life will change.'

'Wait a minute,' I said, shocked. 'If this is true, then I should be able to … Stir the Cauldron?'

He nodded at my ring. 'And you are able. To a degree. That thing. It's a shackle for magical beings. Tal's family found it after Hel's War and took it as their own. It did them no harm, as they cannot Stir the Cauldron. To you? It does harm. It negates your powers. Not so much your skills, though it does stop you from changing size and anything but your face. I am not sure why. You could turn into many things, my boy. That you can change at all, is a miracle.'

'It's broken. It was broken, at least a bit, by—'

'Show me,' he rumbled. I did, and he bent down to squint at it. 'The stone has been tampered with. The whole thing is different, subtly so. It has been altered. Remarkable. Perhaps the stone has been changed? And then, after, someone broke the stone. Never heard of anyone tampering with dverg treasures. Almost like someone was skillful enough to allow you the ability to change your face. I must study this.'

'I … someone did break it,' I whispered. 'A girl.'

He laughed and looked at me shrewdly. 'One of the people you stayed with?'

'Yes,' I said with a blush as Bjornag laughed rather rudely.

Morag grinned briefly. 'Well. They probably lied to you like true bastards about your abilities and mixed you right up, poor boy.'

'Yes,' I whispered, though I felt angered by the slight mockery.

'Calm, boy,' he laughed and tapped his huge foot. 'Someone did something to the ring to allow you some power. Then someone broke it enough to let you access some more of your true heritage. The rage, certainly. They quarrel amongst themselves. Must have liked you, that one. A pretty, lovable girl?'

'She was. Is.'

'Was,' the Jotun rumbled. 'Was, Maskan. You should be happy she did not break it more. If you try to remove or destroy it, it will kill you. Tal's cursed ring. Imagine. It was perfect to fool you. They took you, placed it on my baby's finger, and began corrupting you. This girl took a risk with the ring. Perhaps she liked you; perhaps she sought freedom from her masters? I know not. Matters not. She will obey them when given an order. But it is good to know they still know how to love.'

'She likely sought to help me,' I said. 'And I think she loved me.'

'You have a good heart, boy,' he said. 'But it is a human heart. Weak for lies. That thing stops you from casting spells. That … sense … is lost to you. And should you one day see them? The rivers of ice and fire filling the Void? Be careful. As I said, there are countless spells one can learn, but it is a slow process, and you might die if you fail. If you had the gauntlet, Black Grip, it would be much easier for you to learn the ways of magic. But that too, was stolen. It's what I mentioned. It is precious to us. Have you seen it?'

'I … no,' I said. 'Only this staff and the ring. And an earring.'

'Earring?' he mused. 'Well, they have our most treasured bit of magic, Maskan. It is sad it is so. We might need it one day. This gauntlet is important.' He scowled and looked like a rock that had a grudge.

Eventually, I spoke. 'Lord,' I began but went quiet. 'Father?'

His face looked startled at that and then aggrieved, and he looked away. 'Son.'

'I—'

He rumbled on, his voice intense. 'I am sorry I could not find you. Whoever held you, kept you hidden very well. Their kind have spells as well, many ways to conceal themselves and those they wish to hide. When I learned you had been seen? I knew something was taking place. I also rejoiced for you were still alive, not a skeleton in some unknown ditch. You have no idea what it does to a … a man to lose his child. His baby.'

'They want to kill you for Red Midgard,' I told him. 'They wish to restore the alliance of the north. They claim you are mad.'

He roared with mirth. 'Mad! Yes, I am crazy. Mad with rage. They have been spreading these lies for two decades, as long as the High King has been trying to brew trouble. Not only does the High King threaten us with his heresy—and I have attempted to appease him—but also these things try to topple us from within. The rumors are false. Ygrin and Red Midgard have no outstanding issues. You have been lied to. They set up a huge web of lies to trap you. They played and toyed with you, always pushing you. I killed your father. I hang the poor. I am mad and wish for war. The only thing they can actually blame me for is trying to placate the Balic fellow, our High King. Now that is a mad human.' He pointed a finger at me. 'And now. Tell me. Who are they?' He leaned forward. 'Of the Ten? Or some lesser house?'

'They are of the Ten,' I breathed. 'They—' I began and hesitated.

He struck a fist on his chair so hard the chamber echoed. 'Who? I tire of the mystery.'

'The Blacktowers,' I said.

He leaned back, shocked. 'I see. I see. It is no wonder I have not seen her in my court for ages. I only know Illastria is still alive.'

'Not even Shaduril Blacktower?' I asked, holding my head.

He shook his head, sad to his core. 'Oh, gods. She is walking?'

'Yes,' I whispered.

'You will see, Maskan, soon, why that should not be possible. No, not one of them should be about save for Illastria. Tell me, how old is she?'

'She is very old and very mad. She fears,' I told him and felt terribly sorry for the old woman.

Magor shifted so fast it left me dizzy. He changed to a man-sized version of the King. He shuddered and shook his head. His hands glowed; he moved and glided down to me, aided by a strange wind. He stepped before me and grasped me. Then he embraced me. 'Listen. Hel is the lady of the dead. She hates the gods; she hates her life, and while she is often fair to those who cross the bridge over Gjöll to her kingdom, the theft of her eye, it left her mad. We were abandoned here when they blew the Gjallarhorn on the gates. Our army was betrayed. In the end, we were up there on the hill. Inside it, in fact. Their soldiers had driven us back, the human armies. Their general fought my father, your grandfather who died. But I tricked her and sealed her in with the gauntlet, the Black Grip. We, the shapeshifters took Red Midgard for our own, unknown to men, except for the Blacktowers. And I have to say, I have learned to love humans. I have been a good king.'

'Truly?' I asked. 'I lived in the Bad Man's. You hung men. My family. Them,' I stammered and cursed them for their lies. 'You hung The Bear. Without a trial.'

He laughed. 'We found the Bear. He had already been hung. So were the two women. Both were local peasants. You have been fooled there as well. Crec has been cutting many corners with the laws of the land, but a king has to have tact. We need him.'

'I hate him,' I spat. 'Hated him.'

He scowled at that and went on. 'Yes, I see. Good. You should. We are Jotuns. Not beasts. Being a king, Maskan, is not easy, and mistakes happen, sometimes for the lack of time. But Red Midgard has been a nation for thousands of years. Due to us.'

'You live for thousands—'

'So will you,' he chuckled, and the Red Brother echoed him. 'But Hel's terrible spell? It is her way of resuming the war. She threw a seed to Midgard, probably all across Midgard, perhaps across the Nine Worlds. And that seed, my lovely boy, is that of death.'

I stared at him blankly.

'They are draugr. The family is elder draugr, raised first, stronger and much more terrible than many other undead. All the Blacktowers died twenty years ago,' he said softly. 'All of them. Save for the old lady. Illastria. And she is afraid. No wonder, since she sees the dead walking around the new keep I built her.'

'No,' I said miserably, thinking of Lith and Shaduril. 'It cannot be.'

'Yes. Balan is dead. His wife is dead. Lithiana Blacktower died, and your Shaduril did as well. I am sorry, for she was a truly lovely girl, and I showered her with gifts. She was twenty when their keep was wrecked. All you have been told are lies. We attended their funeral, though none else did, for they were not high and popular.'

I swooned, and Magor grasped me. I shook my head, denying his words. 'Dead. All dead.'

He nodded. 'We could not detect you when we learned your name at the mint because the dead mask the living. There was always one of them near you. Always, save for when you visited that burnt down hall.'

'I have been with Sand plenty. He was alive. I know it,' I said softly. 'They were not always around.'

He smiled. 'Borlein might have found you, but you didn't have a name yet, Maskan. We had not named you. We would have, that night. And perhaps they had dead around you, even when you thought you were alone. It was Tal Talin who we thought was the main culprit behind Hel's attempt to grab the world, but I killed him. I killed him, his followers and boiled their skulls as a warning, but occasionally, we still catch the dead. The red skulls are those of the draugr. The rest are traitors of humankind. But I was worried, as you were still lost. Either you were dead, or they had you. And if the latter was true, it meant someone was holding you for something.'

'My mother—'

'She sleeps here!' he yelled and shook me hard. He pointed his finger at the rock. 'You will be the Beast of the North. That is a name that resonates from Nifleheim. Your mother was my queen, our tribe were the rulers of Nifleheim's northern ranges, once. Hers was our strongest ally. You will be a king, one day. A king. Do not call a draugr your mother.'

I sat down, dazed. I held my head in my hands. 'Do you realize how hard it is to understand this?'

'Yes,' he sighed. 'I am sorry. Now, tell me this. The trouble they have given us has been small and mean for years. They kept you for twenty years. Now, they finally employed you. What else do you know of the plan?'

I nodded feverishly and grabbed my letter from under my belt. I thrust it to him. He opened it up and walked back and forth as he read it. He chortled. 'Crec and Gal,' he whispered. 'Very well. And Balan kills his villagers?' he mused and looked worried. 'Have you seen how many men they have?'

'I saw what was in the Crimson Apex,' I said. 'Balan owns properties that bar the way to the Old City. It belongs to him. Thousands?'

'He is raising an army,' he said softly. 'His own people. Did you know Valkai and his hundreds disappeared from their graves and the scaffold?'

I shook my head. The shipments to the old fort. They were corpses. And then I saw them march out. I shuddered with fear.

'He has raised his own people, and dead thieves and gods know what else to fight us,' Morag growled. 'He will pay. An army of draugr. In my city. And I was to die before they attacked.'

'Listen,' I told him feverishly. 'They killed Gal Talin and Crec Helstrom. They hoped to supplant you with Crec and Gal to make sure they could get to the Tower. I was to kill the Queen, and Shaduril was to kill you, and Gal's mint was the gateway to attack the brothers in the Tower. But since they killed Gal and Crec, I was to take Gal's face and lead them to the mint. But if they already knew the Queen is dead? Then everything they planned was a lie.'

'They know the Queen is dead indeed,' he said. 'And yes, they enjoy theater. The more elaborate the lie, the happier they are. Crec and Gal are dead?'

'I was to take their place. They got greedy. Balan killed them. But this makes no sense. They must have some other plan. If I were to kill you—'

'They sent you here to kill me. That is their plan. Nothing more. That was always the plan,' Morag said. 'They must have known I don't walk around looking like my wife inside my own home. Perhaps they hoped you would see me, recover from your shock and then try to spare your Shaduril, and I know you are in love with her,' he said and waved the letter where it was stated she was to kill Morag. 'Perhaps they hoped you would actually see an opportunity to poison me as you saw me eating. I bet they told you to improvise. Or perhaps they hoped you would use Larkgrin in despair. They made many mistakes, being quarrelsome and driven, but perhaps they hoped you would see me dead for your dead family, no matter your surprise at seeing me here. They hoped I would not know you. They were wrong. But now we have to act.'

'They hold my friend,' I said softly. 'Perhaps they hoped I'd kill you for Sand.'

'And for him, then,' Morag pondered. 'But you are right. All those men they have? Thousands?'

'Yes,' I said.

'Thousands,' he agreed, pondering. Instead of being elated, he blanched. 'We are in trouble. The Mad Watch is not to be trusted.'

'Why?'

'They can cast spells,' Morag told me. 'Did you know that? The draugr. Some can charm, others give you nightmares, and likely Bear was so charmed all through the past twenty years. They need time to do that properly. The human mind succumbs to them eventually, but Gal fought it and wanted something for himself, and that doomed him.'

'He and Crec wanted the throne,' I said. "Balan is after it, I think.'

He nodded. 'Not surprised. They want to rule the city, and so they now hold the Watch in their hands. And yes, with Gal they have a way to the Tower. That is bad. Hellish place to retake, Jotun or not.'

'Gal and Crec are dead,' I said. 'Mad Watch has no commander and I won't help them by taking any faces for them. Tower is safe.'

'Wait,' he said. 'They are dead, I believe you. The draugr are wicked undead who have human appetites for power and riches and mighty goals. Their lords and ladies rule them: though they all wish to rebel. All can hide their undead skin. They are dangerous, boy. They can Stir the Cauldron. Humans cannot touch magic, but if you are an undead, you are no longer human. The night they died, they discovered their magic and their skills. They are all driven by the goals of their old life, the things they once wished for, and they all want to fulfill those objectives.

Desperately. It is an undead thing. But they also have to obey their lords, especially the one who resurrected them. That spell is the evilest of Hel's spells. And so, Maskan, I regret to tell you I saw them this morning. Both Gal and Crec are in the Temple, and they will likely obey Balan. We need the army. Hawk's Talon. One of us will fly to the Spur to fetch them.'

Bjornag growled. 'And then we will break them. Purge them.'

'I need to get this ring off,' I hissed. 'I cannot fight like you do if—'

'It goes off with your life,' he whispered, touching it. 'I told you. That is its curse. It's old, timeworn and meant to cut off criminals from magic.'

I stared at him blankly. 'But that means I am helpless.'

'I need time,' he said sternly, 'to study it. I remember one Talien getting rid of it by nearly dying and coming back.' He looked anxious as he addressed the Red Brother. 'Get the word out. Ready the Brothers. Crec is to be beheaded at a sight. Gather Hawk's Talon and all the Mad Watch that can be trusted, and then we march off to the Tower of the Temple. If they have taken it, we will retake it, bloodily.' He turned to me. 'Listen, boy. They should not go amiss, but if things go really wrong, find the gauntlet. It is called the Black Grip, as I said. Call it and it will accept you. It's dverg-made, of course, as is all our armor and weapons, but this one is ancient. It is fit for the gods. It holds memories of the Ymirtoe's past; it whispers to you, occasionally. It contains knowledge of spells its previous wearers cast. And perhaps it can find a way past this ring. *And* it holds a secret to a powerful spell of guardianship. I mentioned it. It once locked the cave beneath the Temple. It can unlock it. The price will be steep, but there might be help down there if you are brave. And if I die, remember I love you. Mother did as well.'

'Father—'

He grinned and pushed me heavily. 'But enough of that, boy. You and I? We have some murdering to do. You have our armor, good, well. It changes with you and protects you. So do the weapons.'

'I can only change my face,' I told him. 'I am strong, but not immortal.'

'Nobody is immortal. We will find a way,' he assured me. 'The whip is a great weapon and would hurt a goddess. Come, son.'

Father. He was my father. And there was also my mother. I had seen her image, at least. 'Yes, Father.'

'We must be away since they have finally found their balls,' he said. 'Why have you not already left?' he asked the Red Brother.

'Lord, I cannot leave you alone. Let us go up together,' he told his master stiffly.

'Fine!' my father said and touched a long-handled long sword resting against his throne. 'A fine blade. I call it Tear Drinker. Magical. Soon it shall drink their blood and it shall drink their tears. Cold, lifeless blood, bitter, false tears. Let's go and free the Danegell tower from their stench. They will pay. Dearly. Pay with blood and guts, and I'll hang them. There must be limits to how many the draugr elder can raise, but I'm sure they have raised all they can. Their own men, villagers. We will exact heavy toll for such a crime.'

'I won't object to making them pay,' I said, though I was anxious for Sand. 'Will you have your scepter?' I asked him.

He hesitated. 'Yes. Give me Larkgrin. It has powers of protection. We will need it. Do you have it?'

'Yes,' I fished it out of my gauntlet. 'Larkgrin,' I breathed.

It grew in my hand. The staff was glowing, the dark wood cut sturdy, and Morag stared at it in stupefaction.

'No, it is the same thing,' he said, touching it with his finger. 'What are these glyphs?' He touched them.

'Lord!' Red screamed. 'It has been tampered with! Like the ring!'

The weapon trembled in my hand. The King slapped it away from me and grabbed me. The Red Brother grew up to his full height. He pulled on his helmet, drew his sword, and stood before us like an armored bull.

'Run, son,' Morag screamed fiercely, and I felt him draw strange energies. Upstairs, something happened. The house rumbled, dust fell, and we nearly fell. A horrible scream could be heard and then the clap of thousands of feet and sounds of battle.

Bjornag cursed. 'They are attacking us! The Brothers will be hard pressed without you, Lord!'

'Run, and find help! And remember what I said if I should die!' Morag said sadly.

But I refused to run. 'I won't abandon my father now that I've found him.'

The staff stood upright. It was changing, growing thicker, sharper at the ends. The frame cracked into an oval shape; the bird sunk into the well-grained wood. The Red Brother kicked it with his huge foot, but it had no effect. 'Steady,' Morag said, his sword swaying from side to side. The golden symbols melted and ran across the frame to create a golden, rippling center for the oval. A strange light shone in the middle and then, suddenly, the room rocked.

A dark, evil-looking mirror stood on three legs in the room. The frame was dark gray, it shuddered ominously, and darkness reigned where we should see our reflections.

'Damn idiot boy!' Morag spat. 'Go!'

'No!' I told him. 'I'll fight for you. With you. Finally.'

'Fool,' he said. 'But thank you. I hope they can hold the enemy above.'

'There are traps,' Red said. 'They can hold off an army. But we cannot!'

The mirror shuddered, just barely. The golden skin writhed slowly as if maggots were busy devouring it, and we knew someone was going to visit us. It happened so fast. People entered the room from the mirror. It sort of flashed, and then they just appeared. They looked disoriented at first but quickly regained their senses of direction and spread out, drawing weapons, holding dark shields high. There were many people, and they were not people at all. They were all dead, and my skin crawled as they had no masking spells. Many were rotten, dry; others' skin was tight around their skulls. They showed old wounds. They were Blacktower vassals, and at least one was a pageboy of Crec's, his eye gone. In an eye blink, there were two dozen, more, all armed to the teeth, gazing at the two giants and me with calm hatred. They were dressed in the familiar dark leather mail, or peasant garb, and one was the man Gray had called redundant. He was right. They would have killed and resurrected him in any case. The Blacktower coat of arms adorned their helmets, the white lily on red. One was the man I had stolen the sword from I used in the Dark Sands. He grinned at me like a human would, though his jaw was split from some old fight.

Then, Balan entered with four other people, all hooded. One stood to the side, arrogantly folding his arms over his chest. Taram, I thought, not an outsider to his father's plans after all. Well, perhaps to the part about Shaduril. He had nearly ruined everything for them. I might have died.

Balan was a strange, desperate-looking cadaver. His eyes were sunken in his head, skin yellow with white spots, and his chest strangely caved in. His eyes burned with unholy joy, and his thin lips smacked nervously. He snapped his fingers, and men marched left and right of us, surrounding the mound. Father pulled me back, and we clambered over our buried kin. Despite their dangerous looks, I was not sure they could hurt the two, armored creatures. And me.

'Greetings, your rightness,' Balan said with a strained voice. 'How did you like my tinkering with your staff? It is my particular skill. To see ways to change and enhance old magic. I did work for fifteen years on it, and it is superb.'

'It was deft work, dead one,' Morag grunted. 'Never seen that done unless by a dverg. I am impressed.'

Balan smiled, immensely happy. 'Well. All your Jotuns will be gone to Helheim. Nearly so,' he said, eyeing the Red Brother. 'They are still up there, fighting, but surrounded, and we will get them all from down here.'

'If you win,' Morag spat.

Balan nodded and bowed. 'Indeed. So here we will decide it. For years, you have been so careful. Never letting anyone near you, little less alone. When you touched the staff,' he said and fingered his strange, thick emblem, 'I felt it. I knew we could succeed. We needed you to turn him around from his hate. That must have been terrible for you, King. We knew you would do it alone, or nearly so. Too bad it took so long to build the staff to my liking, but it was worth it. I loved this show. And it was a fine, elaborate show. Lovely.'

'What do you want? A commendation. I said I am impressed,' Morag spat. 'Shall we get to it? You wicked shit.'

Balan laughed. 'We had the same mistress, Jotun. Hel.'

'We were mercenaries. You are slaves.' Morag laughed. 'And now, you are intruders. Shall you leave, or shall I show you the grave?' The house rocked, and we heard Jotuns screaming challenges above. Morag grinned. 'Many of yours go back to Hel.'

'Your poor boy,' Balan chuckled, ignored the taunt and nodded at me. 'The only thing he truly understood is that we wanted the King dead. At first we hoped to blackmail him into saving his poor Valkai imprisoned family and working with … the Horns, but he was resourceful. He escaped. So, we took the opportunity to build a finer play and to check out the mint to make taking the Tower easier and to clear Valkai's gang out quicker than we would have. Nobody missed Valkai's men and it was easier than killing our own villagers, though we killed quite a few. We got so many corpses,' he said and waved his hand at the troop around him, 'and made a more elaborate ruse. We enjoyed it. Maskan, dear Maskan. Your grief over your mother was delicious. Your sordid love affairs, your budding realization of your powers? It was fascinating. You have served us well.'

'You must be proud,' Morag spat. 'Draugr liars. You built a show for him and now you gloat?'

'Sand?' I asked them.

Balan shook his head. 'I know nothing of your friend.'

'Ask your boy,' I said and nodded at Taram's dead, white face. 'Sand was alive, and he nearly ruined the plan.'

Balan looked at Taram, who shrugged. The lord laughed. 'Morag here told you about us. The dead, my friend are creatures of old and new passions. They obey when they must and rebel the rest of the time. I am a lord of the draugr. He has to obey a direct command. But when he is alone? Such controls weaken. And besides, Taram there is not my boy. He was Shaduril's betrothed. Before Lith took him.'

The young lord shook his head at Balan. 'I tell you, Lord Balan, that I was in love with Lith before you and my father ruined it by agreeing to marry me to Shaduril,' Taram said softly. One of the hooded dead stiffened. Shaduril. It all made sense.

Balan shook his head, not really caring one way or the other. 'Here we are, nonetheless. It all worked out in the end. How did you like our funeral, King Morag? How you wept over our empty caskets? Amusing.'

'It was boring,' Morag said sullenly. 'Shall you show your faces, you filth?'

'Shaduril,' Balan said.

She flipped back the cowl. She looked alive, vibrant, if sad. She had kept her spell of concealment. She looked at me. 'Maskan,' she said with a small, frightened voice.

I bowed to her. 'Riding after the King is dead, eh?'

She smiled. 'I am sorry. I would have escaped with you if you had killed him. It was possible, but he expected you and it went this way instead. Now we have no chance.'

'She gave you a chance,' Balan snorted. 'By breaking the ring. Tampering with my tampering. Take heart, boy. She loved you. Before Lith broke her again.' The Red Brother was looking at Morag, who shook his head carefully. Above, a strange sound as the dead had apparently reached the house proper. A clang of steel, and explosions could be heard.

'Did you have some specialty, witch?' Morag asked. He was gauging our chances for an escape.

Shaduril bowed. 'The women in the family can cast charms.'

'Oh yes,' I agreed darkly. 'Charms.'

She looked at me and shook her fair head. 'No, Maskan. You are a Jotun. You are beyond such simple spells. And I did not lie to you. You just simply ... loved me. Remember, you were only to see me once. Then the Horns was to guide you here. But you escaped. I love you as well. And hate you. I cannot help it.'

The Red Brother saw my face and leaned to me. 'Don't worry. That is magic nobody is immune to. She was lovely. Is. I don't know.'

The enemy rippled with impatience.

'And you tinker with magic. Craft items?' Morag went on, his eyes going over the enemy lord.

'Yes,' Balan said. 'I can do that, sometimes. Create things that are useful. Your staff is my greatest achievement.' He tapped his pendant. 'I can feel who touches it, you see. I worked for nearly two decades on it. Three taps on this pendant, and it opens up.'

'Lith?' I asked them. 'Come, step up.'

'She is not here. She is, they said, gone,' Balan said. 'She rebelled. She won't be able to refuse us when we see her and give her a direct command, but she is gone for now. She and some of our men disappeared. It does not matter. I will miss her. But our family keeps walking. Shaduril and my wife and eldest daughter.' He nodded at the two last hooded figures.

One stepped up. She lifted her slender hands and pulled back the cowl. It was Ann. She smiled at me coldly.

'She is Sand's sister,' I whispered.

A familiar voice tittered. 'No, but eventually poor Bear was sure she was. He was not immune to my charms. And spells. It took a long time for him to start believing my lies, but he did. In the end, he had very little will of his own. I am the Queen of the Draugr and a hard corpse to resist,' said the last one, and I knew who it was. It was Balan's wife. I shook my head. 'Yes, it is I.' The figure threw back the hood, and I found myself staring at the Horns. There was a golden mask gleaming on her face, the horns glinting in the dim light. She grasped the mask, for it was she and pulled it off. It was Mir. 'Hello, my boy. Too bad you escaped that day in Valkai's place. It would have gone much smoother had you just come here to save your family. But we do like theater and perhaps your hate of the King did indeed make him think you were the only threat worth considering.'

I stared at the woman I had thought of as Mother, the dead one that had raised me. She was lean as a wolf, mean, and her hair was in tatters, a great slab of meat missing from her scalp. She was sickly yellow. There she stood, arrogantly staring around at the hall, and then she just simply ignored me. 'So, Danegell. The dance is over. With the Jotuns gone, we will soon rule Midgard. Hel rules, and we shall govern in her name. It is time for you to travel back to Niflheim, and beyond to the bridge of the dead. There you shall meet your mistress and mine. I hope she will have forgiven you.'

Morag snorted, a sound like huge bellows blowing dust and cinders. 'Twenty years you have haunted our realm. You filth. And you think the men of Red Midgard will just hand their home to you? You think they will succumb to your betrayal forever? You may raise a few of them, charm some, but they will fight you.'

'Yes,' Mir said coldly. 'Of course, they will. But this is the beginning. Your Tower of the Temple is ours. Thanks to the mint. And Crec and Gal, who I was fortunate enough to bring back. They don't always return, and you need a living person to raise a dead one. I raised Valkai's men and quite a few of our villagers, but many failed to return. Now,' she said, cherishing the moment. 'Know this. The new king will march the troops to Stone Home, muster the armies of the north, and take the war to Ygrin and Falgrin. They will fight, but each other. Not us. But enough of this, Jotun. Kill them. Spare Maskan.'

'No need to spare me,' I growled. 'I won't spare you.'

'No, we won't spare you,' Taram said steadily. 'The people will need to see a man hang, won't they, for this crime? The last Brother.' He nodded at my armor. 'They shall.'

My father turned to look down at me, his eyes betraying his fear. I shrugged my shoulders at him. For some reason, I was at peace. 'We will see in Helheim.'

'Sentimental,' Balan noted. 'But you are no true Jotun, so perhaps it is excepted. Kill the two. Then we go up and surprise the rest if they hold. Let none escape!'

Mir nodded, and the soldiers stepped before the five undead lords. There were a hundred of them, and the dangerous Blacktowers. They roared gutturally and charged up the mound, a wave of dead coming at us with murderous intent.

Morag roared, the floor shook, and I felt him calling for strange powers.

The Blacktowers called for them as well.

The Red Brother jumped before me, his huge sword swiped down at the charging enemy mass. There was a flash of deadly metal, then grim screams and six undead men fell in a heap of limbs, indeed dead again. One was the man whose sword I had taken, another the guard I had had killed in the Apex. The giant growled and charged through the milling mass of enemies. Gravestones shattered, corpses tumbled under his foot, and swords darted like lightning around him. He jumped up and leaped for Balan. Spears reached for him in the air, but he shifted to man-size, the sword as well and he came to crouch just before the dead lord, the weapons having missed him. Mir was backpedaling; Ann as well, but Balan was not. Another spear missed the Red Brother as Magor's spell turned a group of the enemy into pillars of ice at the Red Brother's back.

I felt useless as the dead all turned to look at the Red Brother.

A dead man speared at the knight's back, but the man toppled as he hit empty air. The now gigantic, blond gargoyle had shot up from the floor, its hand around struggling Balan, and the sword was flashing in the air. I felt Balan touching the powers, Stirring the Cauldron, as my Father had called it, and a fiery field of energy surrounded Balan.

The Red Knight shrieked as his armored hand was burned, and he tossed Balan across the room, where the former man crumpled at the base wall. Mir pointed at the Red Knight, and Shaduril and Ann turned to face him while Mir stalked for Father with Taram. I stepped forward, holding the White's whip. The Red Brother went into a berserk rage, and draugr corpses fell in heaps around him. Above, something exploded, and the dead shrieked in pain. I heard Jotun voices up there and prayed some would know what was taking place below them.

'Come, Maskan,' Taram laughed disdainfully from beyond some of his soldiers. 'I have some payback to be done. You were flirting with my wife! And my mistress!' he said and nodded at Shaduril. 'I don't forgive these insults, never will I.' His eyes glowed, he pushed past his men as we squared off. In the meantime, Mir put on the mask and faced Father.

Magor called for power, he danced like a furious, two-legged tree around the top of the grave mound, and a savage wind tore through the room. Three dead men were cursing as they climbed up the mound. Blade-sharp ice formed at Father's hands, his mouth growled, and the men flew away, stiff skin torn from their faces, flesh peeling. The ice statues Father had created of some of the undead toppled in the storm. Father was calling for more of the winds, but he was also harnessing a spell of guardianship. He had to. Mir was swaying, and a pillar of fire reached to lick at the Jotun king's face, but to no avail as the ice around Father sizzled. Shaduril and Ann were surrounding the Red Brother, and there flashed a spell of icy spears, which the giant dodged as he crushed a group of draugr soldiers. More loped from the mirror. *There would be hundreds,* I thought and despaired, hoping there was some limit to the mirror's capacity for moving the evil ones.

Then, Taram was before me.

'Don't know how to change your size. Only your nasty face, no?' he said and moved fast as a shadow. 'I'll carve some of it. To the skull.' I cursed, for he had cast a spell. He moved like a shadow and, in fact, he was a shadow, I decided. He had been standing before me, then he was behind me, and the blade cut the air as I barely managed to dodge his strike and turn to face him. 'Always wanted to kill a king. A prince will be an excellent appetizer. But then, after he dies,' Taram said and nodded at Morag, 'you will be the king. And perhaps I shall get him as well?'

'Alive!' Mir yelled at him while calling for more fire pillars, which Magor's protective spell absorbed. The storm wind faltered but still scourged some undead soldiers, who had tried to reach the King.

'Alive, alive,' Taram cursed. 'If she was not here ...' He stabbed his sword forward again, trying to impale my shoulder. I fell away to my back, felt the blade skitter on my chest armor. I rolled and flicked the whip around where he had been standing. He still was, and the deadly whip was tearing for the pale foe.

It passed through him as the shadow darted forward again.

I instinctively kicked up and hit his chest hard just as he was coming back to our world, and he flew back, rolling into a ball of shadowy nothingness, only to appear at my side, grinning manically.

Mir's golden mask glowed as she raised a true inferno around the gravesite. She put everything she had into it. She weaved a mighty amount of power into the spell. It sucked air and ripped ice out of Father's spells, and Morag roared in anger as he staggered. Mir was laughing hollowly, her movements jerky as she kept the fire going, pushing ever-increasingly into it. I was suffocating. The dead would not. I tried to catch a breath and spat drily. Taram rushed before me and rested the blade on my neck, eyeing the mound where Morag went to his knee, holding his throat, trying to concentrate amidst flames and his last protective spells.

Mir flew on her face as Shaduril was hurled on her back. Both rolled over Mother's stone.

The Red Brother stood before the smoking grave mound, bleeding from many wounds, his blade high up in the air, growling. I saw Ann was holding her head in the corner, apparently having been kicked there, her arm useless, judging by the strange angle. A heap of dozens of the draugr twitched on the floor. Taram growled at me as he looked up. There, The Beast of the North still stood, his clothing was simmering and partly on fire, his armor was gleaming, and his massive chest heaving as he turned to Taram. 'Shit,' Taram whispered, and sharp particles of ice lanced from the Jotun's finger, spearing Taram in the chest. The magic tore off flesh and clothing, and Taram flew back to the dark, screaming. I got up and backed off for Father, and so did the Bjornag.

All around the room's dark corners, the Blacktowers crept up, relentless. The golden mask of Mir gleamed dimly; Ann climbed up unsteadily, Balan as well, and Taram was leaning on a sword in the deep shadows of the room. The others were dead, torn.

'Can we do anything?' I breathed as the Blacktowers flickered in the shadows. They were chattering inhumanly, their movements jerky.

Morag wiped the sweat off his face; it came off with soot from the flames. 'We can only fight. Or I can. I wish I had the gauntlet. It would make all the difference.'

'Matters not,' the Red Brother said, grimacing from his wounds. 'They block the doorway. I can try to fetch help, but—'

I sobbed, holding the whip tight. 'This is my fault. I brought that weapon here.'

Father scoffed. 'This is all they wanted. You and I near alone. They hoped you might poison me or kill me, that would have worked well for them, but they wagered I'd see through you. That I would want to make you love me. That I would forget to be careful with someone who has been lied to so much about his father. I could see through you. But not through his craft. Lies upon lies. It worked. Get him out of here,' he told the Red Brother.

'We must get out,' the Red Brother said calmly, his sword at the ready. He eyed the hulking lord behind him. 'Come with us. Charge together.'

'I'll not let them defile my house,' he spat. 'No Danegell would let them crawl over our home, our bones. I'll damn them back to Hel. Take him. Run!' I had no chance to protest. The Red Brother cursed and grabbed me. He pulled me along and he loped for the door lightning fast. The dead ones moved, and he had expected them to. He threw me high, rolled on the ground, his sword coming up and down, and that strike tore an arm off Balan, who had moved to block him. The dead thing shrieked. His eyes were burning in his head as it held the dry stump. Balan flopped to the ground as the Red Brother caught me. Flames licked at the Red Brother from Balan's remaining hand, but we were past the bastard and stepped to the doorway.

Ann laughed with a hateful voice. I felt her calling for strange powers, and the floor glowed.

The Red Brother stepped on it. There was an explosion that rocked the house. The hallway before us fell apart, and then we flew in the air. My guardian was torn into bits and pieces. His armor rained around the chamber in rattling and clanking wreckage. I struck the ceiling and fell to Balan's feet. He grasped my throat and grinned without humor or emotion. He ripped my head up to look at Father.

A swarm of men rushed from the mirror. 'Mir's Bones, that's the mirror,' he whispered. 'I renamed it. I don't like my wife. Don't tell her. But at least she lets me sit on the throne.'

'You have no soul,' I whispered. 'There is nothing real about you.'

'As long as I get to sit on the throne, even once, I am fulfilled. Damn your souls,' the draugr panted. Their goals, they all had them. I struggled, but two undead came to hold me down, and no matter the rage I felt, I could not move. 'The mirror can bring some dozens at a time, and then it must rest for a moment, but they will suffice.'

A dozen, then two dozen armed dead came through the mirror. They moved like animals, slithering, loping, running, and they surrounded Father, who was casting spells, his sword in his hand. He summoned a whip of ice and more whirling ice to cover him. Mir was also casting spells, so was Ann, and Shaduril, and gouts of flame tore at the shields of Father, roasting him in places, leaving his armor smoking. He roared so loudly some undead fell on their knees, but then they all charged him. The whip went up, then down, slaying ten of the enemy, then more as Father held his place and tore the stream of dead into shreds. He cursed and spat and laughed like a dying king would, proud and noble amidst vermin. Mir danced strangely and summoned fiery arms from the ground to grasp at his ankles, which tore off armor and skin and meat. Shaduril and Ann summoned scorching energies, and thin whips of fire grew from their hands. They pushed after the remaining soldiers, and all of them began whipping and stabbing at the huge Jotun. Ice and fire whips went up, smoke and fumes filled our nostrils, the dead fell into pieces and Father bellowed in agony. Ann hissed and moved to the side; her whip came up and down and tore a wound in Father's face. Shaduril stopped her attack, concentrated, and raised a flame wall across Father, and his ice barrier collapsed. Mir came forward, and from her hands grew a tall molten spear. She hovered at the edges of the fight, and I struggled wildly, but Balan held me tight. 'Watch! At least this time you get to witness the death of your father.'

Father went to his knees; the fiery claws were tearing at his legs.

The enemy howled victoriously and charged.

And Morag changed.

He twisted into a ball, sprung up as a bleeding, enormous white bear and wiped his claws across Ann's head, which flew to the dark corner. Then Father jumped for Mir. His mass buried the draugr queen from sight; the claws raked at the woman's body, and she shrieked in surprise and pain.

The fiery spear appeared from Father's back. Taram's shadow slithered across the bear's back, he appeared and a sword thrust through Father's head. Taram hollered incoherently, his goal achieved.

Morag slumped, and he died.

It was over.

He changed as he died, his sword nearly man-sized as was his body. Taram grabbed the weapon and stared at it feverishly. The draugr pried Mir from under Morag's still formidable physique. She was alive.

I hissed in rage and struggled but could not move. I tore at the ring on my finger, but it did not budge but burrowed under my skin instead. I howled in pain as Balan looked down at me. 'All hail the Beast of the North!' he laughed, and the dead turned to look at me.

'Bring him up,' Mir said drily from the side. She was twisted to her side, eyeing the damage to her chest. Half was missing, her throat ragged. Not enough to kill her, though.

'What shall we do with him?' Balan asked his wife. 'As planned?'

She twisted her head to the side. Shaduril was ignoring me until Mir pulled at her and spoke with her. 'Get up and kill the rest. Then tell Crec he is the Beast of the North. Tell him he must lead the Hawk's Talon to Hollow Stone pass as soon as possible and then north for Ygrin. He won't like it, but persuade him. There is trouble from the northerners. And tell everyone, the Brothers work for Ygrin and must be captured and killed, should any survive. Then go and resume your duty.'

'Yes, Mother,' she said softly and nodded at me with a small smile that changed into sorrow. She waved farewell. She had wanted to see me die, perhaps? She would not, and that made her sad? Or did she regret what was happening?

'Balan,' Mir said, and the lord nodded at her. 'Sit on the Rose Throne. Govern the city while we are gone.'

'My pleasure, wife,' he told her, though in truth there was no love between the dead things. *She was leaving?*

'Taram?' she said.

'Mother-in-law?' he said and grinned.

'You are the new Lord Commander of the Mad Watch. Gag and hang the King Killer. Then hunt down the remaining Jotuns,' she said. She glanced at Ann's body as if she had worth. 'Bury her. And Lith if she is dead instead of a rebel. It was a heavy price, but Red Midgard is ours.'

'Yes, I shall,' Taram said, smiling wickedly. More dead entered the room, many dozens poured in. They turned to rush upstairs and when they did, the battle was soon over.

## CHAPTER 16

The Harlot was unhappy.

I could not see her fuming at me, for they had placed a sack over my face so people would not see me changing my looks. There was a noose that was tight around my neck so no hair would spill out, should I play a fool and try to make life hard for them. *Life,* I chuckled in panic. *They were living dead.*

'You have silver, gold? Gold will get you gone really fast. Silver will do it pretty fast,' the fat executioner whispered to me. 'Or you can just hang there. Lord?'

'Yes,' I heard Taram say languidly.

'The armor, it is heavy. Might break his neck too quickly if he does not pray for mercy,' she whined.

'Ah, do not worry about it. The rope is extra thick. And you, Lord Gal, you will not be needed,' Taram called out.

Gal. He was there. Dead as well.

'My Lord Captain, it is the rule of the land I oversee executions and take his possessions for the treasure—'

'For your treasury,' Taram laughed. 'But this is irrelevant. At least in this case. He hangs in his armor.'

'You have a new sword, my lord,' Gal said morosely.

'Yes, I do!' he laughed. 'Tear Drinker!' He had taken Father's magnificent sword. In his hands, it would be deadly. 'And stop delving too deep into my business, my lord, or you shall find yourself explaining your greed to my mother-in-law.'

A resentful grunt told me he was about to launch into a further argument, despite Taram's threat. The undead had a hard time letting go of their desires. But then, there was a high-pitched female voice. 'He is mulish. Won't say anything. But my silver—' the Harlot intervened in the discussion, but only for a moment.

'He is gagged,' Taram told her impatiently. 'He cannot answer you. And he has nothing. Never did. Only in his dreams did he have something. Get on with it. You get paid extra if you do it slowly.'

'Oh!' the Harlot said, and I could imagine her licking her fat lips. 'You should have said so, my lord. Sorry, Brother.'

'You knew you would be paid,' Taram growled. 'You wanted to see if you could rob him before the hanging. On to the Sun Court. He will meet the tree.'

Shit-skulled bastard. I resisted the urge to struggle as hands pushed me. They were taking me to the First Ring, to the Singing Garden and the Sun Court that was the heart of the city, filled with the most influential houses and people. They were showing me off to the old houses, and there I would die. There was a constant drone of yells and screams around me. I was pelted with vegetables; people were crying, and I realized they could not comprehend the King was gone. Then I was hit in the chest by something that smelled like excrement and likely it was. I stumbled on, my feet dragged along. I felt someone was casting spells far, far away and felt the ring in my hand, resisting my giant's senses, and it drifted off, the brief glimpse of magic. Had they killed all the Brothers? They took the Tower. And the Tenginell house. Yes, possibly. Gone. My kindred. My father?

*Dead.*

They marched us through the gates, our steps were echoing, and I heard the Mad Watch curse me. The stupid bastards didn't know what they were allied with. Then, I heard cliff birds shrieking and knew we were before the very walls of the Tower of the Temple, the top of the hill. They marched us to the right, for the Sun Court and the final gate to the Temple, no doubt held by Blacktower and Crec.

'Behold,' Taram said, 'but you cannot! Your Brothers,' he yelled to the benefit of the crowds, 'failed. There they hang, and you, king killer, shall hang with them!'

'Rip his entrails out!' someone yelled.

'Hang him from his balls!' another echoed the murderous sentiment.

'Law and justice shall be served!' Taram yelled. 'We are no animals. Like they are, the traitors to the land!'

I had had no justice at all; no formal court of law had heard my case. But that was moot, apparently, as the people around me either agreed or disagreed with Taram, the new Lord Commander of the City.

I cursed as I struggled with my binds. They were of thick steel, and I could not bend them. 'Tell him to be quiet,' the Harlot said. 'I hate noisy customers. Makes me look like a butcher. Dignity, self-constraint, and modesty will set a good example. Don't be a screamer,' she whispered in my ear helpfully and even playfully.

'I said he is gagged,' Taram sighed. 'Here, get it over with.' I felt the cobblestones give way to marble, and I heard a hundred bells clinking magically. The tree was very near. And so was my demise.

'Sure, let me do this my own way, my lord,' she said. 'There are rules to this art, you know. They will talk about this at their dinner tables all across Dagnar this evening. They will whisper about it in the taverns. And if they find this was done improperly?'

I heard Gal snicker. 'They will hang the Lord Commander instead.'

'Or the Lord of the Harbor,' Taram said with a clear warning.

'The king slayer,' Taram spat, 'has to die. Do your best? Hang him, step back, and let the folks enjoy it. None must see his face.'

'Who is the king?' she asked.

'King Crec Helstrom,' Taram told her, his voice utterly bored. 'He is watching from the wall of the Temple with my mother-and father-in-law. Make it good enough.'

I struggled. I did not want to, but I did. I tore free of the Mad Watch escorting me, ran and fell heavily and hit my face. They grabbed me up—very roughly—to the amusement and jeers of the crowds around me. They threw me around, guiding me in the right direction, pushed me on, and I kicked desperately. The familiar rage was gnawing at the edges of my mind, but it was not enough to break the shackles. I was too afraid, and I felt the cursed ring resisting all my attempts to escape, to do what a Jotun should be doing. Fight. Jotun? I laughed. I was nothing of the sort. I was going to die a human. I kicked around again and connected with a leg that broke in two, at least judging by the crack of the bone and the howling of the man. Then I was lifted. They carried me on; the jingling of the bells mixed strangely with the cacophony of the crowds. The feet of the men who were carrying me thrummed on planks now, and I felt I was lifted higher. The wind was not only rustling the bells hung on the skulls, but also I could now hear the bony clack of skulls brushing each other and the rustling of the leaves. Then, I felt a rope on my face. They slid it over my head, and I could not help it from happening. I sobbed, cursed, and spat and then—amidst shouts, jests and the clanging bells—they hoisted me up on my toes.

'Waaait!' the Harlot shrieked. She came to adjust my armor, the gorget that was hampering the rope, and then I felt something strange. Her fat finger slipped under the hood, pressed against my lips, and there was something in it. A pebble? 'Take it you damnable idiot fool. You'll die, but it's painless,' she hissed, and I knew she was trying to help me for some reason. I opened my mouth and swallowed the pebble. It was acrid, then tasteless, and it felt like a ball of molten lead was going down my throat. Then I forgot about it as the Harlot stepped away.

'All yours!' she laughed. 'Amateurs. He would have escaped! This is why you pay me, Lord Commander.'

'And I thank you!' Taram laughed. 'Make him a hummingbird, boys!'

I struggled to find a footing, but could not. Panic welled inside me, and I cried like a baby, cursed the Blacktowers to Hel, where they belonged, and pissed myself as the pain intensified. I hung there for a long time, listening to the jests and mocking laughter of the crowds. I changed my face and thinned my neck, but the rope was not letting me off its clutch. It had been well designed, and it just followed the size of its prey, getting as tight as was needed for the job. I begged the Harlot would not crack my neck by jumping on my legs, and then I cursed her for not doing so because the poison she had given me was not working.

Then it was.

I cramped, twitched, and screamed into the gag, for I was on fire. It was like a molten inferno, but only for a second. I felt something break inside, and I remembered little. I heard Taram speaking, very close. 'You slept with my lover. With Lithiana. You wanted my wife, Shaduril. Now I have killed a king. And another. Die, you piss-sodden excuse for one. King of Fools. Oh, and I was the one in the woods the night Sand died. I tricked the archers to fire, and White could not do anything to stop me. I gave Sand nightmares of your perfidy. I can do that. I wanted him dead before you died, just to torment you and I did, didn't I? And he did die, Maskan, your Sand. He is a draugr now. He was at Dark Sands and he was dead already. But you will not come back. I'll get your corpse tomorrow and make a robe of your hide.'

*I will see Father*, I thought as I could not draw another breath.

# BOOK 5: THE TIDE

# THE BEAST OF THE NORTH

*'She dreamt of children and happiness and living by the sea. Now she only desires my life.'*
**Lith to Maskan**

## CHAPTER 17

I woke up to pain.
*That was to be expected*, I thought. *Why would death be painless?*
Then I realized my head, my thoughts were filled with something strange. There was a thrumming, sentient power living inside my skull. It was vast as an ocean, wild and careless as war. It was like a new sense. I could see and hear it, smell and touch it, even taste it. I heard the rumble of an indescribable mass of primal ice, ancient and strange, rivers of power rumbling over icy beds of rivers, tumbling into the bottomless void. And there was the fire. Fiery rivers flowed, all made up of molten stone, and they all fell from Muspelheim. They met, somewhere, mixing in great mystery. To see that. To feel that. It was an incredible thing, a terrific sense, but one that simply overwhelmed me. I sat up with my eyes wide open. I held my head as I tried to make sense of it. I attempted to push it back, and for a moment, I saw Sand's drawn face. He too was dead.

Then the powers consumed me again and I gazed at the brilliant streams of icy and fiery powers, all cascading before my … eyes? Soul? I lifted my hands and groped forward to tuck at the beautiful things. I pulled at the powers and felt them obey my call. There was ice, water, wind, all freezing and mighty, and a million ways to grasp some of it, to combine it all together.

I pulled at the glittering streams, grasped icy drizzle, and then plunged into the core of the coldest stream of ice I could find. I tore at it, pulled some to me. Then I called some winds into it and wondered at how both streams tingled in my hands.

'That was the spell your father used,' Lith said calmly. 'I remember how it felt seeing it for the first time. Magic.'

I lost my focus. The spell escaped my hands, and I saw Sand scrambling away. A bitter gust of wind tore from me, dragged me to my knees and forward, and the walls of the underground stone cell frosted over and cracked and groaned as the plaster crumbled to the floor.

The room was dark, and I turned in panic, looked around and tried to find Lith. I saw Sand, his one hand a bloody mess, the wound on his face quite ghastly. He was a corpse, in fact, white and haggard. Then I saw Lith, crouched on the side, her eyes burning softly in the shadows. I gathered the ice and whirling wind again. I overshot the spell, made a mess of it, braided too much of something, and let go of it, but at the wrong place. I felt my breath freezing, and then some stabbing pain at my feet as they were encased in ice.

Lith chuckled.

I tore myself free so hard the floor buckled, but the ice kept me still. I growled like an animal, felt an urgent need to change and felt myself growing. The ice cracked off as I filled the room, hit my head on the ceiling, and fell under a small avalanche of stones.

'He will get us killed,' Sand said warily. 'Blue? White blue? His skin?'

'Jotun. Ice giant,' Lith agreed. 'That is what he is. Always was, but for Tal's old ring and Balan's craft. And our charm spells to fool you and your father, Sand. That was his world. All fabrication. Now? He is the last Jotun. In Midgard at least.'

'They never found Black Brother,' Sand told her. 'Fled from the Tower as they took it.'

'Yes, that is so,' Lith agreed. 'But he is alone in his burden. The last king, then.'

I pulled myself up on all fours, my face level with Lith and pushed stones and rubble off my back. 'You—' I began. 'Bitch.'

'I'm going to get spanked now,' she said, with a bit of worry in her voice. 'I killed the Harlot for you! Took her place! Gave you some of the poison you used in the Mint!'

I rushed forward and grabbed her inside my fist. She flinched and stared up at my face. I resisted the urge to squeeze her. 'Draugr? Not alive?'

She sighed. 'No,' and laughed. 'I still sigh, even if I have no breath to let out. It's hard to be dead and still alive, Maskan. It's confusing. But we pretend. We act. Perhaps we miss breathing.'

'You will look a confused mess of mangled flesh in a bit, love,' I said and thought about smashing her to the wall.

'She changed sides,' Sand told me. 'Or she never had one.'

'She did?' I chuckled. 'They are all mad. They are obsessed, driven by their needs. If they want something, they cannot easily let go of it. That is why you had me, no?'

'Yes, I wanted you. Still do. It is strange,' she said. 'And it was pleasurable. And I wanted to get your help, in return for me not telling Shaduril about that evening. Now I can only ask nicely.'

'You mad thing,' I growled.

'Hold,' she said as I squeezed. 'Just hold.'

'Why?' I asked her spitefully. 'You have to make a will?'

'No,' she said, 'my will was executed after we died. All went to Illastria.'

'Poor woman.' I laughed.

'She went mad. Quite mad,' Lith told me. 'She saw us walking, and her mind could not grasp it. She is the head of the house in the eyes of the world, but truly, she just draws the same words over and over again in her journals.'

Sand grunted. 'I saw it. It says: "They died. Why do they speak?"'

'You won't walk again,' I told Lith. 'Nor speak. She will be happy.'

'I saved your life just now,' she said with reproach. 'That is worth consideration.'

'Your kind killed my family and lied to me. That too is worth consideration,' I told her with a feral growl. I wanted to bite her head off. 'I'm not a fool anymore. Why did you rebel?'

She patted my hand affectionately. 'When Mother, your Mir—and that is her real name—died that terrible night, twenty years ago, the spell chose her. There are other elder draugr all across Midgard, but she is the Queen. We are always second to her, and that cannot be changed. We must obey her if she commands us, and only by hiding and running can we have our independence. But as you see, the dead do not give up. She knows I rebelled. Shaduril is after me. They will find me sooner or later. It's dreary. I do not enjoy it. I can help dethrone her,' Lith said calmly, and I stopped squeezing, despite myself. 'If she dies, then she won't command me.'

'So you wish to be the eldest draugr in Red Midgard?' I sneered.

'I wish to be free.' She grinned.

'You cannot speak yourself out of becoming stuffing for a hole in a wall,' I said. 'That would free you, no?'

'I don't want to die. And I can help you,' she said with a note of worry I found refreshing.

'Speak,' I said, cursing her under my breath. 'I doubt you can help me, you conniving corpse.'

She ignored my foul mood and smiled widely. 'Of course I can! You have few allies. Even fewer who love you!' she said with passion, her eyes gleaming maniacally, and I shuddered in disgust. 'And I did not kill your father. I did not. I was not there, remember? I could not stop it, no because Mir made us and we mostly obey her if she so commands, but I did not take part in that. I have some former Jesters with me, as they remember what it was like to rule their own world. We have ways to help you indeed. As long as we don't run into Balan or Mir, we will. I want to.'

'And what is your agenda?' I asked her.

'Mine? I wish to kill Mother.' She grinned. 'Kill her. I want her dead. She raised us from Helheim. I did not ask for this. Neither did Ann nor Shaduril. My agenda is to kill those who can shackle us.'

'I know,' I hissed. 'I meant after. Will you be happy after I kill your mother and father? What other hidden goals might you have?'

'I had a few,' she sulked. She put a hand on my cheek. 'Still have quite a few.'

'I think you really need me for something else as well, don't you?' I spat.

'Of course, I need you!' she insisted caressing my face, and I resisted the urge to bite her fingers off. 'I need you to help me get the two bastards first, though. And that should be fine with you.'

'No,' I said and squeezed her. 'I don't trust you. Not one bit. Tell me more. You mentioned Shaduril is after you.'

Her eyes bulged, and she stuttered. 'Well. If we kill Balan and Mir, she will be equal to me. And as you know, she has it in her head to kill me. Get it?'

'I don't,' I grunted.

She swallowed. 'I'll want Shaduril dead as well.'

'No,' I told her.

'But I want it,' she hissed.

'I said no,' I barked. 'That is all. You won't get everything you wish for. You're going to have to risk something as well.'

'But—'

'Let go! And then you shall take Mir's place?' I asked her. 'You will rule the dead, along with other ... elder draugr. What will you do with them? Tell me all now, or perish. I'll make rat feed out of you. Beef jerky. They will enjoy a snack, no matter how old.' Her magical earring was shaking wildly as I shook her.

She rubbed her face and nodded. 'I want to run a kingdom. Underground. Deep down here in the shadows of the land. Without anyone to command me. That's what I want. A crew of my own.' She hesitated and upped her bid. 'And I want you.'

'You cannot have me.' I grinned ferociously. 'Only my animosity. And what can you offer?'

'That gauntlet,' she said with a small grin. 'Black Grip. Let me down?'

I let her down, keeping an eye on her. I had few human frailties left, right that minute, I realized, and squashing her would be very easy. 'Go on.'

'Balan had it. I know where it is,' she said.

'Where?'

'Secret,' she sulked. 'Do we have a deal?'

'And has he tampered with that as well? Black Grip?' I sneered.

'That artifact is different,' she said nervously. 'He was tempted to try to use it for this scheme they pulled on Morag, but Black Grip was beyond him to understand. Larkgrin was a simple weapon. Black Grip has … power of its own. It's not entirely dead.'

I was nodding. I needed it, no matter what. I looked at my poor friend in the dark shadows, staring at me emotionlessly. 'Sand?'

'Maskan,' he answered.

'She is party to the killings of our family,' I told him. 'They lied to you, to me. You and your father are as much a victim as I was. Do you wish to kill her?'

'No,' he said reluctantly, and I looked at him in surprise. He looked away.

'I'm a draugr elder,' Lith said helpfully. 'He is a lesser thing. He will obey me when I ask him to.'

'I see,' I said, eyeing Sand. He looked pale, strange, and his eyes gleamed. I had failed him. 'What was that thing you fed me in the hanging?' I asked her.

Lith poked me. 'I told you. The poison I gave you, Maskan, is what you have used once. It puts you in a very deep sleep. It was the same essence Ann created for the mint job.'

'Ann,' I said. 'Poor girl.'

Lith nodded. 'She was always the odd duck in the family. Awkward and smart. We loved each other once, but as you know, she never found love. She did love you. We all do. Did. Perhaps we like danger and tall men? Though Taram is short. I—'

'Shut up. About the poison?'

'It's an ingenious thing. Ann was good with bright things, alchemy, and poisons. You should be grateful I stole some of it from her. I thought it might be useful one day. The effects took time to wear off, and much has happened in the meantime. Are you listening?'

'Grateful,' I whispered. 'I'm not grateful to you, Lith, not for anything,' I told her. 'Who raised Sand?'

'I didn't,' she said, looking uncomfortable. 'Mir has the power, a strange spell to raise the dead. Unique. Possibly Hel's personal favor to the draugr kings and queens. I don't know. It is not as simple as it sounds. She can only raise some twenty per day, and it always consumes a living soul. We harvested Valkai's kingdom for corpses and used the villagers to raise them and each other. Sometimes the spell fails, and it was a real problem with Crec and Gal resisting our charms enough to plot against Balan, but Mir managed to raise them. Sand here, with him we succeeded as well. I fetched his corpse and had Mother raise him. I claimed he might prove useful, and she agreed. Taram, the reckless idiot, risked everything by grabbing him and forcing the poor, just raised boy into that event. He hates you so much. He cannot help it. As much as I love you, he hates you.'

I ignored her words, turned to look at my friend. He shrugged. 'Don't look at me like that. It's probably as weird for me as it is for you to be a magic casting … Jotun. And the arm? No need to worry about that, either.' He indicated his cancerous flesh. The arrow wound in his face looked dreadful.

'Our flesh dries, the wounds remain but the bones mend, eventually, unless we are slain,' Lith explained.

'We are friends, Sand,' I reminded him, not sure if that were true. There was something really odd about him. His movements were jerky, his mood dangerous. 'And now you follow her?'

'I must.' He frowned.

'This is his wish?' I asked her. 'To serve you?'

'I am his draugr elder, Maskan. Will you help us?'

*Them.* Sand *and* her.

'And what can you offer me?' I asked her. 'I cannot imagine myself at the head of your army of mongrels. And perhaps all this is just a cruel joke. I say yes, walk out of here, and Taram grabs me again. Probably get hanged once more, eh? You are a strange and wicked lot.'

She shook her head empathetically. 'No, Maskan. No. This is no joke. I admit some dead might enjoy torturing you so. Imagine you agreeing to our terms and marching out of here only to be mocked again by the multitudes? That would tickle our sense of humor. It would. You saw the wonderful play we put on for you. We love such theater. But no. We need you. You get revenge, and perhaps we can come to some agreement. I will rule the underworld. Maybe you can try to take power above? It won't be easy.'

*The gauntlet. I needed it.* And so, loathing myself, I nodded.

She grinned hugely and shrieked with happiness. Then she hugged my knee, for I was still over ten feet tall. 'So, here is the plan. I cannot kill them. They have power over me. But once you get the gauntlet, you will be very mighty. You will shape-shift, fly up to the Pearl Terrace, and smash them to bits. You can, you know. With the gauntlet, it is all possible. Then the city will fall to the chaos, and we can sort out the new ways to rule it. I get to slay Taram. You don't have to worry about it; I will be cruel. He and I were in love once, but he is still a problem for me. He can make life hard for me, as he also is a lord. And Shaduril—'

'No,' I said.

She shuddered. 'I guess Shaduril is then for me to deal with. Eventually. But you kill Balan and Mir. I will deal with Taram.'

'Yes,' I whispered.

'You won't regret this, my love.'

'Thank you … love,' I answered with dripping sarcasm. I looked at Sand, who said nothing. 'You can cast spells?'

'I hear this thing faintly,' he told me.

'He is not a very talented draugr with spells, my dear,' Lith said. 'He is a bit like Taram was, adept in shadows and disguises and perhaps betrayal.' She walked to Sand and stroked him affectionately.

'I see. What do you look like without your spells?' I asked her.

'The Draugr are not all rotten and dry,' she said happily. 'Just dead. They are not mindless zombies.' Her face paled, the skin went to white, and her eyes were red and fierce. Otherwise, her hair remained red and lustrous. She touched it affectionately. 'I oil it daily. I suffocated that night, twenty years past. Left me unblemished.'

'Your mother is uglier than she used to be,' I told her. 'I want something first.'

'Anything!'

'Sorrowspinner,' I whispered. 'I—' I began and then stared at my finger. There was no finger.

She grinned widely. 'The ring kept you in control as you know. As the poison did rather kill you, I took a chance it could be removed. I was right.' She showed the finger to me. It was swollen and ugly, and the black ring was still there, glinting dully.

'You cut my finger off,' I said dangerously. 'Give it here.'

'Wait, I'll remove the ring,' she said and began tugging at it.

'No, give it here,' I growled, and she hesitated and handed it over while glowering at me.

'Technically, it belongs to my family—'

'Technically, your family is dead.' I laughed. 'They should not own anything.' I ripped the ring off the finger and dropped it into the dust. *Damned finger*, I thought. And I truly didn't care. 'Now. Where is the gauntlet?'

'At the old keep, High Hold. In Father's workshop,' she said with a smile.

'And is it guarded?' I asked her.

'It is well guarded,' she told me. 'And we will have a small army to help us enter, but we will need you to fight. You are, after all, the Beast of the North. After you get the gauntlet, you will use its powers to help us kill off the enemy in the Tower of the Temple. We will loot Crimson Apex as well. Lots of gold there, and I shall need it later. I'll spare Illastria. Poor aunt is sort of a mascot. And she knows things.'

'Very well,' I told her.

She nodded. 'Good. It is settled, then. I'm going to help you. Sand will as well. And so will they.' She nodded at the doorway out of the cell. We were under the city, in Valkai's tunnels. Out there, a dozen eyes glowed. Then scores. More. 'They swore themselves to me, after the battle. Mir could force them back to the fold, but she cannot force you.'

'You have been very busy,' I breathed, eyeing the dead eyes, and Father's ending came to my mind. 'Let us leave them. I'll have to see if any Brother escaped. And—'

'Black Brother did,' she said. 'Flew out of the battle in the Tower, the last of them. They are looking for him. Perhaps we will find him first. We will sort it out, love,' she said and giggled. 'I wonder how you will introduce me to your kin, should any be alive.'

'Gods laugh,' Sand cackled and flexed his hand. I could see bone under the skin, and the human part of my brain protested.

'Valkai?' I yelled. A pair of eyes came forward. He stepped up to the room, wearing chain. He bowed to me, his eyes devious and evil. 'I need a route out of the town. And your boys and girls should come armed.'

He turned to Lith, who nodded gravely. 'We will use the mining route we always used. It leads to your Green Hall.'

'So be it,' I said, and we traveled to Crimson Apex.

## CHAPTER 18

The night stank of death.

That was due to the army of misshapen rogues behind my back. A host of bright, if dead eyes flickered in the dark as we stared at the High Hold, the ruins of the Blacktower's ancestral home. 'I know what Balan and Mir want. And what you claim to want. I know Taram wanted to kill kings,' I told Lith, who was crouched near me. I was thinking about Sand.

'Yes,' she said. 'Your Sand still wants to have his own house one day. He told me about his wishes after he was raised. I ordered him to.' She smiled at poor Sand. 'Perhaps he shall?'

'What does Shaduril want?' I asked her. 'What did Ann?'

'Ann? To die,' she smiled. 'She got her wish.' She was right. She had always been so sad. 'Shaduril hoped to kill me.'

'With good reason.' I grinned.

'Yes. She hates me for taking Taram. I did an idiotic thing, really, but I loved him,' she whispered and leaned closer to me. 'He is really a rotten, whore mongering bastard. He cheated both of us with so many women. That's one of the reasons I want to kill him myself. And the fact he can disturb my plans.'

'Anything else?' I asked her. 'For Shaduril.'

She looked uncomfortable. 'She dreamt of children and happiness and living by the sea,' Lith said uncomfortably. 'Now she only desires my life. And yours.'

I laughed mockingly. 'She had mine already. Perhaps she is sated?'

Lith stammered at that and looked suspicious. Then she shrugged and pointed at the ruins of High Hold. 'Look. There will be a guardian. It's on the top floor. You have to deal with it first. I'll tell you where to go. And be careful with the magic. We all hear and see the Dark Mistress. The dead call the magic that, by the way. We tap the Mistress and call forth spells, and it is easier for us than it is for the living. The dead are clever magicians. Your kind Stir the Cauldron, which sounds idiotic, by the way. Makes you lot sound like some sort of gluttons. Elves speak of Glory, the denizens of the undercrofts, of Svartalfheim, they See the Shades. But a Cauldron?'

'Shut up,' I said.

She clapped my shoulder. 'Be careful when you try these powers. Do not try to invent new ones while fighting unless your life depends on it. You might die.'

'And why do you not follow me in there, if I may ask?'

She shrugged. 'As I said, the guardian has to be dealt with. But there is also a key. I'll go and fetch the key to Balan's workshop. The house holds but a dozen men now.'

'The butler?' I asked her. 'Gray?'

'He is a draugr, an elder one, raised that first night, so do not worry,' she grinned. 'He is not there. Ready?'

I eyed Sand, the boy I no longer quite knew. He was strange, intense, a member of the pack lurking in the night. Terrifying. But an ally.

For now at least. She was not telling me everything.

'I am ready,' I said.

'Sand comes with you. To help you,' she explained. 'Well then. Let's get to it.' She turned to the dead and the hulking Valkai. 'Take the thugs to our house. Rip it apart,' she told him. 'Let none escape. Pack up the valuables I listed. Meet in the foyer when we are done. Don't eat Illastria. Must hurry.'

Valkai nodded. He sent men around the darkness, in pairs and threes. 'Lead on,' Valkai told Lith, who grinned.

'Good luck, Beast,' she told me, leaned on my chest and kissed me full on the lips. She broke it off and disappeared, an army of dead behind her.

Sand chuckled. 'I don't envy you. She is a handful.' His eyes were glowing. 'I'm not sure what will become of us.'

'We will not part ways, Sand,' I told him bravely if sadly. 'You are hers. But you are my friend.'

'Didn't have much choice,' he grinned and indicated his ruined hand. 'But this … the condition can be useful. No pain, really.' He smiled wickedly, and I agreed wordlessly. 'Shall we go deal with the guardian?'

'We shall,' I told him.

We marched through the ruins of the fort. The curtains were still flapping in the windows, spookily, making a strange sound. Mice ran up and down the walls as we entered the gate. We walked on, crossed a dark yard full of swaying flowers, bones and debris. 'Has seen better days,' Sand noted.

'We go in and up there to that room,' I told him.

'Up?' he said and followed my eyes.

There on the top floor, a light flickered. It was weak, frail, but still there. We entered the doors, rotten and ajar, and witnessed a half-crumbled fortress. Excellent paintings had been burnt, the stones cracked and melted in places. There were rows of dry corpses in the great hall, all tied in gray sacks, their feet showing. Some were hoary, near skeletal; others were fresh.

'The ones who had to die to make us,' Sand whispered. 'And the ones who stayed in Helheim, despite Mir's power.'

There were over two thousand of them. Some were villagers, many were Jesters. 'Oh my gods,' I whispered. 'And they cannot resurrect the ones they used to give you spark?' There was a stench of death wafting up from the room, and I retched. Sand cocked his head curiously.

'No, they are gone, and we stumble on,' he whispered. 'Hel's curse and blessing. I am not sure which, yet. There,' Sand said and nodded at a dark stairway leading up. 'Make no noise.' He skirted ahead, treading softly. He hesitated, and I felt him grasping at the flames of his Dark Mistress. He blended with the shadows and shot up to the roof. He looked down at me. 'This is really strange.'

'I am a Jotun, Sand,' I grinned up at him; despite the fact he was not the man I had known. 'I know it is strange.' He nodded, looking severe and I missed his sense of humor.

We navigated the staircase, climbed over some dark rubble, and finally ended up on the third floor. There, silence reigned. Ways ran left and right, silent, dead, old, and cold. A breeze fluttered the cobwebs, and rats were silently making their way in the remains of the rafters. Half of the fort had crumbled. To our left, there were rooms, and from the last one, something threw a bit of light to the floor outside the room. I nodded at Sand, and we trotted that way, as silently as we could. A cat crouched by the door, staring at us. Sand stood there, staring at the thing, whispered a word, and the cat fell asleep. He looked at me, shrugging.

'Mad,' I whispered, very softly. He did not argue.

I reached the door, glanced inside, and there stood the guardian of the fort.

Shaduril.

She had sworn to kill me for sleeping with Lith. She wanted to kill Lith for her crimes. She was dead, and slave to her desires and would likely not listen to reason. She loved me; she hated me. And Lith had sent me there to deal with the guardian. *Bitch*, I thought, and Sand was nodding as if he had read my mind.

She was looking out of the window, humming gently. She held a hand across her chest. The room was neatly arranged but looked dead. Just like Balan's had been, in the Crimson Apex. The flowers in the vase were ancient. There was just a hint of their old color remaining, shades of red, and yellow. The bed had yellowed sheets, and the pillow was faded with red stains, and I guessed that was where Shaduril had died, for there was a hole in the roof and starlight glittered high up there in the sky. There were chests and armoires in the room; one was open with dresses and shoes. She was singing, chanting actually, softly, as if not awake and likely, she was not.

*'Sunlight, sisters, is what we shared, once in past when we were paired,*
*Nighttime came, the stars grew dull, out in the ocean there flew an ivory gull.*
*Now we are still, lost and cold, and bereft of any former goodwill.*
*Sleep well, Ann,*
*My undeath alone will be dull as a dry bone.'*

She swayed and giggled, dreaming, perhaps stalking the dreams of others, alone, and missing her sisters.

Then, there was an explosion.

Dust rumbled down around us as the Crimson Apex came under attack. I felt the dead calling out for magic. Spells of death and destruction were hurled at the gates, the guards and Draugr rushed to take or to hold the home of the Blacktowers.

Shaduril shook as she awakened. She rushed to gaze out of the window. 'Lith,' she breathed and turned.

And flew back as my rock-sized fist smashed her face.

I grabbed her roughly, feeling regret and threw her. She tumbled over her bed, over a chest and landed on her back in the corner. Sand rushed by and scuttled along the walls and shadows, strange and fast. The echoes of alarmed men rang in the night; the fort was on fire, but I had to deal with the girl I had loved. Or still did? Shaduril shot up, but Sand's scimitar rushed down from the top and impaled her hand to the floor. He craned his neck and chuckled. 'Didn't you once feel so superior to me?'

'How?' she breathed. 'Sand?'

'Lith's treachery,' he said darkly. 'And now we have business with you.' Her eyes settled on me.

'Lith?' she cursed. 'She is out there. First, she took Taram. Then you. And now she sent you here—'

'She took your face,' I said patiently as I crouched over her, huge and menacing. It still felt strange to change my size, but also very natural. 'And she saved me by taking the Harlot's face. You, on the other hand, killed my father.'

'Lith is out to rule, you idiot! That's all. You are her willing tool,' she said and grinned madly as she struggled on the floor. 'I loved you. You made an undead piece of filth love you, and then you betrayed her. Didn't you know the difference between her and me? Would I have–'

'No,' I agreed. 'You would not have done what she did. I made a mistake.'

'A bad mistake, Maskan. You should not make a draugr your enemy. We don't forget quickly,' she laughed as she struggled with the scimitar piercing her hand.

'If you struggle, Shaduril, if you make this hard, if I have to fight you, you are doing Lith a favor. She sent me here. And all I need is the gauntlet,' I told her empathetically. 'And you? You lied to me.'

'Yes,' she hissed. 'As I was ordered.'

I spat. 'You told me lies to my face. Lith is rebelling, but you did not.'

'Lith is stronger than I am,' she said quietly. 'I did want to run away with you. But would you have? I am dead.'

I shrugged. 'I don't know. All I did for your family was to spare you from Morag, who loved you but not as a lover. All for you and Sand.'

'And to avenge your family!' she hissed and looked forlorn as I mentioned how Morag had liked her. 'Sand,' she glowered at the boy above her, 'was supposed to make you feel sorry for robbing me. He found me in the harbor, suggested you rob me, and then he would have led you to save me. I did not ask for you to love me!'

'I did. And you did,' I told her. 'You are dead. Can you even love? I—'

Her eyes flashed, and she turned away with an unreadable expression. There was grief, loathing, hatred on her face. She spoke with a small voice. 'I am. And yet, I still feel such distant memories. I loved Taram once. He was careless, amusing. I was dutiful and shy. And then you came along. With that grin. I love you still.'

'The gauntlet, Shaduril,' I whispered. 'And I shall spare you Lith's attentions. I will need you against her.'

She shook her head. 'The Black Grip. That gauntlet was beyond Father's powers to tinker with. Yes, it is hidden. And no. I'll not give you the thing. I cannot.'

'Shad—'

'I rejoiced when I saw you led away,' she sobbed with conflicting emotions. 'I hoped for your death. And Taram's, but the gods took Ann instead. I have been waiting for Lith since she disappeared. She knows I want her dead. And she sent you to me? She will regret it. So will you.'

'Do not,' I told her. 'I'm not as I was. I might not care to spare you if you try to hurt me. Calm and help me.'

She was nodding her head. 'I'd be with Ann, Maskan,' she told me with angry intensity. 'And while I want Lith dead, I am sure she will die one day and join us in Helheim. She will suffer. You would keep me? With you? No. You would not love a husk of a woman who looks like this. Look!' Her face changed. It was dry and yellow, her hair was lustrous, but in places white, and there was an old gash running across her face, and it had taken one of her eyes. I flinched, and she saw it. She smiled sorrowfully and looked away. 'I died right there on that bed, love. So, do you desire me?'

'I desire the laughter of the girl who ran to the beach,' I told her honestly. 'I don't know if I can love what is left of your body, but I loved that person. I am your friend, at least.' She stared at me in confusion, and then cackled and struggled, and Sand kept her there on the floor, though with difficulty.

'It is guarded,' she said. 'The Black Grip. And you have no magic …' Her eyes enlarged as I showed her my missing finger. 'You can—'

'I can hear and see the power. I can Stir the Cauldron, or the Dark Mistress, Shaduril. And I can change my size, looks. I don't know anything, really, but I am much more than I used to be. I am learning to be something of a Jotun, even if the human part still lingers there inside my skull,' I told her darkly and picked her up. Sand's scimitar left her hand. 'I don't want to hurt you. I care for you. But I will need it. The gauntlet. I'll use it to kill Mir and Balan.'

'I don't have it.' She laughed.

'Take me to the gauntlet or I'll pluck your legs off,' I said sweetly and perhaps even meant it.

'You will take the gauntlet and do what with it?' she said dubiously. 'Dagnar is too far gone for you to reverse that. You cannot get into the Tower, even.'

'I am a shape-shifter,' I said. 'All Jotuns are. I can fly,' I told her with a growl, and she nodded reluctantly. 'With that gauntlet, I can kill them. Father told me it would help me.'

She considered it, struggling with her emotions. Her face softened, then hardened, and finally she shook her head. 'I won't,' she said with manic intensity. 'Not after you slept with her.'

I thrust her out of the window, and she fell with a shriek. I hesitated, wondering if I knew what I was doing. Then I jumped after her. My form blurred and changed. It was strange, going from one into another, from a giant into a bird, and all my senses thrust out the old fears. I knew what to do and how, and I glided down as a huge, dark raven, flapping my wings, feeling the wind ruffle my feathers. It felt so natural. It was draining, but not unlike running. The feeling of flight was wonderful for all the few seconds it lasted, though unfamiliar enough for me to make a very ungraceful landing. Shaduril was picking herself up; her leg bent unnaturally. I changed back, taking deep breaths. 'See? No tower is blocked to me.'

'You might have a point,' she hissed and sat back, looking at her twisted leg with incredulity. 'That hurt, Maskan. It will take time for the bones to mend. Not sure why you would think I fear to fall, though. My turn!' Then she took a deep breath and channeled a spell that surrounded her in a fiery, multicolored ball of flame. She rolled towards the doors, hopped up, and half walked and half ran that way. I collected the one familiar spell I knew, braiding the ice and the wind, in a certain, delicate way. I let the spell go after collecting as much of it as I could, and it burned in my veins. The result was far stronger than the one I had used previously. I flew back on my rump, but the ice tore at the castle wall, the ground, and the flowers. It ripped through to pockmark the rock itself with savage strength. I did not see what happened to Shaduril, but a shriek could be heard as the undead thing flew forward by the force of the spell. There were bits of clothing swirling in the air, and then the fiery shield around her dissipated as she rolled across the gateway to crash into a wall. She turned on the ground, and I felt her releasing something. Indeed, a fiery wall grew under me. I shot forward, but the flames followed me. She was cackling, not the beautiful thing any longer, but a hideously twisted thing of death bent on unreasonable revenge. She cast another wall, boxing me inside walls of fire and I cursed, as I did not know spells that were more useful. My calf was burnt; it hurt terribly, even inside the dverg-made wondrous armor.

She shrieked and the fires were extinguished.

Sand had cut off her hand at the wrist. She stared at the limb in horror, and I grew to my twelve feet and rushed forward to grab her. I pinned her with my hand. She shook her head in brief terror but swallowed bravely. 'Ann. I'll see her again.'

'I'll spare your damned undead life,' I told her, 'if you give me what is mine. We shall wait for the keys.'

She sneered at me. 'There are no keys. As you said, she wanted you to face me,' she spat. 'She is out there, watching this tragedy, enjoying every moment.' I resisted the urge to look at the darkness, but she was probably right. 'The door. Go to Ann or go on living in here until she dies.'

She looked down, weighing her options, holding her hand, thoroughly a miserable thing. Finally, she pointed her stump of an arm towards the banner of the Blacktowers, hanging faded and forlorn over the fire pit. 'Pull it.'

Sand cocked his head that way, walked past torn tables and crushed chairs. He stopped before the fire pit and squinted up towards the roof. Then he reached out and pulled the banner. A loud click was heard. The end of the fire pit fell; darkness opened up below the trapdoor and dust billowed out. Sand took a tentative step that way. 'What is down there?'

Shaduril smiled under my fist and eyed the darkness. 'Balan's temple. His treasure room. His workshop. Mir's shrine. But it is guarded.'

'Guarded?' I asked her. 'Since you are not the guardian, what is? Do you know?'

'Oh no.' She grinned. 'Only that it is quite dangerous. I don't know what it is, to be honest.'

'Fine, as you are going first,' I told her and carried her down. She struggled, cursed and then went quiet. We reached the downstairs where darkness reigned. I shuffled and took a man-sized form, but my grip on her was just as strong as it had been. She did not struggle, but I sensed she was regaining her will to fight. I dragged her to the edge of a dark, musty room. Sand was near, his eyes glowing. He looked down to what I thought was just a more shaded spot on the wall, but what was actually a stairway down. 'See anything?'

'Nothing alive,' he told me and grinned. 'Nor dead. A room with tables, something massive in the middle. A statue?'

'A statue with a function,' Shaduril said with a small grin. 'It guards the gauntlet. Balan's thing.'

'It has the gauntlet?' I asked her.

'*Guards* it. It's not alive, but not dead, either. Nor undead. It's magical,' she told me smugly and then shrugged as if ashamed of her wish to see me fail. 'There will be weapons of your kind there. Their armor as well. I brought them after we took them from your brothers. There is a hole where we bring our offerings to Hel. Perhaps such a weapon can help? Your father's sword is with Taram. Larkgrin is with Balan, but there are others.'

'Can you light up the room?' I asked her.

'Never had to, before,' she said dubiously. 'But yes. That will have repercussions.'

'Balan's craft?' I chuckled. 'I'll break it.'

'Not easily,' she said softly. 'Good luck, then.'

She channeled her powers, and globes of light slid around her, thrust down to the floor and up to the ceilings and illuminated the room, and some floated down towards the statue. 'Keep an eye on her,' I told Sand.

'I will,' he said and placed a foot on Shaduril's hurt leg, so she fell on her face, cursing at the indignity. 'Silence,' Sand said with a grunt. 'That looks dangerous.'

It did.

Down in the circular room, there was a shrine made of dark stone, and it was actually a statue. It sat on its haunches; an erect and dangerous looking thing of eight arms, a snake-like tail and the bust of a female. In its hands, there were eight swords, and its face was that of an innocent girl. 'Hel?'

Shaduril shrugged. 'I hear the goddess rarely leaves the Spire of Rot. Balan, Father, of course, used his imagination. I imagine she looks much less dangerous in reality.'

The thing looked up, empty eyes full of careless brutality.

'Shit, oh damn,' Sand whispered. 'I can wait up here for sure.'

I stood up and Stirred the Cauldron, trying to find the one familiar spell I knew. The thing below stood up to its full ten feet height, the swords at its sides, glinting evilly. Its innocent face did not so much as twitch with emotion as the magical thing moved for the broad staircase I was standing on.

'Do it, for Hel's sake,' Shaduril spat. 'Cast spells at it!'

'You are safe from it, are you not?' I asked, terrified to death by the thing. 'Can you make it sit down?'

'Mother and Father alone are allowed to come here,' she said as Sand blanched and dragged her back to the tunnel leading to the castle. 'It will cut us to ribbons,' she hissed as she went.

'We will wait here,' Sand yelled.

The thing reached the stairs and loped up them, wordlessly, soundlessly. I gathered my bravery and released the spell of ice and winds at its innocent face. The spell tore at the dark stone but did nothing more than make it topple onto a knee. I kept calling more and more of the windy power, wondered at the ancient ice flows and blazing fires as I did, and nearly forgot the urgent need to keep the spell going. I struggled with the weaves but managed to intensify the spell. The thing was crawling up; the wind was grinding at the stone, creating a haphazard storm of debris in the room below. The noise was terrible, and I felt drained, tired beyond anything I had previously experienced. My arms were drooping, but I pushed more wind and ice at the thing. It was still crawling up the steps, the swords clanking on the stone and soon, very soon, it would lunge at me. My eyes sought the room beyond the thing. I saw the mound where the creature had been sitting. Beyond it, there was a huge table, what was probably Balan's seat, and chisels and hammers, jewels, and strange tools he used to craft and tinker with the many beautiful artifacts.

I realized my wind had scoured the mound's surface, and there was a brass handle on a wooden trapdoor.

I sobbed with the effort, weaved more ice at the thing; it got up to its knees, the stony was face rimmed with ice, pockmarked by the ferocity of my spell, and it lifted a sword, a long, tapering thing. I prayed and jumped down towards it. I changed into a raven again, and it felt so very natural. It was as natural as breathing, and I passed the thing's sword by a feather's breadth. I fluttered down for the trapdoor, changed to myself again, but human-sized, landed heavily, and ripped at the trapdoor savagely.

It flew open.

I jumped down and heard stony scratching above me. The statue was fast and was already scaling the mound. I felt, rather than saw a sword reaching after me as I fell down a set of stone stairs. One of the glowing lights followed me down, and I cursed as I ran into a doorframe. I dodged inside and looked around.

It was a treasury.

The room was heaped full of Blacktower treasure. Like a pitiful husk of a human, Balan and Mir had hoarded all their former memories. There were portraits of their children, silver and gold busts of their ancestors, wooden toys, and their happier memories. All this was heaped at the end of the room. The middle of the room held another statue, a masked woman, the real figure of Hel, the actual shrine, I suspected. The ground around it was laden with other more recent sentimental trophies, and on the roof, there was a hole where they deposited such loot. There were skulls, rotting and mutilated. Many were formerly Jotuns, others just those of men, their foes. Weapons of their enemies were there also, some tall as a horse, swords and axes made for my people. I saw armor there as well and then I had no more time to think.

I heard steps behind me.

I turned to look that way and saw a large shadow crawling down the tunnel.

I rushed forward and fell on some ancient tapestry. I nearly cut my face on a rusted ax blade and dashed for the Hel's statue. The magical guardian entered the room, spotted me, and began to walk for me remorselessly.

'Shit,' I cursed and sobbed, and groped for the base of the statue. I reached for a long, two-handed sword of intricate make from a pile next to me, and knew it had belonged to the Red Brother. It was stuck, and I pulled at it until it came out. It felt perfect in my hand, the blade keener and less thick than that of an ordinary sword. It would not break, not quickly. I turned to fight and to die. The statue came for me relentlessly, crushing skulls and bones underfoot, and its weapons went up, then down as the thing tried to slay me. Fours swords punched for me, and I fell back, avoiding them. The rest slashed down, and I rolled away as a shower of old silver coins flew high into the air. I rushed at the thing, and swiped the blade across to block its next attack. There were clangs and sparks as the massive sword intercepted three of hers. As I went forward, I grew in size to match the thing and instinctively crushed it in a hug. The sweet female face turned to look me in the eye. 'Stone-hearted bitch of Balan,' I spat. It rewarded me by dropping its swords and crushing me right back. It was stone, I was flesh under the armor, and so I howled. I grabbed its face, wheezing in pain and tried to twist it aside. The snake-like tail curled around my knee, nearly breaking it, and I fell on my back. I attempted to think, to talk, to beg and to threaten it, and then I decided I would die silently rather than beg. I twisted at the magical stone, it did not give in, and the thing groped for one of the swords. It pushed me across the debris of weapons and bones and treasure, squeezed hard, and the sword rose with deadly intent. I managed to block the hand, and if the thing could have shown frustration, I was sure it would have. I managed to keep the sword from piercing me and hoped my ribs would not crack. The thing changed tactics. It stopped squeezing, apparently having no patience, and picked me up. I could not regain my balance due to the tail squeezing my knee and thigh, and it pushed me to the statue of Hel's lap, holding me still with several hands. The sword thrust for my throat.

I shrunk in size to a man, slithered away from her grip, and the tail, and heard the blade sinking into the Hel's statue, splitting it with a grating noise.

I groped around in the legs of the thing, and cursed, for I was nearly finished, hurting, and tired and had no hope.

The statue of Hel fell in two pieces around us.

And there, amidst the rubble, was the thing they had hidden so very well.

It was gray-white, near a plaster-colored leather glove. *Was that it?* I thought, and decided it was my only chance. The statue's many hands grabbed at me; I rushed forward, tore off a gauntlet and smashed my bare hand on the glove. It glowed briefly and changed into strange, cool metal, studded with yellow gems, segmented to make it supple, and then it was all black, old as time, and it slithered over my hand, covering it.

The statue grabbed my hair, but I barely noticed.

My head was filled with memories of past times, past places, ancient deeds of the Jotun kind, the history of our lineage, our stories. I saw my father, sitting amidst a tribe of hundreds and I saw Mother, standing over a snow stormy glacier, laughing merrily. What shot through my head was a jumble of emotions and knowledge, and I knew the gauntlet was indeed somewhat sentient, for I could feel it respond to my feelings with a joy of its own. Then, I felt pain. The statue had thrown me to the ground and placed a foot on my chest. Sharp rocks pricked at my neck, grated against my armor by the statue's brutal power. I felt I was bleeding on the stones. The gauntlet tightened around my hand. It was more than a device to bind memories. It was one to bind spells. There were so many ways of stirring the forces of the Cauldron, so many strange spells you could achieve. One could study it for many lifetimes and only discover spells by experimentation and testing over slow centuries. But the gauntlet remembered all father had learned, and his father and his kind before.

A sword was coming down at my chest.

I called forth a spell of fire and ice both. I mixed simmering heat, pulled at flowing lava of Muspelheim, and added freezing hail of Gjöll to the weave, and a shield of stone covered my skin. The statue struck down, sparks flew, and the sword shattered on impact. I felt the hit and knew the spell was much weakened by the attack, but it had saved my life. The magical thing fell back; the stone eyes were seeking the other weapons, which it rushed for. Then it bent down to pick them up, relentless in its duty. I shuddered with fatigue as I climbed up. I grew in size, yelled so hard the chamber trembled and attacked. As I did, I called for fires again. I created a spell that twisted the old heat of ancient lava, brutal and simple, and stone grew out of my hand and solidified into a deadly stone maul. I crashed the heavy, terrible weapon down on the statue's back. It came down so hard the weapon shattered, but so did the statue. It fell onto the ground, split in half at the waist, and looked ready to crawl, its few remaining arms holding it up. I kicked it hard, very hard. It flew to the wall where it shattered, finally dead, though bits of its stone seemed to shudder still. I breathed hard; trying to hold myself together, dizzy with fear and exhilaration the gauntlet gave me. I turned to find Valkai and Sand staring at me, and Shaduril was dragged behind them by one of Valkai's dead. Lith edged to the chamber and avoided looking at her sister. I picked up a helmet, saw it was that of Borlein, the White Brother and wore it.

'You found it?' Lith asked innocently.

'You lying bitch,' I told her.

'Sorry,' she said sheepishly. 'I told you I need you for many things, and most should be to your liking. I am surprised she is alive,' she said with a grin. 'Or dead and alive. You know what I mean. Now I have to finish her myself.'

'I told you I wish to spare her,' I growled.

'Let's not get stuck on semantics,' she sighed. 'She is beyond saving. Well done, Maskan.'

'The Crimson Apex?' I asked her. 'There were no keys, of course, but I hope you burnt it.'

'Burning brightly.' She smiled thinly. 'Illastria is safe. Riches as well. Though as you noticed, there are many here as well. Pack them up, boys.' She eyed Shaduril. 'What do you plan to do with her? I said I want her dead.'

I pulled Shaduril away from her, and her eyes never left her sister. 'Shall we go and kill your parents?'

'So that is how it will be,' she whispered. 'You just ignore me.' The dead glowered at me and I spat at their feet.

'Yes,' I said. 'And there is more. The plan has changed.'

'Really?' she asked me, tapping her foot. 'How has it changed?'

'I've decided I do want to take the crown. I will purge Dagnar. We will kill your parents, but before that, we will take the city,' I told her while ignoring Shaduril.

That got her attention. 'What?' she said, looking at me as if I were mad. 'There are dead guarding the Tower of the Temple. Many, many dead. We are but a hundred. A few more! And Balan can command these men, and they will forget me. He can command me. Shaduril and me. You were supposed to fly up there and kill them. Now you have the tools for a proper fight. Do not—'

I nodded. 'I won't be happy with that. I want the city. You will have your kingdom below, I shall have the one above, and so I have a plan.'

'You?' she said with wonder. 'You have a plan? A pup still wet behind his ears? We have no time for such schemes, boy.' She eyed Shaduril with hatred. 'Did she put you up to this?'

'Shut up. Listen. I want you to go to Dagnar, Lithiana. Come here. I shall whisper to you.' She did, though cautiously. She hesitated before me, looked at Shaduril, and draped her hands around me. She pressed her lips to my helmet, and I whispered to her. She was nodding, uncomfortable, and I pushed her away. 'Can you do this?'

'I can,' she said softly. 'But—'

'Do it, or I will release her. She will forever haunt you dreams,' I told her wickedly and felt Shaduril shudder with a desire to slay her sister.

'And by implication, you will give her over to me, if we try this?' she whispered. 'You ask us to risk all for something we could probably take right now?'

I laughed at her. 'Yes, I will give her to you after. As for taking it right now? You could try.' I looked at the smashed statue, and she followed my gaze.

She frowned, very human-like, but she got the message. 'I see. I hoped we could sneak there, just you and I. But now you want to make a war out of it. Fine! I will do as you said. But I won't show my face.'

'Coward.' I laughed.

'I have plans,' she hissed. 'Perhaps even with you.'

'You want the under lands. I want the mountain,' I hissed. 'And now I can have it as well.' I turned to Sand. 'I am still your friend. Remember it.'

He nodded and spoke. 'Find a way to free me from Lith. And we can be friends again.' Lith raised her eyebrows at that, but seemed unimpressed otherwise.

I hesitated and opened my arms for him. He hesitated as well, and I leaned on him and crushed him in a brief hug. His eyes glowed wickedly, and we laughed together. It would be strange if we would indeed be friends again. Then I whispered a request in Sand's ear and pushed him away. He did not say no. Nor yes. He just stared. That would have to do. I grabbed a sheath for Red's sword. Then I noticed the whip. I took that as well.

'Come wench,' I said and dragged Shaduril out and pushed past the undead. We walked out of the halls and into the woods and traveled through the night to the Green Hall. I turned to look down at Shaduril. 'I wasn't going to give you to her.'

'I'd like to think so,' she said morosely. 'But I am dead anyway. You cannot guard me forever, and she won't give me mercy when you fight.'

She looked hideous and maimed, especially her hand. She nodded at my scrutiny. 'The bones will knit. Only massive damage will kill an elder draugr. The hand might grow back as well. I have been told it is so. Though there will be no flesh.'

I looked away from her. 'I am sorry I did not know you when you were alive.'

'Had you done so, you would have married a giantess eventually,' she chortled. 'And I have not forgiven you for Lith. I cannot. It's in our nature.'

'Here,' I said and gave her something. It was triangular and had a silver hoop. 'I'm still a thief.'

She looked at Lith's earring. 'You are sparing me?'

'You will come with me, Shaduril, and here is what you shall do,' I told her, and she listened.

'I will,' she whispered and held on to the jewel and then put it in her ear.

'Stay near me this day,' I told her. 'And be ready to act.'

'Done,' she said as I walked on. Gods, but I still loved her. In some strange way, I did. I would worry about it later. I stroked the gauntlet and found what I was looking for. I hesitated a bit, but then I cast the spell and what I found, was hopeful. I sent out a call. It was answered.

'Lith?' I yelled.

'Love?' she said, avoiding her sister.

'I will need to look like the Black Brother,' I told her. 'The horsehair has to be black when they see me.'

'You look like one,' she said, confused. 'But I am sure pain will do the trick.'

'Tenginell stables,' I said. 'I need Black Brother's horse. It will look authentic. It will have to be … perfect.'

Her face brightened. 'Perfect? Yes! I will have it brought to you before we get up there. I'm happy,' she said with admiration, 'that you have grown so devious. You have reached far from the Mint, Maskan. Perfection. We love perfection.'

I nodded. She did not know the half of it.

## CHAPTER 19

There was a great throng of people around the Sun Court. The barracks were lined with Mad Watch soldiers, near two thousand of them, it seemed. Their conical helmets gleamed and red cloaks fluttered in the wind. Nobles and even braver commoners stood around the place, lounging under cover, for snow was falling. The Tower of the Temple was a square, red tower on the cliff's end, tall, thick, and imposing. The wall before it was tall, though not like the Ring walls around the hill. This one bristled with ballista and other siege weaponry. *Gods help us if we don't manage a surprise*, I thought. People wore dark clothing, leather, and heavy wool, and the somber mood was strangely expectant. I glanced up at the Temple's walls. There stood the flag of the Helstrom's and that of the Blacktowers, Balan in front of them, their thousand disguised undead men staring down at the multitudes. Lith's rogue Blacktower militia was standing around us, holding their swords, spears, and halberds, their tunics dusty with travel. It was risky to have them there, but for now, they obeyed Lith. Taram was by the gate, frowning at the helmeted last Brother. I had taken a face under it just in case, that of a beggar, my hair white with a broad brow. Shaduril was near, so was Sand, all disguised under hoods. Sand held my weapons. And Illastria, she was somewhere with Lith, who dared not show her face.

Crec had led the army out as Mir had instructed him, but not the Navy. But where was Mir? *Had she truly left as he had hinted?* I wondered.

Gal Talin was there, though. He was seated on a horse, sitting before his house guards, all eyeing us expectantly. His guards were broad and strong men, all undead, draugr, slain in the butchery where he died. Gal was there for my belongings and amusement. Valkai stood forth and bowed to the lords, Taram and Balan, and even Gal. There was a rustling sound as Lord Commander of the City mounted a horse and soldiers squeezed their weapons nervously, whispering to each other.

'Valkai?' Balan finally said, his one good arm making an elaborate greeting that managed to seem superior.

'This one was caught fleeing the city,' Valkai told the lord proudly. 'He was hurt, severely injured.' I slouched in the saddle, and the blood glistening on the horse's flank was obvious to everyone.

Balan chuckled. 'Lith? You served her, no? You were assigned to her? And she is not here. Is she far?'

'Yes,' Valkai lied with cool familiarity. 'She is hurt, my lord. We chased after this one during the battle for the Tower. It is the Black Brother, one of the murderers.' People muttered unkindly around us.

Balan nodded, his eyes gauging Valkai, wondering if Lith had been loyal or was just trying to cover for her own agendas and perhaps cowardice. Finally, the lord bowed back and pointed a finger my way. 'I am grateful. In the name of Crec Helstrom, The Beast of the North, I, Balan of the Blacktowers charge you with the murder of our king.' He turned to Valkai. 'I am disappointed you did not kill him immediately. They are dangerous.' He looked nervous as he said the words, wondering how to hang me. I had access to magic, and he was anxious to see one of the Jotuns in the very heart of the kingdom. I saw he was cursing the stupidity of Valkai under his breath.

'He is weak. Too weak for any surprises,' Valkai said heavily. 'And yet, we do apologize for failing you, my lord.' I made a great show of weakness by nearly falling from my horse.

Balan ignored Valkai and pointed his finger at me. 'Have the archers stand ready. Hang him. And justice shall be served.'

'Hang him,' Taram said with a grin. 'For justice. See to his gear, Gal Talin?' he called out, and the thousands of people around us looked on as the regal lord rode forth. He came forward to stare at us.

He nodded. 'His belongings, and then hang him.'

The Mad Watch shuffled forward, their tall spears aimed at us. Their conical helmets glittered in the light, and I prayed things would go well. People were whispering, and there were some calls for justice to be had. Their earlier ferociousness had lost some of its edge.

A Talien guard of Gal's rode to me through the wary ring of the Watch, a tall wide man wearing a wide-brimmed helmet. I stared at him, sullen, morose.

'Your riches then, my lord,' the Talien man said, 'for the state,' he added. His eyes were blinking greedily. In my fist, there was my pouch. I dropped it in the guard's outstretched hand, and Gal nodded and beckoned for the man; the wall of spears around him parted for just a moment. The Mad Watchmen shuffled in indecision, their thousands of men murmuring at Gal's blatant greed. Gal seemed oblivious to their disgruntlement, grasped the pouch, and poured the contents in his fist. He eyed a golden chain, and nodded, congratulating himself for the valuable thing. I grinned softly. Should I die, I doubted Gal would keep any of that, as it came from Balan's own treasury.

Taram ignored Gal. 'You want to hang from your horse, Brother?' Balan called out. 'Your friends hung there, just now,' he said and nodded at the massive, ancient tree where I had just hung as well. 'Alas, they were mostly dead when we began. You get to choose the limb.'

'Do not stretch this, Taram,' Balan called out. 'Take him.'

My eyes stayed on Gal as I shrugged.

The lord was rifling through the rest of the items from the pouch, no longer interested in the execution. His fingers were going over gold, silver, and finer things of an intricate make. Then his eyes grew large as eggs, and he licked his dry lips.

*Gods, let him not resist the temptation*, I thought.

The Mad Watch pushed through the Blacktower Guards around me, and Valkai, the leader of the guard of dead men, was cursing. It was taking too long.

Gal pulled out the Sorrowspinner.

He was mumbling to himself as he admired it, a pitiful greed-driven beast that did not for a moment stop to think why I had had it. Instead, he coveted it, his brother's long lost ring, and the mark of the lord of his house.

And then he put it on his finger.

Many things happened.

Balan's face distorted with panic, for he had seen the ring; the yellow-stoned, black thing with inlaid gold carvings. The people around us opened their mouths in shock and terror, and the Mad Watch faltered in confusion, men getting turned around by their mates, who were pointing at the thing seated on the horse. Gal was clearly dead. His face was half missing and his chest showed a ragged wound. Gal was rotting and drying, the skin tight around his skull, and there was no doubt he was gone and yet living at the same time. His eye glowed with unholy light. In moments, thousands of people all stared at Lord Gal, who did not fully fathom he was under such scrutiny. Instead, the abomination was admiring a bracelet, giggling softly.

I rose up in the saddle and yelled, my finger pointed at Balan. 'That, my lords, people of Red Midgard, is Lord Balan's ally! That is Balan's creation. He is as Balan is, a traitor in the guise of a man, a murderer, and a thief, and they are here to betray you, as they killed the King and Danegell brothers. My brothers! We were framed. All Blacktowers are like him. Kill them and see what they turn into! Take back your city,' I yelled. Gal still did not fully comprehend why everyone was staring at him until he tried to weave a spell and noticed he could not. His dead eyes looked utterly astonished, and he groped at his face, only to notice the white, shrunken fingers. Some people were screaming. Others were exhorting the troops to hack the thing to pieces.

People turned to look at Balan in the wall. 'Wait—' he called out, but I interrupted him.

'For the King,' I yelled, 'kill the undead lords Balan, Taram, their men and that bastard there!' I nodded at Gal. 'All his men. They are all like it.' Valkai's men had discreetly dropped the lily on red symbols from their armors.

People hesitated. It was only natural. Sand rode to me, and I grabbed Bjornag's sword from him. He offered me the whip, but I shook my head. 'I told you. Help her.' He frowned and shrugged, and I thanked him with a nod. I turned to Gal and guided my horse forward.

Balan squeaked. Gal shuddered in surprise. And after an excruciating moment of indecisive silence, a woman screamed. 'Down with Blacktowers! With the Talien's!' It was Lith's voice. The Mad Watch turned in unison, their spears high in the air. I whipped my horse and pushed past the Watch, and the battle began. I rode by Gal and his confused house guards, all of whom were looking at their hands in shock, fearing they too, were exposed. I raised Red's sword and sliced a man's head off. There were screams as the man fell from his saddle, and the truth of his nature became evident in the ghastly, real condition of his face as he lost his spell of disguise. Gal raised his face to look up at me, stammering and chattering strangely in fear. I gave him no quarter. He shrieked as he raised his thin arms to fend me off, and the blade went up and came down with a giant's strength. I slashed him so brutally, he fell in two pieces and even his horse bled and died. The remains fell and were forgotten. I gazed up at Balan. 'He is like Lord Gal! Kill the Taliens! Kill the Blacktowers!' I shrieked again at the fighting Mad Watch and the hesitant nobles.

A crazy melee ensued.

The Mad Watch pulled down all the Talien guards, hacking and slaying the surprised men, all of whom confirmed my words by their haggard, dead looks. Taram, meanwhile, was whipping his horse for the gate. 'Lord!' a young noble yelled at me. 'The gate!'

'Take it!' I screamed. The Mad Watch reacted quickly, surprisingly soon as we charged forward with a slap of feet. The Blacktower men were slow to act, and only after Taram's repeated yells, they were pulling at the massive gates, their white lily and red tabards flashing in the shadows of the massive doors. 'Heyaah!' I screamed, the horse slammed into the doorway, trampled a man, and pushed inside. There, the pandemonium of the Sun Court was not apparent. Blacktower guards, some eight hundred were lining the walls and the yard, not fully comprehending what was taking place. Outside, I heard Valkai and Sand exhorting the troops to form up and enter.

'Inside! Save the Kingdom! Kill Balan and Lord Captain Taram! All the Blacktowers. Hack them to pieces!' Valkai yelled, and a ragged scream rose high into the air, and a deep thump of feet and jingle of weapons and armor filled the air. Two ballistae shrieked as their missiles tore through the crowd, changing ten men into heaps of dead meat, but that was all they could do.

Before us was the Temple courtyard, and then the massive tower, the Tower of the Temple, which reached up in its intricately carved detail. It was red, and now, closer up, I saw each stone was carved with pictures and symbols, and the brilliant white Pearl Terrace was far up on its side. Above that, birds shrieked. The gate bells were tolling across the city.

The Blacktower Guards turned to look at us. Some four hundred of them. They formed a wall across the entrance as a dozen or more were filtering in through the heavy gate, the magical gate that could not be opened by anyone else than a Brother. My gauntlet, the Black Grip was whispering to me of a spell, designed for such an opening. On the walls, a great number of men were running about, and I spied Balan and Taram running for a doorway connecting the wall to the higher level of the tower.

I spat at the enemy at the gate. It looked like a terrible fight.

Archers were pointing at me; men were jostling to a thick shieldwall, many rows deep, their white on red tabards and armor flashing. Mad Watch members began to push in with high numbers. I turned to look at them. 'Form a wall. A shieldwall, men,' I told them with supreme confidence. 'Then we shall kill the murderous dead.' Some officers nodded and began barking orders. I was looking around, for the one man who might stop this happening was missing. Crec was not there, and they needed a leader.

And they obeyed.

They had just hung my brothers, and now they obeyed one quickly enough.

The gates banged as red-cloaked soldiers rushed in. There were hesitant ones with them, some shook their heads and gestured at the barracks, preferring to stay out of the war that was possibly a mistake, but most had seen Gal and Balan endorsing him, and so we had nearly a thousand men coming into the Tower's courtyard. I dismounted and pulled out my sword. I pointed it at the shieldwall of four hundred enemies, and the Mad Watch shuffled forward to settle in a thick wall of spears and shields around me. 'They are not of us. Do not hesitate. They do not belong here. So send them to Hel.'

'What are they, Lord?' asked a captain with a dark horsehair helmet.

'They are abominations. Inhuman. Evil. They tricked you into killing the Danegells,' I hissed, and soon, some five hundred men had settled with me, in three ranks of bristling spears. I saw Valkai was leading more men, now even armed noble citizens to the walls and there, the killing began on the stairs without any real ceremony. Blacktower militia smashed their axes and swords down at the first of our men; they retaliated, and a ferocious mood took over the men around me. 'Sing!' yelled a captain and lifted his sword.

'Sing, boys!' yelled the sergeants, and they did.

The song was savage, old as Red Midgard, and a ferocious drive to slay and maim filled our hearts. I was not sure how many of the enemy were draugr, probably most, for they did not look at each other, did not hesitate, but stayed put, doggedly. An excellent tenor voice led the men in their song.

*'Hearts of old, hills so cold,*
*here we stand, our merry, bloody band.*
*Ready the spear, cast away your fear,*
*And the enemy, the dogs, shall fall like logs!*

*Call out: kill them!*
*Twist their stems!*
*Eat their hearts!*
*Rip their parts!*

*The night will soon fall,*
*Away the dead shall we quickly haul.*
*For the taverns await,*
*And the victors shall not be late!'*

'Kill!' a high officer screamed.

'Kill them!' I echoed him, and so we charged. It takes courage to charge a bristling wall of sharp steel and blunt edges, to throw away all that you hold dear, and they did so willingly. They fought for the dead King, for each other and for all living men; for they had seen Gal, the slain Talien guards whose spells no longer masked their nature, and no human can ignore such a thing, knowing in their hearts there is no love or mercy in such a foe's heart. We tromped towards the enemy, who banged their shields together savagely, the sound echoing above the clanging of the bells and the battle sounds on the walls. Bells were clanging wildly down in the city as well, and I thought I heard distant screams.

'Take them!' I yelled, wondering how much I wanted to hurt the enemy, to burst through the tower doors and find Mir, Balan, and Taram. The ground trembled at our charge, arrows flew at us, and spears were thrown, rocks even. A man hollered next to me, holding his face and then fell down in a heap. Another died behind me. An arrow struck the chain in the hem of my breastplate, a rock bounced off the sword blade. I charged and yelled, hard as a Jotun could and the Mad Watch answered it, and the shieldwalls crashed into each other. Men fell back to their fellows, some dead, others dying, some stunned. Blood spattered high in the air, cold for the draugr, steaming for the living. A groaning voice of the dead and the wounded filled our ears and the panting of the fearful and the excited screams of the killers made for a mad cacophony. Swords went up, then down, axes struck shield, hundreds of tapering spearheads thrust at throats and faces, and the coppery smell of blood and entrails filled the crisp winter air. The shieldwalls steadied for a moment in a desperate push of shields. The merciless hacking of panting men and their long weapons turned to a competition of shorter blades and spears over the shoulders of the first ranks, flashing at faces and for guts beneath the shields. The dead were hard to vanquish as only massive damage would kill one, but slowly, our numbers told. The Mad Watch had taller spears and the men in the second and third ranks were brutally effective in pushing them over the shoulders of the first rank and into the faces of the Blacktower men. They began falling, in high numbers, and then the enemy buckled on the sides, where the Mad Watch pushed them relentlessly. Soon the wall was curling around the tower door, and we were stomping on the fallen of the undead.

I raged in the first rank, and the dverg-made armor made me near impregnable. There was a dead Watchman to my left, standing upright in the press, hampering my movements as a great many larger enemies were gathered before me. Spears nicked at my armor and chain as they all tried to take me down. A huge, embossed shield slammed at me from the front. It pushed me back, and I saw a surprisingly quick maul coming down at my unarmored head. I grabbed it from the air and hewed down with my sword from high, and the man's face flapped open. As he fell back, he spat blood on me. I laughed and felt raging joy, released from all bounds. It was a brilliant, utter joy of carnage as I charged forward. I swept the sword through the enemy ranks, and the beautiful blade chewed through the shields, be they metal or wood with unholy hunger. This is what a giant is made of: utter, ruthless carnage. I cleaved an enemy in two with no mercy. A sword stabbed at me from the left, then right, and the men fell as Watch soldiers stabbed at them with spears over the first, ragged rank of men. I grimaced at the pain of the few wounds I had received; roared, and laughed spitefully as I pushed to the less steady second rank of the enemy, where I kicked a foe so hard he folded in two. I slashed and slashed, like a butcher, growled away nicks and wounds and killed with glorious abandon. Men cheered my progress and pushed after me. I grabbed a huge man with bristling, greasy hair, one who had been charging for me with a ball and chain; his shield was broken, and I squeezed his throat so hard he bit off his tongue. A man jumped on my back, stabbed with a dagger, and I howled as the blade found a hole in the armor and slashed into my shoulder. Then, a Watchman speared the man. I growled, grew thicker, and swiped my sword across a wall of spears, men holding the doorway. Two fell apart; the sword hummed with brief resistance, and a third man spat blood as his ribs were broken. I roared and fought my way to the door, stepped on an enemy skull and the Watch followed me to the breach, turning to the sides of the foe, pushing and hacking wildly with ax and sword, many of their spears gone and twisted. They lived up to the name of the Mad Watch, howling and laughing at the enemy, who were giving up in places. The door was closed, and I searched for a spell to open it. It came to me.

But then, the door boomed open.

I slipped on blood and guts and fell on my back.

Three draugr stepped up, and they were not bothered by their hideous, dead looks. They were the elders; those Mir had resurrected that first night after dying. They were the most gifted of all the creatures, and they were all Touching the Dark Mistress. One was the butler, Gray. There were four hundred men standing amidst the piles of bodies, all staring at the creatures and not one knew what was about to take place.

I Stirred the Cauldron, and the shield of stone covered me as I scrambled away, and then the disaster struck. One draugr released a whirl of fire that tore through the heart of the Mad Watch troop. It started out as a small campfire and grew to a height of ten feet. Men fell all over the courtyard, smoking and screaming as they burned, some cooking in the air. The acrid smell of burning hair and skin filled my nostrils. Another draugr changed the air to scorching hot across part of the courtyard, and men screamed as they rolled, steaming in their armor. The last one, though, killed most with his magic. It was Gray's spell. He grimaced and gathered a great deal of power. His spell was made of simmering, deepest embers, poisonous fumes and patient fires, the gauntlet whispered to me. It was a strange spell, and I guessed it was a rare one and very, very deadly. He kissed the air and released a spell of blue-tinted wind, which thrust ghost-like past the screaming men, and billowed for the gates. Gray was trembling, the spell difficult and draining, but the spell kept going; men were coughing, weapons were dropped, and some few managed to crawl out of the way. Then the flames cast by the first of the draugr met the billowing cloud and a conflagration blast through the yard, toppling people from the walls, roasting the dead and living, in such terrible heat I could see skeletons running around before they turned to cinders. Hundreds died.

My spell saved me. It was strained to the very edges of its endurance; I felt the stone guard losing its potency as the fires licked at me. I charged forward as I saw the outline of the gate that was swinging shut. I grew into a Jotun. I saw the butler's eyes grow wide, the draugr guarding the three lifted feeble spears and shields, and I landed on them, taking down many of the enemy and a healthy part of railing of a fabulous stairway. They squirmed under me, biting and thrusting, and I pummeled anything that moved and the two spell-casting ones were soon nothing more than mangled flesh. I spied the butler, who was trying to flee up the stairway. I ran after him, breaking chairs and gilded vases decorating the vast bottom level of the Tower. Some guards converged on me, but I ripped them off the stairs and grabbed Gray. He was raising his hand. 'No you don't,' I laughed and grasped the limb. It broke apart while he was staring at it incredulously.

'Why did you help me?' I asked him.

He smiled wickedly. 'I told you. I loved Shaduril. And she loved you,' he explained. 'I saw her grow up, you see? Almost like my own child. Is she—'

'She is not gone, no,' I told him.

He smiled. 'She is as fine as she can be under the circumstances. She is best of the lot. Though Ann was a good sister, if sad. Some children are miserable all their lives, sir.'

'I will spare Shaduril,' I told him.

'Thank you, sir. Spare her if she desires this life. Kill the rest,' he said sadly. 'And myself, sir.'

'Speaking of which, where are Taram and Balan? And the pretender mother,' I spat, 'who made a fool of me?'

'You are Jotun.' He chuckled. 'Imagine that. I have taught manners to one. How to dress and to eat. I am sorry I tricked you. Though I did little. I smiled at you, and that was a genuine smile, sir. I liked you, sir. They are on top. Save for Mistress Mir.'

'Where is she?' I demanded. I noticed the battle was still ongoing outside, but apparently there were still some hundreds of Mad Watch alive, and they were killing the remaining enemy, despite the catastrophe at the gate.

'They left yesterday. In the evening. King Crec and she? They took Hawk's Talon north. They will march and pick up our armies and take a war to Ygrin. In the winter, even. The passes will be closed any day. Madness, sir.'

I stared at him. 'They want to make war on our allies and then rule what is left. There is nothing mad about it.'

'Rule? They? Mistress Mir?' the butler asked and then shrugged. 'Not really.'

'No?'

'No, sir,' he said with a weak smile. 'Killing your father was just the first step in a far more elaborate plan. You forget. There were many living mercenaries in the Crimson Apex. The ones that always changed? So far, only the undead have fought. Where are the living men who work with them? Think about that, sir. Quickly. That mask, sir? The horned mask? It is that of—'

Lith appeared and hacked off his head.

He flopped down on the stairs, and I grabbed her. 'And now you appear?' I said. 'What is the Horned Mask? And where are the mercenaries? The living ones. I saw hundreds in the Apex.'

'We have no time for this now, Maskan!' she said with rippling anger as she struggled in my grip. 'Ignore him. Did you tell him you will spare Shaduril? I cannot find her outside.'

'Yes,' I hissed. 'Why were you looking for her?'

'I would have had her killed,' she hissed. 'So what?'

'You won't get her. She is safe. Neither one was prepared to keep their word so stop weeping, girl,' I told her.

'I was only going to take what is mine in advance. You would spare her. That was not the deal,' she cursed. 'Liar. But fine. I'll leave my men in the yard. The Mad Watch is nearly done there.' She looked down as two of Valkai's men pushed Illastria inside. One was an undead woman, in fact. Illastria looked confused but smiled politely at me. 'They will keep Illastria safe. Let's go on.'

I shook my head at the creature. She had some devious plan concocted. But I was not unprepared. 'Yes. Let us deal with the rest of your damnable family.' I laughed as she was still fuming.

'Yes,' she hissed. 'Up there. The bottom is clear. I checked. You first. If they see me, they can command me.'

I nodded and got up to walk the stairs.

'You and I, love, will probably have to settle some scores at some point,' she whispered. 'I love you, and cannot help it, but I will flay your hide if you displease me too much.'

'I think I am beyond such concerns,' I told her with a grin. 'Be careful, love.'

I nodded for the upstairs and hesitated as I saw Sand standing by the doors. I winked at him as he eyed Lith and me dangerously. *Gods, do not make it so I have to slay him for the bitch.* 'The wall is safe? The city?'

'There is a Mad Watch guard at this Tower gate, keeping people out. Lith's people are at the wall gate,' he agreed darkly, his eyes on Lith. 'She giving trouble?'

'You serve me, Sand,' she reminded him.

'I forgot, mistress, sorry,' he told her.

'We are going up. You stay down here. Keep my horse by the gate.'

'I will,' Sand agreed with a sickly grin. 'Good luck, my … friend.'

I nodded at him, dragged the huge two-hander out, and marched up the stairs. Lith followed me, her eyes burning in the dark, her face pale and dead. The Danegell residence was surprisingly sparse, barely worthy of a king, but then, it was also a practical, surprisingly homelike abode. The stairs were made of lacquered wood and slabs of stone and dignified, simple furniture sat every now and then in wide, homely alcoves. 'What do you need Illastria for?' I asked her.

She laughed softly. 'She owns the Blacktower lands. I think she had better be under my thumb. Where did you hide Shaduril?'

'How many stairs?' I asked Lith, loathing and ignoring her question.

She nodded up. 'I'll find her. Or she will find me. She cannot help it. The Throne room is up on the third. It is colossal. The Pearl Terrace is also up there, behind the Rose Throne, and there are halls and banquet rooms set around the area. They hold court there. There are a hundred rooms on each floor. The work areas are below with the gate guards. This second floor is for officials. There will be draugr up there. It will be very hard to find them if they are hiding.'

'I see. But it won't be that hard,' I rumbled and changed. Lith gasped as I fell forward on my fours, my claws grew to the size of long daggers, and I turned entirely dark; my snout was elongated and full of razor sharp teeth. Gods, how much power my skills gave me. I sensed everything, smelled the smallest of scents lingering in the corners. I turned my snout towards her and she retreated, blanching in satisfactory terror at the sight of a huge, powerful wolf. Then I padded my way up. There was a door and beyond it only shadows. I smelled the air coming from the partly open doorway and knew we were not alone.

'He in there?' Lith whispered, stalking the shadows near me.

I growled and went through the doorway in a rush. My eyes were superb. The draugr were creatures of the night, but I was darkness itself. I saw them. They were in the huge room, standing in the shadows of the pillars framing the walls, and there was a dozen of them. All Blacktower men, some women. One, I saw, was a hauntingly beautiful female, her eyes in slits as she tried to understand if a lumbering Jotun had entered. I remember having seen her in the Apex, one of the servants and the one that had given me the clothes the day Lith had tricked me. I smelled others moving carefully, their weapons at the ready, bows aiming at emptiness. I padded forward, felt the thrill of a coming kill thrumming in my chest. I was recklessly anxious, powerfully savage, a slayer in the dark, like they were. I calmed myself, restrained my need to slay them and stalked closer. The woman was calling for magic, her hands were flickering, and the Black Grip, my gauntlet that was part of me told me she was seeking light. She had sensed something was wrong.

And then there was pale light in the middle of the room. The dead turned to look at it, then at the door.

But I was behind the woman, the strongest, and the most dangerous of the lot.

I jumped on her back. She shrieked in surprise, and then in pain, her dry lips drawn in a mask of terror as my blade-like claws raked her neck, and then her spine and the corpse fell, releasing a whiff of fiery spell at a curtain. The dead turned to me; two arrows flew, but I was past them.

They had no chance.

I bowled over one, raked his head off, turned, and bounded at one rounding a pillar, and the corpse actually shrieked with horror as my maw ripped at its face. Several shadowy warriors were coming at me, spears, axes, and hammers up. 'Kill the Beast!' one shrieked with chattering teeth and let go with an arrow. I growled and yelped as the point grazed my leg, jumped in the lot as I shifted. I landed on the group, their arms flailing desperately, and I pummeled them with my gauntlet, clawed at some that tried to crawl away and roared happily as the bowman let go another arrow, only to hit my sword. I pulled the massive weapon, rushed forward while shifting to a man-sized version and rammed the smaller blade through the draugr's chest.

A shadow flickered past.

I rolled away, cursing.

A beautiful Jotun's blade ripped my forehead open. Tear Drinker came at me from the front, then behind, and I danced, jumped, and thrust my sword around me, luckily thwarting the blade while wiping blood from my forehead and eyes. I put my back to the wall, near-blind, called for powers, saw the cascading ice and blazing fires in eternal fall to the abyss, and pulled at a desperate spell the gauntlet whispered to me. I drew in mighty molten forces, twisted them rudely together, and let them go.

The tower quaked and rumbled.

Dust flew, stones groaned and so did I, for the spell was hugely draining. I saw Taram fall to his side in the small earthquake, his sword scraping at the stone so hard sparks flew high up to the air. He tried to get up, but I released the rest of the spell; a pillar fell with a tumble, and the draugr lord fell again. He saw me coming, for I charged like a mad thing for him, my sword high, then coming down. Then, the bastard turned to shadow, slithered away and the sword split the wooden floor. I saw him streaking to the side, into a room, where a woman screamed

Then died, for a servant girl fell on the doorway.

The lights went out in the room.

I laughed and stalked in. I pondered the dilemma. A wolf would be easier to stab by a thing of shadows. But I also needed the senses. I chuckled and tried something creative. My head flowed and changed into a wolf's while I kept my armored body. It felt a strange mix, the body less dexterous than a wolf's, more human—no, Jotun—than an animal. But I saw and smelled everything, even over the scent of blood spreading from the hapless servant girl. I resisted the urge to lope as I had no paws and kept focus on my weapon.

I smelled Lith. She was close, stalking just outside the room, finally joining the battle. In the room, there were bunks in neat rows, a thick carpet that smelled of wet wool and also trunks for servants to keep their gear in. On one wall there were weapon racks. I snarled with a feral intensity, for I smelled rot and blood at the far right corner. I stalked forward, keeping my eyes on a suspicious shadow. I was close, jumped over bunks, and laughed, the sound coming out with a curious, dog like yelp. 'Run, little skeleton. Run!' I howled, and the growl was enough to convince Taram his hide and seek game had failed.

The shadow shuddered. Then moved. It flickered; I felt a spell being cast and saw vine-like tendrils grasp at my feet. I jumped out of them, ripped them up, and thrust forward, for Taram was flickering forth by the wall, trying to escape. I turned with the speed of his movement and swished my blade, which clanged with his sword. It didn't hit him but was enough to stop his flight, as he fell against the wall. I roared, my strength savage and bitter, and hacked down again, with terrible effect as a bed was sundered into bits. I kicked it aside, looking at Taram's shadowy, dead, and yet still strangely handsome face backing off. He danced away from me, and I saw him glance at the door. 'Lith?' he said. 'Care to help me?'

'No, you shit sucker,' she hissed. 'I will enjoy the show.'

Taram laughed and gathered spells. The fires spread left and right of me, and he charged forward. He dodged under my quick thrust, and rolled up to bump at me. I howled and grabbed him, pulled him towards my jaw, but his dagger stabbed at my face; his knee kicked my mouth shut, and we fell over rubble, rolling. I was a Jotun, savagely strong; he was lithe and agile as a snake. I dared not change; he was so close, and it would take a moment to do so, and that moment would be all he needed. He laughed, let his façade of calm disappear, cursed, and spat drily at me, again rolling on the floor. He hacked down with the dagger; my hand blocked him, the blade stabbing a shallow wound through my armored arm. I howled and kicked, and we rolled again to break another bed. He tried to get away from my grasping grip, his sword aiming down to slit my face. I butted my fanged face forward, and the dagger went through my snout again. I bit down on the blade and held it, and his victorious smile disappeared. I grasped his hair. He shrieked. I welcomed the stabbing, terrible pain as I yanked him closer, his dagger held by my teeth. If a dead man can grow pale, he did. I growled and pulled; he resisted, but in vain. He let go of the sword and again yanked at the dagger in my face, which sent stabs of blinding pain through me, but I had him, and then my bloodied, wounded maw opened up, clamped on his jaw and throat. The dagger was free, but he had no chance to hit with it. I bit down hard, tasted rot and old bone and ripped most of his face off, leaving one eye and forehead. He stumbled away as I choked on the terrible fare. He tried to melt into the shadows, sobbing in his strange, undead pain, hoping to dodge the smirking Lith.

My gauntlet came up with a solution.

I called a spell, one of ice and icy rocks, of frigid waters and vapors, and Taram fell forward on his face. A grasping pair of cold hands held onto him, and then more as I gave it a good, last push, released the spell, and he was held in a powerful vice of many hands. I shifted, taking my gigantic form and shuddered with fatigue. There were savage wounds in my face, and one tooth was loose. I stepped on him, placed my foot on his back, and pushed, his bones cracking. He howled, giggled, and addressed me, lisping strangely. 'Well, worm. It was different from what we used to share in Crimson Apex, this fight. Lith betrayed us?'

'Yes,' I said. 'And Shaduril will outlive you. Both of them will.'

'I should have taken Ann when she lived. Much more sensible than those two. Well, I guess I'll get my chance in a bit. She's already there, and I would have company in Helheim.' He laughed. 'But she was a prude, and I hope Hel's land has cured her of that.'

'She'll hurt you for her sisters in Helheim,' I said with murderous rage. 'I doubt you will enjoy her company. And the girls here? They'll laugh over the remains of your miserable corpse. Think about that, you slimy shit, as I see how deep I can smear you into the cracks.'

'Maskan—' he began, but Lith interrupted me.

'Go and take out Balan,' she said with an ice-cold voice. 'Leave him to me. You promised.'

'Why would I?' I laughed. 'He killed my father.'

'He is broken, Maskan,' she said slowly. 'We need to know more about Mir's plans. And then I will slay him. If she is not here, we will have to prepare for her. He might know more.'

'I know! I know it all! Spare me!' Taram howled as I cracked a rib.

I considered him. He shook his head and let go of his disguise spell. His skin was white and yellow with old wounds, leaving dry flesh hanging out in places. He had lost the fight, but he was still dangerous. I bent down and took one of his arms in my hand. 'Ready?'

'Spare him! For now!' Lith said, and I grinned.

'Here,' I told him and tore his arm off. I handed it to him as he looked in shock at the thing. Outside, bells were tolling.

'I'll take him to the guards, and then I'll join you,' Lith said, smiling at Taram.

I shrugged and stepped away. 'Fine.'

She hesitated as she came closer. 'You going to survive, love?'

'Wounds, you treacherous bitch, love,' I told her with a grimace. 'Nothing serious, I suppose. Perhaps not,' I said and felt my face was badly wounded.

'Makes you look handsome,' she purred, and I pushed her away and picked up Father's sword.

'None of that, now,' I told her, and she nodded, hesitant, chasing away that obsession. Then she was staring at Taram, who was spitting strange mucus from his dry lips.

'Go,' she told me and concentrated on Taram. She walked around him, thrust her short spear through his leg and began pulling him towards the doorway. He howled; Lith giggled, and I left. I stumbled across the hall, drew breath, and prepared to fight Balan. I walked up a staircase, met nobody, passed gilded couches in small alcoves of the higher tower, and made my slow way towards a doorway. It was a wide, silver thing at the end of a hallway, illuminated by Lifegiver's brilliant light. I spat as pain twisted my side, and I pushed over to the door.

I kicked it in, and it flew open with a bang.

Inside, the heart of Dagnar.

It was a huge circular room with dozens of doorways leading out of it. The walls were adorned with well-crafted tiles, inscribed with silver runes. Heavy arches supported the high, blood-red ceiling. A road of yellow bricks led to the opposite side of the huge chamber, and any visitor walking the path would at all times be thinking about the king on the throne, and he would be flanked by a row of courtiers and guards. The throne itself was a simple thing. It was large and dark red, and it had a simple back of well-grained wood. It was made of rosewood and rumored to have been the seat of Odin in the ancient times.

The vast chamber was empty.

There were torches burning on sconces, casting light to the chamber, but it felt dead. I shifted to a wolf, fell forward, and sniffed the air. I moved around carefully, eyeing the Rose Throne, the shadows, and the rooms beyond and around the perimeter. The kitchens were not far; I smelled spicy soup had been prepared there a day or so ago. I also sensed there were corpses in the other rooms, but they were different from the draugr. They were truly dead. Only one dead was standing, I decided, as I thought I had found Balan.

There was someone beyond the throne.

I loped there, spied window frames made of twisted dark iron flowers. The glass panes were crystal glass, yellow and white. Beyond the beautiful windows, a figure stood. I spied a door, a simple one and thought I saw Balan standing on the Pearl Terrace. I walked that way; wary of the many tricks Balan might have up his sleeve. He was a crafter, a maker of miracles, and I had carried his tools to my father. So many dead.

I stepped behind the draugr lord but stopped to look out over the town, to the mountains and the sea. The sight was unbelievable. The terrace itself was simple, broad and barbarically adorned with crude iron and rough wood, yet the wonderful sight gave the terrace its name. The

Arrow Straits spread out to the south and the east, glittering as if a thousand tiny pearls were bobbling across its surface. The many cascading waterfalls, the Hard Pass, and its lake land were things of wondrous beauty, and I could see why my father had prayed there, each morning for the gods. I momentarily even forgot Balan.

But not for long, as the Lord of the Blacktowers turned. His hand was gone, of course, and yet the dead thing raised it to ward me off. Then he realized his mistake and frowned, shrugged and put the stub down. He was not grasping at power, only standing there, and he let his human face disappear. He looked drawn, yellowed; his skin stretched and rotted, and his lips were curled back into thin flaps of skin. He leaned back tiredly and wiped lank hair from his eyes. 'Well, if you wish to kill me and send me on my way, do it. If you wish to talk before the nastiness, you should do something about your shape.' And so I changed. Tear Drinker was under Balan's chin, and he did not flinch. He grinned. 'Well. We fooled you well, didn't we?'

'You manipulated a child, but I suppose that is accurate,' I spat. 'You stole a baby from his family because you wanted to kill his father. You waited and crafted your spells and cast your web over an innocent, surrounded him with a fake family, pushed him over to hate his own, then struck when both Father and I were vulnerable. You did it for the throne. And here you are. But it is over now.'

'My quest is over,' he said softly. 'Mir made me a draugr lord, and I obey her. I was offered a lifetime of crafting wondrous things, but I am tired. What would be greater than Larkgrin, ever? I was driven to seek the seat of the King. So often, I saw him sitting here, dealing with Red Midgard, and I admit it, I envied him. And his queen. I was but the keeper of the secrets, an official of no name and no admirers. I wanted the seat. And now I have sat there. It was nothing. The dead watched me; I ordered them to bow, and they did, and I felt nothing. I am bored. Tired. And hate my family. They were always unkind, quarrelsome, conniving and scheming bitches. Save for Ann. She was so sad, all the time. I am happy she got out. And now it is over.'

'You failed in taking Dagnar,' I told him, prodding him with my sword. 'Utterly. And I will stop Mir from taking our army to fight the northerners. Mir will not benefit from your madness. No matter what you are planning, you will fail. I'll stop the pretender king.'

'The pretender king?' he chuckled. 'I suppose you guess Crec will lose the army.'

'They won't get into battle. I'll stop them. And the weather will not kill the army before I warn them. They are hardy men, no matter if it is winter,' I spat. 'Crec will never come back here. Everyone has seen what you are. The armies will mutiny when I get to them, and I will make sure Ygrin knows what—'

'Die,' he laughed drily. 'The armies will disappear. Ygrin won't kill our men. Neither will winter. For the High King is out there.'

'What?' I asked him, trying to understand what he was saying. 'The High King?'

'Yes, the High King Balic,' he confirmed. 'The Hammer Legions are coming. At least thirty thousand veterans. Six to seven legions. Almost half the troops of the Verdant Lands. They will land in Red Midgard, and they will rip our armies apart one by one. Crec and Mir will make sure they won't fail. And as for Dagnar?' He laughed. 'We have it. But we really want more.'

'What do you want, you undead filth?' I asked.

'Didn't you ask Lith?' he growled.

'Yes,' I grimaced. 'She lied, of course.'

He smiled sadly. 'Lith's rebellious. Like she always wanted what Shaduril had, she wants what her mother and father have. There is something else hidden in those tunnels below the city. And when you kill me, she will lead them. She will rule the city. Though there will not be a city left.'

A drum rolled.

It was a dull sound, odd and ominous, and disquieting blasts of a blaring horn; an ululating, disconcerting, strange sound that chilled all who heard it into silence, followed it.

'What is that?'

'I was supposed to rule Dagnar,' he said ruefully. 'Lith will. She is a One Eyed Priest, Maskan. We all are. We all serve the High King. That mask? It's the mask of a southern priest.'

'The High King?' I asked him. 'Does he know what you are?'

'Mir is the draugr queen,' he laughed dryly. 'He, the High King is the draugr king. I lost my wife to him the night we died. They planned this together across the continents. You don't understand, Maskan. Blacktowers do not want to rule this land. We want to destroy it. And we do so at the command of the King. The High King. He seeks to topple the one subject of his that could lead a rebellion. Magic-using Jotuns. Later he will destroy everyone, one by one.'

'You bastards. What was that blare?' I asked him as the sword pricked his face. 'The troops that have not yet shown their faces?'

'That is an army. Not all the legions will land in the north. We smuggled some here, little by little, and after the Old City was cleared, it was an ideal place to hide them. That gauntlet,' he nodded at the fabulous armor, 'will give you spells and powers to fight the army that is descending from Valkai's dungeon, but it won't last. I was to oversee the destruction. Lith wants the honor. She is making a bid for me and Mir in his eyes.' I heard commotion far down. I walked next to Balan and looked down to the city.

It was on fire.

The army Mir had created of the dead was a paltry joke in comparison to the Hammer Legion raging all across Dagnar. They were emerging from the recesses of the Old City. They climbed all over the place, free to reign terror now that the Danegells were truly gone, and the army had marched out. They were the men I had seen changing in the months leading up to the Yule feast. There were foreign black and red standards marching in the haze of the harbor, the Fourth Ring, the Third Ring and even the Second Ring. The gates had fallen, and I saw pockets of Mad Watch running about, fighting as they did, dying as Hammers of the High King struck at them ferociously. They were powerful, and savage men in black, wide helmets and long chain mail and cuirasses, their shins and arms covered in leather. They howled in their shieldwalls, crushed all resistance, pounced on the mortally surprised populace, and marched forward. Always up the hill. They were taking the rest of the gates, the harbor, but thousands were streaming through the streets for the Temple.

'It is useless, Maskan. There are nearly four thousand of them. You never saw but a few of them. Fly away; find a new life for yourself. Your relatives are gone,' he said as he saw me looking down and followed my gaze. There down at the Tower's gate, Valkai's men had taken it. A man, a draugr, was leaning on its side, hurt and battered, his face gone. Taram. Sand was there, next to a confused looking Illastria. And Lith was there as well. Balan snorted. 'Just do not trust the dead. I see you hurt Taram? And gave him to Lith? She wants him as well. Cannot let go. Now she truly has him!'

'I will not trust anyone ever again,' I told him coldly.

He sighed. 'Yes, you will. Now, Lith will rule for a while. They will tell Mir I died in battle as you attacked us, but she hopes to take as much power for herself as possible. She will blame it all on you if the High King or Mir might ask why I died. They will get power as the dead only really care about the results. Lies are in our nature.' He chuckled sadly. 'You made a mistake, again.'

I grasped his neck and bent his face down to the gate. There, some two to three hundred Mad Watch soldiers stood by my horse in front of the Tower. They were likely the only band of organized soldiers available to the city. They faced the four hundred enemy undead, survivors of Balan and the men who had served our cause. Valkai was growling, and they thickened into a column at the gateway, determined to hold it. And they would. I saw Lith gesturing at my poor friend Sand, ordering him to step away to help Taram and to guide Illastria to her, and he did, though reluctantly. The Mad Watch looked on, shuddering with indecision. 'Look below.'

'Hah,' Balan said. 'Less than three hundred soldiers? What good will that do? Is that Sand? Your last relative. So to speak.' He squinted.

'That is Sand,' I told him.

'Lith's now.' He chuckled. 'I could go down there and order them to step down. Will you spare me if I do? It won't matter due to the Legions, but perhaps you want to see Lith executed before you die?'

I watched as the Blacktower men chanted in a thick column of bristling shields and spears, some of the dead anxiously looking back towards the Sun Court. I saw the Hammer Legion marching resolutely through the gates of the First Ring, slaying men and women, even children as they went, streaming right and left, the majority, several thousand coming from the Temple. 'Sand is not family. He is a friend. My best friend. But I do have family. A sister.'

'Are you mad?' he asked softly, eyeing me with undead intensity.

'She is my family,' I pointed at the warhorse. 'I did not trust Lith. And as for your offer? No, thank you. I don't need or trust you. I'll do my own executing.'

'What? A horse?'

'That down there is the one who you called the Black Brother. But it is not a brother at all, but a sister.'

The horse changed, and a giant emerged. The saddle fell to the bloody ground, broken. It was she, a sister, the Black Sister, in fact. She was an ice Jotun like I was; one of the great warriors in the lost armies of Hel's war, the last Jotun in Midgard, in addition to me, of course. I looked at her gleaming, tall armor; the dverg-made magical armor of a giant; a tall spear, as tall as the gates. She laughed so harshly it rang in our ears. The giantess's name was Balissa Danegell, and she had answered the call of my gauntlet, enraged, and alone out in the mountains. None had been suspicious when I demanded to be seated on the beast in the Tenginell stables that I claimed was known to be Black Brother's. The deception had to be perfect, and the dead love such perfect deceptions, and they never doubted they had been fooled. It had been perfect, for me.

Valkai stared at her in shocked anger, hissing at Lith. Taram disappeared into the shadows, and Sand pulled Illastria out of the gate and far from the bristling band of undead blocking it. Lith pointed her spear at Balissa, shaking her head, giving commands. I felt Balissa draw in an enormous amount of power, weave and fold the icy winds and frigid ice of our homelands, and then she blew the enemy a kiss as she released the spell. She quickly cast something after, which was a scorching hot wind.

It was a powerful, terrible combination of spells.

A horrific gust of wind whipped through the enemy ranks. It was a spell like mine, but it was her specialty. The cold wind tore off cobble stones, grass, mortar from the walls. Then it hit the thickly packed enemy troop. It froze some; the following scorching hot wind burned others, and the mix of the two opposite powers was not unlike a hammer blow on a roach. Bones broke; faces froze, flattened, necks were severed, limbs ripped off, and what remained, burned. Hundreds of spears rattled together as a significant chunk of the enemy column practically flew out of the gates, frozen and burning. Balissa tottered, near exhausted, and then walked forward to kick at the remaining, dazed enemy who were running, fearless undead or not. She picked up stragglers and smashed them, brutally speared some, and finally casually closed the gates. She looked up and frowned.

I waved at her, and she nodded back at me, stiffly. She blamed me for the loss of my father and our brothers. But I was all she had.

Balan gawked at the gate. Balissa was yelling at the Mad Watch to man the gates and the walls. They were scared of her, but most ran to obey. 'Doesn't matter. It is hopeless! There are thousands of the enemy. The Mad Watch is scattered all over the place. The Temple and the town will fall! You had best fly away!'

'Here,' I told him. 'Give me all your toys.'

'All my toys?' he asked, confused.

'Toys,' I told him and searched him. In the end, I had all I wanted.

'What will you do?' he asked, curious.

I leaned on him. 'The Temple. There is something special down there. I know. Father told me. Many wondrous artifacts. A throne, I hear. The real throne of Morag.'

'Oh no,' he breathed. 'The book was always a bit vague about that place. Apparently, they made their home there during the Hel's War and …' he began, and I saw he was curious to know more. I could see it from his excited eyes. He had developed goals for himself, ones he could not ignore.

'But you won't see it,' I told him flatly, and I saw I had broken his cold heart.

I picked him up and tossed him far, far from the wall, where he splattered on the wall of a blue mansion. I saw Lith supporting Taram outside the gates, limping away, and I made a throat-cutting motion to them both. Sand was keeping Illastria safe. That was the only thing I had asked of him. That did not break his oath to Lith. And he was doing it.

The drum boomed. The first of the southern enemy soldiers were in sight, and there was a brief scuffle at the gate as Lith struggled to explain they were allies. Soon, there would be a thousand Hammer Legionnaires gathered before the gate. And more.

I looked down to the yard. To the left, the remains of the old temple were nestled, sad, and forgotten. Weeds were growing amidst the stones, and carvings were faded in the surface of the rocks. There once stood the gateway to one of the other worlds, perhaps Asgard. And below it, the home Hel's armies had carved in the stone lands of Dagnar, thousands of years past.

'They had better be there still,' I whispered and ran down the stairs. There I found an old lady and ordered a Mad Watch member to take her up. After that, I walked out and to the walls.

## CHAPTER 20

Balissa sighed as I climbed to the wall. I held Bjornag's two-hander, my hand on sheathed Tear Drinker and I stared at the massively tall female, whose helmet was under her armpit. She had bright blue eyes, the blue-tinted skin of a Jotun, and a superior, noble bearing of an arrogant bastard. Her eyebrows were lively; her face lean as ice and her mouth had a perpetual pout. Her tall spear glinted as she pointed out to the Sun Square. Wind ruffled her red-blonde hair that was thick around her shoulders

I saw an army of dark-armored men; all hefting round, embossed shields of gray and black make; spears, javelins and heavy hammers, their helmets very wide, the rims reaching to their shoulders. Most had chain mail draped across their mouths. 'That will be uncomfortable when the air freezes,' Balissa said, observing the armor over the lips of the enemy. 'Steel and ice and sweaty skin. Perhaps they can piss on each other's faces to remove the frozen chain.' I chuckled dutifully, but in truth, they were too many. They stood in blocks of nearly five hundred men, and there were four such blocks. Some three hundred undead soldiers formed their own block. This was the Bull Legion, judging by the horned beast in the black and red standards. They might slaughter us with ease, I thought. Balissa spat at them. 'You know we are buggered, right?'

'I know,' I growled at her.

'Because of you,' she whispered. 'Your inability to tell truly evil from good.'

'I don't know what to tell you, Balissa,' I told her tiredly. 'I trusted my family, the people around me and never knew the truth. Shut up and tell me how to win this battle.'

She eyed the enemy, the shaken Mad Watch and remained silent. 'You know how.' She eyed the gauntlet with fear and wonder.

'If I open the vaults,' I said, 'what will happen?'

She sighed. 'It might go very ill for Dagnar. It will change things. It might save us.'

'How?'

'You are the Beast of the North.' She chuckled. 'No matter if you do or do not open the vault, Dagnar will change; the humans will suffer, and the north will shake to its foundations, but perhaps something good will grow out of it if you do open it? Do not, and the dead will rule. You might bring us all something different, very, very different, if you open it up. The dead? They won't give us mercy. You have to remember …' she said and cursed as the army before us rippled in anticipation; a great drum began to beat, and an officer wearing a blue cape appeared. Then I saw Lith, in a conical garment, walking for the man and pulling on a golden, horned helmet. 'One Eyed Priest,' she said with a pouty grin. 'It means Hel's Priest, for her eye is lost, and hence are the worlds shattered from each other.'

'You were saying?' I asked her.

'I was saying,' she told me, 'that you are a Jotun. You are of the Ymirblood, a Toe of a Giant, a Jotun of Nifleheim, scion of Jotunheimr and foe to gods and their creations. Men are not our friends. Magor felt responsible for them, some of our kin agreed, but in the end, we are not friends or kin. They will turn on us.'

'I have a hard time believing they would choose those dead over a Jotun,' I told her, eyeing the enemy officer walking forward.

'They will choose us,' she affirmed. 'But abandon us when we have done their dirty work. Should you decide to save our asses and open our former base, their lives will change. Some will die. There will be more conflict in the world. The High King will face stiff resistance, but it will break all of Midgard. But at least many will survive. Death will come either way, but some will live if you go there and succeed.'

'How?' I asked.

'You will see,' she said softly. 'The general the gods sent here is formidable. Might be a prisoner now, but if freed, it will change men's perceptions and allegiances for good.' She chortled, shaking her head, and I began to get irritated. She slapped the wall. 'But if you do not, they are sure to die. What is down there can possibly spare them, but there will be conflict later.'

I shrugged and wiped my hand across my face. 'I was a human. Still am, partly. I say we spare most of them. And take risks.'

'Some of them, I think. Not most. And no, you are not a human at all, you damned fool,' she hissed. 'We live amongst them, for here we were royals and lacked nothing. We do not love them.'

'Magor felt responsible for them,' I told her. 'You just said so.'

'Magor was a great king,' she agreed, 'but he would never choose his slaves over his own people. And his true allies. But free them and it, Maskan, and let us not worry about Dagnar and the north. The old ways will be gone. Midgard will change.'

'You cannot tell me anything? What is down there, exactly?' I asked her again.

She shook her head. 'Something we once surrendered to. But Magor tricked it and sealed it in there with the Black Grip, your gauntlet. It was the base of war in Hel's War on worlds. Remember. Whatever happens to humans, as a result, we have nothing in common with them. You are responsible to your people. Me. And those we locked in there.'

'I will—'

'You? On the wall!' yelled an imperious voice with a strange, clipped accent. The officer.

'They want you, my king,' Balissa chuckled. 'Look kingly.'

'You lost?' I yelled down at the officer, who wore a full, golden helm with a bull painted in the middle. 'Dagnar has a king, and I cannot remember inviting you.'

'Dagnar,' the man said with a growl, 'has a king indeed. Always did. Danegells are traitors, and the High King condemns you do die. You inhuman vermin.'

'The whore,' I laughed and nodded at Lith, 'is no human.'

The officer glanced at Lith's golden mask and the contingent of dead. 'They are more. The god touches them. Our god. The High King, the one Lord over us all, is the true god of men. They are like him, his seed, and his kin and serve his will. Now. Fly away, I know you can. And you men!' he yelled, and the Mad Watch stiffened. 'You have our word you will be spared, should you throw down your weapons.'

I laughed hugely as the men on the wall eyed me. 'Yes! Go down to them. Look at your city, men! My father always guarded Dagnar, and never once burned it. Hear the screams of your women and children out there?'

The officer stiffened and spat. The Mad Watch remained quiet, pondering the words of their strange new lord and those of a savage conqueror. 'Choose now!' the officer yelled.

'We are no longer Balic's subjects, my lord! Not since he burns our homes,' I yelled and was rewarded by a ragged, rumbling scream of the Mad Watch. They raised their swords and axes to the air; spears thrust up to the sky defiantly, and they laughed at death. They should have been enjoying the Yule feast. Instead, they would soak in blood. The two thousand Hammer Legionnaires banged their shields together, and the officer turned to confer with Lith.

'So, they will come and dance,' Balissa stated. 'What now?'

'Can we hurl them back?' asked a timid Mad Watch captain. 'We have only a few hundred men. Many died out there in the city and in the battle. And they destroyed the ballista.' I looked at the mighty things. They were broken beyond repair.

'The walls are not very tall,' Balissa said. 'They are more ceremonial than anything.'

'We can lock the Tower, no?' I asked and turned to look that way.

The doors had been hacked to pieces.

Balissa snorted. 'Once they are open, they are like any door. Now they are useless. I say we fight them here and then retreat to the tower anyway. Easier to defend unless they bring siege. And they will, but not today, maybe. There is a store of food and arms there, I think, to last a good while. Unless they lost that as well.'

I nodded and looked at the wall. There were now some three hundred Mad Watch guardsmen on the walls, barely enough to man it. The gate was propped by slabs of stone, debris, and corpses, and fixed to the ground by spears and wedges.

I pulled the captain to me. 'Give the orders. When the time comes, we retreat there.' I nodded at the tower.

'Can you …' he began and stammered.

'Use magic?' I asked him. He nodded. 'Yes, we can. But—'

'It's not enough,' Balissa said darkly. 'It would be sufficient if we had more Jotuns working for us. I'm exhausted already. So are you.' She glanced at me as the captain went. 'Go and change Midgard.'

'The place was closed twenty years ago, Balissa,' I told her. 'Whatever is down there, they will be starved.'

'They won't,' she said. 'They are not Jotuns. Neither is the one we tricked. She will not need to eat often, and the others are quite ingenious.'

'Woman? What are they?' I asked.

'Useful,' she said. 'Push them back!' she screamed, and I realized the enemy had suddenly charged. Two thousand iron-studded and leather-shod feet trampled the ground; drums were banging madly behind the ranks and golden-helmed officers screamed at their men to take the walls.

Balissa turned me. 'Good luck. I will fight until it is hopeless. Then I shall flee if I can. Hope to see you again, numbskull, my king,' she said with a small grin. I nodded at her, eyed the Temple dubiously, hoping to decide on a suitable course of action. I could not go yet. I had to do something first. I ran through the gatehouse, cursed the disabled siege ballista, the empty caltrop boxes and kicked at what had been arrow racks. They had done an excellent job in dismantling our defenses. I reached the other side of the wall, where men of the Mad Watch looked mesmerized as the enemy carried ladders for the wall. I grew in size to twelve feet and pointed my sword at the foes. The guard stepped back from me. 'Those fight for the dead. Some of us shall die, but they have to come over the wall. They thought the Tower would be theirs already and have not prepared for this.' I prayed that was true. 'They were not expecting trouble. They would have slaughtered you where you slept. This is a gift to us. We shall fight like the mad, and mad you are, are you not?' I asked them with a bellowing voice. They looked dubious and fingered their weapons nervously. Some nodded. Most of the Watch was gone. Scattered and dead. 'Are you with me? Or shall your damned king fight alone?'

They hesitated. They had seen Balissa standing tall as a giant. They had seen me hurtle through the doors to the Tower as a Jotun. They had seen our powers. I saw the first legionnaires reach the wall.

'Kill the sons of bitches,' a Watch officer growled. 'For Dagnar!' *Not for the king,* I thought, but it would do.

The enemy was not totally unprepared. They had ladders.

They went up. Then they crashed down, trembling, despite their sturdy make, for men were already scaling them. A throng of dark-armored enemies milled around the base of the wall; a dozen men were hammering at the gate, and there was a thousand men waiting a little way from the Tower of Temple's wall while the others made ready to break us. I heard Balissa scream a challenge, and then I felt air rippling with a spell and saw a blistering hot and freezing cold ice storm whip up in the middle of a pushing group of enemies. Flesh froze, others burned spectacularly, and men screamed and flew around. I knew Balisssa was tired and could not throw many such spells, and this had not been as strong as the first one. I noticed Lith dancing as she also was casting a spell, and a fiery spear grew from her hand. She threw it; it flew to smash against someone, and there it exploded. The rock broke, a crenellation fell on the legionnaires, and the Watch suffered injuries and no doubt deaths. Then she did it again at another spot, and the officer of the Hammers rode back and forth, eyeing all the efforts until he disappeared below and stood in front of the gate. A man screamed in the gatehouse, an apparent victim of a swift javelin or arrow. Lith ordered Valkai to lead men to the gate, men with heavy mauls. He did. Sand and some of the dead, who did not join the battle, guarded Illastria.

I turned to look at the ladder right in front of me. I heard steps and curses below and hazarded a glance over the rim. An arrow went by my face, but I saw a burly man clambering up. I grew large and thick, and his eyes went from madly brave to shocked as he saw the size of the enemy waiting for him, but up he came until I hacked down at him. His helmet split; his hauberk was rent, and he fell to take down the next man on the rungs. Another jumped up soon, grinning with terrified determination, and I roared as I kicked him far, a broken man. I leaned over to grab the ladder and spat as javelins rained around me, hitting my armor. I pulled the ladder up. There were men holding it, and they came with it. I pulled it, dragged it over and squashed the men still clinging on. I reached for the last of them, a tall man trying to escape to the gatehouse and threw him in a high arch at the enemy ranks below. The Mad Watch cheered wildly, their voices tiny amidst the howls of the pressing enemy, and they truly began to fight. Spears waited for the enemy to appear over the ladder, and then men died. Many fell, a dozen. Dark, deadly javelins flew in swarms over the wall, striking sparks off the stone, a few impaling and wounding Watchmen.

'Keep killing the motherless goats!' I screamed and noticed something out of place. A chanting concentration of troops were marching for the middle part of our wall, two hundred grim men, pushing their milling companions aside. They were holding shields high, and I saw there were ladders, very tall ladders amongst the group. They were determined to take the wall, as determined as a starving thief, and then they acted. A hundred men lifted a dozen ladders up while some held onto them. The ladders were already full of men as the Hammer Legion lifted them high, grunting with the effort, and they landed high between two previously embattled ladders on the wall. It looked like a bridge, full of scuttling, armored beetles. The ladders crashed down on the wall. The impact shook some of the enemies off; others fell over to our side and the stone below. But many of the savage fighters jumped to the wall itself, amidst Mad Watch, who were suddenly fighting a desperate battle to repel the enemy. Several enemy linked shields in the middle of the turmoil, wielding heavy, deadly hammers at the less experienced guardsmen. A man fell, his face caved in. Another followed, his neck was broken as he tottered to the side. More men clambered up the ladder, holding their shields up, and some five Mad Watchmen were caught between the men on the wall and the legionnaires who were climbing. Two of my men fell in confusion; one ran away only to die as a javelin pierced his neck. Two more dropped their weapons and begged for mercy, but there was none to be had. A golden-helmed officer jumped up to the wall, ten of his men braced themselves, and I acted.

I ran for them. The wall trembled; they threw javelins at me, their eyes full of terror. My sword went up; they hid behind their shields, and I swiped the huge weapon at them. There was a jarring crash, a thrumming noise as the sword shuddered redly and three of the enemies were dead or dying, limbs hacked off, shields rent. I roared and went in kicking at the enemy, stepping on one, and faced the officer, who hacked desperately at my midriff, drawing blood with his ax. I kicked him so hard his helmet flew off with his head. Yet more and more of the enemy came to me, and then I heard an officer of the Mad Watch screaming.

'The gate! It is breaking!' A group of Mad Watch turned to repel men at the ladders, and that was when Lith joined the fight in our stretch of wall. I felt her, rather than saw her, for she was holding a great spell, and I knew I had to move. Her mask appeared at the top of the ladder at the other end of my wall.

A wall of wickedly hot flames spread to the left and right of me. Men burned indiscriminately, to their bone, their soul, perhaps, for they screamed hideously. A hundred perhaps less were charred by Lith's spell. She was pushing the fires towards me.

I jumped off the wall. I had to, anyway. I jumped to the enemy side. I thought desperately as I saw the shocked opponents look up from under their broad helmets at a plummeting, armored giant was about to break into them. A wolf? A bear? What was the limit? And then I decided. I changed in the air as I came down, and when I hit the army below, it was not a soft-bellied wolf or a furry bear that hit them. It was a sauk, the lizard. There was slithering power in the form. It was a ferocious, merciless killing machine. I had the dark, leathery, and horned skin, powerful ripping claws, and bursting speed. It was perfect for the chaos. A hammer struck my skin but bounced off. A spear went wide as a man fell over my back. There were many desperate men trapped under me, and I clawed them to death, roared so hard some of the enemy dropped their weapons and toppled over. Then I slithered forward. To move like that, as if the world was still, was an empowering feeling. I was fast, flexible, strange, and I was soon lathered with blood, theirs, and mine. I moved through groups of men, crushing them under my claws and bulk, drawing flesh and meat from quivering bodies with each step, biting swiftly and savagely at limbs and heads, and I roared when I tried to laugh, for the hammers were feeble indeed against my leathery skin. One struck my snout, though, and I went into a berserk frenzy. I loped, jumped, ripped, and bit at the enemy; slit gullets, slashed shields to pieces and ran around wildly in the helpless milling mass. I hunted officers, the golden-helmed, sturdy men, and bit off their arms and heads and felt blood flow as the enemy swarmed me with daggers, swords, and spears now. I killed thirty, maybe more, and while many legionnaires died and some even ran, I sensed the walls were falling. A horn blared desperately, a call to retreat. The gate broke. I heard a Jotun scream for men to run, and so I realized—even in my bestial rage—that I had to run as well. I loped right, then left, screamed as a flurry of javelins hit me. I saw two hundred men marching for me, using spears and hammers to herd me, and so I charged. I crushed spears, took hammer hits and bowled over a dozen enemies. They screamed, hit at each other and me, and so I transformed in the chaos, crawling around in the pile of twitching bodies to take the face and armor of an officer I had killed. They yelled in confusion, all around me, urged each other to kill the beast but suddenly they realized there was none to kill.

'Where in One Man's name did it go?' one asked, bleeding.

'Turned into a bloody mouse?' another, a man with a lip torn off answered painfully. Men jumped around, looking for a mouse. I was trembling with exhaustion and took a breath, then another, covered in nicks and wounds.

Then I saw Taram.

He was limping along the men, his eyes burning with hate, his arm missing. He had disguised his torn face, but everyone saw he was not entirely human. He looked confused for a moment, and then his eyes brightened in understanding. 'Men, ware! He—'

'This way, men!' I bellowed and guided the confused mass of men to the gate. 'Half stay at the gate, the rest join in the attack on the tower. Riches and women, boys, to the one who kills a giant!'

They yelled agreement and loped off in a confused mass, the reluctant half staying by the gate, locking shields to hold it, missing an opportunity for riches and women. There was an officer there with men already, and the confusion helped as the rest loped after me. The enemy was flowing for the Tower, over the walls, through the gates. I sensed Taram was running after us, cursing us, yelling at us to stop, but few did. I was looking for Lith and saw her, gathering men for an attack on the base of the wall. And Sand was there, guarding Illastria.

The tower was under siege.

A thousand enemy soldiers milled around it. Javelins were thrown at the defenders of the gate; some hundred bedraggled Mad Watch soldiers, and I saw Balissa there. A spell flickered in the middle of a group of Legionnaires. They slipped and fell, cursing as a pool of water froze, trapping many. At the same time, Lith's spell of fire burst in the doorway, intense and fiery, but Balissa countered it with snow hail, and then the mighty Jotun cast another spell of icy wind, throwing a dozen enemy into a terrified, dying and dead pile of shivering, bleeding men. I saw Lith was tottering aside, holding her mask.

I pointed a finger at the gate to the Tower. 'Reinforce them! Do not let them shut the doors!' Men ran forth to obey; I pushed them, eyed them, growled at them as I imagined a Hammer Officer would and saw Taram running forward, his face raging.

'There is a Jotun out here!' he shrieked, his sword trembling in rage.

'Where?' I asked, and he saw me, ran to me, and pulled at me.

'The thrice damned idiots thought the sauk just disappeared into the thin air! He took a new face—' he began and tried to yank at me to follow him. I grinned at him, saw him blanch, and punched him so hard he flew through a troop of men. I dodged out of sight, bellowing at men to charge the tower, which they did, and I wondered how to get in. I ran past Sand, bumped into him and poor Illastria, then changed direction and ran for the Temple.

Three Hammer officers raised their weapons; javelins were drawn back, thrown, and men hollered inside the blazing doorway. A hundred enemies charged after the charging officers, and even though some fell under the feet of their comrades, pierced by a few javelins and spears thrown back, they charged through with manic intensity, even through the fires. I saw Balissa's spear flicker, thrusting aside five enemies into red ruin; some fell to the flames, dead, but then, after moments of battle, the sounds receded, and I knew they were retreating up the tower.

I stopped. There were hundreds and hundreds of the enemy, and there truly was no way for us to defeat them. I turned to look at the Temple. It was standing forlornly on the side of the tower, once rumored to be a gateway to other worlds. There were many like it scattered all over the world, but this one had supposedly led to Asgard, where Odin ruled. He too was a god of one eye, like Hel.

I cursed myself and went forward. I pushed and pulled through a throng of men. Screams could be heard as men died in the tower. I caught a glimpse of Hammer Legionnaires rolling down stairs as the desperate defenders fought a hard fight to survive. There were no prisoners to be taken; none would surrender.

Some of the enemies were marching around the tower, others were running, all looking to block any possible escape route. I joined a group, passed through the ancient stones of the temple and slunk away from them. I concentrated on my gauntlet, and it answered. The door. It was close. My eyes sought the image it had shown me, and then I saw it. Not far from me, there was the red stone slab the size of a man, which I approached reverently. It was not part of the temple; no, it was easy to see. It was not as skillfully built as the Temple had obviously been, but cruder, more primal, closer to what a giant would revere, strong and naturally intricate. I stepped near it, trembling and hesitating. I changed my hand to reveal the gauntlet, and it whispered to me of a complicated spell that was tied to the artifact itself. I called for deep embers of certain molten rivers, combined them with heat and hot winds in a certain strange way, and released it on the gauntlet. Then I pressed it on the stone.

It clicked.

There was no mighty show of lights, or explosions. No pillars were growing out of the sand, nor was there a bizarre guardian with a weapon, accosting me, demanding a passphrase, denying my right to enter.

I took a breath. The stone shot open.

Then I went down to the dark and tapped the stone as I did, calling for the same spell again. The door closed with a click, and the sounds of battle faded. Shadows fled along the walls; I went down broad steps, and I felt magical wards renew themselves, flitting thought the stone, sealing the place tight.

# BOOK 6: HEL'S HORDE

# THE BEAST OF THE NORTH

*'The Jotuns trapped you here and have ruled above ever since.'*
**Maskan to Baduhanna**

## CHAPTER 21

I walked down stairs that were dusty in most places, but not in all. I bent to the dark ground, realized there had been people walking on the steps, for there were shuffling marks; feet had been dragging through dust, and I decided I had to see better. I fell on my fours, shed my skin, and took the stealthy form of a gigantic wolf once again, feeling every fiber in my body shrieking from pain and exertion. I looked around. All around the doorway, the stone had been hewed, torn, scratched, and hauled away. In places, the quarrying work had reached an entirely smooth stone, and that did not show a single scratch mark. The spell was strong. It created a cocoon around the area. I felt a brief bout of panic as I thought of being caught there under the rock. What if the spell did not work again? I shook my head, abandoned the doubts, and made my way down. The stairway was surprisingly short, ending in a crude doorway, which I crossed. I sniffed the air and smelled strange things.

There was life down there. Down, for I was on a ledge.

And below, there was a city.

It was multilayered, spiraling down and down, filled with stone houses, all bluish-gray, dark and pale white, lights burning inside, doorways open to the trails that inevitably led to the bottom, where a dim light shone. I gazed that way and smelled a sweet body of water. There was a lake deep inside the hill, far, far down. I stalked to a bridge, spanning a crevasse of dreadful depth. All along the way, similar quarrying work had been attempted, only to meet with the strange, smooth rock. I smelled and now heard movement in the nearest of the houses and walked towards them. There was speech, guttural speech, dark and gritty, like stone speaking. I slunk along the routes and spied a carved, tall building guarding the road. There was a chair outside it, leaning on a doorway and a bitter smelling mug of ale. I went forward and gazed inside.

There were creatures there. They wore no shirts; they were dark as night, their hair brown, and white, and silver jewelry adorned their beards. They were superbly crafted specimens, their necks thick like trees, arms gnarled and heaped with glistening muscle. Their faces were haggard, bony, and their lips were thin. They were chuckling, obviously drunk, and they were perhaps four feet tall.

They were dverger. They were legendary creatures, to be sure; the very best of smiths, strong warriors, and rumors said they were evil and selfish. Those were the stories. *Like stories of Jotuns,* I laughed, and that came out as a growl.

The dverger turned, having been engrossed in a small feast. One groped for a wicked scimitar, the other grabbed a maul, and they eyed me. They said nothing, did not move, and I decided one nodded at me, carefully, ever so slowly.

I walked past the doorway, smelled food being cooked, and more and more of the guttural speech invaded my ears. I passed shops, taverns and heard a flute playing. I stalked past a smithy, a fabulous thing full of steel weapons, intricate cups of excellent make, plates and jewelry, the smith a white-haired, entirely gray dverg, who turned to stare at me with an appraising, sharp look. I went down the spiraling ways, stalked over rubble and debris of a building being constructed.

Behind me, a horn blared. It was a strange, non-threatening sound; one that was intended to alarm the strange city of my presence, but seemingly in a non-hostile way. Hundreds of the dverger appeared, holding tankards of drink and plates full of mushroom-like food. I noticed some were fat and short; strangely squat, and I decided they were not dverger at all, but some other race. I stalked past the staring troops of dverger, and I heard them following me in the shadows, filling the path behind me.

So it went on, seemingly for a long time, and I despaired, for the tower would undoubtedly be fallen, and Lith would be seated on Rose Thorne. Balissa would be slain or fled, the city burning and Red Midgard gone. Did it matter? Yes, I decided. I was both human and a Jotun. The dead had made me a strange mix of the two, raising me as one of the men, and then thrust me to the intrigues of the Jotuns and the dead, and so I was determined to stay confused, a man and a giant.

And a wolf; I chuckled and growled as I stalked through the strangely harmonious town. What were they? Remnants of Hel's army? From where? Dverger? Mercenaries long lost in the wars and imprisoned? Did Father command them? What did they think of Hel now? And would they fight against the feral dead, who served their former mistress?

'They will if they wish to leave this hole,' I said and realized I had again growled, but this time so loudly the army of dverger had stopped. I slunk along, eyeing them carefully, but none raised a weapon. And they, I noticed, were all carrying them. Many were armored now in thick, tight-fitting plate and chain, and many were armed with mattocks, shields, tapering spears, wicked axes, hammers and mauls, many eyeing me from under their dark helmets. One pointed at the bottom of the pit, and I glanced there and saw the luminescent lake. It was shining with blue and green lights, deep and alive with fish that swam lazily in its shores. In the middle, there was a flat island, not very large, and filled with strange stones. I sniffed the air and sensed there was something else down there.

It was alive.

I spotted a haze in the middle of the island. Then I realized the stones scattered across it were skulls. I changed my skin and grew to my size of twelve feet. The dverger made a rumbling sound and I realized they were speaking excitedly. I looked at their faces, and there was a strange mixture of hope, savagery, and glee in the furry smiles that greeted me. Their teeth were very white. 'What is down there?' I asked them in the common and saw them blinking their eyes, then nattering something to each other. They finally pushed forth a dverg who was armed with a long-hafted hammer, bare-chested and wide as a barrel. His face was dark as coal, and I could not understand him, as he bowed and spat and tried to make some point.

I looked at the gauntlet and searched for an answer. Visions of a legion of such warriors, marching in dark tunnels filled my mind, and I knew I saw visions of long past. There was another, the Old City burning as the savage warriors hacked through stone and flesh to take it from men, in eras long past. I saw a battle in the city, a siege and dverger being burned on pyres by their kin. I saw my father, and another like him, as they fought against something I could not make out. In the dark by the lake.

Here.

I also saw a spell in my mind, a subtle, small thing of wind and ice mixed with some of the heat of Muspelheim, and I grasped the spell, gathered it, and released it at myself.

'Do you understand?' the dverg was asking. 'You damnable great lummox.'

'Yea, you runty snot-nosed, shit-snuffling bastard,' I growled at him.

His eyes brightened, and he flashed a quick grin. 'Thrun Tain Shug,' he pointed a finger at his own chest. 'You?'

'Maskan,' I said. 'Danegell,' I added. 'Son of Magor. And the Beast of the North as he is dead.'

Thrun nodded and stroked his beard shrewdly. 'Yes. I see. Or smell him in you. Hel's own general, Lord of all the Ymritoe kin and leader of our armies in Midgard. He and your grandfather,' he said and nodded ominously towards the lake, 'left us here. That was not so long ago, but it has been tedious.'

The human in me blinked. 'That is thousands of years past.'

Thrun nodded suspiciously. 'I see, I see. You think that is long? There is a story here to be told, and gladly we'll hear it at another time. How goes the war above? We don't know, you see, since your father locked us in here with the bitch. He made peace, a pact with her after your grandfather died in battle, then escaped like a mouse and left us behind. Granted, we should have moved quicker, but there you are. You owe us.'

There was a thrumming sound coming from the boulder-like creatures. 'I know nothing of such matters,' I growled. 'I was born twenty years ago.'

'Man-years?' Thrun asked. 'A baby giant? Lok's tits, how amusing!'a

'Do I look like a damned baby?' I yelled so hard his beard flew over his shoulder. 'There is war above, but the Danegells ruled the men since they left this place.'

He bowed in some form of apology and then froze in shock. 'Rule men? We stopped killing them?'

'Yes!'

He huffed. 'You smell like a man. Ruled the men?' He did not look happy.

'Yes, ruled them. Ruled them well!' I yelled. They all looked at each other.

'And so I take it the war above ended after your father shut the doors?'

I went to my knee before him. 'Yes. He took over the north. I don't know why, but he abandoned Hel's War. And now he is dead. Because Hel decided to try again, and there is Hel's own dead above, attempting to take over Midgard. And I hate them. I will fight them. Have already.'

Thrun growled and stared at me intently. 'We made a contract with the goddess Hel. We would fight for her. Always for her, until she releases us. That is the deal.'

'Is that so?' I growled back. 'Fight on, then. You shall not get out of the tomb until I say so. Keep quarrying.'

Thrun let his maul fall to his side with a thump. 'For your father and long years we have lived here, you owe us better. And—'

'You just said years do not matter to dverger, didn't you? Stop weeping,' I spat.

He scowled at that, and the army around him growled and hissed. It was an uncanny sound. Thrun nodded at my gauntlet. 'We might find it in ourselves to betray our general, to slay you, take that thing our best smiths crafted in times past, and hope to learn to use it to go up and help Hel's armies.' He was trembling with rage, eyeing me despondently, his people of like mind. There were hundreds of the dverger by then.

I snorted. 'Yea. You have a lot to be upset over. My father commanded you and left you here, for you are single-minded and unyielding, just like the dead, only less subtle.'

Thrun sputtered. 'Subtle! I'll have you know—'

'The dead rule, Thrun,' I told him slowly. 'They are subtle. They'll trick you, fool you, and make deals with the living, only to betray them in the end, and gods know what is genuine and false when one speaks. You and your contracts with Hel. Bah! You are dolts. The army above might have you. They would welcome you. Then, when all the living are gone, they will eat you. They only want to purge all the living from Midgard. Where is your home? Do you not wish to see it?'

'Svartalfheim, the lands below and under the root and stone, and a fine home it is. My clan left it; we were paid well,' he said with a scowl. 'And there is no way back. None. Unless the gates have been reopened.'

'They have not,' I told him. 'They are still closed. Closed, dead, and lifeless. And the dead will take the worlds until no living thing breathes. You are no friends of them.'

Thrun said nothing for a time, struggling with his honor, his promises, and his very nature.

I looked down to the lake. 'What is in there?'

'The bitch,' he said darkly.

'What do you mean?'

He pointed down to the lake. 'She was Odin's general. She rallied the humans to fight us. She brought them back from the brink of defeat. She gathered thousands under arms and sieged us here for years. Finally, they broke in, killed thousands and your grandfather …' he stammered. 'He died here. He fought her, challenged her to a duel, and she won. Your father swore an oath to her, and while the foolish cow thought she had won, he raced away and locked her in. Tricked her. Under lock she was, no matter her power.'

'With you,' I stated. 'She let you live?'

'Yes, with us,' he spat. 'Occasionally, she challenges us to fight her, and of course, we do, for it would be dickless to refuse. She gets bored, you see.'

'What is she?'

His wrinkled face took on a speculative look. 'Tell you what, boy. We will follow you to hammer at Hel's toes if you beat the wench.'

'We can just sneak out?' I asked him.

He laughed. 'She would know. She would. Looks docile, but she is awake. She would attack us, she would escape and once free, she could just rally the humans again up there and have us killed.'

'Can't you kill her?' I growled. 'Dverg weapons are supposed to be legendary.'

He looked very glum. 'We could. It would be too costly. And yes, our weapons are superb. And we have people who can See the Shades. But only the greatest of our smiths can create weapons to kill such a creature with ease. Your weapons,' he said and eyed the Red's sword, 'were made by Katal Killtar, ages ago, and we have nothing like it. Only your average man slaying things. It would take hundreds and hundreds to kill her without such weapons. A feast for the lizards. We wish to live.'

'So,' I said slowly. 'I should talk to her.'

'Either fight her or make a deal. You should. I think it's fair. A payment for your father's betrayal, I believe. And, if we leave this place, and fight for you, of course, you promise to carry our crime of oath-breaking when you meet Hel. It's a pact. Our souls will not be punished for abandoning her.'

'Deal,' I said, not really caring about Hel and her deals.

'And the gauntlet stays with us when you do fight her,' he added with a twinkle in his eye.

'I thought I was to either fight or make a deal,' I growled. 'I'll need it if it is the former.'

'Yes,' he said with a grin. 'But perhaps she is happy with swordplay alone. You might not need the Shades.' He laughed politely and looked away. He thought it would come to a fight. There would be no deal.

'No deal,' I breathed, the deal deteriorating. 'What is she?'

He laughed, and so did a thousand throats, filling the air with guttural noise as the throng kept growing. He leaned on me, and I knew I was dead by the look on his face. 'She is called Badwahenae, Baduhanna, or the War Maiden. She is Odin's ilk, one of the lesser gods, spawned as a First Born, a thing of the Aesir, mistress of Spear Dance. She is, Jotun, a demi-goddess. She is not immortal, nor all-powerful. She is a soldier of Asgard, not an actual god. She was a fair match for your grandfather. She is, however, very strong with the Shades. More, humans will fight for her. They see her as one of their makers.' *Balissa had said she would cause more wars amidst humans*, I thought. Thrun went on. 'And she will likely kill you. But we take this chance to escape, nonetheless. Eating mushrooms while the damned fish down there swim in circles and mock us? No more. Leave the gauntlet. Come, it's fair.'

*A demi-goddess,* I thought. *Gods help me.*

'Leave the gauntlet,' a brown-haired dverg grumbled and took a step forward. 'And swear you will take the blame for all of our crimes.'

I pushed him back. 'I take full responsibility, by Hel, for all of your oath breakings,' I said, laughed, and jumped off the ledge. I changed in the air, feeling very drained and fluttered down towards the lake as a raven of immense size. I skimmed the lake's pristine surface, felt the droplets of cooling water reach up to me and saw the vast bounty, schools of fat fish that were so torturing the dverger, scoot off for the depths, spooked by my approach. I crossed the boundary of the island and landed on the skull of a Jotun.

And waited.

The mist in the middle of the island dissipated while darkness surrounded the water's edge.

I was not alone.

There was a statue sitting on a pile of bones, all gray and very mystifying. It was a small woman with ethereal, delicate eyes and pouty lips. The head was tilted up, thick, long hair curled around her shoulders, back, and thighs. She wore a long tunic that reached to her knees, and her feet were shod with simple sandals. She was a rare, indescribable beauty. She might make me feel peaceful, but for the bones she sat on. She was beauty and death combined. Like Lith. Unlike Lith, she seemed the type to stand and fight bravely.

I changed to the size of a man. Red's dverg-made sword was clutched in my gauntleted hand, long and dangerous; deadly, but not as deadly as the delicate thing before me.

She was not like Lith.

She was alive.

The eyes opened, and a puff of dust fell on her cheek.

'Shit,' I told myself as the Aesir got up and stared at me curiously. The dust rolled off her skin and twirled around her left, glowing hand, and the grit formed into a shield of silver and black. She looked astonished as she saw me.

'Shit?' she breathed. 'This is all you can say, you stinking Jotun when you meet a First Born?'

'I—' I croaked, but she slapped her hand on her chest. The last of the dust fell off.

'You come with a bared sword. So did Garok Danegell, a fool Ymritoe, once. I think your kin? Ah! He was your grandfather, was he not?' Her eyes went to a pile of bones and armor on the side. 'He fought well. Briefly, but well. Where is your traitorous father? I smell him in you. That liar owes me.'

'Lady—' I began, but she shook her fair head, and her hair billowed around her as if it were alive. It was. Alive with magic. A weapon grew out of her hand, a red-hafted flail that radiated strange power.

'The dverger have been keeping me amused for long years.' She grinned. 'They yearn for the fish, and I won't let them touch them. They grow mushrooms and probably would kill for meat. They are so predictable. But a Jotun is much more entertaining, of course. Your father was talented. Despicable traitor, but clever. I did not think they could block a goddess from leaving this hole, but they did. That is the artifact, no? Truly old thing. I underestimated it,' she said and gazed at my gauntlet. 'There is something strange about you. Son of Magor? Yes. But strange, nonetheless.'

'I've barely met my kin,' I told her honestly, my sword trembling.

She nodded at my gauntlet. 'Ingvir crafted that eons ago. It is a powerful, sentient thing and meant to signify the kingship of the Jotuns. It will grow with you. If you will grow.' I gritted my teeth together at that. *If.*

'I came to fetch my army,' I told her brusquely. 'I need them. I need you to allow us to leave. And not to fight us,' I said, and her beautiful eyes grew large with surprise. She laughed with a voice that tingled and carried across the mountain.

'Your army? The dverger? The mercenary scum I once routed from this city? You know their history? You do, some of it, surely,' she said as she walked around me slowly. I turned to her, feeling foolish at being afraid of the tiny female. But she was a demi-goddess. Whatever that meant. 'You know my name, of course?'

'I heard it,' I said.

'What is going on up there in the world?' she asked, with poorly hidden curiosity in her voice.

I breathed deep and tried to steady my nerves. 'Midgard is beset with the Cult of the One Man. We ... some men believe there are no gods and the High King is the god.'

'What?' she tittered. 'A god?'

'The god. But he is undead,' I said. 'Hel's thing. Draugr king. Something happened twenty years ago. A spell washed over the land. And it changed something. It was like an evil seed, and now the seeds have grown discontent and evil spreads across the land. Father died fighting it.'

'Your father left me here,' she hissed. 'You ask me to weep?'

'No,' I spat, and she grinned. 'He thought you would be as bad for Midgard as Hel is. He did not want to serve you any more than Hel,' I said and nearly chuckled at the incredulous look on her face. 'We distrust the gods.'

'You know anything about the gods?' she whispered. 'About my kin?'

'I know little of Odin and the Aesir and Vanir, my lady,' I admitted. 'I was a thief.'

'A thief?' She chuckled. 'Calling me a lady is a mistake,' she hissed. 'Your lady, indeed. You know I once struck a bargain with Thor. I would lay with him if I did not slay as many Jotuns—your kin—as he in a span of hundred years? We are no gentle, peaceful things. We slay and hold grudges. We are not friends to Jotuns, who blame us for their losses in the early ages. We are no friends, Jotun. And I am no simpering lady.'

I bit my lip and decided things could not be much worse. 'So. How was he? Thor?'

She looked astonished at my temerity. She kept walking around me, but her weapon was now leaving a string of chain behind it; glowing, red-hot chain which she was looping around us and over the skulls that sizzled with heat and let out a noxious stench. She shook her head. 'He is a god, Jotun. A warrior. He knows how to get to the point.'

'Siff the Golden is not your friend, then?' I asked her, hoping I recalled Thor's wife's name correctly.

She chuckled. 'My, but you are brave. She is kind, patient, and a friend to wisdom, but who knows her heart? She might care for Thor, she might not. I suppose she does not like me. Are the ways still shattered?'

'The ways? The Nine Worlds are shattered from each other as far as I know. We are lost and stuck … gods, dverger, I am, I suppose. This is my home but …' I shrugged.

She was nodding. 'The Nine were sundered in Hel's War. The Nine Worlds are all lost. Some had champions, like me, some not and none knows, not even the Fates what takes place in them. But here? We won. There was but a pittance of her army left after Magor—'

'Fooled you, goddess. Trapped you here,' I told her as her face hinted at a rising storm of fury. 'The Jotuns trapped you here and have ruled above ever since.'

'Have ruled?' she choked. 'Above? Not killed men? They have likely made a mess of it.'

I grinned. 'The Beast of the North, the King of the Rose Throne, was Magor Danegell. He and his remaining Jotuns have governed the Red Midgard. It is a nation, my lady, of the north. He has ruled well.'

'Ruled well?' she hissed. 'They came here to ransack the land. To take it from the gods. There were tens of thousands of them. And you say they blended in?'

'They cast spells, they Stir the Cauldron, lady and none else can. We are shapeshifters, and I suppose Father fell in love with the land.'

'Lies,' she hissed while the coils of spellbound chain tightened around us. 'He was a liar. An oath breaker. You are here to fetch the dverger to—'

'To fight the enemy of all the living people,' I said. 'I told you. As I said, something happened twenty years ago. A spell? A storm was—' I shuddered as a vision of a beautiful, red-headed girl was fighting a strange, powerful female with snakes for hair, releasing a complicated spell in her desperation. 'A spell. It affected all the Nine, despite the sundering. Death is still the one thing that holds across the Nine, lady, and Hel has a power that spans death. The spell raised dead here, in Midgard. Draugr. And they have been plotting and killing and slaying as they go, and the High King is their lord. We have nearly lost Dagnar.'

'Magor …' she prompted me.

'Dead,' I said. 'My mother died twenty years ago when they stole the gauntlet to—'

'Keep me here,' she said happily.

*Yes, she was right,* I thought. They would have wanted to make sure the Jotuns were the only enemy they had to topple. 'How did they know of me?' she asked.

'Unlucky chance,' I told her. 'The dead family whom Hel's spell chose had been keeping the history of the land, and so they knew all about the Jotuns and you.'

'How unfortunate,' she smiled. 'And this High King is another abomination?'

'Yes, lady, that he is. And now I need that army,' I told her stubbornly, nodding at the ranks of dverger. I was aware her mood was swinging from murderous to intrigued and then murderous again.

'I will leave this place,' she spat. 'Perhaps I shall fight the bastard armies of Hel. I shall seat myself as the Queen of Midgard instead? Perhaps. But they shall stay.' She nodded at the dark mass of dverger on the outcropping.

'No,' I told her. 'And Red Midgard has a king. Not a queen. You were a general, not—'

She stopped in front of me, the red-hot coils now burning the skulls around us. They flared up to dreadful flames of dark red and black. She stood there, slender and beautiful, full of god-like anger. 'I am an Aesir. That makes me the queen of men. You came here to ask me for my throne and an army. And what will you give in return?'

'My fealty to Odin?' I asked her and saw she was skeptical. I frowned. 'I can bring you supper?'

'Odin might accept, but I do not trust you. Your family is sworn to Hel,' she hissed. 'What of that?'

'I was raised a human,' I told her stubbornly. 'And I just told the lot there I'd take the blame if they abandon her. It was good enough for them, maybe.'

'If Hel finds you on her doorstep,' she laughed, 'she will declare a feast. Traitor. Your father betrayed her, me, and now you would do the same to Hel.'

'I can swear fealty to Odin,' I told her mulishly. 'He can surely see my worth? Hel be damned.'

'Curse Odin,' she hissed. 'And damn Hel. You swear to me.'

'You seem to have plans for your own world?' I asked her.

'I deserve the world,' she said as she cut off a spontaneous giggle, the flames dancing around her now. 'The gods are not here. I am. I fought for this world. You come here to make demands on a goddess, on an Aesir. You know who I am?'

'A demi-goddess,' I said arrogantly. 'I suppose you can die?'

'What?' she asked me, her lips thin with rage. 'What did you say? Die? Yes, I can die. That might kill me.' She tapped my dverg-made sword. 'Thousands of the dverger might do it. But I don't die quickly. Say my name.'

'Baduhanna, Badwahenae or just the Bitch, as they call you,' I said. 'A goddess who tortures the living with plenty while they eat mushrooms and mold for thousands of years? I know which I would use if I ate shit for your maliciousness. I swear you nothing. Give them to me. My army.'

'I'll let you join your relative, Maskan,' she said breathlessly. 'I'll leave you here to have a long rest with him. Then I'll go up and put things right.'

'You were trapped by a Jotun.' I laughed at her, terrified to my core at her now burning eyes. 'The dead will find a way to kill you. Or trap you again. Possibly in a place worse than this.'

'The junk,' she said and nodded at my gauntlet. 'Give me the piece of scrap. It will obey me. And show me the spell to get out of here.'

'No,' I told her and lifted my sword.

## THE BEAST OF THE NORTH

She giggled madly, filled with power, and yanked at her weapon. The glowing coils shot up from the burning pile of skulls, lightning fast. I jumped up in the air and felt the heat scalding my armored calves as I landed before her. I swiped the sword down at her, but the shield was there, and a thunderous boom echoed in the cavern. I thought I heard the dverger murmur, and I realized they were making bets, most all against me, no doubt. The burning chain was twirling around me, about to split me in half, but I changed to what Father had changed to and came down on her shield as a huge ice bear. Sparks flew from the thing as we fell over her throne of bones and tumbled away to the darkness beyond. As we rolled, I lost sight of all the bones, the lake, and the dverger city. I heard nothing but her laughter in my ears as I raked my claws at her, but the shield was impossibly fast, and sparks ignited my fur. Worse, the fire chain was curling around my rear legs now. She slammed the shield at my snout, and I fell back. I scrambled on the skulls, felt the chain retreat, and as I looked up at her, I saw her shining figure slamming the flail at me. It struck me on the side, and I roared with molten, insidious pain as I was scorched to the bone. I fell on my side as she giggled happily, danced to the side and aimed a swing for my neck. I shot forward, turned into a Jotun, and howled as her hit took a piece of my armored back with it, though I was spared decapitation. I felt blood pouring down my back, and the terrible woman was licking her lips in anticipation, fascinated by the battle, her short tunic fluttering with the power and speed of her movements. She pushed me away, and I skidded on skulls and bones. I swiped the blade at her, the long and deadly sword thrumming with power, dangerous perhaps even to a goddess, and she blocked it again with her shield. I charged forward again, threw all my weight at her, and it was a lot of weight.

'Mad as your grandfather.' She giggled. 'Mad as any Jotun when death calls. No dignity, just animal rage,' she added, goading me as I pushed against the Aesir, raining hits on her shield. Bones were flying as I heaved against her. I pushed, bleeding, grunted and raged, and she silently countered my strength, a smile flickering on the edges of her mouth. I'd used all my strength, and instead of striking her shield, I docked to my fours, changed to a small sauk, and slithered forward and under her shield to tear at her face. She dodged, shrieked and slapped the weapon on my snout, tore a chunk of teeth and bone and skin off, but I managed a hold on her shoulder, and so we finally fell over together, rolling on the ground, bones splintering beneath us. My claws raked at her as she howled in pain. I kept a hold of the Aesir, enduring the beating her weapon inflicted on my back and legs, cursing the terrible pain in my head. But I did not let go, ground my teeth together, and raked at her with my claws as we rolled. We stopped at the edge of the lake. I heard the dverger shouting now, excited. There was a scalding fury burning in the Aesir's eyes, and she was actually bleeding from my attack, though the wounds seemed shallow and supercilious at best. She slammed her fist in my snout so hard I nearly died, and I let go of her neck. She whispered to her flail and turned it into a fiery spear that was going to puncture my skull. I nearly passed out from fatigue as I changed again into a man-sized jotun, and she missed my head, the blade sinking deep into the stone. *I was a thief, a thief*, I told myself in terror, trying to accept the fact I should just give up. She cursed and yanked at her weapon. I stumbled forward, holding on to Red's sword and struck down with all my remaining strength at her exposed side. I gave it my all. She yelled in surprise; the shield came to intercept my weapon, and I felt a jarring crash as Baduhanna's shield met the sword.

They thrummed with the power of the impact, and I grinned, for my blade had sunk into the side of the shield, tearing it, and the end of the sword was in her side, sunk deep. She looked at the blade incredulously and then she was struggling with her own, stuck blade, and I grunted as I leaned forward, pushing the sword with my remaining power. We struggled thus; she was sweating, a demi-goddess. 'Perhaps,' I lisped, for my face was badly hurt, 'you are out of practice?' I asked and laughed, spat blood and bits of teeth and knew I was severely wounded. I felt my armor was broken in places, and I bled profusely. But I refused to give up.

She cursed softly, my blade cut deeper as she stopped pushing back, but her blade came off the rock. My sword dug deeper into her, but she endured the pain with a grimace, held the spear towards my face, and whispered.

White flames shot out from it, and I was burned in my arms and under my helmet's rim. My face was terribly blistered.

I flew to the side, ripped off the helmet, rolled to the water to douse the flames, and spied her running to the side, her hands glowing with energies of the First Born as she tried to heal herself. I could not see anything with my left eye and sobbed for I was beyond repair. She was gagging, in terrible pain, her clothes burned off. Despite her wound and pain, she looked magnificent, like a queen of war, a battle maiden of no regrets, a goddess of bravery and ancient grudges.

*I had nearly slain her. That was something.*

I tried to get up, to stop her, but I was too weak and could only crawl for her, dragging my sword with me. She turned to look at me, her high breasts heaving with incredulity as she regarded her shield, her side still bleeding from a deep cut that looked like it was scarring over. She walked around me, and I tried to follow her movements. I managed to fall on my back, my face a mass of pain, my back a mound of blood. She stepped on the sword, and I could not move it.

'You fought very well, Maskan,' she said surprisingly gently. 'I underestimated you, of course, but very well indeed. Jotun's blade is excellent and occasionally, even a god can die of it. You nearly became a legend.'

And then I saw Taram.

I looked at a shadow shooting from the side, a spell tingling in the air and saw a blade, thrusting for the back of the goddess. It was one of the blades of the Jotuns who had fallen in the island so long ago. He had killed a king. Now the undead thing was after a goddess. He hawked a small laugh as Baduhanna looked up, surprised, the blade coming for her unprotected back.

I grabbed her and pulled her to me. The blade followed her, Taram's one hand brought it down with deadly intent. I pushed her off with savage strength.

The blade split my chest, and I fell back, mortally wounded.

I dimly saw Baduhanna's weapon flash. I saw a shadow escaping; then flames dance with dark and orange flames around it, and Taram screamed. He fell to the side, not far, a miserable thing. I spat blood as I saw the nude goddess step on his face, smashing it to a pulp.

Then I remember feeling her very close, and I remember I kissed her lips. 'Ann was right,' I said weakly. 'Just kiss the girl.'

Darkness. Warmth. I am not sure how much time had passed, and then I felt a caress of a warm hand on my face. I opened my eyes and felt invigorated, and I could see with both my eyes.

Her face was grave. 'You are right. Undead walk the land. That one? He was out to slay me. Incredible. It was a draugr. A bright, nasty creature.'

'He killed my father,' I said, feeling strangely invigorated. 'They all have goals. And they cannot let go of them. They awaken to death, and they have to obey their lords, but they are always rebelling against their wishes. They want something for themselves. He wanted to kill a king. Then, a goddess. He almost killed his second king, though.' I groped weakly at the excellent plate armor and found it was shattered in the chest. 'How—'

She put a finger over my mouth, silencing me. 'I find you very strange, Maskan Danegell,' the goddess said huskily. She sat over me, clad in a tunic again, a creation of magic.

'They plan for many things,' I said. 'Mir, the queen of the draugr, has led the armies north to war against our allies. And the High King is waiting for them. And the city above? It has likely fallen to the Hammer Legions.'

'Hammer Legion. A ridiculous name. Unimaginative,' she murmured.

'So I need that army to save my last sister and people who have called the Danegells kings for thousands of years.'

'And now they failed,' she said, eyeing my father's long sword appraisingly. 'Dverg-made, like most great weapons. Your two-hander nearly killed a goddess. You have good swords, Jotun.' She kicked the blade Taram had used, frowning. Even a demi-goddess can be shocked by a near death. She shook her head and rubbed her face. She was drained. 'I wonder why they make the blades so long, being short.'

'Being short, you need a longer reach,' I told her. She laughed brilliantly.

'True,' she agreed and left the sword on my side. 'You feel alive?'

'Barely,' I told her thinly, touching my face.

'A few scars. That's all you get, my vain little Jotun. Nearly as cute as it was, Jotun,' she said with a groan. 'Shape changers have this problem. They usually take an animal form, and such a form so often gets stabbed and slashed in the face. But you are fine now. If nothing else, I can renew skin. Replacing flesh is harder. And I spent a lot of my powers in saving you and healing myself. None else can heal, boy. Only an Aesir. That is our skill. But it is exhausting. So you owe me.'

'Didn't you want the fight?' I sulked. 'I only denied you an oath.'

'I cannot recall.' She giggled. 'Perhaps so. But you owe me. Restoring spells are far from easy. You are rarely blessed like you just were.'

'I do owe you, lady. But not a kingdom,' I groaned.

She nodded, sulking. 'So. You are saying Red Midgard has a king.'

'I said that once, and I am the damned lord of the land,' I told her.

She pursed her lips thoughtfully, clearly amused. She poked my chest so hard I was sure there was a dent in the metal. 'And the High King? Another enemy?' she asked, and I nodded, suspicious. She leaned closer and batted her long eyelashes at me. 'Would you allow me to carry that crown?'

'That would mean I serve you,' I told her glumly.

'You will,' she said thinly. 'I won, didn't I?'

'I think it was a tie,' I told her stubbornly.

She shook her head dejectedly. 'You might have lived like a man, but there is something very Jotun about you. Noble and idiotic at the same time. You kissed me?'

'You kissed me, no?' I asked.

'No, you grabbed my hair as I healed you and kissed me,' she insisted. 'Are you saying it did not happen?'

'I remember it did,' I told her and shrugged as she tilted her head at me. 'Not sure why. Perhaps it is because you are a goddess and I was dying, and I am sorry,' I sighed. 'I don't care who sits on the throne of the High King in Malingborg, but Red Midgard is free now. I just told the enemy army that as well. Take any land, and leave us to ours.'

She giggled. 'I think you are very brave. Here is the deal, you sorry fool. I will give you this Red Midgard you keep talking about. And the dverger as a guard,' she told me frankly. 'And you will kneel before me, under their eyes. You will uphold your father's broken oath to me.'

I sighed, eyed the ceiling, and saw the host of the dverger looking down at me. I thought of Red Midgard, of the suffering of men, the dead Jotuns, and the dverger lingering there, dying out slowly. I decided there was nothing to decide. I climbed to my feet, shuddered to my twelve feet, and sheathed the Red Brother's two-hander. Then I grabbed my father's sword. She eyed me bravely, seemingly unarmed, and got up as well, barely reaching my waist. I laid the sword before her, kneeled, and bowed before her. 'I, Maskan Danegell, of the Clan Danegells, people of the Ymritoe,' I bellowed so hard the cavern shook, 'pledge I keep my father's oath to Aesir Baduhanna of Asgard and break our family's pact with Hel. I shall be called the Beast of the North, the Cursed, the Traitor, but this I shall endure until Hel claims me.'

Baduhanna smiled at me and touched my face. 'And I shall give you your crown. You will serve me and together, love, we shall make war and build law across this land of ours.'

'Why would I serve you?' I asked her. 'I just said we should fight together but rule separately.'

She laughed. 'You swore an oath to keep your father's, boy. He swore to marry me and serve me, his queen. Jotuns and gods, Maskan, often marry. And now you agreed to this. Husband. We will settle the matter of the rulership later. You shall have the crown, but I am not sure you will rule alone. It depends on my mood and how honest you turn out to be.'

I gawked. She ignored me and turned to look up at the dverger. 'Will you honor the lord of your people? His word is your law, and long have you served without praise, with no hope, no reward. Shall you go out to the light and be free of this misery? Or shall you stay here and rot? He broke your vows, and no punishment will come to you for that.'

There was silence for a long time. They stood there, some two thousand strong. They were all armed and armored now, to the teeth, and I saw many had packed, in the hope of a fool Jotun finding their freedom. I had, but not the way they had hoped. Thrun stepped up, reluctantly. 'If he faces the wrath of the goddess for us, we shall obey him. And you, Aesir. But we will one day wish to go back home. If the ways open, we shall leave. This pact binds us until such time.'

'So be it. He shall endure Hel's rage,' she grinned. She spoke to me gently. 'But not alone. Take your grandfather's armor. I'll find something from some of your other relatives.'

'I am happy I made an ally,' I told her as I approached the Jotun's bones and the magnificent suit of dark armor that was inlaid with gold. 'But you tricked me. And a marriage—'

'Is a fine thing, boy,' she said. 'As long as you obey your woman. I'll show you how. And I am happy we are allied as well. Not all couples are.' She grinned as she tapped her foot, looking for a suit of armor that might fit her.

I stared at her. Married to a demi-goddess. Sand will laugh.

Or not. Much depended on Sand. And ... Illastria.

## CHAPTER 22

The Tower had not fallen. Not totally.

There was a guard of Hammer Legionnaires on the steps, all eyeing the open doorway. There were many more inside the tower that was fast turning into a charnel house. The legionnaires stood in a rank of five hundred and occasionally, I could hear Balissa yell a challenge on the top of the tower. That was followed by screams and then booms and the gauntlet gave me a vision of her. I called out to her, and she stiffened briefly, then I spoke to her, and she was relieved. I let go of her mind, and I knew she was holding off the enemy at the very top of the stairs with whatever remained of the Mad Watch, but now more ferociously.

We stepped out into the open, wearing the dark armor. She had taken some from the dead Jotuns, which fit her magnificently. I held my father's sword, Bjornag's two-hander strapped to my back. Baduhanna had her dangerous spear and the strange shield. We stepped closer and one man in the legion pulled at another, and they turned to stare at us. An officer in a golden helmet stepped closer, uncertain of our allegiance. He pulled at an under-officer, a sergeant with a transverse crest of white hair on his golden helmet. The man shook his head and spoke with a burly standard bearer.

'By Frigg's hem,' Baduhanna breathed and shouted, 'Yes! We are with the enemy. The King!'

The officer took another step forward. 'High King?'

'High Queen,' she corrected him. 'With the High Queen!'

The officer looked stunned. 'You are calling the High King a woman?'

'I am a woman, you egg-headed traitor,' she hissed. 'And you should bow down before me.'

From behind, we heard the slap of feet, and guttural voices were chanting eerily. A priest of the dverger stepped into the light, wearing a chain mail as long as he was. In fact, it was partially dragging behind him. He cast spells, pulling weaves from the blazing fires of Muspelheim, called out darkness to cover the tower, the walls, and he shuddered with glee as he looked up at me.

'See them,' I told them. 'The men who would take the land? They will eat all the food in this city and leave you with mushrooms. Kill them before they do. Form up.'

And they did.

Thrun came out. He was armored head to toe, his beard plaited and adorned with silvery skulls. An endless stream of short warriors followed him, and their chanting took on a ferocious edge. They formed a neat, compact column. Tall spears were hefted, thick shields banged together. Lighter armored priests and mages spread to left and right, hiding under cowls and every single one held wands and talismans. Baduhanna saw me staring at the artifacts and chuckled. 'They are useless,' she said. 'Likely good for scratching their asses. But it's some silly ritual of theirs to hold twigs as symbols of power. Svartalfheim is a strange world.'

Useless or not, there were soon a hundred dverger in the ranks. The Hammer Legion recovered quickly from their shock of seeing the strange, non-human enemy forming on their side. Being professional soldiers of high repute and veterans of a hundred campaigns in the south, they were brave and did not falter. They banged their shields together and formed into a column that grew in size as men inside understood there was an enemy outside as well as inside the Tower. Others ran from the gate, an officer was yelling at a man to ride to the city, and I knew they were fetching more men.

The officer shouted a howl-like command at his men. They shuffled forward into the dverg-made darkness, matching the dverg chant with their own. 'Kill them,' I said as more and more of the dverg poured out.

The enemy charged instead. Their officer shouted, and they ran at us, hundreds of them.

The dverg casters released their spells, holding their bizarre talismans high. I felt fire being called, and so the legion screamed, for there was a wall of flames that split the legion in half and another spell, an enormous hand of fire that slapped down in the middle of the ranks, scattering burning men left and right. And that is when the dverger charged. They were but two hundred now, more joining them all the time from the hole, but they were deadly. The enemy was confused, split and terrified, and the long-suffering dverger army looked like a fist of darkened steel, their spears thrusting forward with strange unity, a near mechanical deadliness. The legionnaires thrust and slashed back, men and dverger died, but the short men grunted, pushed, stabbed, killed, and crushed those who got past the spears. They were faster, shrugged off wounds that would put down a bear and defended each other like they were connected. Perhaps they were. Legionaries were strong men, used to fighting in a shieldwall, charging in a column, but never had they met a wall like they did that day. It was like fighting a hill of rock. Shields hit together, hammers raining down on the dverger, but the short men were powerful, strong beyond any human, and with a terrible grinding sound, they stomped forward, crushing the first ranks of the legion together, unable to fight. Then they killed them. At the same time, the mages cast fiery walls on either side of the legion, a whirling field of fire that hemmed the enemy together, and the butchery was terrible for the poor bastards. I gagged at the smell of dead men burning, blanched at the horrid sound of roasting fighters. I saw the officer gesturing with a sword at the mages, and javelins were readied by the troops in the rear of the enemy column. 'Look out!' I yelled as dozens went up, whirring in the air. Most were aimed at the first of the dverger casters and two hit, felling the casters, and giving the rest a reason to stop casting and to retreat away. Some javelins whirled in the air, aimed at us. I conjured the spell of warding, and a stone shield guarded me, and I stepped before the goddess, who snorted at my protection as a javelin snapped on my chest. 'I have my own, boy. Husband.'

'I know, but am I not supposed to guard my wife?' I said with a grin, for I was happy, superbly happy, ferocious and alive and I screamed for the dverger to attack. 'Kill the southern bastards! And then into the tower!' Thrun grinned back at me, as they heaved against a wall of legionnaires. A dverg fell on his side; his head caved in.

Thrun yelled back at me. 'They die, King Maskan! And they will tell Hel of your betrayal!'

I laughed at that, not sure, I should, but I was not thinking about dying.

Then, a horn rang in the city. There were many, but this one was unfamiliar and came from the direction of the harbor.

'What is that, then?' the goddess asked, and I had a premonition of doom. I skirted the enemy formation, and some legionnaires countered me, firing bows. My stone skin deflected them, shattered them with impunity, and I walked for the main gateway as the men fled before me. Baduhanna followed me casually as the legionnaires fell back, leaving heaps of dead behind. More and more of the dverger emerged from the dark, and mages and priests sneaked back, forward, and threw more darkness around, so much it seemed there was no Lifegiver in the sky. A group of Legionnaires rode to the gate, their flags up. They were not Bulls, but Griffins with a hammer, and Lions with spiked tails.

'Different unit,' Baduhanna said. 'Units,' she added.

'Another legion?' I whispered. They rode forth to see better, and the gauntlet instructed me. It showed me a uniquely useful spell to deal with such as they, and so I gathered powers. I let go an intricate web of ice, which shot across the gate and clutched the beasts' hooves, and then grew to encase the horses, then the men's legs and in the end, they were left beautiful statues.

'Nice touch,' Baduhanna said encouragingly. 'The gauntlet? No novice could use such spells. But you must be careful. Don't overextend yourself. You will burn up if you don't take care.'

'You can give me lessons later,' I said as I toppled one of the icy statues to its side. I looked up to the gate, and I shifted. I took on a hawk's form and flew up into the air, relishing the giddy freedom for just a moment. Then I forgot the wonderful feeling. I circled the gate, then the tower, and looked out over to the city.

It was a battlefield.

The whole city was fighting, in fact. There were dozens of pitched battles in all the Rings against the Legion, and many raging fires. The original Bull Legion held the gates, and they streamed off from these rallying points to disperse any sign of people causing trouble. There were bodies everywhere. People fought them, for no northerner gives up his home without a fight and Dagnar, despite being surprised housed tens of thousands of hardy people.

But there was a real battle ongoing in the harbor.

Red Midgard's navy, partially manned by Hawk's Talon Marines was fighting. And they had an overwhelming enemy. A vast fleet was trying to enter the harbor, and some had, in fact. The riders I had killed had likely been looking for the commander of the Bull Legion. Elements of the two new legions were moored in the harbor, but some six Hawk's Talon galleys had bravely shut off the harbor behind them. There was a hellish and desperate battle below the Fat Father, the massive tower that guarded the harbor. Enemy galleys were trying to force their way in, and there was a vicious melee rolling in the decks of three of four ships blocking the entrance. There, in the sea, wide transports and boldly painted galleys were trying to make their way in. They had likely thought the battle was already won, and indeed, it should have been.

And there, in the high, flat tower called the Fat Father, the one overlooking the entrance to the harbor, Lith was standing. I saw her with my hawk's eyes, and there were Valkai, Sand, and dozens of Blacktower men. And Illastria, the poor mad woman, she was there as well. Lith was swaying. She was casting spells, raining fire down on the embattled ships. One broke in two, and sunk, taking a hundred men with it.

Countless masses of men were on board the transports.

There were ten thousand of them. Some thousand had managed to land earlier, before the navy had begun to fight back. *Two legions.* With my keen eyes, I spotted the army commanders standing in wealthy gear on the decks of their battle galleys, lining up to enter the harbor. The commanders were coaxing their captains to take the fight to the few remaining defenders. I tried to fathom what I was seeing, the terrible implication of the extent of tragedy falling on the city.

My kingdom was dying.

I saw the army commanders all over the city were conversing with scouts and pointing up to the tower and the darkness enveloping it. I fluttered down to the gate, and Baduhanna greeted me as I changed. 'How bad is it? It's always bad, mind you, but how bad?'

'There are many enemy soldiers in the city. A few thousand. The people are fighting them. There might be enough spirit in the people to drive them out, but not if the others land. There are ten thousand out in the harbor, and the Hawk's Talon Mariners are fighting them. And the One Eyed Priest, Lith, is there.'

'Lith?' she asked. 'A woman?'

'A corpse, elder draugr,' I said.

'One of those who fooled you?' she asked. Behind us, the Hammer Legionnaires finally broke. The dverger roared and split in several direction to chase off the running soldiers. Hundreds charged up to the tower, and there, calls of the dying surged to the air. A dverg pulled at me. 'King. There is enemy marching up for the gate!'

'Man the gate!' I called out, and the dverger turned to look at me. I pointed my finger down to the city where I imagined standards of the enemy coming for the tower to investigate the darkness and a possible new enemy. 'I have to get to Lith,' I told Baduhanna.

'Love, you cannot beat them alone,' she said.

'Can you fight?' I asked her.

'I'm feeble, Maskan. Healing drained me. I can defend the walls,' she said with a grin. 'But you are right. We must stop them from taking the harbor. You can probably lift a few people there, but—'

'No, I can do more,' I hissed. I showed her Balan's thicker, golden-edged amulet.

'Looks terrible. I'd rather not have it,' she said with a sniffle. 'You can find me a better one later. But I sense it's been sprinkled with Glory.'

'Get me the Jotun and a hundred dverger,' I told her. 'Your Highness,' I added as she scowled at me.

## CHAPTER 23

The dverger were blocking the gateway to the Tower and legionnaires were inching closer, launching weapons at the dark dverger mass. More were arriving, but it would take them time to muster the courage to charge us.

Balissa was exhausted. Her hair was plastered to her forehead, and she was eyeing Baduhanna with hostility. 'It is customary, King, to ask for advice before getting married to an Aesir. It is not unheard of, but still. Freyr married a Jotun, but—'

'I'm not sure how I married her. She just says it is so,' I breathed as a troop of scowling dverger assembled before me. 'My father's oath, and I took it on me. She tricked me.'

'You kissed her, you ice-brained idiot,' she said and eyed the beautiful Aesir enviously. 'Must not be a terribly harsh duty, eh? What are we doing?'

'I think it might be, actually. But hear me. There are ten thousand enemies coming to the city,' I said, and the dverger looked at each other.

Thrun spat a tooth on the cobblestones and rubbed a bruise he had received in the battle. His eyes were glowing with ferocity under the helmet. 'Ten thousand? We can take them. We have the gear. Unless they land. Then we die.'

'I'll see to this mess,' Baduhanna called out as she walked up to the wall. 'And join you later. Fight well.'

'If things go wrong,' I called out to her, 'hide in the hole.'

'Never!' she laughed. 'I'll go to Valholl if I die, husband. It will take hundreds of them to kill me without dverger weapons and magic, but I will never go back down there.'

'Not unlike the undead,' Balissa growled. 'Stubborn and driven.'

'She saved me,' I said.

'And nearly killed you,' she returned.

I decided it made no sense to argue. 'We will go down to the harbor and kill Lith.'

'You and I?' Balissa asked, shocked. 'Ten thousand enemies?'

'We kill Lith,' I growled. 'And they will come as well.' I nodded at the hundred dverger, who grinned up at the Jotun.

'I don't get it,' she said. 'There are limits to the size of the creature we can change into. Unless you suggest we eat the little bastards and then vomit them all over the enemy.'

'I've not had Jotun for thousands of years,' Thrun said darkly, fondling his spear. 'I fancy Jotun brain in Astan wine. Though there is probably no Astan wine to be had anymore. But—'

'I have this,' I said and struck the Blacktower medallion. Balan's medallion. I closed my eyes. 'Ready?'

'What is it?' Balissa asked.

'This thing killed my father,' I said. 'We go first. Follow as soon as you can. It can only take a dozen a time. A bit more.'

'He has gone crazy. I knew it. I—' Thrun began, but then I tapped the thing three times.

They stared at me. Then at the shimmering air that solidified into a golden doorway. I pulled my father's sword, called for the shield, which covered me, head to toe. I blew a kiss at Baduhanna and stepped in.

I came to stand in horrible chaos. Valkai had been hammering at the dark mirror as I barreled into him. Sand was on the ground, a gash on his undead face. His pocket was hanging loosely as Larkgrin, which I had stolen from Balan and hidden in Sand's pocket when I bumped into him in the battle, had been activated. Lith was over him. Dozens of the enemy were staring at me feverishly. We were on the top of the Fat Father Tower, and beyond Lith, a pair of thick masts were passing into the harbor. It was a huge war galley, and Griffon was emblazoned in the flapping standard. A quick glance told me two Hawk's Talon galleys were bearing down on the ship.

Lith looked up at me. Her mask was gleaming as she stood above Sand. 'Very deft, Maskan. You learn quickly. Kill him, Sand.'

Sand got up and drew his sword. He hesitated, his greedy eyes flickering. 'I—'

Lith stared at him, disbelieving. 'You obey me!'

I snickered while I struck an undead from the tower. 'He has doubts, you see. He always wanted his own house. I promised him what you did, and one more house.' Sand slumped, holding his head, half swayed by his need to obey and by my promise.

'Ah, how kind our rebel. But he cannot disobey,' she hissed. 'Kill him!' Lith shrieked. Sand hardened his face and came at me, until Illastria grasped him and spoke to him softly. Sand stopped and did not move, looking at me, Illastria, and Lith, each in our turn. 'Kill him!' Lith screamed.

'Do not,' Illastria said. Sand stood still, shivering.

Lith turned to me, hesitating, confused. 'What is happening? How can she command Sand?'

I didn't answer. I didn't give her time to think. I charged her.

She ran away from me, her robes flapping in the sea breeze. The enemy charged me in mass, and I fell on my face as they swarmed me. I swiped the sword across some legs, lopping them off. They stabbed at my armor, some went through, and I cursed them. Lith was hesitating on the brink of the tower, and then her eyes widened. Balissa came through the portal. She roared, and her spear split the foes in my back. I crawled up and slashed through two of the draugr that were distracted by the Jotun. I turned to Lith.

She fell away from us.

The reason was Thrun. He and his men charged out and began dispatching the foe with gleeful grunts. Illastria stood before Sand protectively, and they left them alone. One dverg fell in a heap of heavy armor as two Blacktower dead hacked at him from the side, but they did not last long. The tower was slick with blood. I ran to the edge of the tower and looked down. There, a deck full of rovers and a hundred elite legionnaires were working to destroy the Hawk's Talon galleys. Some men were pulling Lith to her feet. She was screaming warnings and pointed a finger up.

And they all looked at me.

I prepared a spell.

It was the icy prison spell, hugely drawing on my strength, and I released it, swaying on the wall. Lith released a spell at me at the same time, and it was a suffocating, nauseating spell of filthy odors of the fire side of magic. I gagged and staggered, but noticed my ice spell hit ten or more rowers and a ballista crew, who turned into lumps of ice. The galley turned and wobbled, the legionnaires fell into the water and some to the rover's pits. Lith's spell was lost as she fell on her rear. The galley hit a burning vessel and tore a hole in its side. A dangerous looking general of a legion pointed his sword at the rovers; a flutist ran to blast notes in her instrument, and men were screaming below to extract the ship. A Hawk's Talon ship was dashing in, arrows raining down on its deck, felling men, but their ballista tore a bloody path through a group of legionnaires.

'You alive?' Balissa asked me as she slashed a dead man down with the spear.

'I am,' I spat, feeling tingling in my mouth. I would have died of that spell, had Lith finished it.

'She knows spells no others can touch. She is dead, and their Dark Mistress is stranger than our Cauldron. Look out!' I looked down, but Lith was not casting spells. Instead, I fell forward, as Valkai pushed me over. We plummeted down; he was clutching me with mad intensity, laughing like the maniac he was, and I knew we would hit the deck of the ship. I spun in the air, then again, and then we hit the deck.

And went through it. And the next level as well.

I was hurt, but not so badly as Valkai was. He had fallen on two bench rowers, and I had fallen on him. He was dazed, his dead face unmasked. The rotting and yellowed skin showed his true nature to everyone, and all the stunned rowers around us backed off. I spat at Valkai. 'You liked to jump on your victims, no?' I stepped on his so hard his chest caved in, and he went silent, water leaking from the planks beneath him. A burly man with a claymore appeared, looking confused at the huge knight getting up before him. Father's sword was still fast in my hand, and I made my allegiance clear as I hacked it through the man. The rowers swarmed me, their rowing master speared at me, but I grew to my full height, and they fell off. I felt bones crunching under my feet as I climbed up the sundered deck. I heard a strange sound, water gurgling, men shouting warnings, and then a ram's head punctured the ship's hull. I flew forward by the terrible hit, water drenched me, and I realized the Hawk's Talon were trying to withdraw the ship to ram again, but could not.

Upside, there was a sudden sound of battle. I looked up and in Lifegiver's light saw the dverger pour up to the tower. More and more came, and they were assembling something that folded out, repeatedly. Perhaps Baduhanna had routed the enemy in the Tower of the Temple in Dagnar. Some dverger, the mad ones jumped down to the ship. Some fell to the sea; others made it. A weird whistling sound could be heard, and I saw projectiles tear up from the tower for the ships at the sea. 'The bastards have siege machinery,' I whispered and laughed gratefully at the clever dverger. Arrows by the dozen rattled up the tower, and many of my dverger paid with their life, but they kept attacking.

Then, I saw Balissa flutter down to the ship in a bird's form.

I tore myself up to the deck.

A wild melee was raging there. A hundred Hammer Legionnaires struck at the desperate attacking Hawk's Guard; a dozen dverger were slamming their shields at the enemy on and under the afterdeck and there, above me, Balissa was leading some dverger up, stalking Lith and the gorgeously armored general. Arrows rained on her, with little effect. Dverger died, but so did the enemy as they found their footing and charged the afterdeck officers. I changed and ran on as a wolf. I loped past enemies, dodging their hits, mostly. I yelped in pain at a dagger that sliced thinly across my flank, wielded by a panicked rower. I reached the stairs and rushed up. There, Balissa was stabbing her spear at the captain of the ship and the guards. Many dverger pushed after her, mattock, sword, and ax heaving, and the deck was awash with blood. There was the other huge warship looming just behind ours, trying to edge past us, but the dverger on top of the tower hollered happily, and explosive bombs rained down on it. That ship's captain screamed orders, the general of the legion agreed, and they pulled off reluctantly.

Lith joined the fight. She was moving fast, trying to get past the legion's general, but could not. Balissa stabbed and hacked at the enemy guarding that man until many fled, others jumped to the sea, and some tried to get past to the deck, but the dverger slashed them open.

Balissa speared ahead, taking hits from the general's last two burly guards. The mighty spear twinkled forward; it impaled one guard, then the second. The general screamed—an enormous man with a bristling beard—and he pushed forward, holding a mace, his red and gold armor gleaming redly as he rammed his shield at Balissa. She grabbed the shield, crumpled it in her fist and two dverger stabbed the general from both sides. He cursed softly and fell forward, dead.

Lith gathered powers just as I got up to the deck and changed my form into a Jotun. The powers were of ice and wind, rain, and she weaved them together so fast. The air crackled crazily, her hands let go a stream of sizzling lightning. There was a huge bang and we were all suddenly disoriented. The light ran through the men, the dverger, and cooked them in their armor with the incredible stink of burning shit. The air clapped again, our ears screamed, and we could not breathe for the shock. Most of her enemies did not move after they fell on the deck.

Balissa fell as well, after an agonizing struggle with the torturous pain of burning from the inside out.

She fell at my feet, panting dreadfully, her chest smoking. I held the railing, trying to stand up, still dizzy from her horrible spell. I took a resolute step forward. Lith saw me come, she cursed and wove another spell, this time wholly of fire, and Balissa tried to crawl away. I grabbed her, pulled her away, but could not save her from Lith. The spell was released with a cruel laugh. It waved over us. Balissa was encased in stone, from her chest to her feet, and the spell touched me as well. I felt heavy, so heavy and knew my legs were encased in stone. I heard Lith giggling behind her glowing mask. The afterdeck buckled under Balissa's new weight; she shrieked and the deck gave way with a crash. She plummeted down to the hold, and then I heard a crash and the roar of water, and she went through the ship to the sea.

The weight, the stone mass around my legs pulled me to the hole. I grasped at the deck, desperately. I got hold of a structure that had been a heavy chair, bolted to the deck. I held on to it and knew I'd die.

Lith kneeled before me. Her eyes gleamed with the intensity of undeath. She placed a hand on my cheek and caressed it. 'It was real, Maskan. I really wanted you. As soon as I heard Shaduril did, I did as well. Is it any less real for that? But now, I will have what Father wanted. The city. And I tell you now. I'll not let Sand have a house, little less two! Well fought, Jotun.'

'Get on with it, evil bitch,' I spat at her.

She gathered heat, fires, and I knew she would pour molten death into my skull. I tried to concentrate, but could not. I was beyond exhausted, and could barely hold on. 'Goodbye, Maskan,' she said. I smiled. I had a reason to.

'What have you done to my city?' a woman asked behind her.

Lith turned to look at Mir's enraged face. 'Mother?' she said and got up. 'I have—'

'Mutinied against your parents,' Mir said, and Lith bowed in panic. 'Stand up!' Mir screamed.

Lith did and took her mask off. 'Mother—' Her face screwed curiously as she stared at the weapon Mir wielded. It was White's whip, and Shaduril's sword was on her belt. Then she frowned and stammered as Mir's hand changed. There was only a stump where there had been an illusion of a healthy hand. The whip went up.

'Shaduril!' Lith shrieked. 'Wait!'

But Mir-faced Shaduril did not wait.

She whipped the whip and ripped it through Lith's face, throat, and chest. Mir's face changed to Illastria's, and she mocked her with a lopsided grin, then she changed to the vibrant, alive-looking Shaduril—minus her hand—and Lith cursed in her dying pain as her beautiful sister smiled at her crookedly. The damage was terrible, massive. Shaduril looked at her sister, as the earring twinkled with the strange magic. 'Our aunt is safe in the throne room, sister,' she said softly. 'We switched during the battle. Thanks to Sand. You see, he did help Maskan here out of love, but I too, am an Elder Draugr, and he did not stop me from playing with faces. It has been delicious stalking you, love. Tell Taram hello for me.' Lith staggered and fell before me, blood dripping from her slashes. She was trying to speak. She collected great powers and released them dangerously, out of control. Fire burned in her hand, and Shaduril laughed in her face, apparently happy to die as well. I reached out—desperately—and slammed my hand on Lith's head. Her skull crumbled, the magic left her, and I slipped and hung on to the broken chair by one hand.

Baduhanna and Thrun appeared and dragged me up. I changed my size—totally spent—and the rock fell away from me to splash into the sea.

It was over. I heard the strange joyful, guttural laughter of the dverger as they kept firing at the huge army out in the sea. I saw two ships burning. The Hawk's Talon yelled as they finally took the deck of our ship. Out in the town, the enemy legion was pulling out, leaving dead and dying behind.

We would win.

## CHAPTER 24

I was standing on top of the tower. The huge enemy fleet was, if not fleeing, then careening away. 'They will not go home,' Thrun said darkly. 'We lost two hundred brothers.'

'We will honor them,' I told him. I was tired to the bone. 'Balissa?'

'Healing,' Thrun said. 'She changed into a fish. A big one. Teeth the size of an ale tankard. Hurt, though. Burned badly.'

'I'll help her,' the Aesir said, though she was weary as well.

I looked at Shaduril. She was one-handed, but still the beautiful girl I had once loved. In a way still did. Sand was there as well, fondling Larkgrin. He did not bother to hide his face, but he would when we returned to the city.

Baduhanna leaned on me. 'They will be dangerous, you know. You can never trust them. If this Mir sees them? They will obey.'

I looked at Sand. 'Shaduril disguised herself as one of the undead soldiers. I asked him to help the disguised Shaduril to save Illastria during the battle. To help Sharudil take Illastria's place. To give her my whip so Shaduril could help me and gain her vengeance. He did. He didn't know I would put Larkgrin in his pocket, but he did help. Even by not stopping Shaduril. Of course, he could not since Shaduril has power over him just like Lith did, but he didn't try to fight her. Their own quarrelsome nature was Lithiana's downfall. Perhaps it will be Mir's?'

'They might help. They might rebel,' the Aesir said.

'He is also a friend,' I told her. 'So is she.'

'So be it,' she said unhappily.

I nodded at her and watched a hundred dverger operate strangely efficient ballistae. There was a ship that was too slow to turn and follow the fleet now sailing to the east, and it shuddered and groaned as dozens of long missiles hit in with a steady, deathly barrage. Men fell into the sea.

Baduhanna scowled as she turned to look at the city. 'So, there is a war,' she said. 'Well, I've had peace for far too long anyway.' She smiled happily at the thought of the carnage, and I felt a twinge of worry.

'We will need to save the army,' I told her carefully.

'And reassure the allies as well,' she said with a grin. 'We will have years of work ahead of us.'

'There is much to do,' I agreed with her. I turned to look at Dagnar as well. It was still blazing in places, and especially the harbor and the Second Ring, they had suffered greatly. What remained of the population was chasing after the Bull Legion, putting out fires, or standing in haphazard ranks at the former Harbor Market, staring at their King, a twelve-foot tall thief. 'Some will blame me for this.'

'Then,' Baduhanna said, 'you will hang them. Be a king.'

'Yes, goddess,' I told her with a neutral voice.

'Come, husband,' she giggled. 'I'll convince the majority of the dolts of your merits. You will get your crown, but for now, let them choose whom they will follow.'

'I thought we agreed that already,' I said, surprised.

She laughed. 'We did. We will find a way to please everyone, Jotun. We will make them hopeful of their future. We shall prepare them for war. In that war, you will sway many of them to your side, and that is the only way to become a king. A Jotun king over men. Most will hate it. Those will fall. But—'

'I might be a Jotun,' I growled at her and stopped her in her tracks. 'But I understand men.'

She shook her head sadly. 'Look out there, love.' And I did. The sole remaining Hawk's Talon galley was holding steady in the bay. The men stared up at me. Others looked at us in wonder. Others scowled. Some turned away. 'There will be a civil war before any other war. Some will choose to follow me. Others will love you. Yet, many others will disdain both. You know this. If we are allied, Maskan, as husband and wife, we will be strong. You need me to govern this small piece of the world, for now. Let us be on the same side in the war.'

'Yes, goddess,' I said, feeling like a ship lost at sea.

'Come!' She laughed. 'And we shall spend the night together. I am entitled to that, at least, after these years of staring at the hairy faces of the dverger.' I saw Shaduril scowl at that, Baduhanna noticed it as well and scowled back at her, and I decided I was in trouble. She walked to the wall near where Balissa was on her side.

Sand chuckled and whispered in my ear. 'You are a king and a thief, my friend. I think you have to steal your kingdom back.'

'Will you help me pickpocket Red Midgard?' I asked him with a smile.

'I have time,' he answered.

Shaduril shook her head as she looked at the Aesir. 'I hate her.'

'Don't get any ideas, Shaduril. I'll take my whip now,' I said and took it from her.

'She will not love you forever. And you will be her puppet,' Shaduril said coldly.

'Your nature, dead,' I smiled, 'is to scheme. You see enemies everywhere. But I agree. That is why I did not mention your family's book to her. Neither will you two. In there, there is bound to be interesting information to make me allies if my wife will not give me what I want.'

'Be careful if you plan to cheat her,' Shaduril said.

'What will you do now?' I asked her. 'Will you stay?'

'No riding off, then, I think,' she said wistfully.

'No,' I said, looking away. 'We will stay and deal with the issues.'

'I too, have time,' she told me softly.

I turned to Shaduril. 'At least we got rid of Lith and Taram.'

'We did,' she said uncertainly. 'Thank you.'

'Will you be my friend? You ought not to hate me. I did get hung, and Lith is dead. You should be at peace,' I said.

'I love you,' she whispered.

'I care for you,' I told her and looked away. *She was dead.*

She smiled, but the smile changed into a deep scowl. 'But you are married. That is hard to forgive.'

*Gods help me.*

## EPILOGUE

Times changed for Midgard. What was the world of humans and had been for thousands of years, was at risk. The dead had invaded it, and a giant and a goddess had saved part of it. Its beliefs, and people were forever changed. There were those who cherished the changes. There were those, who would have nothing to do with non-human races, not even goddesses. They would not abide giants calling themselves kings of men. Some would even serve the dead.

And Maskan and his alliance with the Aesir? His unsteady friends Shaduril and Sand? His enemies Mir and the High King?

Well, there is more.

Wait.

*- The story will continue 2016 with the Queen of the Draugr.*
*Be sure to check out the books The Dark Levy and Eye of Hel, which are tales related to the Beast of the North -*

Thank you for reading the book.

Do sign up for my mailing list by visiting my homepages. By doing this, you will receive a rare and discreet email where you will find:

*News of the upcoming stories*

*Competitions*

*Book promotions*

*Free reading*

Also, if you enjoyed this book, you might want to check out these ones:

**Grab them from my AMAZON HOMEPAGE**

## AFTERWORD

The ancient Germanic and Norse mythology are wonderful sources of fantasy stories. I have lived and breathed these stories for decades, and love the Nine Worlds with all its creatures and magic, some subtle, others heavy-handed. Making a fantasy series centered on this trove of treasures was a quite natural step for me.

Hence, there are TWO "sister" storylines, walking hand in hand though one day they will meet. One tells the story of the Ten Tears, and the first book in the series is called "The Dark Levy." The second book is called "Eye of Hel" and will be out in fall 2015. That story begins in our world, "The Tenth" world and much of the action takes place in the world of Aldheim, the Jewel of the Worlds, home of the elves.

This series, the Thief of Midgard, takes place in, as the topic says, Midgard. Nothing is what you expect in Midgard. That I can promise.

As you read this, you will notice many similarities with the classical fantasy genres. Lord of the Rings ladled many of its core values from the ancient religions, like mine, and you will probably see some similarities in the magic system with the Wheel of Time though it will be different enough. Also, the creatures you are used to from other books will not be all familiar. The Germanic legends are not as black and white as many of the classical stories. Gods can be good or evil, impulsive and brooding and happy, like humans. The ancient race of the giants might not be lumbering idiots, dragons need not covet gold above all, and the dwarves might be mad as hell. Or Hel. You choose.

Hope you enjoy this.

I am always on a lookout for reviews. Reviews make or break us. An excellent review pushes an author to excel, brings tears to his/her eyes and makes our day. Give one in Goodreads and amazon.com, and I am very grateful. You will also enter a review competition, where you can win Amazon Gift cards. A constructive critical review is a brick on which to build a better story and to make our work keener and more considerate. Let us have them, join the mailing list at www.alariclongward.com and check out the other competitions that are ongoing. For one thing, I hope to give a character of your making life in one of my books.

See you soon.

Printed in Great Britain
by Amazon